The Tutor

Kathryn Mattingly

Winter Goose Publishing
45 Lafayette Road #114
North Hampton, NH 03862

www.wintergoosepublishing.com
Contact Information: info@wintergoosepublishing.com

The Tutor

First Edition, August 2018

Cover Design by Ladd Woodland

ISBN: 978-1-941058-82-4

Published in the United States of America

ALSO BY KATHRYN MATTINGLY

Benjamin

Fractured Hearts

Journey

Olivia's Ghost

Kathryn Mattingly
2019

For my daughter, Anna,
who lived on the island of Roatan, *and has shown me*
how to be an empowered woman

CHAPTER ONE

Matti felt like a stalker peering into his mother's studio when he should have been in bed asleep. He stared at the rows and rows of books neatly aligned on shelves that ran floor to ceiling. He could inhale their musty scent from where he stood. As a little kid he pretended to read them. The older books had smelled of glue when he opened their hardbound backs. It was a pleasant memory, sitting cross-legged on her studio floor surrounded by little stacks of books. At nearly twelve he could now boast having read them all, including those in his father's library. What a shock it would be for his father to know he had smuggled books out one at a time and returned them after his mom had tucked him in for the night.

Something was causing Matti to linger. Maybe it was the lure of linseed hypnotizing him, or watching his mom sketch at the antique table where she gave private English lessons. Roaming around after bedtime with his Gameboy would end abruptly if she discovered him in the doorway. Matti pulled himself away and across the sprawling home. Expertly he missed every piece of furniture in the looming dark by a mere hair's breadth.

He grabbed an apple from the basket on the counter and ate it while staring out the screen door, just as he did every evening about this time. Stars winked at him through the mesh until he tossed his apple core in the waste can and headed for the stairs behind the garage. They lead to the guest loft, which housed a plush mahogany pool table in the front room. He could easily spy on his father from the window beside it, which overlooked the driveway. This was his nightly ritual, waiting for his dad to return from the docks, where he managed the night shift of workers unloading crates of imported olive oil.

Matti dreamed about playing pool in this room with his dad, even winning sometimes. He imagined them laughing and eating snacks while they played, or sharing opinions on interesting topics. Mattia Antonio Giovanni was an overwhelming name to live up to, and he wasn't sure he wanted to. He had no desire to dress in perfectly fitted Gucci suits like his dad, yet he wished his father didn't see him as a scrawny nerd in baggy shorts and t-shirts. His dad had never said as much, but it was always right there in his eyes.

Matti blew up countless aliens on his Gameboy while sprawled across the sofa in the guest loft. He tried not to think about last Saturday, when his dad took him to the docks. *It's time you pitched in and learned about our family business. You can start by helping unload oil crates.* The men hired to do the unloading teased him about how small he was and not strong enough to lift the heavier crates. Just when Matti thought things couldn't get worse, his father pulled a gun from his pocket to shoot rats scurrying in and out of empty crates. In no time at all there were dead bloody rats everywhere. *You try it boy. It will help make a man of you.* The gun had felt awkward and heavy. He couldn't hold it still, even with both hands. The crew stood around laughing because his shots went nowhere near the rats. It was the first time he'd felt humiliated by his father.

The garage door opened and Matti rose from the sofa to peer out the window. His dad didn't pull straight in, like he normally would. Instead he maneuvered the car around and backed it up the driveway. Matti didn't dash down the stairs and dodge a landmine of furnishings in the dark until reaching his room. Instead he stayed put and stared out the window. The car disappeared into the garage and Matti wished he could greet his father at the door, where he would smile and say *Hello son. How was your day?* More than anything Matti wished he wasn't such a disappointment as a namesake. If he had street smarts it would endear him to the Giovanni clan. His dad hated how he was a freaky genius, especially since his obsessive-compulsive behavior was nearly diagnosed as Asperger's Syndrome. Everyone in his sixth-grade class teased him for being smart, or being small, or else they had made fun of his perfectionism. At least it had been established that he wasn't on the autism spectrum. *He's just a very bright, sensitive kid with a lot of compulsions. He might outgrow them or they may get worse, in which case we have meds for that.*

Matti couldn't believe he was still in the guest loft just because his father chose to back into the garage instead of pulling straight in. The thought of getting caught because he'd decided to hang back was nerve-wracking. He listened for the ignition to shut off while staring out the window of their home in the hilly San Francisco neighborhood. When he couldn't hear the steady hum of the motor anymore, Matti grabbed his Gameboy from the beveled glass table—and froze. Goose bumps spread over his arms from an eerie sound seeping up through the ceiling of the garage. It was a dull thudding noise, like a trapped bird flying in circles. He crept down the stairs and onto the cement walkway. Part of him wanted to bolt for the house but instead he peered into the back garage door.

There were weird shadows on the wall from an overhead light and the car trunk was open, which was odd because his father never brought anything home with him except a briefcase. Matti could see something in the trunk was moving. He sucked in a gulp of air and held his breath. It was a woman! She had duct tape across her mouth, and on her wrists and ankles. Why was a woman bound up and stuffed in his father's trunk? Matti started sweating from an adrenaline rush, just like that day on the docks, shooting at rats. He swiped at his wet forehead with the back of his hand while gawking at the woman struggling to free herself. She caught sight of him and their eyes locked in a frantic stare until his father appeared out of nowhere.

Matti jumped away from the door and squeezed against the garage wall. He shut his eyes and had a panic attack. His last one had been on the docks last Saturday. He'd leaned against the crates while his body went haywire, like it was doing now.

"What am I supposed to do with you?"

Matti stiffened against the rough stucco.

"Stupid woman. A deal is a deal. Now I have no choice. You should've stayed where you belong."

Relieved it wasn't *him* his dad was talking to, Matti peeked inside the door again, just enough to see his dad reach down and grab the woman's neck. Her bound hands and feet flailed against the sides of the trunk. There was a snapping sound, as if her neck had broken. Matti slid down the outside garage wall. *How could he have hidden in the dark like a coward while his father hurt that poor helpless woman?* It wasn't long until he heard his father wrestling with a garbage bag. Scooting closer to the open door, Matti peeked in and saw the woman's limp body being shoved into it. Her bound hands flopped out to one side. *I can't believe this is happening* swirled around repeatedly in Matti's brain. He put his head in his hands and tried to focus his thoughts on what to do. Maybe he could sneak into the house and dial 911, but what if his dad saw him? He could end up killed and stuffed in the garbage bag with the woman. His dad never liked him anyway, and he wouldn't want a witness to his murder. Matti watched his father drag the body down their hilly front yard, stopping beside a large hole recently dug by the grounds crew. His mom had mentioned at dinner that the cement truck would come in the morning to install a fountain.

Matti half crawled to the corner of the garage. Hugging his badly shaking body he watched dirt fly up into the star-studded night. His father was burying the woman where the fountain would go. Once the cement was poured no one would find her. Fearing his dad would return soon, Matti ran back to the kitchen walkway. He was stooped over so as not to be seen and nearly fell from shaking so hard. His hands were numb as he fumbled with the screen door, which finally opened. Tripping over a chair in the kitchen, he stood still while listening for anyone who might have heard it. Nothing stirred in the darkness so he made his way to the stairs, pausing briefly outside his dad's den. His father had a constant stream of visitors to his office. Matti assumed they were businessmen buying olive oil, but now he wasn't so sure.

He had been to the groves where the olives grew, back in Sicily. Matti saw a flash of himself a couple summers ago, dodging in and out of the gnarly, bushy trees while playing tag with his cousins. He was certain he could never feel that carefree again, knowing he had watched a woman die and made no attempt to prevent it. The light was off in his mom's studio on the other side of the stairs. She must have gone to bed. He wondered if he should wake her up. But it was too awful, too unbelievable. How could he explain *letting* it happen? How could he say he'd done *nothing* but watch? Tears flooded down Matti's face and he nearly exploded trying not to sob out-loud. He couldn't remember the last time he had cried like a baby. Boys weren't supposed to cry. The girls in his sixth-grade class cried over everything, but not the boys.

Matti climbed the stairs while wiping his snotty nose and wet eyes with the bottom of his shirt. His teeth chattered uncontrollably from being so cold. How long was he watching his father *kill* a woman, throw her in a hole, and cover her with dirt? He'd completely lost track of time. The only thing he knew for sure was that tomorrow morning fresh cement would entomb her forever. His own mother would never know about the body under the fountain. The body of a woman his dad *murdered*. Matti stumbled at the top of the stairs and leaned against the wall, thinking maybe his severely shaking body would break open and spill onto the carpet.

Lights along the private driveway shone in the upper windows and made the eyes on the portraits in the hall look alive. It was as if they were taunting him about what a weak coward he was. Matti was convinced that the people in the portraits believed he should hang beside his father on the thickest limb of a dead tree. Why didn't he run down the road screaming for help, or grab something to hit his dad with? The woman thought he'd save her, that he'd take action—*be a hero.* Instead he just let her die.

He looked away from the three sets of eyes because he couldn't bear to see the judgment in their expressions. He wanted to get up and run back to his bed, pull the covers over his head and pretend to be asleep . . . for eternity. But he couldn't move. He'd stopped shaking and instead was just numb, inside and out. Somehow Matti convinced himself that the portraits weren't alive and judging him, mainly because he needed to get a grip on his sanity. He tried to forget about . . . what just happened . . . and instead thought about his mom. She had sketched her students while they read aloud to her, explaining that it improved their pronunciation. That calmed him a little—thinking about his mom, who seemed to like that he was a scrawny pointless nerd. She claimed to have been just like him as a little girl. Matti took comfort in knowing his mother was no longer scrawny, and he didn't believe she could ever have been pointless.

The first portrait in the hallway was of Emmy. He stared into her soft brown eyes and it helped to slow his breathing. She was never his mom's student, but her father had been. Matti nicknamed Emmy's father "the Honduran" because he was from Honduras. He'd wanted a portrait of his daughter and Matti could still picture his mom sketching Emmy in the studio while the Honduran read to her. He could still hear the Honduran laugh. The man laughed deeply and often whenever he came for tutoring. It was an odd sound, because *his* father never laughed. The Honduran had graduated recently with a degree in architecture and was returning to Honduras. Matti wondered if he would take the portrait of Emmy.

Next he focused on Kim, on her round Asian face, while trying desperately to block out that poor woman's eyes staring into him from the car trunk. His heart began to pound again. Matti strained his ears to listen for his father downstairs, but he heard nothing. The master suite was at the other end of the house and his dad never came upstairs. Matti couldn't remember his father ever being in his room—not to say hello or how are you, or goodnight if he happened to be home one evening. Matti never thought he'd be grateful that his dad didn't like to spend time with him. Even if for some odd reason he did come upstairs, Matti knew he wouldn't be able to run and hide from him. His body had tightened up like a cripple. He wasn't sure he could even drag himself down the hall to bed.

Matti stared at Kim's half-smile from his position on the floor. She would never have understood him doing nothing for that poor woman. Kim would have barreled into the garage and beat his father with her fists. She'd have *done* something. He looked away, feeling shameful, and stared at Faraji, the African doctor. Matti wanted to crawl into the painting with him. He could hear drums, just like the ones Faraji had said his people played. He even felt the hot sticky air and smelled the dry dusty earth like Faraji often spoke of. The doctor barely knew English when first coming to be tutored. By the time he'd finished medical school and returned to his own country, his English was perfect. Matti had liked him and his stories about where he lived. Oh to be in Africa with Faraji right now!

Matti watched the lights along the driveway dim and knew it was almost dawn. The sky out the hall window was slate gray and blanketed in morning fog. He must have dozed a little while scrunched up against the wall. Everything that had happened was still very clear in his mind. He wished his father had strangled him after all, stuffed him into a garbage bag and dragged him down the hill along with that poor woman. He longed to be tossed into a shallow grave no one would ever suspect was there, buried forever beneath a fountain. Half crawling he dragged his body down the hall and into his bedroom, where he climbed into bed, sprawled out on his back. African drums played in the distance and he knew he was losing consciousness rather than falling asleep. Just before his world went black Matti realized the drums were only his own heart, banging loudly against his chest, as if begging to get out.

CHAPTER TWO

Intuition told her the answer to Matti's current mental state was right there on the front lawn.

Natalie awoke to the sound of a cement truck and was annoyed that she'd overslept. Observing the workmen below her bedroom window made it clear Antonio was in full command of everything. It was odd he didn't leave that responsibility to the crew hired for the fountain project, and even odder that he didn't come to bed last night. She tried not to think about where he'd been instead of home in bed. Antonio rarely returned from the docks before midnight these days, but he'd never stayed out all night before. Maybe he was having an affair. She wondered what physical prowess he could possibly have left for another woman, considering how voracious his sexual appetite was for her. Natalie wished he were as ravenous for her thoughts as he was for her body.

It was a lonely, emotionally deprived marriage. Antonio was never open with her regarding his business affairs or personal goals. These days he seldom talked at all except to share his views on what he read in the paper each morning at breakfast. After that he saw a string of visitors in his den. They were always polite, but cool and withdrawn, not much different from her husband. She put on jeans and a t-shirt, ran a brush through her hair, and went to wake Matti up. Their son filled all the empty spaces of her heart. If only Antonio saw in Matti what she saw. Instead he often expressed his disappointment about the boy being nothing like him. Matti reflected so much of her it hurt to have Antonio adamantly unhappy with their only child. Life would be easier for the boy if he'd inherited his dad's outgoing and assertive traits, but she couldn't bring herself to want Matti any different than how God made him.

After opening the blinds, she turned to take a good look at her son. Watching Matti sleep always made her wish he would never grow up. Today, however, she was dismayed to see that he'd obviously been gallivanting outside after his bedtime. Her son lay sprawled across the crumpled sheets with his muddy and grass stained pajama bottoms quite exposed for all to see. He hadn't even taken off his shoes when returning to bed. She sat beside him, thinking how small he looked for almost twelve. Natalie reached out and smoothed back his dark hair, which was identical to her own. His face was quite pale. Did he hear the cement truck and decide to get a closer look? Maybe standing around in the cold morning air made him sick. She felt his head but it wasn't warm.

"Matti . . . wakeup." Natalie shook him gently and he opened his eyes—not wearily, but widely. He popped them open as if afraid of something. Considering the muddy shoes and grass-stained knees, Natalie assumed whatever he was afraid of happened earlier, outside. Adrenalin shot through her veins and put her maternal instincts on full alert. "Are you sick, honey?"

He stared up at her, blankly.

"Were you outside to watch them pour cement?"

Matti didn't respond, and Natalie could sense something was wrong.

"Sweetie, what happened? Did someone hurt you . . . one of the workers on the lawn?" It was all she could think of. They did look a little rough around the edges. It wasn't a fair assumption to make, but there were no other logical explanations for his obvious distressed state.

Matti shifted his gaze to stare at the ceiling instead of at her. Natalie's mind raced through a gamut of possibilities. What could have happened since tucking him in last night? Every evening their ritual was the same. She'd sit on his bed and they'd talk about the book he was reading, or the report he was researching for school. She wondered when he'd be too old for the bedtime routine that she cherished. Right now he looked more like a frightened child than an adolescent. She couldn't think of what might have transpired in the past few hours. After one last penetrating stare, Natalie sprinted back to the master suite and grabbed her iPhone off the nightstand. Her hands shook as she called Henry, who was a family friend as well as their GP. While waiting for someone to pick up, she returned to Matti's room. He was still staring blankly at the ceiling.

"Henry?" Natalie's breathing slowed a little once she heard his familiar voice. "Can you come to our house right away? It's Matti. There's something wrong with him, Henry, and I just don't know what it is."

Natalie stood by the window and observed the invasion of workmen on her front lawn. Then she looked at Matti, stiff as a corpse, with his eyes open and staring . . . just staring . . . at the ceiling. She could hear the men shouting orders and scraping wet cement. If one of them had somehow abused Matti, she would kill him with her bare hands. She could hear Henry's voice at the other end of the phone and tried to focus on his words. *Don't panic. I'll be right over. Just keep the boy still.*

Natalie nodded, as if Henry could hear that, and then she hung up. She set the phone on the dresser and stared at her son. He was everything that mattered to her. Without him she had nothing, nothing at all. Fear took on a whole new meaning as it became glaringly obvious Matti's mental state had crossed a serious line. There was nothing normal about the boy sprawled out before her. Henry had mentioned antidepressants and how Matti might need them one day soon. She'd asked why Matti's behavior should be expected to get worse rather than better. Admittedly he was shy and nervous by nature, but he was not *crazy*. Henry assured her Matti was far from mentally ill, but puberty often brought its own mixed bag of issues with highly intellectual children. Observing him now she understood what Henry meant. But such issues would surely not appear suddenly, overnight?

She sat beside him on the bed, hoping Matti might turn his head to smile at her and say it was all a joke. But that wasn't Matti's style. He wasn't bluffing. This strange behavior was quite real, and she had to find out what caused it. Natalie leaned down and kissed his cheek. Her whole body began to shake as waves of panic swept over her. She feared for his fragile, beautiful mind that never quit absorbing knowledge at an unstoppable pace. His intellect wouldn't have frightened her except that Matti was so *affected* by everything he learned, and learned in excess. He was often overwhelmed by the many injustices of the world, by the cold hard facts he couldn't get enough of yet couldn't accept or change.

Maybe he was self-destructing. Maybe he'd crossed a line from which there was no way back. Maybe her Matti just simply could not accept . . . whatever he'd witnessed or experienced in the last twelve hours. Natalie glanced across the room at the open window. A coastal breeze straight from the bay moved the curtain playfully. Sounds of machinery and male voices floated in with the wind. What happened on that sloping hill? Intuition told her the answer to Matti's current mental state was right there on the front lawn.

Natalie took Matti's shoes off and pulled the covers up around him. She smoothed back his hair again, although it hadn't moved a fraction, and silently willed her introspective boy to awaken from his dazed state. Matti's OCD had been diagnosed early and watched carefully. What more could she have possibly done to protect him? And yet, here he was, all but incapacitated. Natalie shuddered to think what abuse he might have endured if attending public rather than private school. At Bayside Academy, concessions were made for Matti's incredible intellect, allowing him to research and absorb all the knowledge his heart desired, through long hours in the science lab and media room. He'd been isolated in a protective learning bubble. Gratefully, it gave few circumstances for schoolmates to focus on Matti's quirks and rigidity that frequently played out like underdeveloped social skills.

She headed downstairs praying Henry would meet her at the door. Hopefully he was a miracle worker, for surely nothing short of that could fix whatever horrible thing had happened to her son since last night. Antonio entered the kitchen just as she told Kim to let Henry in the minute he arrived and bring him straight to Matti's room.

Antonio put bread in the toaster. "Why is Henry coming . . . is Mattia ill?"

"He's acting very strange, Antonio. I'm worried about him."

Antonio shrugged. "The boy always acts strange."

Natalie studied her husband, who appeared to be distracted. His quick glances out the window at the yard project belied any concern for the boy.

"Why don't you let Kim make your usual breakfast?" she asked.

"I don't have time. They're going to pour the cement soon. How is Mattia behaving stranger than usual?"

"I went to wake him for school and his pajamas were filthy. He'd obviously been outside. I thought maybe he'd gone to see the cement truck. He seems to be in some sort of shock."

Antonio stared at her, his steel blue eyes squinting. That last comment had gotten his full attention. The toast popped up and neither noticed. Natalie met his gaze and tried not to indicate how taken aback she was by his cold stare. Did he have something to do with Matti's condition? Immediately she felt ashamed. Antonio was a complicated man. Not especially affectionate or warm-hearted, but certainly not someone their son should fear. Yet, something about the look in his eyes frightened her.

"That would explain his Gameboy on the lawn this morning. Has he said anything?" Antonio grabbed the toast and buttered it sloppily. He took a bite while staring at her again. Natalie thought his behavior was nearly as strange as Matti's. He'd only begrudgingly accepted their son's diagnoses as highly intelligent with a good deal of anxiety related issues. Antonio had made it clear he didn't want a physically frail boy who suffered from phobias and knew more than most college graduates by third grade. He had every intention of molding his son into a *real* man he could be proud of. Natalie wasn't sure how to interpret what a *real* man was, in Antonio's estimation, but she was fairly certain Matti would never fit that mold.

"No, he hasn't said a thing, and he isn't responsive when I talk to him. He just stares at the ceiling. I'm wondering if one of those men out there might have . . . might have . . ." Natalie couldn't finish her sentence. It was unspeakable.

"Might have what?"

". . . molested him, maybe after finding Matti in the bushes spying on them."

Antonio rolled his eyes at her. "You have an overactive imagination, and so does that boy. That's probably what's wrong with him—his own imaginings. I'll go up there and check on him myself. Let me know when Henry is here. I want to speak with him before he sees Mattia."

Natalie stood there grimacing. Alarms were sounding in her head. She couldn't shake off the feeling that Antonio was more involved than he was letting on. Something about his eyes . . . eyes she knew so well—all the moods behind them—and yet she couldn't read his eyes this morning. Something foreign had crept into them.

"Perhaps he will confide in me, if someone actually assaulted him. Adolescent boys are not going to share that with their mother." He gave her a no nonsense look and she decided not to make a scene.

"All right then . . . but be gentle with him, Antonio. Matti has obviously suffered some sort of mental breakdown and we don't want to send him over the edge." Antonio nodded as he climbed the stairs. Natalie wished he were nicer to the boy, more tolerant of his timid nature. Matti would never be cold and calculating like his father. How did she overlook this about Antonio when he was her student? She admired him back then, his determination to lose his accent and speak perfect English. He was quite romantic in the beginning, taking her to candle lit dinners at expensive restaurants, whispering how he got lost in her large emerald eyes. Yet she was the one who'd gotten lost in the cold, steel blue of his. She'd been silly to think two people from such different worlds could understand one another. Only in fairytales did the privileged prince and working-class peasant girl live happily ever after.

Maybe it was as much her fault as his. If she'd spent less time absorbed in her tutoring and painting, she might have gotten Antonio to share his hopes and dreams. He frequently complained of her being as reclusive as their son, stashed away in her studio for hours on end. Antonio hated that she still worked for a living. He didn't approve and would often complain about it. *Why do you still tutor when I have more money than can be spent in a lifetime?* It was true she didn't need to earn a living, but at least she could do as she pleased with her income, whereas Antonio measured and counted every penny she spent of his family wealth.

Natalie heard the door to Matti's room close, and shivered. Why was she frightened at the thought of Antonio alone with Matti? She couldn't remember the last time he'd been in the boy's room. His concern for their son's sudden traumatized condition didn't feel like concern at all. If her instincts were correct, then somehow, Antonio might be to blame for their son's condition. She paced back and forth by the front door, waiting for Henry to arrive. Kim watched her from the kitchen door, looking worried for the boy.

"I won't be able to tutor you this morning, Kim. We can reschedule."

"I understand, Miss G. I hope Matti be okay."

"Me too." Natalie stood still, and the two women looked at one another somberly. Neither had to say anything about how concerned they were for Matti. Words weren't necessary. "Please, Kim, go home and do your college report. I won't need you today. I'll keep you posted about Matti."

"Yes, Miss G." Kim nodded and turned from the doorway. Natalie watched her back down the drive a few minutes later, just as Henry pulled up. Not able to contain herself, Natalie unlocked the front door and flew down the walkway to greet him.

CHAPTER THREE

Henry almost wished he and Antonio wouldn't get away with it—stashing Matti in a mental ward.

Matti had never thought about the *flap flap flapping* of blinds opening, like a sail in the wind or a deck of cards being shuffled, until this morning. He'd never realized just how dazzling his mom's green eyes were until staring into them. It was too painful—staring into those eyes, which were unaware of him being an accessory to his father's crime. The *flap flap flapping* of blinds transitioned into the *crack crack cracking* of bones. It was a sound that grew louder and louder in his head until he wanted to scream, but nothing came from his throat. His mouth didn't open. His body wasn't working. It was like a bad dream. Matti stared at the ceiling, at the little crystals in his overhead light that hung down all dangly, and then he saw a flash of the dead woman. He saw her taped hands flopping out of the garbage bag *again and again and again.* He thought his head would explode from the sound of her bound limbs *thump thump thumping* against the sides of the trunk, then he heard a new sound. It was his dad's voice . . .

"Mattia." Sweat broke out on Antonio's forehead as he waited for a response. The boy must have witnessed his events of the late night. He watched Mattia stare at the ceiling light and feared what he'd say to his mother when the shock wore off. Most twelve-year-olds would shove what they saw deep inside somewhere and share it with a therapist one day. But Mattia wasn't like most twelve-year-olds. His son would more likely dig up the dead woman from under the fountain and given her a proper burial. The boy's heightened sensitivity to just about everything was annoying to say the least.

He needed to be sure his son didn't snap out of it and confess all. Some day he would convince Mattia of the necessity for last night's messy little murder. Exactly how he'd keep the kid silent in the meantime was not clear yet. Perhaps heavy sedatives would work for now. The only thing clear to Antonio, as he stared at his traumatized son, was how Henry owed him. He would have to help with this dilemma by providing the sedatives necessary, and possibly a place to house Mattia away from Natalie. As long as the boy kept his mouth shut, there was no way for Natalie or anyone else to discover what had happened. Antonio sat beside his son on the bed. "Your mother tells me you're sick."

Matti didn't divert his eyes from the crystals in the ceiling light, but a whiny sound erupted from the back of his throat. Antonio lowered his head beside the boy and whispered in his ear, "I know where you were last night, Mattia. I found your Gameboy on the lawn." He took it out of his pocket, slipped it beneath the sheet, and pressed it into Matti's hand. "Let's keep whatever you saw as our little secret, because you were my accessory to a crime, Mattia. I think your mother would be very disappointed to know that."

The sound coming from Matti's throat grew louder and higher pitched. Antonio stood up. He ran a finger under his collar, which was damp with sweat. The boy's reaction to him was quite unnerving. "Dr. Henry is going to examine you." He peered down at the underdeveloped adolescent and saw a strong resemblance to Natalie, with his dark hair and pale skin. Mattia's hair wasn't wavy like most Giovannis', and there were no olive tones to his complexion. The large emerald eyes staring at the ceiling light were what really made the boy a dead ringer for his mother. "Don't tell stories no one will believe. Do you hear me?"

The guttural sound in his son's throat stopped. He shifted his gaze to stare at Antonio. Had he sufficiently stopped the boy from spilling all he knew in some hysterical manner? Feeling squeamish from the pathetic emotional state of his only child, Antonio left the room, just in time to see Natalie coming down the hall.

"Henry is in your den. How's Matti?"

"He's sleeping. I think we should let the boy rest until after Henry examines him." Antonio was not at all sure he could keep his headstrong wife out of the boy's room, where she'd see firsthand how he was far from sleeping. In fact, he was more agitated than ever. It wouldn't take much to conclude that Mattia's condition had everything to do with him and nothing to do with men working in the yard.

"All right. I'll wait in my studio. But please notify me the minute Henry is done with his examination."

"Yes, of course. I'll come and get you."

Natalie headed for the stairs and Antonio glanced over the railing at his den below. It was time to orchestrate a plan with the good doctor.

Henry couldn't imagine what had happened to Matti. The adolescent was more than just bright—he was brilliant, which always had a significant downside. The Giovanni fortune didn't appear to give any of them peace of mind. Whenever he'd been there Antonio was a bundle of nervous energy, while Natalie brooded over half-done portraits in her studio. No wonder the boy had issues that reached beyond his unusual intellect.

"Henry . . . thanks for coming." Antonio extended a clammy hand while his eyes darted about.

"Where's Matti?" Henry stood up, eager to examine the boy and see for himself why Natalie had called.

"I need to talk with you first." Antonio sat down on the leather sofa without apology and waited for Henry to reseat himself. Henry begrudgingly collapsed back into the buttery leather and studied Antonio's ashen face. "I know what put Mattia into shock, Henry."

Henry didn't respond. Somehow he was not surprised.

Antonio tapped his foot on the lush Asian rug while Henry waited patiently for him to speak again, but then Antonio jumped up and pulled back the heavy curtain on the front window. He stared at the expansive lawn where Henry had noticed a newly cemented fountain upon his arrival. The crew had left, their work done. He imagined gardeners would appear next and tidy up the landscaping. Water would cascade down the tiers by the time tulips were in bloom.

"Mattia saw something . . . unfortunate, here, last night."

Henry waited for him to go on, but the hard-body Italian hesitated. He thought it odd for Antonio to be speechless. Generally, that was how he rendered others. "What did he see, exactly, Antonio?"

"A murder."

"Say what?" Henry turned in his seat to get a better look at Antonio, still standing at the window peering out.

"It has to do with the babies from Romania, Henry. One mother got it into her head to get her infant back."

"And you *killed* her?"

Antonio shot him an angry look, his eyes burning with self-justification. "I had no choice. She might have gone to the authorities. We'd all end up in prison over a simple misunderstanding. I couldn't take that chance, Henry. Unfortunately, a life is expendable if it puts too many others at risk."

"And that's how you justify killing whoever gets in the way?"

"I'm not asking for your blessing, my good doctor. What's done is done. Just remember that if I go down, you go down with me."

Henry put his head in his hands.

"No one has any way to trace this woman. She smuggled herself over here on our ship full of olive oil." Antonio began pacing from the window to the door and back again. "The woman was a peasant. No one will miss her except for a few other peasants, and no one will listen to them."

"I thought the babies were voluntarily exchanged for money, enough money to keep a roof over their birth family's heads, and food in their pantries, for quite some time." Henry sighed. He didn't approve of this baby trade the Giovannis had stumbled upon, purchasing newborns from former Soviet countries struggling financially. He'd only agreed to help distribute the smuggled infants because his own daughter was childless, and desperate to adopt. Now it would seem he might pay an even higher price for the two grandsons he adored, higher than all the unsuccessful in-vitro fertilization treatments and exorbitant foreign baby fees. Perhaps surrogacy would have been a better solution.

"Yes of course it's voluntary," Antonio agreed. "I don't know what happened. Either this crazy woman changed her mind, or someone slipped up." Antonio sat down across from Henry again. "I need you to heavily sedate the boy until we can get him into a psychiatric unit at a hospital somewhere."

Henry nodded. "I must examine him before I can prescribe sedatives."

"Of course, but regardless of what you diagnose, my son must be inaccessible for a while . . . at least until I'm able to reason with him."

"There's a program for disturbed adolescents at St. Mary's. It's called the McAuley Crisis Unit."

"No. I can't have someone actually *curing* him. He might confess to what he saw. I need you to place him in some mental ward where no one will bother with him and only you will visit." Antonio stood up. Henry thought he looked shorter than usual. Perhaps it was the weight of his crime that physically diminished him. "You have to convince Natalie this is the right course of action. I'll arrange to have someone official come take him away in an ambulance. You can't let him have any visitors, Henry."

It was a ludicrous idea to lock up an emotionally disturbed adolescent with mentally dysfunctional adults, but Henry didn't share that with Antonio. The normal course of action would be a combination of counseling and drug therapy. It was not unusual for the exceptionally gifted to develop various forms of mental illness in puberty, especially if exposed to the type of drama Matti just witnessed. Fortunately, in this day and age most conditions were quite treatable. But then proper treatment wasn't what Antonio had in mind. "Let me see the boy." Henry had no desire to ask Antonio how it was he murdered this poor peasant woman, or what he did with her body. The less he knew about it, the better.

Antonio led him upstairs where he found Matti lying on his back, staring at the ceiling light. Whatever despicable behavior he witnessed from his father, something more was probably going on with his young mind. He recalled Matti's psychologist recommending they find a good psychiatrist in the next few months, explaining to Natalie that psychiatrists were licensed to administer drugs. While examining the boy he decided to appease Antonio. As much as it disgusted Henry, there was no safer recourse for any of them. If Matti came to his senses and confessed what he knew about the murder, they would all pay the price. And he couldn't afford to let that happen, not with grandsons to watch grow up.

Henry studied the boy lying there looking at the light fixture without really seeing it. He spoke softly to the boy throughout the examination, as if Matti were awake and coherent. He asked the boy questions, despite knowing he wouldn't answer them. It was clear from Matti's vital signs that his brain was the only obstacle to normalcy. Shock from watching the murder, perhaps coupled with the fear of being caught, or the overwhelming guilt associated with feelings of helplessness to intercede on the woman's behalf were no doubt contributing to his mental breakdown. It was hard to say what else was going on in that complex, quickly developing adolescent mind.

He'd tell Natalie lots of tests were needed in order to make a proper diagnosis. Somehow he'd convince her that Matti would heal much quicker there, among medical professionals, rather than isolated here at home. Henry almost wished he and Antonio wouldn't get away with it—stashing Matti in a mental ward. On the other hand, he hoped fervently she would go along with such a plan.

Natalie wheeled Matti out to the front porch and waited for Diego. She was grateful to have a friend in this hour of need. Of all her students, Diego studied the hardest and learned the fastest. He'd graduated with his architecture degree and would be returning to his family's coffee plantation in Copan, Honduras. Whoever would have suspected she'd end up going with him, exactly one week after Matti's emotional breakdown? It had been the longest week of Natalie's life.

She watched for Diego to enter the private lane and hoped everything would go off without a hitch. Antonio was out running errands on the other side of the city, and so she'd cancelled the hired help for the day. Natalie prayed there wouldn't be any unexpected visitors. She'd convinced Henry not to stop by anymore, reassuring him that she'd give Matti his medication. He'd hesitated at first, but finally agreed to let her start medicating the boy. Of course, she hadn't given Matti as high a dose of the prescribed drugs Henry left in her care. In fact, Matti no longer was so drowsy as to need a wheelchair, which she'd rented for excursions out to the pool. But she didn't want Antonio to know that, so she continued to use it when taking him from his room to get a little fresh air and change of scenery. If anyone did happen to see her there on the porch with Matti, perhaps having him in the wheelchair would avoid suspicion.

"It's going to be okay, sweetie. We're going far away from here." She patted his hand and observed him for a minute, forgetting about the rescue van. Matti was staring at the fountain. Somehow it disturbed him. He'd resumed the whiny sound in his throat, predictable now whenever agitated—specifically, whenever Antonio was in close proximity. Whatever happened to Matti must have coincided with pouring cement for the three-tiered structure. According to Henry there was no evidence Matti had been abused, but Natalie didn't trust Henry at this point. Nonetheless she thought the doctor was probably right. Whatever happened had nothing to do with the workmen and everything to do with Antonio. It chilled her blood to consider such a grave thing, but there was no mistaking Matti's fear of his father. Why else would Antonio want their son constantly sedated? Why wouldn't he agree to admit Matti to the McAuley Crisis Unit at St. Mary's? She'd researched the facility and it was the perfect place to get the best care for a mentally troubled adolescent, yet Henry wouldn't back her up. He was going to have Matti committed somewhere far away and none of his explanations for it were reasonable.

She had no idea what they were ultimately plotting for Matti's fate, she only knew Antonio was using Henry. Natalie couldn't fathom why. She only regretted being naïve for so long regarding Antonio's abuse of power. Tears welled up in Matti's eyes and the whiny sound escalated. Natalie smoothed back his mop of dark hair and kissed him on the forehead. "We're leaving and never coming back. I promise." Natalie almost wished she'd given him a portion of his sedatives. But she needed him to walk through the airport and not appear so lethargic as to draw attention. It wasn't long until a generic looking white van pulled into the private drive. Diego rented the vehicle just for this occasion. It couldn't be traced. Their plane tickets would not be traceable either, and Natalie didn't ask why not—she was just grateful. All that mattered was getting out of the country, before they were caught.

Diego's daughter, Emmy, was sitting in the back seat of the white van. His ex-wife had given him full custody of their only child when leaving for L.A. to become a movie star. Since Natalie had never heard of Diego's ex-wife, she could only assume the woman was yet to be discovered by Hollywood.

"Are you ready?" Diego stepped onto the front porch. Natalie nodded as he knelt beside the wheelchair. "It's good to see you again, Matti. I wish it were under better circumstances, but Emmy's happy you'll be coming with us." Matti didn't respond. He stared at the fountain while making the high-pitched sound in his throat. Diego helped Matti up and walked with him to the van while Natalie hid the wheelchair behind a bush and grabbed their suitcases off the porch. She placed them in the vehicle while Diego seat-belted Matti next to Emmy. No one said a word as they backed down the long drive lined with tall, feathery date palms. Natalie watched from her window for anyone who might have seen them leaving.

The airport seemed like an eternity away. The further they drove, the more keyed up Natalie became. She expected to be pulled over any minute by a policeman Antonio had paid off. It was something she wouldn't put past him. Scrutinizing Matti in the backseat, she could see that he was visibly calmer. He was staring at Emmy, as if he recognized her. Emmy was watching trees speed past the window, but occasionally she glanced at Matti with half a smile. Diego had said that Emmy was a sixth-grade honor student. She missed her Aunt Mira and was glad to be returning to Copan. He'd told Emmy about Matti's condition and how no one knew what triggered his emotional breakdown. He didn't explain why Matti and his mom were coming to Copan with them, only that they'd be staying in the summerhouse on the island of Roatan and she must not tell anyone.

Antonio would be livid when he found out. Retaliation would be his sole quest. Now Diego and Emmy were involved. It worried Natalie. She didn't want to bring any harm to her good friend, or his daughter. Antonio would never quit searching until he found them. He had the resources to make it happen. But maybe . . . just maybe, they would leave no trail to find. At least, this is what she prayed for.

CHAPTER FOUR

Matti played his video games until they became his dreams, and he didn't know the lights were out and the game was off.

Matti stared at Emmy and saw flashes of the portrait in the hall. He was sure it was the same girl. Her brown eyes sparkled at him just as they had in the painting, and the dark curls lay about her shoulders in nearly the same way, only longer. He tried to picture the other portraits but all he saw was himself crouched down in the hall, shaking, scared out of his mind. And now here he was, in this van. The man driving was obviously the Honduran with the coffee plantation, and Emmy of course was his daughter. His mother was taking him away to where they lived. That much he understood.

Ever since *that night* his life consisted of coming in and out of a fog. His mother was always there by his side, and a few times he'd seen his father hanging around. Thinking about his father caused him to unconsciously begin making a sound in the back of his throat. Emmy glanced at him and then he realized what he was doing and quit. His mother turned around and stared at him with her eyebrows scrunched together. It was her worried look. He missed her warm smile that could heat up a cold room and couldn't remember when he'd last seen it.

"Everything will be fine, sweetie. Roatan is an island off of Honduras. It has beautiful forests and white sand beaches. You can rest there, Matti, and get better."

Matti knew the only thing that could make him better would be to forget that night when his father . . . *when his father* . . . he couldn't finish the thought. There was a flash of that poor woman's eyes pleading with him, *finding hope in him* . . . but he couldn't save her . . . *he couldn't.* It felt odd to be so awake . . . so alert. He wanted to sleep forever. Thinking was too painful, too frightening . . . *his father was frightening.* Maybe he would come for them. Maybe he would hurt him, or worse, hurt his mother. And he wouldn't be able to help her . . . just like he couldn't help that poor lady.

Matti focused on the blue sky outside the car window. He wished he could forget about his father. He wished the man were dead. Then he could never find them . . . *never hurt them* . . . never hurt anyone ever again. Matti's heart nearly jumped from his chest and his hands had become sweaty.

Watching the trees wasn't helping him forget *what happened.* It kept rewinding in his head. Maybe because he was so *awake.* He wished they'd give him whatever had kept him in a fog.

The sound in his throat began again, but he couldn't stop it, and then his mom turned around and handed him something. It was his Gameboy. There was a buzzing in his ears and her voice sounded far . . . far *away* . . . but it was soothing, sweet, comforting as always. Sometimes he thought his mother was an angel. He pictured her floating in the clouds dressed in a shimmering white gown, smiling at him. But then the hands in the garbage bag flopped over again and he jumped, his breath caught in his throat and it was *hard to breathe . . . hard to breathe.* His mother was staring at him, alarmed, but then Emmy reached over and turned the Gameboy on. She smiled and said something, but he couldn't make out what.

Matti stared at the screen and remembered how to play. He immersed every fiber of his being into the game, becoming lost in it, and never looking up. Not when they helped him from the van, not when his mother led him through the San Francisco airport, not until she turned it off to get him through security. Even then he stared at his Gameboy. He watched it move along the conveyor belt in the ivory container and stared at the gray metal machine that seemed to have swallowed it. Matti watched his Gameboy roll out the other side and snatched it from the plastic tub.

He turned it on and played the game along the corridor to their gate, and while waiting to board. He blew up aliens until his mother shut it down for takeoff. He stared at the dark screen and imagined the game, every step, and how he'd maneuver through them to get more and more points, until finally his mom turned it back on. He played while eating a sandwich inflight. He played the game until it was time to land and then he stared at the blank screen until they touched down. Once the plane was grounded, Matti played his Gameboy through the airport terminal to another gate for San Pedro Sula, and the entire time on the flight. He played it while they waited for Diego's friend to fly them to Santa Rosa de Copan in a private jet, and all during that final flight while Emmy slept in the seat beside him. He refused to eat dinner and continued zapping aliens all evening while sitting on a sofa beside his mother in the main house on the Honduran coffee plantation.

Matti played his video games until they became his dreams, and he didn't know the lights were out and the game was off. All he knew was that he had a way to fill his head with something other than that fateful night. He finally had a way to push his fears into the furthest corner of his mind, along with his conscience, which caused him great anxiety because he'd failed to save that poor woman . . . her grave now a fountain in his front yard.

Antonio pulled his Mercedes into the garage as usual at almost midnight. Earlier in the day the trunk of his car was completely refurbished from paint to carpet. He smiled before turning out the light and locking the garage door. Walking through the dimly lit house he went over the details in his head concerning Mattia's move in the morning to the mental ward. Natalie was his wild card. She hadn't wanted the boy transferred there. He always shuddered at her reaction when Mattia became visibly upset in his presence. He would never have run into Mattia if Natalie hadn't insisted on getting a wheelchair and taking the boy out by the pool "for a little fresh air and sunshine."

His son's fear of him was the only flaw in an otherwise flawless plan. It caused Natalie to be distant and unusually quiet even for her. She didn't respond to his advances when he slid beside her in bed, nor would she carry on polite conversation during breakfast. Every spare minute was spent in Mattia's room or her studio, which wasn't entirely unusual, but he was almost certain she'd stopped tutoring her students. There weren't many, but the few she had were invasive, in his opinion, and normally he'd be thrilled to see her quit tutoring. Right now, however, it worried him. The more she obsessed about the boy, the better the chances he'd spill the beans about that unfortunate incident, which Antonio had worked diligently to erase any trace of.

Sneaking quietly into the bathroom to shower as usual, Antonio decided he must be prepared for a scene in the morning with his wife. She had never caused one before, but she never had a reason until now. He was always more than happy to comply with her wishes, feeling fortunate to have such a reasonable and pleasant wife, even though it annoyed him that whatever sparks were between them originally appeared to have cooled. He missed the raw passion of their early years, before Natalie focused all her attention on their son. But then his lover in the little house on Landover Street more than made up for the lack of attention he was getting from Natalie. Antonio quickly dried and felt his way through the dark to the bed. He dropped his towel on the floor, like always, and slid between the sheets. But Natalie was not there. Turning on the light, it became clear his wife hadn't slept in their bed this evening. Panic set in quickly as Antonio grabbed the towel, tying it about his waist while dashing to Mattia's room. Flipping on the light he discovered what he'd already feared.

The boy was gone.

Sitting on the bed he shouted several obscenities for no one to hear, and then returned to the bedroom, angrily reaching for the phone. Antonio swore upon his grandfather's grave that Natalie would not live long enough to tell anyone she'd left him and taken Mattia with her. There'd be a price on his dear wife's head before the morning sun rose over the San Francisco Bay.

Mira pulled gently on Emmy's hair as she twisted it into a single French braid. It felt good to have her niece home again, standing in the kitchen getting her hair braided. She'd missed Emmy terribly while away in the States. As brothers went, Diego was a wonderful sibling. If only he'd be content to run the coffee plantation, especially now that their father had passed on . . . but no, not Diego. He had high aspirations of designing and building homes on Roatan, where he recently announced his English tutor from the States would be living. Mira could tell his feelings ran deeper for this tutor than mere affection between a teacher and student. He had that starstruck look she'd seen once before. Considering his taste in women thus far, it was a concern.

Emmy's mother Amanda was more self-involved than any human being Mira had ever met. It was a relief not to have her under foot anymore playing princess of the plantation. Nonetheless Mira felt bad for Emmy, who might never see her mother again, now that she'd run off with her portion of Diego's fortune. Thankfully Emmy didn't seem to miss Amanda all that much, which wasn't surprising. During the four years Amanda lived on the coffee plantation she'd spent almost no time with her only child.

"Emmy, tell me about this tutor who is going to live in our summerhouse."

Emmy shrugged. "What do you want to know?"

"Is your father . . . dating her?"

"She was his teacher."

"Do you want him to date her?"

Emmy shrugged again. "She's nice. I like her, and I especially like Matti."

"He seems like a strange boy to me," Mira admitted. "So quiet . . . but he has beautiful dark hair and big green eyes. There's no mistaking he's his mother's child."

"Didn't Daddy tell you something happened, to make him not quite right?" Emmy asked.

"What do you mean by not quite right?" Mira put the brush down and poured Emmy a glass of orange juice.

"Well . . . he's sick, sort of. Daddy says he's been 'traumatized' . . . but no one knows exactly what happened."

Diego strolled into the kitchen and commented on Emmy's pretty French braid. "Thank you, Daddy!" She finished her orange juice and skipped down the hall while he poured himself coffee.

"What happened to this little boy that does nothing but play video games?" Mira asked.

Diego sat at the kitchen table bathed in sunshine and stared into his coffee. The beans were grown just outside their door, and the aroma was like none other. "We aren't certain what happened." Diego took a sip of their special blend. "Probably, his father had something to do with the emotional breakdown he seems to be experiencing."

"And that's why Natalie felt she needed to leave without a trace?" Mira asked, wanting to demand her brother confess his obvious feelings for her, but not daring to approach that subject.

"Yes. He was going to have the boy hospitalized and wouldn't listen to Natalie, who disagreed."

"She must be more than a great tutor for you to reciprocate in such a generous manner." Mira observed her brother carefully, but he gave no indication of his feelings for Natalie, if indeed he had any. Her brother was more charming than she could ever hope to be, but she loved him anyway and was content to walk in his shadow. Diego was a good man and he encouraged her to be an independent woman, which was something almost unheard of in their country.

"She had no one to turn to, Mira. You would have done the same . . . a helpless woman with a troubled boy and no living family. She suspects her husband has acquired at least part of his fortune in unscrupulous ways. And then there is the question of why Matti seems to be afraid of him. The boy must have witnessed something or was somehow made to fear the man."

Mira poured herself coffee and sat at the table. "That's quite a lot of imagining Diego. It's a jump from not wanting her son hospitalized all the way to blaming her husband for his condition. How much of his money did she run away with? As much as Amanda took from you?"

Diego shook his head. "Amanda wasn't cut out for this kind of life—isolated on a coffee plantation. As for Natalie, she has her own money from tutoring . . . and her paintings."

Mira raised an eyebrow. "She paints?"

"Yes. Natalie is a very talented artist. You should see the portrait she did of Emmy."

"You didn't bring it with you?"

"No. We didn't want to give a reason for anyone to suspect where she and her son had gone. Originally, I told her to hang on to the painting until I graduated. The little house Emmy and I rented these past two years while I was in school would never have done such a grand painting justice."

"I see." But Mira didn't really see at all. How long would this tutor be allowed to stay in the summerhouse on Roatan? Did her brother hope to move in with this woman, even knowing they could never marry as long as an estranged husband was out there somewhere?

"Mira, I'm taking Emmy with me to Roatan this afternoon, when I bring Natalie and Matti to the summerhouse. Emmy and I will stay in the guest quarters on the back of the property."

"For how long?" Mira asked.

"Jake and I want to build homes on the island."

The mere mention of Jake sparked feelings in her that she couldn't ignore. "Will you ever return to run the plantation, like our father planned for you to do?"

They stared at one another from across the table until Diego finally answered, "Not if I can help it."

"I thought not." Mira shook her head. "You've wanted to design things ever since you were a little boy building Lego cities. And you hate the family business almost as much as you despised our father."

"It's not that melodramatic, Mira. Yes, it's true I don't like running this coffee plantation and I never understood our father, who mistreated not only the men who worked for him but our own mother. The truth is you have all the passion to keep this place afloat. It will never mean to me what it does to you."

"Promise you'll visit often." Mira's eyes filled with tears.

"Of course." Diego walked over and kissed his sister tenderly on the forehead. "I won't be that far away. If you need me, I can be here in an hour. Bryce can bring me in his charter plane . . . that is if he's sober. Otherwise it might be two hours, so I can pour coffee in him first." They laughed, but Mira thought perhaps it was not such a laughing matter that Diego had turned his back on the business, to let a mere woman run it. Surely their father and his father before him were screaming obscenities from beneath their elaborate tombstones at this very moment.

CHAPTER FIVE

She could stay forever if the island wooed her son out of his self-imposed shell.

Nicholas Salvatore Giovanni reread his half-brother Antonio's e-mail requesting that he immediately begin searching for Antonio's missing wife and son. Nic couldn't believe his half-brother had the nerve to summon him to do anything at all, even in the name of family business. He'd never met his older brother's wife, Natalie Northcross Giovanni, having been at college when they married. Having a different mother than his older brothers made him nothing more to the Giovannis than a pawn to push around, at least where the family business was concerned. He didn't know any of them on a personal level. His mom raised him in a white stucco villa on the coast of Greece, where she'd cushioned him from all the Giovannis except his old man. Salvatore had been there occasionally. Lately however, when visiting his mother in the two-story home surrounded by cliffs jutting straight up from the sea, Salvatore was nowhere to be seen. Although vague about the details, his mother indicated she didn't care to know where Sali was these days. He'd probably taken up house with yet another woman half his age, which nobody wished to discuss.

Despite his mother's dismay, Nic joined the family business right after college. He'd spent the last ten years in Puerto Vallarta selling olive oil to vacation resorts. They couldn't get enough of the rosemary, garlic, or thyme infused extra-virgin oil for their restaurants that catered to rich Americans. In truth, Nic was mostly busy spending a portion of the family fortune on housing for the poor. He managed the work crews while hammering nails right beside them. When in Mexico on his first family assignment, he'd been touched by the children living in abject poverty. He could have been one of those little vagabonds, growing up penniless with little to eat. His mother's family had almost nothing. Had it not been for Salvatore Giovanni's need to trump his first wife's scandalous affair by marrying the young peasant he'd gotten pregnant, Nic would not stand to inherit anything but the dust of the road. He'd be one of the barefooted boys who begged beside the posh resorts.

Where did the last ten years go? Several girlfriends and many modestly constructed houses later, he'd grown the family business considerably among the oceanfront resorts, spending a large chunk of the profit on his housing construction for the poor. In a way he felt like Robin Hood. The wealthy resorts were paying extravagant prices for his oil, and he was then spending the money a mere ten miles down the beach on their fellow countrymen. He didn't really mind the nervy summons from his half-brother living in San Francisco. He had tired of his adventure here and was ready to find another project to take on. Perhaps he would discover where, and what, his next building project would be. Nic loved rolling up his sleeves and working with his hands, as much as he despised the import/export business of wining and dining clients. He was grateful the family business funded his projects of passion, exactly why Gucci suits hung next to the blue work shirts in his closet. Shuffling between the privileged and the less fortunate made his life exhausting, if nothing else. A little time off would be nice.

He answered the e-mail by saying he'd begin his investigation ASAP starting with a visit to San Francisco. Why not? Girlfriend number three just moved out, and the last housing project was finally complete. Besides, if he ignored the family in their hour of need, there was no telling what the backlash might be. He could end up picking olives off the trees himself, back in Sicily, just to pay his rent. The Giovannis weren't the kind of family you wanted to cross, even if you were related to them.

Izzy watched Diego's black SUV pull up in front of the Espinoza's summerhouse. She couldn't bring herself to stop staring while he exited the vehicle with Emmy and two strangers, whom she observed to be a pale-faced woman and half-grown boy. They had dark hair and slender bodies. Diego and Emmy were soon carrying luggage into the guesthouse at the back of the property, indicating that whoever this woman was, she wasn't really *with* Diego. Izzy's husband Solomon poked his head into the kitchen. "What you starin' at? We got customers out front, Izzy. They's signed off the Internet and want cold Salva Vida's on the deck."

"In a minute," Izzy mumbled, thinking there were only three kinds of people in Roatan: those born on the island with no hope of ever leaving, those looking for a diving adventure along the reef, and those praying their sketchy past would not catch up with them. Izzy had a feeling this lady wasn't a diver, and she certainly wasn't born here. Nope. This woman had damsel in distress written all over her. Both she and the boy looked more somber than excited to be on the island. Izzy shook her head. *That girl is runnin' from somethin' . . . or someone . . . fo' sure.* She pulled two cold beers from the refrigerator and smiled. Everyone used the Internet café at some point in time, and theirs was the only one on this part of the island. If she didn't gather up a basket of avocados off the tree out back and take them over as a neighborly gesture, then surely her new neighbor would come to her.

Izzy put the beers on a tray and began to hum a tune. It was going to be a fun summer, with strange new people next-door and all. Maybe she'd even get a chance to visit with Diego now and then. She truly missed their childhood days of romping on the beach down the shore, when his family stayed in the summerhouse. Izzy had wanted to buy this parcel of land beside Diego's summer home for as long as she could remember. Thanks to her daddy's wedding gift, the land was now hers, and the café. Izzy carried the tray out back to waiting customers while lost in thought about her new neighbors. She'd find a way to put a smile on their faces, even if it took all summer to do it.

"Thanks, Diego . . . for everything." Natalie looked him right in the eye while serving fried rice with shrimp, thrown together from the food Mira packed. They'd been sweeping, cleaning, and arranging things all afternoon until hunger got the better of them.

"I just hope you and Matti will be comfortable here." Diego's brows were knitted together, and his eyes swept over her in a worried, protective way.

"How could we not be?" Natalie smiled. "The view alone is stunning." She glanced out the front window at the sea, with its white sandy beach and emerald green water. The laissez faire mood of the island had already helped abate her anxiety from having deserted Antonio.

"It doesn't begin to compare to what you and Matti are used to," he argued.

"No. You mustn't think like that, Diego. I don't come from wealth. It was on the estate that I felt out of place. This feels like a real home to me.

It's more than I ever hoped for, when first realizing Matti and I must leave San Francisco." She looked at her son sitting next to Emmy, eating the spicy shrimp and rice as if he'd had it every day of his life. In truth, she wasn't sure he'd ever had either one before. Antonio wasn't a fan of Cajun food. The Gameboy sat idle between them and Natalie wondered why it had been on the front lawn that morning. Why had Matti taken it outside with him? Where exactly had Antonio found it? She should have asked more questions when she had the chance, but something told her Antonio wouldn't have answered them anyway.

Diego continued to study her, while peeling his shrimp, as if she might disappear into thin air right before his very eyes. Maybe he hadn't quite accepted that they were really here, on the island, over two thousand miles from San Francisco. "Natalie, don't look so worried. There's no way Antonio can find you. We left no trace of your journey here."

Natalie shook her head. "Antonio won't give up looking until every stone is unturned." She took a drink of the big and bold Chilean wine Diego had poured for them and decided it was just like the summerhouse—cheery and bright.

Diego folded his hands on the table and smiled at her. "You're safe here, and you're welcome to stay in this house forever if you wish."

"Diego, don't be silly. As soon as I can, I'll find somewhere else to live and give your family back this lovely home." She put her fork down and looked at him determinedly. "In the meantime, I'll pay you rent. I have money from my tutoring, just as I told you before. You need only tell me what you wish to charge."

"Nothing." Diego quit eating and sat back in his chair. "I didn't realize how hungry I was or what an amazing cook you are."

She ignored his compliment. "I have to pay rent, Diego. Matti and I cannot possibly stay here for free."

"Well, then, we have a problem, because I can't possibly charge you rent. This property has been in my family for many years. It's seldom used anymore." They stared at one another in a deadlock of wills. Finally Diego spoke, his eyes soft and pleading. "Natalie, listen to me. Mira hates the beach, and I've scarcely been here myself. It was my parents who loved to come for the summer. But they're gone now, and I'm just happy it's not vacant."

"I can't take advantage of your generosity, Diego. You've already been too kind." She didn't add how the idea of being dependent upon anyone right now disturbed her. If nothing else, her marriage to Antonio had taught her that self-sufficiency was much more desirable. She'd been such a Rapunzel in an ivory tower all these years, with the dark mysterious Antonio becoming more distant by the moment. It had been just the opposite of what she'd hoped marriage would be. How silly of her to think Antonio would be a soul mate, sharing his deepest thoughts through pillow talk. Fairytales had ruined women for reality. That was a certainty she could bank on. Natalie shrugged, as if intentionally shrugging off her joke of a marriage. "You could be living in this beautiful beach house yourself, with Emmy, and not in the tiny guest quarters on the back of the property. That's where Matti and I should be," Natalie added, as she stood to clear the plates.

Emmy coaxed Matti out onto the porch swing and Diego helped clear dishes, setting a handful on the counter. "If you don't wish to live here as only my guest, and I can't accept your money, then perhaps we can work out a compromise," he suggested.

"What do you mean?" Natalie filled the sink with soapy water, thinking it felt good to do things by hand again.

"Well . . . you know that I've just started a business with my friend Jake. We're going to build vacation homes on the island. I think I mentioned how we grew up together, and that his family owns a coffee plantation just down the road from my family." Diego picked up a towel and started drying dishes. "Anyway, I have nowhere for Emmy to go during the day . . . and your cooking . . . what a treat that was for me and Em." Diego laughed. He had a beautiful laugh, deep and rich. Natalie had always loved to hear it and see the sparkle in his brown eyes. Antonio's laugh was usually at someone else's expense, and his eyes never indicated lightheartedness. However, they did frequently gleam with anticipation. Right now, Antonio's eyes were no doubt gleaming with the anticipation of finding her.

"Emmy grew very tired of frozen dinners in the little house on Juniper Street," Diego continued, "while I studied for my degree." He stacked the dried plates in the cupboard and grew silent, as if hesitant to finish his request.

"I'd love to watch Emmy and have you both stay for dinner. It's a wonderful idea." She grinned at him. "I'll agree to this compromise, but only if I can make you a hot breakfast, too. I think such an arrangement would serve both our needs well—for now at least, and I will homeschool Emmy for you."

"It's a deal then." Diego's eyes were on fire with self-satisfaction at the arrangement and Natalie wondered if this had been his plan all along. If so, she didn't mind. She was only glad she could be of use to him and Emmy.

They finished the dishes and peeked out the door at their middle schoolers, seated together on a wooden swing hanging from the wraparound porch. Emmy was pumping the swing high into the air while staring up at the rosy sky and setting sun. Matti, however, was focused only on his game, as if there were no other world except for the one on his tiny screen.

Natalie looked past the kids to the swaying palms and glistening sea. She listened to the cooing doves in the thick tangle of bushes beside the porch, and inhaled the sweet fragrance of supple blossoms, their strong floral scents wafting by on a lazy breeze. She could stay forever if the island wooed her son out of his self-imposed shell. If this magical corner of paradise could do that, then she would happily never leave.

CHAPTER SIX

Mournful tears of countless mothers wailing for their stolen infants cascaded down the fountain.

Nic first met his half-brothers, Mario and Antonio, while attending their Uncle Martin's funeral in Sicily. Uncle Martin was instrumental in the family olive business and had been the only brother of their mutual father, Salvatore Giovanni. Natalie didn't come with Antonio to the funeral, being nine months pregnant at the time.

Although never having met his Uncle Martin, Nic was nonetheless shaken on that sad occasion when learning of Giovanni business dealings far beyond olives and oil. This education came while smoking cigars and downing whiskey late into the night, long after women from the church had put away their condolence casseroles and gone home. Regardless of still being an ideological young man, Nic knew he'd never help promote their lucrative baby trafficking. He wanted no part of these shady business transactions now entangled with the groves that Giovannis had pruned and plucked for generations.

It sickened him that infants from republics abroad, struggling to recover from communism, were smuggled in on cargo ships of oil. Wealthy Americans paid exorbitant prices for these babies sold by their destitute mothers for a mere pittance. He didn't blame the recipients of those infants, who were desperate in their own way for a child, but he did blame those who would exploit the poverty-stricken young women who felt they must sell their children in order to eat. Mario and Antonio insisted they were only taking infants offered to them for a price, but taking advantage of such desperation could only be defined as extortion, in Nic's opinion.

He stood in the marble foyer of Antonio's home overlooking the San Francisco Bay and thought about how odd it was to have a family you barely knew. Especially a family so rich and powerful it nearly determined your every move, and gave you privileges merely by birthright.

"Nicholas! You look just like your mother."

Nic wasn't sure how to answer. "Then I guess that makes me prettier than you," he replied. They laughed, easing the tension of their strained reunion comprised solely to track down Antonio's wandering wife and half-grown son.

"I need to speak with the staff, Nicholas. Please, look around and I'll catch up to you. Natalie's studio is here, off the foyer." With no more pleasantries than that, Antonio dismissed himself. Nic didn't know where to begin. He'd never played detective before, but if he had any hope of finding Natalie, he'd need to detect a few clues about where to look. After snooping around in her studio, it became evident that his sister-in-law was a very interesting woman. She was well read, sketched with great passion, and had several impressive portraits of his nephew, Matti, hung above her desk and bookshelves. Each one portrayed him at a different age and not only captured his features, but gave you a sense of who he was.

He skimmed through her day planner and carefully studied several unfinished canvases leaning against the walls. Family photographs kept in albums on her bookshelves showed Natalie Northcross Giovanni to be a slender woman with thick, dark hair and haunting green eyes. He knew she'd graduated college with a double major in English and Art. Natalie, he'd heard from his mother, was a private tutor that painted. Antonio had been one of her students. Nic's old man had once mentioned that Natalie's mother, Lydia Northcross, was shipped to America after having an affair with a married artist back in Italy. Lydia gave birth to Natalie while living with an aunt in New York, after which she joined a dance company as their lead ballerina. She'd probably been taking ballet lessons since she was two, according to his old man, who loved to rattle on about how Antonio's wife was an eccentric painter's bastard child, raised in a traveling theater troupe.

Nic felt akin to Natalie, more so than anyone else in the family, considering the similarities in their backgrounds—eccentric old man takes advantage of younger, naïve woman and *bam*, a baby is born to live with the consequences. That would be him and Natalie. Perhaps if he actually found her they could share dysfunctional childhood stories.

He discovered her laptop in a cabinet drawer and wondered why she hadn't brought it with her. Turning it on he was dismayed to find it password protected and felt odd trying to crack her code with every trick he'd ever learned, which weren't many. But how else could he find her? It wasn't going to happen through osmosis. When Antonio didn't reappear after a half hour or so, Nic decided to expand his search and headed upstairs. He stopped to admire each portrait hanging in the second-floor hallway and was taken aback by them. He felt as if he knew Natalie just from observing her artwork. The subjects she chose spoke volumes about her, and the way she captured their personalities with the stroke of a brush. What did an artist like this find appealing in a thug like his half-brother?

"I see you've made yourself at home." Antonio walked up beside him. "Any ideas as to where she might have gone?"

"Who is this young girl?" Nic asked.

Antonio stared at the painting, as if seeing it for the first time. "I think she's the daughter of the Honduran. He was one of Natalie's students."

"Did you meet him, or any of her other students?"

"No. I never went into her studio."

Nic tried not to look surprised that Antonio was so uninvolved in his wife's passions. After further questioning he found out his half-brother had no inkling of how Natalie spent her days. Any activities not recorded in the day planner on her studio desk were simply a mystery.

"Why do you suppose she didn't take her laptop with her?" Nic asked.

Antonio shrugged. "I doubt she used it for anything but keeping records of her students. Natalie didn't like technology. She avoided it."

Nic nodded, even more intrigued with her—an artist and tutor that shunned technology, and apparently read the rows of thick hardbound books in her studio for entertainment.

Next he looked carefully in Matti's room where classic literature and hero comics were neatly stacked beside a state of the art computer. There were well-penned school reports and academic awards stashed on Matti's closet shelves. It was clear that his nephew had a bright, creative mind like his mother. The boy resembled her in other ways too—with his lean frame, dark hair, and expressive green eyes. Obviously, Natalie had either fled in a hurry, or under duress, or just didn't wish to bring any items of value with her. They must literally have only clothing and toothbrushes with them, but Nic didn't comment about this to Antonio, who stood watching from the door.

When done examining Matti's room, they headed downstairs and across the expansive home to the master suite, where Nic barely opened most of

Natalie's drawers and hardly touched any closet items. It felt like such an invasion of privacy. Antonio didn't appear interested in going through her things either. Perhaps he already had or didn't believe they'd reveal anything. After their unsuccessful attempt to unearth any eye-opening clues, they sat down in Antonio's den, where Nic confronted Antonio about his proposed fate for Natalie. "You can't be serious about having a price on her head?"

The two men studied each other, for it would seem they were of different breeds, despite the same Giovanni blood running through their veins, along with the same square jawline and wide forehead. Nic was taller and broader, his eyes a brighter blue. He had his mother's auburn hair and fair skin, not the dark Giovanni hair and complexion.

"I am very serious," Antonio answered. "Natalie is nothing more than an inconvenient complication for me at this point. If she is found, and if the boy has told her anything of what happened, we could lose our olive oil business, and all go to prison—yourself included."

Nic doubted that, never having been involved in the shadier aspects of Giovanni business, but he said nothing. Instead he walked over to look out the French doors. There was a newly constructed fountain within full view. Its marbled tiers had water cascading down each one, making a pleasant sound through the open window. It was soothing to watch as it flowed from one tier to the next, while specks of sunlight danced along the moving stream. Yet something about the new fountain seemed unsettled, which was exactly how he felt at the moment. Maybe it was the fresh dirt with recently planted flowers that belied a sense of serenity. The fountain almost appeared to be an elaborate tombstone on a freshly dug grave. The thought of someone killing Antonio's wife because she had become a business risk might have been behind his morbid thinking. He would never understand this Giovanni family he was born into.

"What exactly happened," Nic asked.

"Of course. You should know. It might matter later, when you find the boy."

"*If* I find the boy," Nic answered.

"I'm counting on you, Nicholas. At this point I have men searching every inch of the Bay Area, but I'm willing to bet Natalie is long gone by now. I need you to handle this delicate family matter."

"Why me?"

"Because as far as I can tell you spend as much money as you make, so you might as well spend it on your traveling expenses to find Natalie and Mattia, instead of spending it on homes for Mexican peasants."

Nic didn't respond. Building houses beside men with no knowledge of construction had taught him patience. "I could never harm a woman, Antonio."

"Once you find her and the boy I'll send someone to deal with it."

"Well, that's a load off my mind. Better to just give you her address and let someone else do the dirty work." Nic knew Antonio didn't understand him well enough to be offended by his comment. In all likelihood his half-brother would believe him to be quite serious. It made Nic's stomach churn.

This time it was Antonio who stood by the window. He stared at the fountain as Nic had done. "The boy saw a murder."

Nic slouched back on the leather couch and waited for Antonio to continue, while trying to digest the incredulousness of this entire situation.

"You see this magnificent fountain with three tiers of water?"

"It's beautiful," Nic agreed.

"It isn't just a new addition to our lawn." Antonio glanced at Nic. "It conveniently doubles as a tomb for the peasant woman from Romania . . . that I had to silence. She must have followed her baby over here on the next boat. Maybe she had second thoughts, which was a hesitation likely to cost more than money."

"How is it that Matti witnessed this . . ." He wanted to say *atrocity*, but let his sentence end just short of a damaging insult.

"I was in my office upstairs when she showed up, standing there in the doorway looking frightened, but like she meant business."

Antonio sat down across from Nic again and continued with no emotion. "It was late and the secretaries had gone home. She barely spoke English, and soon she was nearly hysterical . . . begging . . . pleading for her baby back. Stupid woman. I grabbed the duct tape off a shelf in my office and stuffed it in my pocket before escorting her to the parking garage. Thank God it was empty. Everyone had gone home for the day." Antonio shrugged. "I taped her mouth shut before she could react, and then her hands and feet. As soon as I had shut her in the trunk I drove straight home."

"Just like that?" Nic couldn't look at him, for fear his facial expression would give away his shock about exactly what a lowlife his half-brother truly was.

"No, she didn't expect me to grab her. I think she expected me to pull her baby out of the trunk and hand it to her." Antonio scoffed. "Unfortunately the ride home didn't suffocate her, so I had to break her poor scraggly neck. It was unfortunate, but what else could I do? Now she's no longer a threat to us, or anyone else."

"And Matti watched this happen . . . in the garage?" Nic carefully kept any emotion from his tone.

"I suspect he was nearby, maybe looking in the side garage door. I considered closing it, but who'd be peeking in after midnight? I found his Gameboy lying in wet grass the next morning, beside the door. He probably also saw me drag the body to the fountain and bury the garbage bag I put her in. The next day they poured the cement. That's the day he lost it . . . and Natalie called Henry."

"I see." Nic nodded. No wonder Matti couldn't talk and had been reduced to a quivering shell of raw emotion, his ability to reason shut down. "Who knows about the murder except for Henry?" Nic asked.

"Mario . . . and Pops."

It sounded odd to hear their father called Pops. Nic had never called him anything at all except sir, to his face at least. Behind his back Salvatore was always his *old man* . . . and he truly was old. Too old to be having more children, which made Nic feel grateful to be born at all, even if it wasn't into a family he would have chosen. "Is anyone looking for Natalie outside the Bay Area?" he asked.

"I have a couple of investigators checking out her theater friends—her mother's friends really. They were the only family Natalie ever had. She lost touch with most of them when her mother died last year, from some sort of cancer I think. It was the dance troupe that paid for Natalie's college, so I'm sure they'd be more than happy to put her and Matti up for a while."

Nic hoped Natalie was out of the country. He hated the thought of thugs gunning her down. He stood to leave, thinking he might be sick to his stomach if he stayed much longer. The new monument to the unknown peasant woman from Romania caught his eye out the window. Mournful tears of countless mothers wailing for their stolen infants cascaded down the fountain. If life were simpler he would turn his brother over to the police. Instead he would have to play by his family's rules for many reasons, including not wanting to go to jail as an accessory. He loathed his need to endear himself to the Giovannis in order to eventually receive a substantial share of inheritance due him.

Antonio encouraged him to take what he needed from Natalie's studio, and any personal belongings of his wife's from the bedroom, if they might be helpful in locating her. Nic didn't think the huge closet filled with tasteful clothing and bureau drawers of elegant treasures gave away any secrets as to her whereabouts, but he did gather up the personal day planner, laptop, and a few other items from the studio. Before leaving he studied the portraits one more time in the upstairs hall. Certainly there was a story to tell in these paintings. Each must have meant something special to Natalie or else why had she chosen to paint them? If they'd been commissioned, she wouldn't have them to display. The quality was excellent, so surely their subjects hadn't rejected them.

Finally, his curiosity led him to pick up a painting and examine the back. Just as he suspected, the name of the subject and date of completion were placed there. According to the information on his list of former students from Natalie's files in her studio, the young Asian woman still worked on the premises. He was sure she didn't know where the mistress of the house had gone. Natalie wouldn't have wanted anybody to know about her plans. The African doctor, however, was a strong possibility. He'd been back in his own country for at least a year, and had a residency in his childhood village, according to Natalie's student records.

Nic ran his hands through his hair with frustration. Staring at the portraits placed neatly back on their hooks, he wondered if Natalie could have made a quick, untraceable getaway to Africa. It seemed unlikely. No one could have orchestrated such an event unless they were savvy to unscrupulous ways of disappearing. His eyes wandered to the painting of the young girl with brown curls and an engaging smile. He hadn't looked on the back of the child's picture, but now, with careful hands, he turned it over to find the name *Emmy*.

Nic returned to his motel room and rechecked the list of students Natalie was tutoring right before she left. He discovered that a Diego Espinoza had recently graduated from San Francisco University with a degree in architecture. It said on his registration form that he had a daughter named Emily Ann. Nic saw in his mind the eloquent longhand of whoever penned *Emmy* across the back of the portrait in the hall. The names were close enough to make the stretch.

Next he made a few phone calls and discovered that Diego had moved out of his rental home recently. The landlord didn't know where he'd gone for sure, but suspected he'd returned to Santa Rosa de Copan, Honduras, where his family had a coffee plantation. Nic decided there was every possibility that this Diego could have personally escorted Natalie and Matti out of the country, which made more sense than anything else. Why would the Honduran leave a portrait of his daughter behind? Maybe Mr. Espinoza planned to take it back to his homeland once he graduated but thought better of it when he became an accomplice in Natalie's escape. Nic booked a flight to Honduras on a hunch, dreading that his fluke idea might be right on target.

CHAPTER SEVEN

It was hard for him to be near Izzy,
for reasons he didn't wish to explain.

Natalie opened the door and saw her neighbor holding a basket of avocados. The woman was of Spanish and African heritage. She was stunning to look at, standing there in a vibrant peach sundress. The luscious green fruit in her sturdy hand-woven bowl was probably just picked off a nearby tree. For almost a second too long, Natalie forgot her manners. "Hello," she said finally, while offering her hand to shake. "I've seen you next door . . . at the Internet café."

"That be me . . . Isabella. Jus' call me Izzy." She handed the basket of avocados to Natalie.

"Please come in." Natalie swung her arm toward the front room of the summerhouse and smiled warmly at this tall, vivacious woman. "I'm Natalie Northcross, and that's my son, Matti." She gestured toward the beach directly in front of the house, where silhouettes stood out against dancing sunrays.

Izzy nodded and glanced at the blue-green sea. A lanky slip of a girl with a mop of untamable hair stood at the waterline talking to Emmy and Matti. "That's my daughter, Angel. She's ten . . . almost eleven. Not a shy girl." Izzy grinned widely.

"I can see that." Natalie laughed. "I'm glad they're getting acquainted. Let's move into the kitchen, shall we? I'll make some guacamole."

Izzy was still standing on the front porch, perhaps not quite sure whether or not to step over the threshold and into Natalie's life, for which Natalie didn't blame her. She was, afterall, a foreigner. But at least staying in Diego's summer home made her something other than a tourist.

"You got a couple cold Salva Vidas to go with that avocado dip?" Izzy winked and Natalie decided this woman, who looked more luscious than the avocados, was going to be just the diversion she needed to forget her troubles.

"Well it's your lucky day, because Diego has filled an entire shelf of the refrigerator with Salva Vidas. He told me it's the most popular beer on the island." Her cheeks felt hot as she quickly added, "Diego is staying in the guesthouse."

"I see." Izzy's dark eyes twinkled. "Well, Diego and I go way back, you know. His family spent summers in this here house, and I growed up down the beach a short ways. Everybody snorkeled right over there." She pointed to a cluster of rocks jutting out from the surf, which lazily lapped at them.

"I'd love to hear all about that, Izzy. Please come in." Natalie nodded toward the kitchen and headed that way, with Izzy right behind. She watched Natalie grab a couple knives, along with a bowl and some limes, sea salt, and cilantro. "Diego's daughter and my son have become good friends," Natalie added, while sitting down at the table. Izzy joined her, and together they began cutting avocados in half.

"I'm hoping it will help him to speak again," Natalie shared, glancing up at Izzy. She didn't quite know what to add to that, but a part of her wanted to spill everything to this tall, bone thin woman who radiated warmth.

"That boy ain't well, is he?"

They looked into each other's eyes. Izzy's were like rich pools of chocolate. Natalie wanted to paint her full, perfectly carved lips, which could be the focal point of a stunning portrait. It was painful, thinking about why Matti wasn't "well." Instead she studied the thickly braided knot at the nape of Izzy's neck, which must have fallen halfway down her back when set free. Finally she said, "No. He isn't well. That's why we're here . . . but it's a long story. Let's save it for a rainy day. It *does* rain here, doesn't it?"

"Oh yes, darlin'. It don't just *rain* here . . . it gushes, like the gods are angry or somethin'." Izzy laughed a long infectious laugh, and it felt like therapy to Natalie, better than all the professional help she might seek out if she could. While her new friend mashed the creamy fruit Natalie chopped cilantro and squeezed limes. After seasoning it with salt, they grabbed cold Salva Vidas and sat on the top step of the front porch.

Glancing at the beach they were pleased to see the kids still together. Matti was between Emmy and Angel, with his head bent, playing the Gameboy. The girls were digging their hands and toes into the white velvety sand. Occasionally their laughter would drift up to the porch.

Izzy told Natalie she and Solomon had been married for eleven years and almost lost Angel in childbirth. "Angel" was her miracle baby, but she'd be having no more. Natalie shared that she never became pregnant with a younger sibling for Matti. It was a grave disappointment for her husband, who had wanted more sons.

"Is you divorced?" Izzy asked. "I ain't meanin' to pry, but why be halfway 'round the world from your man otherwise?"

Natalie swallowed hard. "My husband wanted to put Matti in a hospital for the mentally ill."

Izzy crossed her long, bronze-colored legs and Natalie wondered if she was married to the broad-shouldered black man she'd seen glances of at the Internet café. He had no Spanish in him like Izzy.

"So, jus' like that you done run off?" Izzy's dark eyes flashed with wonder.

"It's another long story for a rainy day." Natalie smiled apologetically.

"Well, my man done run off . . . but not for good I hope." Izzy chuckled. "It's poker night. He won't be back till near dawn."

"Stay for dinner, Izzy . . . you and Angel. I insist. I'm sure Diego would be happy to see you and catch up on old times."

"Well good gracious. Ain't nobody done ask me to dinner lately. Why not? But you gotta let me help you cook, girl."

"It's settled then." Natalie felt happier than she had in years. She anticipated taking all summer to unravel the many layers of this multifaceted neighbor. "We're having chicken, but I'm not sure how I'll prepare it."

"Well then, you's asked the right gal to dinner, 'cause I do chicken like nobody's business. Have to . . . chicken's our main food here on this island. Let's go make a meal Diego will kiss us for." Izzy's eyes lit up and Natalie wondered if there'd been more to her friendship with Diego than sandcastles and snorkeling. She'd wait until a rainy day, and ask.

Diego wasn't sure how he felt about finding Izzy and Angel in his kitchen when he got back to the summerhouse. Certainly, it was a bit of a shock, but the chicken was fried to perfection and served with homemade tortillas, which Izzy had taught Natalie how to make. They were still laughing about Natalie's struggle to flatten out the doughy balls. Not an easy thing to learn, apparently, although Diego had watched his mother and sister Mira do it as if second nature to them.

"Izzy also showed me how to make salsa, with green chiles and tomatillos off the vegetable truck that drove by this afternoon." Natalie looked quite pleased with herself, and even more pleased with her new friend, Izzy, but Diego wasn't so sure he relished them spending a lot of time together. It was hard for him to be near Izzy, for reasons he didn't wish to explain.

Diego grinned. "Seems like you've learned a lot for one day." He studied Emmy and Matti seated across from him. The hot Roatan sun had made their skin a shade darker and their cheeks bright red, despite all the sunscreen Natalie lavished on them. Diego smiled at Angel sandwiched between his daughter and Matti. She had her mama's piercing brown eyes and wild frizzy hair. He had no doubt Angel would be a heartbreaker one day, just like Izzy. "How's the Internet and café business?" Diego inquired.

"Slow, but it keep' us busy. The Internet is down half the time, but my Sunday chicken special bring' in enough to buy groceries."

Diego sighed. "Well, Izzy, you're a lucky woman to have your daddy gift you enough money to buy that property and build the café."

Izzy watched Angel stuffing her cheeks with bites of warm tortilla. "It was your sister, Mira, who left my daddy that money. Your family's been more than good to mine." She glanced at Diego and then looked away, out the front window and down the white shoreline. Diego saw a strong resemblance to her father, Devante, who'd been a tall, proud, hardworking man with a straight back and long neck. He'd managed the workers on the Espinoza coffee plantation ever since Diego was a young boy. When he and Mira went over the books after their father died, they discovered that Devante had barely been paid enough to survive on. Together they schemed to make it right, giving Devante a tidy sum of money as backpay. It was the least they could do to make up for the terrible injustice. Devante had given a large portion of the money to Izzy and Solomon at their wedding, which is why they were able to buy the land and build the Internet café, with living quarters in the back.

"My daddy's from the Mainland . . . has a family there," Izzy explained to Natalie. "But he loved my mama and came whenever he could to see her and me." Her expressive eyes filled with love for her father and were tinged with regret at barely knowing him. Diego was glad Devante gave most of the money to Izzy, instead of leaving it for his large, lazy wife on the Mainland, raising a slew of unkempt children. He suddenly felt guilty for wishing Izzy hadn't attached herself to Natalie, who'd been in a perpetual daze since leaving the States . . . until tonight. Maybe having Izzy next door would be as good for Natalie as he'd hoped the simplistic and rough-hewn summer home would be, with its overgrown palm and persimmon trees that housed exotic birds and colorful lizards. Richly patterned butterflies fluttered past the blooming bushes and flowering plants daily, alongside industrious honeybees. How could she not rejuvenate her spirit in such a setting, or with such a vivacious, warm-hearted neighbor?

After dinner was cleared they sat in rattan chairs on the wraparound porch, except for Emmy and Angel, who ran giggling down the beach. Matti hadn't gone with them. Instead he played his Gameboy from the porch swing. All the island birds competed with their evening heritage tunes, and tiny geckos bathed in the newly lit porch lights. Darkness fell with little relief from the hot humid air, and several Salva Vidas later Izzy took Angel and went home. Emmy and Matti had retreated to the summerhouse where even in Roatan there was a TV to watch, although cable reception was sketchy.

Diego and Natalie walked along the shoreline in the moonlight and said nothing. The enormous sky of stars nearly close enough to touch needed no words. Eventually they sat in the sand and picked out constellations until Diego reached for a handful of Natalie's hair, which shone like silk in the moonlight. He ran his hands down the length of it while she turned to look at him. He couldn't tell what her striking emerald eyes were trying to say. He hoped she yearned to be intertwined with him on the blanket he'd grabbed, just in case. It sat on the warm sand, forgotten, while he gently touched her lips in a kiss that began innocently enough. Natalie's response was surprisingly receptive, but then she broke away and ran back to the summerhouse on her newly tanned feet. Diego was left alone in the heavy night air of the darkened beach to wonder if she would ever love him, in the same way he so completely loved her.

Antonio rolled over and looked at the clock in the bedroom on Landover Street, home of his blue-eyed blonde lover named Sydney Beaumont. He decided she was really quite pretty in a generic sort of way, as he lay there staring at her face while she slept. Her features were not as exaggerated or interesting as his wife's, but then she wasn't as complex or mysterious either. He could rest assured that Sydney would not be running out on him as long as he bought her expensive jewelry.

Sometimes Antonio couldn't believe Sydney and Natalie were nearly the same age, because at times they seemed generations apart, if not different species altogether. Sydney was into basic pleasures and frivolity like fast dirty sex. Natalie was a slow simmering creature worth every mounting moment of foreplay, and although she always looked tempting, somehow never as if asking for it . . . like Syd.

His mind switched gears to yesterday and the heated phone conversation with big brother Mario, who kept swearing that no babies were taken against a mother's wishes. Finally, he'd gotten his stubborn brother to scrutinize the reliability of their hired help. The hardened street-wise men gathering up infants from impoverished mothers were anything but reliable. Mario would be back in Sicily by now, telling Pops about the dilemma that led to Natalie and Matti's disappearance, not to mention the newly installed fountain doubling as a tomb. Pops would be more than a little upset, but he would think sending the audacious and somewhat aloof Nicholas to the rescue a brilliant idea. It would draw him closer in the family circle and demonstrate his loyalty to the Giovannis, which had always been questionable.

Antonio was disappointed his men hadn't found Natalie in the Bay Area when she first disappeared. Any hope of that was now waning. There was still a chance she might turn up at one of the retired dancers' homes dispersed across the country. He had his men looking into it. He wanted his son back. The demise of Natalie would be unfortunate but well deserved. Nobody double-crosses a Giovanni and gets away with it. Besides, he could never trust her again. He'd miss his wife's sumptuous body, but he never understood her as a person. He'd been naive to think Natalie's admirable loyalty to the makeshift family she grew up with could easily be transferred to his Giovanni clan. Instead, she never fit in, and didn't try. As long as she could paint her portraits, tutor her students, read her shelves of books, and fuss over Matti, she was happy not to intrude into his life. She never inquired about his relatives, or the business. It was almost as if she was afraid to learn too much about them.

He tried not to think about what a wild card Nicholas was, although he had never done anything openly to defy the family. He had, in fact, made a respectable showing of profit from new clients among the more elitist Mexican resorts. The only blemish on his record was the generous amount of income he allotted himself. Everyone agreed that as a bachelor he should enjoy life, but rumors had it most of that money went toward housing for the poor Mexicans in the communities near the resorts, which Nicholas helped construct. Such heroism could only be explained as ideological youth coupled with too much time and energy. It was hard to tell whether or not Nicholas was a valued commodity or a liability to the Giovannis.

Antonio rolled over and ran his hand along the contour of Sydney's petite naked body. She opened her eyes and responded by massaging his most valued appendage, which led to a quick round of rambunctious sex. They showered together for another round and then Antonio prepared to leave, announcing he wasn't sure when he'd be back.

"What do mean . . . you're not sure?" Sydney's gaze changed from lovesick to daggers.

"I have lots of business matters to attend to, Syd. It just means I'll be at home for a few nights."

"Why? There's no *little wifey* there to answer to. You could move in here if you wanted . . . or, I could move in there. Who'd care? It's not like she's ever comin' back."

"Don't be ridiculous, Sydney. How would that look for my mistress to move in while my wife is missing? You want me arrested for suspicion of murder? The same holds true if I don't spend most of my time at the estate. Someone might start snooping around, looking for foul play."

Sydney angrily smacked her coffee mug down on the table. "Well, you didn't kill her . . . did ya?"

"No, and I don't want anyone to think I did."

Sydney shrugged. "Fine then. Stay at your dumb mansion for all I care."

Antonio found it easy to see why Sydney never had children and was divorced after a two-year marriage in her early twenties. Although educated and from a respectable Bay Area family, she hid her sophistication and intellect as if it were something to scorn. He figured out long ago that Mommy and Daddy would be on her hit list if she had one, because she'd made it repeatedly clear how much she despised them. They'd both been workaholics, and she'd basically been raised by what she referred to as "evil nannies." That alone spoke volumes about her rebellious lack of direction in life. The one thing she found solace in was art. Sydney had a collection worth a near fortune, and was running out of rooms to display it in. She no doubt had her aim set at being wife number two, so she could fill his estate with her expensive paintings and sculptures. Not to mention spending *his* money on more artwork.

Antonio, however, had no intention of letting that happen. Once Natalie and Matti were found he would need a new reason to keep his mistress out of his home. What would people think if he cut short the grieving process? They might suspect he wasn't all that sympathetic about his dear wife, who had turned up dead. Surely Sydney could understand the danger in that, when the time came.

And then there was the matter of Matti. Anyone he might choose to remarry would have to see raising Matti as a key responsibility of the marriage. Just the thought of doting on anyone other than herself would no doubt sour Sydney's stomach. If nothing else, it would keep Miss Beaumont from clawing her way into his fortune prematurely, or so he prayed fervently, as he packed his overnight bag and left. Antonio planned to keep Syd absent from his life until the end of the week, when his lust would resurface and win over any premeditated plans to abstain from Ms. Beaumont. He only hoped his conviction to keep Sydney on the side was as strong as his desire to hold her near.

CHAPTER EIGHT

If you are not emotionally open to intimacy, it will not happen.

Nic checked at San Francisco University for a forwarding address concerning Diego Espinoza and discovered he had returned to Honduras. Luck would have it they were grateful to let a family friend deliver the trophy Diego had been awarded by the design department. It was for his beach house floor plan, which had been his senior project. Nic wondered why a coffee plantation heir would want to design beach houses, but then, it didn't really seem that odd when considering his own situation. Being raised by a single mother in a multi-million-dollar home hanging over the Aegean Sea was, to say the least, disconcerting by the time puberty set in. Nic had no intention of following in the footsteps of his mostly absent father. His mother had raised him to be as normal as possible, but there just wasn't anything normal about being a Giovanni.

Nic dozed during the redeye to San Pedro Sula, Honduras. He tried not to think about what he was doing—tracking down his half-brother's son so that he could be returned to his father, who was a murderer. Could he really sacrifice Matti's wellbeing in order to inherit a portion of the family fortune? Maybe not, but then again, the one thing he knew about his half-brother was that in the end, he'd want his son to take his place in the business. No real harm would come to the boy by his dad's hand. Matti could simply walk away one day if he chose to do so.

Upon arrival in the developing country Nic wasted no time in locating where Diego Espinoza grew his coffee beans. When finally locating the estate in Copan, he introduced himself to Diego's sister Mira as a fellow university student. It felt odd to call himself Nic Walsh, but he was fairly certain Natalie wouldn't know Antonio's little half-brother Nicholas Salvatore Giovanni was called Nic, since no one in the family referred to him as that. Nor would she be aware of his mother, Deirdre, having the Irish maiden name of Walsh.

Mira was pleased to meet someone from Diego's alma mater, but sorry to say Diego was not there. "He's at our summerhouse in Roatan," she added, with a warm smile. "Would you like to come in for a minute? Have some iced tea?"

"Sure, that would be nice." Nic smiled back. He charmed her with the same kindness he'd used on the woman at the university when acquiring this forwarding address for Diego, and several hours later left Mira with the trophy for her brother's design award. Mira had been fairly tight lipped about her family, and especially little brother Diego, but enough information was gathered to make his stop off in Copan worthwhile. He'd at least learned that Diego was a diver, with his own well-equipped dive boat docked on the island. Nic also found out that Diego was hoping to build summer homes with his boyhood friend, Jake. Together they had bought up a great deal of oceanfront property, and Jake had already built a few homes, selling them for exorbitant fees to rich Americans.

Having been raised on the Aegean Sea, Nic was quite the diver himself, and building houses was second nature to him, despite the differences between a modest home thrown together for poor Mexicans and a sophisticated fortress built for men of privilege. He took his seat on the next commuter plane to the island of Roatan, relieved to have several suitable covers for his being there. Mira hadn't indicated a woman from the States was with her brother, but then Nic wouldn't expect her to. He just wondered what he would actually do with Natalie if he found her.

Roatan, Nic soon discovered, was a diver's hangout more than anything else. It was not yet developed in any of the finer aspects of tourism, with the exception of a few resorts. Anthony's Key was one, with its dolphin encounter for petting and swimming beside the gray mammals. The resort was a cluster of grass-roofed huts built out over the water. It boasted private, groomed beaches and a daily dolphin show in which the intelligent creatures showed off their antics alongside young, educated trainers imported from richer shores.

A reef inhabited with beautiful sea life surrounded the island of Roatan. The protective reef meant there were no breakers, but rather, the ocean appeared as a translucent emerald lake. Nic thought the poverty level of island natives not much different than Mexico. Perhaps islanders were a bit luckier in that they had lush, wild fruit at their fingertips—or at least only a short shimmy up a tree. Living conditions in the hot, humid climate were otherwise not desirable. Young children ran barefoot; their skinny, dust-soaked bodies scantily clad, which was no different than the hordes of barefoot offspring in Puerto Vallarta.

Nic knew he might have known a similar humble beginning, had his mother not married the man who fathered him before the wedding. It was just one of many trysts for the rich and powerful Salvatore Giovanni, but Deirdre had gotten under his skin and held his attention long enough to reach the altar. Gina, who bore Antonio and Mario, had been the only other woman to accomplish that feat.

Nic checked in to a humble set of rooms behind a dive shop on the beach. He spent a week acclimating himself to the hot, humid climate and layout of the island. He was careful not to snoop for fear of setting off alarms among the locals, but instead observed his surroundings carefully, listening with great scrutiny for any word of Diego Espinoza. Nic dove every morning and evening, choosing different dive locations each time along the reef. In the afternoons he toured the island on his new black Harley, oozing with special features. Nic had bought it from Marlon Romolo, who ran Romolo's Bistro in West End. He sold specialty bikes on the side, shipped sporadically from the mainland. Marlon's Italian cuisine was the best food on the island, which Nic had discovered his third night there. He and Marlon soon became fast friends, spending late evenings discussing motorcycles and diving locations over fine imported brandy.

After leaving the bistro, Nic frequented local dive bars a short walk from his rented rooms. They were strung along the beach in-between clusters of boats moored at long wooden docks jutting out from the shoreline. The best gossip by far was to be had at the open-air bars sporting warm, humid breezes, even in the earliest hours of the morning. It was in one such place called Sundowners that he heard his first real information about Diego. Palm trees rustled on the dark beach as if a storm were brewing. Nic found an empty bar stool beneath colorful swaying lanterns that dimly lit the rough-hewn counter.

"You say the man who owns *that* boat will be diving in the morning?" Nic asked. The bartender nodded as they stared at the boat in question, bobbing in the shadows. It was tied to the end of the dock and was a larger, better specimen than most. The alleged excursion for early morning had been a conversation with another customer, which Nic had intentionally overheard.

"Yep. That there fine motorized vessel is owned by one Diego Espinoza. He had me get fresh tanks for him this evening. Ya see I run the dive shop down the street as well as this here bar." The bright-eyed middle-aged man was a head shorter and wider than most of the customers on this Wednesday night. "Course, if this here weather don't calm down he probably won't go out. Ain't much to see if the ocean floor's all stirred up."

Nic downed his local Honduran beer and asked for another. "What does Diego do . . . besides dive?" Nic already knew, but it seemed like an appropriate question. Most people would wonder what a man did to be able to afford a boat like that. Maybe the loose-tongued bartender would have some interesting backstory on the well-known Espinoza family.

"Diego? His family's been comin' to this island fer as long as I've been here, and that's a mighty long time. My own daddy was one of the first white men to stick around a spell. Built and manned this bar himself until the day he died. Now there's a story."

"Answer the question, Ike."

Nic turned to view his fellow bar mate seated several chairs down, and soon found out his name was Jake Banderas. What luck to meet Diego's old friend and new business partner!

"Diego's family owns a coffee plantation in Copan. They have a summer home here and Diego is fresh back from the States. Been a diving fool for the last couple of weeks. I'm going out with him in the morning. You a diver?" Jake asked.

"All my life," Nic answered honestly.

"Why don't you come with us?"

Nic laughed. "Does Diego care if you invite strangers onto his boat?"

"Nah. I do it all the time. He likes the company, and to meet people from around the world. Where you from?"

"Back East. Born and raised in Connecticut." This was not a complete lie, since his mother had uncles who'd migrated from Ireland and become successful there. He was born while she was visiting, in order for him to have dual citizenship. His mother's marriage into a wealthy family afforded such opportunities. They visited the Americanized Walsh clan six weeks every summer. Nic felt closer to his second cousins on his mother's side than he did to any Giovanni he'd ever met.

"What brings you to Roatan?"

"The diving, of course. But I aim to stay awhile. Maybe build some houses."

"You a builder?"

"I've put up my fair share of homes, but I don't design them. And I have no property or permits here. I'm just hoping to exchange hard labor and some management experience for rent money."

Nic had already summed Jake up as fairly laid back in personality. He was lean and looked athletic, probably a good diver. After paying his bar tab, Nic stood up to leave. He didn't want to get too chummy just yet. He needed to tighten down the details of his new identity first, and he wanted a couple hours sleep if he was going to dive off that fancy boat shortly after sunrise. Both men agreed the dive was off if the storm didn't pass over. Otherwise, he agreed to meet Jake on the dock at first light.

Natalie stared out the screen door at the sun rising over the ocean and wondered how she and Diego would ever get through breakfast, after their embrace in the moonlight the night before. What could she say? She found Diego quite attractive, and adored Emmy. Part of her wanted to fall into his arms and stay there, protected and loved by someone genuine and kind. He was exactly the kind of father to Emmy that she wanted for Matti. She would certainly choose to fall in love with Diego, if choosing whom to love were an option. Maybe she just needed more time, to put the sour taste of her current marriage behind her.

Opening a tin on the bottom shelf of the cabinet released a robust coffee bean aroma into the air. It was a special blend made from the beans off Diego's plantation. She scooped it into the filter and added water. Natalie watched the pot percolate and tried to come to grips with just how traumatized she'd been by living in constant fear. She wondered what Antonio did to acquire such wealth and gain such power. It was evident by the type of people who stopped by to see him, and the respect he received at family gatherings. She'd known for some time that old and withering olive groves were not the only source of income for the Giovannis.

Living in the shadow of a quiet tyrant had caused her to shrink inside. She'd closed off her feelings, not daring to be open and exposed. The young woman that had gushed with trust and resiliency was gone. If you are not emotionally open to intimacy, it will not happen.

It was only when painting that she felt free, and so she focused fully on each detail of every person she painted, through every little line or crease in the flesh. Emmy smashed her face against the screen of the back door and Natalie smiled as she let her in. Diego wasn't far behind, entering the kitchen cheerfully as if nothing awkward had happened between them in the moonlight. Natalie avoided eye contact as she poured his coffee.

"Are you diving today, since the storm blew over?" she asked.

"Of course. Shouldn't every morning begin with an extreme pleasure sport?" Diego's eyes sparkled, and Natalie felt immediately at ease. His hopes certainly didn't seem at all dashed. Whether learning better English or how to be an architect, failure just made Diego try that much harder. It was something she had come to know about him as his tutor. Natalie could only hope she was up for the sport.

"Nothing offshore could be more beautiful than what I see snorkeling with Matti and Emmy down the beach." Natalie winked at Diego while serving the eggs she'd gathered from their hens out back, and spicy sausage from a butcher in Coxen Hole, where Diego did his banking and bought groceries. Cutting into the warm sausages reminded her of the dusty one street town with narrow crowded buildings and hordes of locals walking busily by. Her first trip there with Diego had been bumper-to-bumper traffic, which bottlenecked near the end of town before siphoning out onto the main road. Natalie had been appalled by glimpses of poverty behind connected wooden storefronts. She'd entered every tiny shop and rummaged through its special treasures, lightly touching the hand-carved mahogany steamer trunks. She'd especially admired the black pottery made from volcanic clay. Diego had bought her several of the smooth, shiny pots. One was on the table filled with flowers picked by Emmy and Angel.

"I'll teach you how to dive and then you'll see what's so fascinating deep down on the ocean floor," Diego told her between bites.

Emmy put strawberry jam on her toast while Natalie watched, wondering if Matti was up yet and playing his Gameboy instead of coming to breakfast.

"I don't know, Diego. The equipment looks scary to me. I feel light and free with just my snorkel mask and fins."

"I want to learn how to dive!" Emmy pleaded.

"See there? Some girls are up for extreme sports." Diego laughed. "When you're sixteen, Emmy. I will teach you then."

Natalie studied the vibrant red and purple blooms in her new black clay pot as she thought about whether she was up for learning to dive. But then she felt Diego staring at her. For a second they held eye contact. There was something intimate about eating together in the early morning, while doves cooed outside the screen door and other less recognizable birds chattered loudly in the thick foliage beside the porch.

Matti broke the spell as he shuffled into the room, focused on his Gameboy. Natalie jumped up and ushered him to his seat beside Emmy. She kissed the top of his dark messy hair and poured him a glass of juice. Emmy handed Matti a piece of toast smothered in strawberry jam. No smile crossed his face, but there was a twinkle in his eye. It was real progress; not being nervous and jumpy, or looking tortured by some inner pain. This small sign of healing gave Natalie hope.

Diego stood and thanked her for the wonderful breakfast. He squeezed Emmy's shoulder and stepped onto the porch. Natalie followed and watched as he gathered up dive gear. She could almost pluck green bunches of bananas hanging over the rail behind him as he said goodbye. It was hard somehow to look directly at him. Somewhere deep inside she was still feeling very shy—vulnerable perhaps. It certainly felt odd to be a displaced woman at the mercy of his gracious generosity.

Diego took his free hand and gently lifted her face. "Natalie, I promise I will not come on to you like I did last night. If we're to be more than friends, you can make that call, okay?" She smiled and nodded. He descended the steps, glancing back and waving as he walked along the path to the gravel road. He would catch a taxi because his Land Rover was in the shop and he couldn't easily hold the dive gear on his motorbike. Taxis ran along the main thoroughfare at a frightening pace every ten minutes or less. They all looked travel weary and unreliable, but if they didn't break down, the ride was fast and cheap. Natalie watched him from the rail until he was out of sight, and wondered if she would ever make that call, given the opportunity.

CHAPTER NINE

Slowly, her son was rediscovering the joy of living.

Diego grabbed his wetsuit from the taxi and glanced at the docks. He noticed Jake had brought someone along for the dive. It was always nice to meet people from other places and discover how they ended up in Roatan. He shook Nic's hand firmly as Jake introduced them and commented on what a good morning it was for diving. Nic expressed his amazement at the clear skies and calm sea. The impending storm had completely blown over.

"Not unusual here," Diego explained. "Lot's of them blow over unless it's the rainy season." Diego asked where Nic was from and continued to make small talk as they secured their gear for taking off. Once they pulled away from the dock and headed out to sea, Jake made coffee in the galley while Diego took the wheel. He steered at a steady pace through the calm water, which glistened like a green jewel. "What brings you to our little island?" he asked Nic.

"Diving. I've been building houses in Mexico for the last ten years and decided that gig was up, so I had some time and needed to think about where I'll be building next."

"You're a builder?"

"Yes I am. I don't design the houses, mind you. But I can man a crew, while working alongside them."

"Really." The thoughts in Diego's mind began forming quickly. He and Jake could use some help and had discussed looking for a third partner. There was more to Nic than met the eye, of that he could be sure. More than likely, he was sitting on hordes of inherited family wealth, like many of the divers who came to Roatan from other countries.

"Actually, I made a detour in San Pedro Sula before arriving on the island, and that detour had something to do with you."

Diego sipped his coffee and studied Nic. A twinge of adrenaline rushed through his veins, and he suddenly felt quite protective of Natalie. His ex-wife Amanda had been easy to love, and easy to give up. There was nothing easy about Natalie, not her situation or his feelings for her, which went well beyond protective. "How, exactly, have I played into your visit?"

"The university asked if I would deliver your winning trophy, since I was headed here anyway."

"My trophy?"

"You haven't spoken to Mira."

"What does my sister have to do with this?"

"I delivered the trophy you won for having your design selected. It was for a beach house, I think."

Diego thought a minute. "Yes, of course, I did win that award. Why didn't they just mail it?"

Nic shrugged. "I'm friends with a secretary in the front office and we got to talking about the design awards and then one thing led to another."

"So you're from my alma mater?"

"I am . . . but not from the design department."

"I thought you were building homes in Mexico, my friend." Diego hoped he didn't sound too defensive, as if he had something to hide or someone to protect. He grabbed the thermos Jake had filled with coffee and poured some into Nic's mug, and then his own.

"I was . . . until entering the MBA program. How is it you and Jake know each other?" Nic asked.

They looked at Jake, who was blowing on his hot coffee.

"We go way back," Jake offered up. "Diego's family owns a coffee plantation down the road from mine."

"I see." Nic adjusted his ball cap to shade the steadily rising sun.

"We went away to college together in the States," Diego continued, "but then I returned a few years back for a second degree in architecture."

"To design vacation homes?" Nic asked. "I mean, you did win an award for a beach house," he added.

"That's right. Mira doesn't need any help running the estate. She knows the plantation better than I do. My sister has a gift for turning bitter beans into sweet profit."

Nic laughed. "Well, if you're building homes here on Roatan, I hope you'll keep my services in mind. I would love to have a reason to stay for a while."

"Tell me why someone with a master's in business would only want to manage a building crew . . . and on a third world island at that?" Jake asked.

"I have money to invest in whatever projects I manage." Nic shrugged. "My family is well off, and admittedly I don't like to sit at a desk all day. Let's just say I choose my labor-intensive projects carefully."

The boat stopped, and so did the personal aspects of their conversation. Diego used the opportunity of arriving at their dive site to change the focus. He didn't want to appear too eager to know every detail of this Nic Walsh, as if he had a reason for his scrutiny beyond idle curiosity. They secured the boat and put on their gear, discussing a strategy for the dive as they prepared to enter the sea.

The men surfaced about an hour later, after an exhilarating dive in which every type of fish, it seemed, had swarmed along the reef beds. They ate their sandwiches and drank bottled water while drifting near the shore, just far enough out to avoid hitting the sharp-edged and delicate coral. Diego liked Nic, who seemed unpretentious and was definitely telling the truth about being an avid diver. The man was obviously no stranger to the underworld of the sea. Still, he had no intention of mentioning his houseguests. He knew that Jake wouldn't say anything about them either.

By the time they returned to shore, Diego would have pursued Nic's ability and desire to invest in beachfront properties on the island right then and there but thought better of it until eliminating every last shred of doubt about this interesting stranger. They parted ways with only a commitment to dive again the day after tomorrow. Diego needed more time with Nic in order to completely trust him, knowing if Nic became a business partner he would find out about Natalie. Perhaps he would anyway. It was a small island, and although it kept the world at bay for those wishing to disappear from it, anyone actually born on the island knew what everyone else was about. Not a fact to take lightly when you're hiding another man's wife and child.

Natalie and Izzy walked along the gravel road while Emmy and Angel ran ahead, leaving Matti to trail behind. His eyes were focused on the Gameboy rather than the clear cyan sky and gentle surf licking white sand. It left half circles of creamy foam along the shore. Natalie watched her boy obsessively blowing up zombies and aliens and grieved for him, unaware of his stunning surroundings, locked within himself.

They were going to visit Anthony's Key, and more importantly, its renowned dolphins. She'd been looking forward to this outing, chattering on about it while wrapping sausages and scrambled eggs in tortillas this morning. Diego insisted they take pepper spray to ward off packs of wild dogs roaming freely in Sandy Bay. And so it was with pepper spray in hand they took a water taxi to West End, and a land taxi to the gravel road they were now walking along. Taxis didn't like spending much time off the paved surface, because the rough terrain beat up their tires. There were too many customers waiting for highway service that brought in faster, easier money. But no one was complaining about the walk along the ocean through Sandy Bay. The surf was shallow for a long way out, and schools of fish could be seen feeding in the turtle grass. Storm-weathered docks speckled the shoreline and short, fat palm trees heavy with coconuts lined the road.

"My people live up there." Izzy motioned with a nod of her head toward the narrow lane they were approaching. It was a little village of sorts, with shanties on either side, half hidden by low sprawling trees and tall wooden fences.

"Jus' maybe they won't notice us," Izzy whispered. "They don't like me much since I got money from my daddy."

Natalie watched her search every shanty with cautious eyes, on the lookout for something living to stir. Some yards had children as scruffy and scrawny as the dogs that barked nonstop. Others held clotheslines full of billowing shirts and faded towels.

"Are these your mother's relatives?" Natalie asked, remembering Izzy's father lived in Honduras.

"Yes, they is. My mama has three brothers and they lives here with their wives and children, all my age now, raisin' too many kids to bother countin'."

A couple women in one yard returned eye contact with Izzy, but gave no nod of recognition. Natalie felt their icy stares. She sensed they were the wives of Izzy's uncles.

"Is your mother still here, too?"

"No. My mama's dead."

"I'm sorry, Izzy."

"She got the fever and couldn't fight it off."

"The fever?"

"Malaria. Everybody here gets it from the skeeters, and most people fight it off jus' fine, but my mama was extra skinny at the time, lost her will to live I think. My daddy hadn't been around much. I think his family on the mainland found out about her." Izzy shrugged. "I's just guessin', mind you, but it seems likely."

Natalie thought about the malaria drugs she and Matti decided not to take. Diego had said if you lived on the island you couldn't consume the pills all the time. They were poison, just like chemicals in the mosquito repellent. Diego insisted that every evening around dusk, when the mosquitos came out to feed, they cover their exposed skin with a natural cactus juice concoction. So far it seemed to be working just fine.

They were almost through the makeshift village when a man appeared as if from nowhere, leaning against a crumbling stone wall. Emmy and Angel had already reached the shoreline, where they sat in the sand and waited. "Whachya doin' here, Izzy? I thought you done moved away to run that fancy Internet place?"

Izzy stopped in front of the man. Natalie paused beside her. Matti didn't look up from his game.

"Hello, Uncle Roy," Izzy said without a hint of warmth. "These here are my new friends and neighbors." She nodded at Matti behind them. "We's come to see the dolphins."

"Have ya now. Well, last I heard, they wasn't letting the likes of us in that fancy resort."

"I reckon that won't be a problem with my friend Natalie here. She's livin' in Diego's summerhouse."

"Well then, I guess it don't hurt none to have yourself friends in high places. Specially iffin you've turned yo' back on yo' family."

"I ain't done that, Uncle Roy. Best I can tell, my family has turned their back on me."

"We ain't the ones moved away up there where all them tourists hang out."

"I don't hang with tourists. Solomon and I are runnin' a business. You's welcome anytime to visit our café. I'll even give you all a special discount."

"No thanks." Roy spit on the ground and adjusted his sweaty ballcap.

"Suit yourself then," Izzy said as she sauntered away tall and proud, with Natalie at her side, and Matti still bringing up the rear. Soon they were walking along the water's edge again, with the girls running ahead.

"What's his problem?" Natalie asked.

"He's jus' mad that my mama didn't divide her money from my daddy with her brothers."

"Why would she?" Natalie wondered.

"Ain't no reason for her to, 'cept so they'd be civil. My uncles will say family ought to stick together through good times and bad, but it ain't likely she'd of gotten any money from them, had they ever run across any." Izzy tossed her wild frizzy locks. "It's more than jus' the money. My aunties ain't never forgiven my mama for not having a slew of children like them. And my cousins ain't never forgiven me. It seems unnatural for a woman. But Mama must've had the same problems I's had bearin' children. We's jus' broken inside. Ain't our fault."

"Of course not," Natalie agreed. "Izzy, I think perhaps more than anything, they were jealous of your mama, and now of you, not having the burden of so many mouths to feed."

"Whatever the reason, they ain't speakin' to me, so it don't matter why not."

They walked the rest of the way in silence, each occupied by their own thoughts. Natalie realized growing up with a ballet troupe for a family wasn't as sad as she'd once thought. Blood relatives didn't necessarily love or accept you, like the makeshift family she had known.

As they approached the resort, a water taxi sat empty by the dock. It was provided to escort guests of Anthony's Key to the dolphin cove, on the far shore of the bay. Generally, local natives with brown skin were not welcome at the exclusive resort, just as her Uncle Roy had pointed out. But Izzy and Solomon ran an Internet café. Natalie had been on the island long enough to know that business people were never looked down upon by the resorts, regardless of their roots. Surely the local native running the water taxi for Anthony's Key knew Izzy was a respected businesswoman.

Matti, Emmy, and Angel scrambled aboard the taxi, while Natalie watched Izzy saunter up and exchange smiles with the boatman, who helped her step in and sit down. Natalie breathed a sigh of relief. The native running the taxi was well aware of who Izzy was, probably for many reasons that reached beyond her Internet café. It was all right there in his eyes. It occurred to Natalie that her neighbor was a bit of a celebrity. The medicines she made from her roots and herbs would have more impact on islanders than the café, but Natalie presumed it was the café that got her full run of Anthony's Key.

Dolphins greeted them the minute they exited the boat. Two of the mammals swam up to lift their heads in hello, and then dove beneath the emerald sea. When they resurfaced they had seaweed perched on their noses. Instinctively the children reached out their hands and scooped it up, to toss as far as they could across the bay. The game of fetch had them giggling. Even Matti was all grins.

Natalie held back tears as she watched her son become mesmerized by the dolphins. The Gameboy hung limp in his hand and his eyes sparkled with delight at their antics. Slowly, her son was rediscovering the joy of living. She doubted that would have happened in a ward full of other mentally traumatized patients. She even doubted it would have happened while living in their stucco mansion. The house had seemed more like an oppressive and suffocating prison than a warm and cozy home. It was especially true after Matti's world fell apart through some unspeakable trauma, and Natalie's had crumbled along with it.

She could only wonder what Antonio had to do with Matti's breakdown. More importantly, how was Antonio handling their disappearance? She shuddered despite the intense heat of the Roatan sun. She never wished to see Antonio again. The look on her son's face while playing fetch with the dolphins reassured Natalie that fleeing their homeland was a wise decision. Matti was more bonded with the dolphins than he'd ever been with his father back in San Francisco.

Perhaps one day soon he would talk again and share the horror of what he'd witnessed on that night.

CHAPTER TEN

She relished the idea of helping young native girls accomplish whatever they wished.

Nic ordered a drink at Sundowners and chatted with the bartender, Ike, while waiting for Jake and Diego. This was the third morning he'd dove with them in Diego's boat and was pleased that the three of them were becoming more than diving buddies. A hot noon sun beat down on his back at the open bar while he chatted with Ike about the moody sea, until Jake walked up and sat beside him. He ordered a beer and when Ike sat the foamy drink in front of him, Jake raised it in the air and looked at Nic. "Here's to the best diver I've ever met."

"I'll drink to that." Nic laughed and clinked mugs with Jake. This last dive had been the best yet. They talked excitedly about the sharks and stingrays that had swum about their finned feet while gathering up spiny lobster from behind rocks and under beds of seaweed. They were for the feast tomorrow night at Diego's summerhouse, to celebrate bringing Nic into their construction business.

The conversation turned personal while they waited for Diego to join them. Jake confided that he preferred building houses on the island to running a coffee plantation with his older brother in Copan.

"It seems that Diego feels the same way," Nic offered up with a shrug.

"True enough. Even as young boys Diego and I skirted responsibility with our studies at school, or chores at home."

"I don't think following your dreams and using your true gifts is skirting responsibility," Nic pointed out.

"I suppose not." Jake stared at his beer, as if there were more on his mind than boyish antics of the past. "Still, I wonder sometimes where my brain is. I'm in love you know." Jake looked up at Nic and their eyes locked for a second.

"No, Jake, I didn't know. You've never mentioned anyone. Who's the lucky woman?"

"You aren't going to believe this, but trust me, it's too twisted to be anything but true. I am in love with Diego's sister, Mira." He downed his beer and set the bottle heavily on the counter. "Have been, since I was eight

I think, and she threw a ball at me harder than any boy. Nearly knocked me over."

Nic couldn't help but smile. "Is that right?"

"That's right. She's held my attention ever since."

Nic thought back to when he'd nervously approached Mira on the coffee plantation in Copan. She was an intriguing woman, very self-assured. Most men would find her authoritative demeanor intimidating. A childhood friend like Jake probably didn't see her in the same light. He would know all her vulnerabilities.

"Our fate is doomed," Jake confessed, "due to my inability to stay on the mainland and pamper coffee plants for a living."

"That's a tough one all right. Does Mira know about your affections for her?"

"We've been in and out of a relationship since we were fourteen, or at least, since I was. Mira is two years younger."

Nic thought about the implications of this. Diego had a best friend that was in love with his sister, and she with him. Yet the obstacles of daily life kept them apart. Jake was crazy not to do whatever necessary to make his relationship with Mira work, if he truly loved her, and he told Jake so.

Diego joined them while Nic stared into his empty beer bottle, wondering why he'd never fallen in love, although he'd come close a few times. Hearing voices he looked up to say hello. After fresh beers all around, they worked out the details of their partnership. Nic would man the second crew that Jake had put together and would begin a new home, one designed by Diego himself. It would be the very design that had won the award. Nic would fund this endeavor with his own money, and thus buy into the business.

"Tomorrow night we'll celebrate with the Pot of McCoy." Diego laughed, and then explained it was a type of chowder filled with fresh fish and shellfish. Nic found the nerve to ask who would be at the celebration. Diego shrugged in his customary manner and took a few seconds longer than usual to formulate a response.

"You, me, and Jake, obviously. And my sister Mira is coming for the special occasion. I spoke with her this afternoon and shared our intention to form this partnership. My daughter Emmy and our neighbors who run the

Internet café next door are coming. They have a little girl named Angel, and . . . I have a houseguest. She'll be there with her son."

"A house guest?" Nic could feel his heart beat a little faster, and his palms had become sweaty. Why though, he couldn't imagine. It wasn't as if he really wanted to locate Antonio's wife and son. It was more like he was afraid that he might.

"She's a woman friend of mine who needs a place to stay for a while with her son." Diego offered up. "Her husband is some special kind of scum back in the States. Scared his son so badly, the boy doesn't speak now." He took a long drink from his beer before continuing. "Her name is Natalie. The boy's name is Matti. No one knows what his father did, but the man must be some piece of work to terrorize his son so badly he no longer wishes to talk."

"I see." It was all Nic could do to keep a calm, steady gaze on his new partners, while recalling the murder that Matti had witnessed.

"My daughter, Emmy, and I stay in the guest quarters behind the summer home. Friends and relatives of my parents used to stay there. It's small, but we're really never there. Natalie watches Emmy all day, and she cooks for us. She's actually quite a good cook for someone who hasn't done much of it."

"So you have a relationship with this Natalie?" Nic asked.

"I would like that, but so far . . . she seems to need time."

Nic nodded. "Nice of you to put her up. She must be very grateful."

"She was my English tutor in the States. It's the least I could do to repay her." Diego winked. "You didn't think I sounded this good on a Honduran bilingual education, did you?"

They all laughed, and then Jake changed the subject to their college days. He declared it was a miracle that he and Diego had made it this far, on no more effort than they'd put into their studies as youths. Nic didn't confess he had been quite the student, even as a young boy. He'd always felt the burden of wanting to do more, and be more, perhaps because his father was seldom present to care one way or another. It was Nic's way of rebelling, of showing that he was more worthy of his old man's attention than either of his half-brothers. Now he wondered if he really was any better than his half-brothers. Would he turn Natalie in to prove his trustworthiness to the Giovannis? Certainly it would secure his inheritance for future projects to help the downtrodden. Would he make his half-brother's wife and son the sacrificial lambs for those worthy causes? Nic wasn't sure he could live with such a compromise.

Natalie dropped the coffee tin and was grateful it didn't spill. She hadn't been this jumpy since the morning after that amazing and disturbing kiss from Diego. He and Jake had found a third investment partner for their custom beachfront homes. It would be exciting to have a party in their large and lush backyard full of tall, sturdy date palms and colorful Bird of Paradise. Neither species was native to the island and had been brought there by one of Diego's ancestors. Both were thriving beautifully in their foreign environment, just as she hoped she and Matti would. It was meeting this Nic Walsh from America that made Natalie anxious. Diego assured her Nic came from the East Coast, but why should they believe him? It was slightly awkward, despite trusting Diego with her very life.

She tried not to think about the stranger from the States, and instead focused on the celebration. Elders on the island would bring the yucca-yucca root to boil in the Pot of McCoy. Izzy had explained how the elders would prepare the chowder as it had been done for centuries. The seafood concoction was always cooked in a large open pot over hot coals. Coconut mash gave the chowder its unique and revered flavor. Natalie wondered who would shimmy up the trees in their yard and cut down the coconuts, which to her looked like no easy task. She was glad Jake would be coming. Natalie liked Jake, who had been to dinner several times since her arrival here. He was intelligent and thoughtful, bringing her wine or flowers each visit, and once he brought a soccer ball for Matti.

Turning to thoughts of Matti, she realized it was time to collect Emmy and her son, who were next door at the Internet café. Angel had invited them to see baby chicks recently hatched out back by the laying hens. They would grow up to be fryer hens, something Natalie made sure Matti and Angel understood before visiting the chicks. She peered in through the screen door of the Internet café and watched Izzy fill an amber bottle with a syrupy-looking liquid. It was probably a boiled and mashed root of some kind. Izzy dabbled in home remedies and knew the name, origin, and medicinal capabilities of every plant on the island. Her customers always came back for more, and her reputation for curing anything from rashes to paranoia had spread far and wide. She was more popular and better trusted than any local doctor.

"Now you gives this to Anna Marie three times a day, and no more than a spoonful, you hear?" The young, skinny woman beside her nodded while a chubby toddler squirmed in her arms. Natalie wondered if she was the mother, or the older sibling. She hoped the latter but had seen enough young native girls with babies to know better.

"Thank you, Izzy. You's the best cousin I ever had."

"Don't mention it, Sarah Jean. I wouldn't be telling your daddy though, girl. He's none too fond of me since my daddy left me money to buy this here café."

"I knows it. My own daddy's a stubborn man. I don't be telling him nothin'."

Natalie entered through the screen door and Sarah Jean stared at her with deeply set brown eyes, rich and round like a cup of Honduran coffee.

"That be my friend and neighbor, Natti," Izzy said.

"It's nice to meet you, Sarah Jean." Natalie extended her hand and Sarah Jean looked at Izzy.

"Shake her hand, silly girl. That be how Americans say 'nice to meet you.'"

Sarah Jean hesitantly extended her free arm, while balancing the toddler on her opposite hip. Natalie memorized the young woman's striking face to sketch later. There was such innocence there, and a fair amount of fear. Her dark skin glistened from the humidity while her robust eyes shimmered with uncertainty. Maybe she could tutor this young woman. Having the skills to make a living might eliminate all that doubt in her eyes. In that moment Natalie decided she would tutor all the young women. Why not? It would repay the island for being her refuge. She relished the idea of helping young native girls accomplish whatever they wished. None of them had received much formal education on the island. Diego had told her that. Girls left school after only a few formative years, to help their mothers at home, and become mothers themselves at much too young an age. Maybe that cycle could be stopped, and an education would be the best way to start. If they became efficient at reading, writing, and math, they could support themselves.

"I's be goin' now, Izzy." Sarah Jean gave her auntie a big hug, nodded, and smiled briefly at Natalie, and then nearly ran down the porch steps with the squirming toddler. She passed Solomon, who was on his way up the steps. They did not, Natalie observed, acknowledge each other's presence.

"Solomon, it's about time you be gettin' home. Where you been?" Izzy asked.

"Why you keep given that no good family of yours medicines and such, Izzy? Your uncles ain't likely to come 'round thankin' us for interferin' in their lives." He pulled her into a tight hug before she could answer.

"Solomon, let me go. We got company." Izzy giggled while struggling to free herself. He released her and leaned against the long wooden counter in their roomy kitchen, built to cook for a crowd in the adjoining café.

"How's that boy o' yours doin'?" Everyone knew Solomon had a soft spot in his heart for Matti. He'd taken a liking to him, often sitting beside the troubled teen on the top porch step and having a one-way conversation, while Matti blew up aliens on his Gameboy.

Natalie smiled. "He's doing much better than when we first arrived . . . thanks to Izzy."

"That right?" Solomon looked at Izzy curiously.

"Oh, I ain't done nothin' for that boy 'cept give him a little something to calm his nerves."

"Well, whatever magic you've made from those roots and herbs of yours, I'm forever grateful." Natalie walked over and kissed her on the cheek.

Izzy blushed and changed the subject. "Solomon, we's goin' next door to Diego's party tonight. He's brewin' up a Pot of McCoy 'cause he has a new partner to build them fancy beach houses with."

Solomon frowned. "I can't make it, Izzy. You and Angel go without me."

"Why not?"

Solomon shrugged. "I already promised the boys I'd play poker. You know I always do on Friday night."

Izzy folded her arms tightly in front of her. Those perfectly carved lips turned downward. If eyes could shoot daggers, Solomon would be wincing in pain, but instead he rummaged through the refrigerator unaware of her anger. Natalie had envied their touching, laughing, and kidding around the few times she'd seen Izzy and Solomon together. It was something she'd never known with a man, such ease and playfulness. This was the first time she'd witnessed any trouble between them.

"Why don't you *not* go jus' this once? It ain't like they wouldn't forgive you."

Solomon pulled a plate of leftover chicken from the refrigerator. He grabbed a flour tortilla from the bag on the counter and rolled the chicken up in it. Izzy watched him, silently, while Natalie willed herself to blend into the woodwork. He kissed Izzy on the forehead and winked at Natalie before strolling out of the kitchen. Izzy silently stared at the back of him as he left, her arms still folded tightly in front of her.

"I'll be late, woman," he called out from the porch. "Don't wait up for me. You have fun at Diego's." They could hear Solomon's footsteps on the porch and then he was gone. The fire in Izzy's eyes indicated she would have liked to chase after him and beat his chest with her fists. But no sooner had he disappeared around the corner than Izzy broke down in tears, making a mournful sound unlike anything Natalie had heard before. She watched as Izzy buried her head in her hands, sobbing, and then ran to her side. Natalie put her arms around Izzy's tall, narrow frame, which was limp and bent over at the moment. They just stood there, in each other's arms, while Izzy cried it out and Natalie struggled to understand.

Why hadn't she noticed something was wrong between Izzy and Solomon? But then, no one would have suspected her unhappiness with Antonio, either. The difference was in knowing Izzy truly loved Solomon, and unless her instincts were completely wrong, Solomon loved Izzy, too. Why would he play this power game of choosing poker over the party Izzy was so obviously looking forward to? Was it the fact that Izzy was so smart with running the Internet café, and popular with all their customers? And then there was her daddy's money, which had allowed them to buy the land and build the café in the first place. Was being so uncooperative a form of rebellion on Solomon's part, in order to feel more in control? Natalie hoped that's all it was, but something told her, judging by Izzy's reaction, that Solomon's behavior was more than a mere power play.

CHAPTER ELEVEN

"Why, this here's the first time I seen fire in them eyes since you got here, Natti-girl."

Antonio woke up to the sound of dirt being shoveled. At first he just listened, not sure if it was real or part of his nightmare about burying the peasant woman under the fountain. No, that sound was most definitely *real* shoveling. He jumped from the bed and stared out the window at the grounds below, where gardeners indeed were digging. To Antonio's complete dismay he observed them preparing to plant trees as cornerstones to his shrine for the Romanian mother. They would certainly add a charming effect. He vaguely remembered approving plans for phase three of the fountain long before phase one began.

Without a sideways glance to Sydney still dozing in the bed, he nearly sprinted down the stairs and out the door. Antonio flew off the front porch and ran across the yard, stopping out of breath near where the gardeners were digging. He didn't have the time or inclination to feel embarrassed by his shirtless body and bare feet. They'd been chattering quietly in Spanish until seeing the master of the house. Antonio's presence prompted them to be silent and hold their shovels still.

They couldn't know, Antonio convinced himself, that only minutes ago he was struggling to pull jeans on over his naked body in order to stop them from unearthing something regrettable. Looking at their round faces and large questioning eyes caused him to feel foolish about his paranoia, thinking a corpse might have shifted twelve feet in any direction.

"What are you doing?" he demanded in English, for he knew they spoke it well enough to communicate with him.

"We plant cherry trees, like in the plans." The head gardener looked at his work crew for moral support. They each nodded emphatically.

Looking carefully at the spaces marked for planting trees, Antonio recalled that dreadful night when he carried the peasant woman's body to this fountain area and dug her grave. He berated himself for not trying to soft sell Matti on what he *thought* he saw. Anger swelled in his veins again at Natalie's disappearance. She so handily out-maneuvered him, something no man had ever done, let alone a woman. This traitorous wife of his would pay dearly for her distrust. Antonio made a mental note to call Nic when he returned to the house and see if he'd made any connection between the Honduran and Natalie's whereabouts.

"Okay then, plant the trees," Antonio ordered. He scrutinized the area one last time and squelched any insane thought of the body having moved. He was sure, afterall, that he placed it deep in the middle of the cavity awaiting fresh cement, dead center beneath the fountain. It would be hard to reclaim his evidence even if concerted effort were put forth, rather than just a few Mexicans planting trees twelve feet away.

Walking briskly back to the house Antonio observed a white police car turning into the private lane. It was not going to be a good day. What at first seemed routine investigation and sympathetic support was now becoming tedious questioning full of suspicion. And he couldn't blame them, although he was beginning to hate these men in their blue uniforms. Antonio never had any use for the law. He prided himself on tiptoeing around their arsenal of rules and regulations concerning shipping imports and exports.

And then there was the baby trade. It made a mockery of those rules and regulations to say the least. Antonio couldn't believe he'd stumbled upon such a lucrative and easy scheme for padding olive export profit. Of course, it couldn't last forever. His objective was to reap its rewards until the groves, newly planted near the aging ones, were fat with exportable fruit. He had only hoped he wouldn't get caught in the meantime. "And damn Natalie for her role in that very real possibility," he muttered under his breath, as the squad car parked beside the porch.

It was perfect timing for the police. Antonio had just reached the front door with no opportunity to warn Sydney, put on a shirt, or compose himself. It would take all he could muster to appear pleasant.

"Hello officers. What can I do for you today?" Antonio made no gesture to invite them in as they strolled up the walkway.

"Good morning, Mr. Giovanni. You're out early," the larger of the two officers commented. "Can we impose upon you for a few minutes? We have a couple more questions," he added. The officers smiled, but it didn't feel at all genuine to Antonio, and why would it be? He knew these men in their crisp blue shirts found him nothing but an arrogant rich man, trying to skirt laws made precisely for derailing his wealth.

"Certainly." Antonio had flashes of Sydney standing at the coffee pot in her see-through negligee, hair impossibly rumpled from an all night romp in the California king-size bed. With his wife and son gone barely over a month, and under signs of duress at that, it would not look good to have a mistress hanging out in the mansion. Not good at all.

"Yes . . . well, I was just checking on the yard crew planting those cherry trees," Antonio offered up, smiling weakly.

"Umhum." The officers glanced briefly at the Mexican gardeners before stepping onto the porch, where their intimidating badges brightly reflected the morning sun. They were obviously poised to enter the home, whether invited officially to do so or not. Opening the door and muttering something about hot coffee in the kitchen, Antonio only hoped he didn't appear agitated. Fortunately, Sydney was not standing nearly naked at the coffee pot. Surely she'd heard their voices by now and would stay hidden in the generous master suite.

The officers sat down in the kitchen nook overlooking the garden while Antonio poured them stout mugs of French roast. They observed him, rather than admiring the garden view, as if looking for a sign of fear. Antonio prayed they wouldn't detect any. He had passed a lie detector test with flying colors, and why not? He actually had no idea where his wife went with Matti, and like the officers, he could only assume they were together. It infuriated him that she was able to pull off this stunt and disappear with no more trace than a few particles of dust on the wheelchair in the front hall.

Antonio kept telling himself he had nothing to fear, that he wanted the same answers they did, and as promptly as they wanted them. Sitting across from the officers, he sipped his coffee and tried not to consider how his baby trade, and consequent murder, might shed a great deal of light on this very dark situation.

Natalie peeked at the children in the yard while making tea for Izzy, who stared blankly at the tree outside her window. It was dripping with ripe pomegranates. Natalie had recently discovered that pomegranate juice was like nectar from the gods. It was especially good when infused with tequila. She wished she had a little of Diego's spiked juice for Izzy's tea. "Where is Solomon really going, Izzy?" It was a reasonable question, considering that poker night alone wouldn't upset any wife to the extent of Izzy's current misery.

After dabbing at her eyes with a tissue and taking a long drink of the honey-sweetened tea, Izzy answered. "My man has a fancy for that young'un ridin' along in the back of her daddy's vegetable truck." The faraway look in her eyes quickly evaporated as she focused on Natalie. "We buy everything we don't grow here from them two." Izzy sighed, fumbling unconsciously with the tissue in her hand.

"Jessica? She can't be more than sixteen." Natalie couldn't imagine Solomon, nearly forty, seducing this slip of a girl with kinky brown curls.

"Ain't odd at all for an island man to have his way with a girl that age. She would jus' feel privileged to accommodate my Solomon, seein' as he's a respectable businessman."

"Why? Surely there's no happy ending for her?" Natalie meant that Solomon would never leave Izzy. She wanted to reassure her, but what did she know of island ways? Divorce might be as common on the island as it was in the States.

Izzy didn't respond. She just sipped her tea and stared out the window while Natalie admired her profile—the long neck, the straight, flawless nose. It would make a fine painting. She stored the memory to sketch later, with all her other sketches of Izzy. With the lips slightly downturned and her eyes filled with doubt, it would be the only drawing that showed vulnerability. Ever since she'd met Izzy, the woman had been all smiles and boundless energy, her eyes twinkling with secrets. It made Natalie's heart ache to see her this way.

"Men here think they got a right to mess around any time they want. Married or not. And the women, well, if they are young and naive like Jessica, they feel flattered. It's a bad way to think, and it's keepin' our womenfolk poor and pregnant . . . this notion that life is all about bein' desirable to a man. We know how far that will get you on the road to happiness, don't we?"

Natalie silently agreed.

"These women here on the island, they ain't never gonna get anything better for themselves and their hordes of young'uns until they realize it's all about whatcha can do—whatcha can be, aside from pleasin' a man, specially one that ain't yours. He won't feed his bastard children—that's for dam sure."

"I can tutor them, Izzy. The island women can come to me and I'll help improve their reading and math skills, help them speak English properly." Natalie could only hope it would keep her own mournful wail buried deep inside, where she wanted it to stay. She wished her many years of education were all *she* needed to find freedom and independence. Staying hidden from a dangerous husband seemed as precarious as raising a parcel of unplanned babies.

"That ain't no half bad idea." Izzy grinned for the first time since Solomon had strutted into the kitchen and hugged her somewhat seductively.

Natalie nodded. "And they don't have to pay. Maybe I'll paint a few of them, sell their portraits for money. If they give me permission to do that, it will help us all out."

Izzy lit up. "Why, this here's the first time I seen fire in them eyes since you got here, Natti-girl."

It was true. She did feel excited at the prospect of helping island women with their math and reading skills, so they could earn money, and be self-sufficient. Making a living on the island with her painting would allow for her own self-sufficiency. Not that she didn't appreciate Diego and all that he had done for her and Matti.

"We best check on them kids." Izzy looked out the window to see where they'd gone. As if on cue, shrieking came from the far end of the yard. Something more fascinating than chicks must have caused the squealing. Both women headed that way, the screen door slamming behind them. The kids were squatting in a circle near where the chicks were kept. They were all staring at an impossibly large spider, right in the center of their circle. It was quite hairy, and nearly the size of a salad plate, with beautiful black and brown features. Natalie didn't know whether to be impressed or mortified. It moved slightly when Matti poked it gently with a stick. She wanted to shriek herself but thought better of it and caught the near scream in her throat. "Matti! What is that?"

The girls looked up at Izzy and Natalie, and then became absorbed again in their scary find. Matti didn't alter his gaze from the fine treasure in the middle of their circle.

"Look Mama!" Angel pointed. "It's a giant *tranchula*."

It was indeed the biggest tarantula the women had ever seen. Big enough to eat a baby chick for breakfast and still be hungry. Natalie watched Matti, who was fascinated with the spider. He showed no fear whatsoever as he gazed almost lovingly at his find. It calmed her urge to find a large rock and smash the creature before it could do any harm. She had thought of this as self-defense and not murder, until seeing the look in her son's eyes. It was clear Matti would view killing the spider as anything but justified.

"Are these common here, Izzy? I mean, are they hiding behind every serrated leaf in this little jungle of ours?" Natalie hoped she didn't sound as mortified as she felt.

Izzy chuckled. "Natti, honey, these here little critters are the shiest you's likely to run across. If they is on every big ole leaf out there, you ain't never gonna know it unless you surprise them on accident." Izzy studied Natalie's face and looked amused. "I'm pretty sure that ain't gonna happen. So jus' forget about 'em . . . the same way they'd like to forget about you."

All of them became so enthralled with the beautiful, albeit frightening creature, that none of them saw Diego walk up.

"What's this we have?" he asked, smiling. "A pet for Matti?"

The little girls looked at Diego with a horrified expression. Matti, on the other hand, had a glimmer of hope in his eyes.

Natalie's heart softened despite her terror. "I don't know. Can you keep these creatures in captivity?" she asked, looking at Diego skeptically.

"I don't see why not. I can teach Matti what to feed it. And we have cages in the storage shed, left over from my own nature friends."

Emmy and Angel offered to watch Matti's new pet while he helped Diego find a wire cage. Natalie had little doubt the arachnid could easily have moseyed along, for all the threat these two little girls would be in detaining it. She smiled while watching them stare determinedly at the fuzzy spider. If a stare could intimidate, then surely it feared what might happen should it choose to scamper off. Natalie didn't know if she felt relief or dismay when Diego and Matti returned with a cage.

"Who wants to put our little eight-legged friend in its new home?" Diego asked. The girls frowned at him. "Do you want to do it, Matti?"

Matti eagerly nodded.

"All right then. Gently grab his abdomen with your fingers, between his second and third leg, and pick him up."

Matti reached down and confidently did exactly as Diego had instructed. When he lifted the spider off the ground, Emmy's breath caught in her throat and Angel covered her mouth with one hand. No one dared say a word, or even breathe. Matti carefully maneuvered his new pet into the cage and shut the door. Scrunching down on his belly in the dirt, he looked directly into the arachnid's eyes.

"What will you call him?" Diego asked, as if Matti would answer. Natalie admired that about Diego. He never treated Matti any differently than he would anyone else. His belief in Matti's ability to snap out of his condition at any moment had made her believe it, too.

"Call him Harry!" Emmy offered up, inspecting the little beast more closely now that he was behind bars.

Matti smiled, his face nearly touching the wire cage, but Angel had tired of the captured pet. She ran off to watch baby chicks peeping and running around the yard.

"Harry it is then." Natalie confirmed Emmy's suggestion, based on Matti's smile, which was a rare occurrence. Then she headed back to the café to prep for the Pot of McCoy. Izzy, who had generously offered up her large kitchen for party preparations, followed her.

"Well, I guess our little prisoner is one less threat to them baby chickens," Izzy commented, as she entered through the screen door right behind Natalie. They were chopping onions, garlic, and carrots when Diego walked through the door. He'd brought the cooler of spiny lobsters, which he started rinsing in the oversized stainless-steel sink. "These here are the feistiest lobsters I's ever seen!" Izzy grabbed one to rinse.

"They are squirmy, aren't they?" Diego winked at her and Natalie admired the comfort level of these old-time friends as they stood together by the sink, now crawling with spiny lobsters. Diego kissed Izzy on the cheek affectionately and thanked her for the use of her kitchen to prepare for the Pot of McCoy. Natalie gave her thanks as well. She'd finished chopping vegetables and was making guacamole to serve with the salsa and tortillas. She couldn't remember if she'd added salt yet. Watching Izzy and Diego interact in such a playful way was distracting. Why did she wonder just how close the two of them had been in the past? She tried not to let her imagination get away from her while squeezing limes over the colorful bowl of mashed avocados.

Izzy and Diego soon left, each with a large pan of scrubbed lobsters and jumbo shrimp purchased in Coxen Hole that morning. Once they were out of sight Natalie sat down at Izzy's table. She could see Matti out the window, still on his belly, staring at his new pet. All thanks to Diego. She shook her head, wondering why life could be so unfair. Diego was a great role model for her son. He'd make a wonderful father for Matti, but even if she were in love with him, Antonio would never give his son up or give her a divorce. And anyway, there didn't seem to be chemistry between her and Diego like the sparks nearly ignited earlier between him and Izzy. Natalie wasn't sure she was capable of such burning desire. Her feelings for Antonio had stemmed more from *his* desire for *her*. Regardless of whether she'd ever feel the same passion for Diego that Izzy obviously felt, falling in love would just complicate an already impossible situation. She wasn't really free to love anyone at all.

CHAPTER TWELVE

Natalie swung the door wide open and looked her fear in the face.

Nic heard his phone ring while rummaging through things in the tiny rented room. He was searching for the bottle of wine he'd bought in Coxen Hole for the celebration tonight. Finally he scratched his head in frustration and dove for the cell phone under a dive magazine. "Hello?"

"Nicholas, what have you learned about my wife and son on that third world island?"

Nic sat heavily on the bed and stared blankly at the small kitchen. He'd looked in the only two cabinets twice. There was a TV with bad reception sitting on a bookshelf, and a fairly worn loveseat to watch it from. Not many places to lose a bottle of wine. "No one here has heard of her so far." His mind raced to Diego and their last conversation at Sundowners the night before, but he didn't want that information to spoil his opportunity for a new adventure. Nic already had plans to build affordable homes for the native islanders, once his partnership with Jake and Diego took off. Antonio could mess that up if he knew his wife and son were here.

"The police won't stop harassing me about my missing family. They seem to feel I had something to do with their disappearance, but sadly, I'm as much in the dark as they are. I want my son back, Nicholas. Have you no leads at all?"

"I'm going somewhere this evening that might reveal information, if there is any." Nic's vision rested on the bottle of wine, right where he'd left it, sitting beside his laptop on the dresser.

"Call me first thing in the morning, Nicholas. Hopefully with good news."

"Hopefully," Nic answered, and then hung up. He swooped the bottle of wine off the dresser and headed out the door for Diego's.

Natalie heard a knock on the door and then voices. Diego and Mira were exchanging hellos when she joined them.

"Natalie!" Mira walked over and hugged her. "You've done a beautiful job making this old summerhouse into a home. I like your little touches." Mira took a minute to observe the local pottery and paintings Natalie had added, along with the vibrant blooms in a vase on the table, provided by their own yard. "I see you've taken good care of my brother." She glanced up at Diego. "He tells me you're watching Emmy for him and feeding them both."

"Yes, well, I'm glad to do it." Natalie regretted Mira needing to stay at the Italian resort instead of in her own summerhouse. She felt guilty occupying the beach home, which had been in Mira's family for generations. Being Diego's houseguest couldn't have felt more awkward. Being stranded between countries and even continents in order to keep her son from his father wasn't a situation for light conversation. Natalie hoped no one would inquire about her private life during the celebration.

She escorted Mira to the yard out back, focusing her small talk on the many exotic plants in full bloom, a few of which she'd plucked for the vase in the front room that Mira had admired. It wasn't long until Diego joined them, along with Jake, who must have arrived shortly after Mira. The two greeted each other with reserve, but a telltale look in their eyes told Natalie they'd be meeting again later at the Italian resort. Izzy had explained their love for one another, and their inability to merge such very different lives.

The island elders were at the far end of the property, chopping yucca-yucca root and stirring it into a big pot, which hung from a bar over hot embers. Matti had helped Diego gather wood for the fire much earlier in the day, after feeding Harry. Then he'd watched, nearly mesmerized, as Diego shimmied up a tree and cut down coconuts with a large shiny knife kept in a leather sheath at his side. It was the first time her son showed any desire to do something so physically strenuous. She shuddered at the thought of Matti shimmying up palm trees and cutting down coconuts with a sharp dagger. Part of her realized the need to stifle her protective instincts. The more she thought about it, the more she liked the idea of her son knowing how to collect coconuts from tree tops rather than shuffle paper in a Gucci suit.

A soft breeze picked up and rustled through the palms while the elders discussed tourists overfishing their waters. Jake and Mira had wandered over to the porch and were viewing Matti's tarantula. Just then Izzy entered through the back gate and greeted them as if old friends, much to Natalie's surprise, since Izzy had confessed to barely knowing either. But her exotic neighbor exuded confidence and charm much like her father had, considering his two families—one on the mainland and one on the island. It was something he would have been jailed for in a more law-abiding country.

Izzy soon approached her to say the kids were snorkeling down the beach. Natalie nodded, thinking of their lazy Sunday's fishing off the railing of Diego's boat, anchored near the shore. Emmy and Matti would eat tuna sandwiches in their secret hiding place off the galley. By late afternoon they'd grab their snorkel gear to explore the coral beds. She enjoyed such outings with Diego as much as the children. Still, water was not her comfort zone. Natalie was grateful Diego had established ocean safety *dos and don'ts* for herself and the children, especially since they had gone off to snorkel alone. They were smart kids, but truth be known, she didn't want Matti out of her sight for any reason. Knowing how unreasonable that was, she had given in and let him do island activities that took him out of view for several hours. It was her way of helping Matti rebuild his shattered confidence, destroyed so completely by whatever happened that night back in San Francisco. Coddling beyond a point would cripple his ability to successfully maneuver through personal challenges. How do you display courage if never challenged to do so? And how can you believe in yourself without knowing you have what it takes to make a difference? She didn't want Matti drifting through life without even making a ripple on its surface.

It was time to warm the tortillas. Natalie excused herself and went into the summerhouse to grab them off the counter, carefully wrapped in a tea towel. She glanced out the window to see Diego putting shellfish in the Pot of McCoy when the doorbell rang. Mira and Jake were deep in conversation among the Bird of Paradise. Izzy was putting finishing touches on the long wooden table beneath the palms. Everyone was here except for Jake and Diego's new partner, Nic Walsh. She glanced in the front room mirror before opening the door and saw someone she barely recognized. Her dark hair was loosely pinned up because of the stifling heat and humidity. Her milky white skin had a rosy glow to it, despite religious application of sun block. The lavender sundress was more revealing than anything she would have worn in the past, but island ways were all about staying comfortable and cool.

Natalie smiled. It was fun living here. She needed something more productive to do, but she was working on that, on finding students to tutor and paint. Whoever would have thought she'd learn how to fish and snorkel.

They'd hiked some trails on the island that provided such a stunning view of the endless sea, she'd nearly cried. Kayaking at sunset had been the biggest thrill of all. The sky wrapped her up in a tangerine blanket while the rise and fall of the ocean lulled her into a state of calm. Diego opened up a whole new world to her and Matti, one filled with God inspired wonders rather than manmade possessions. If he had found a suitable partner for his business, then she would do whatever necessary to make Nic Walsh feel welcome. Natalie swung the door wide open and looked her fear in the face.

Matti marveled at the sea urchins on the ocean floor. He hadn't seen this type on previous trips. Their spiky backs were bright purple and hot pink. Such a water wonderland amazed him with its treasures. He felt at home here where there were no people, except for Emmy and Angel, stirring up seaweed with their snorkel fins. The three of them had somehow found a secret place to explore on the reef. He'd snorkeled with Diego and his mom near here, but then from the shore Matti spotted a darker blue patch, just a little further out. Diego had taught him that darker blue meant deeper water, perhaps a hole beside a ledge. Fish loved to gather in such crevices. They'd stuck their poles in them before, from the boat, and caught their fill to fry up later. Nothing tasted better than fried fish wrapped in warm tortillas, oozing with spicy salsa. He would never have dreamed of eating anything like that back in San Francisco.

Matti took a huge breath and plunged deeper into the crevice with Emmy and Angel at his heels. He grinned inside his snorkel mask, realizing his theory had been correct; there were endless schools of colorful fish in the hole. It really wasn't much further out than where they usually snorkeled on Saturday mornings. He'd felt a little guilty when Angel said her mother never let her swim past the last buoy, carefully placed to guide boats away from the shallow surf. It didn't matter. They were all strong swimmers, Matti reasoned. He'd taken to the water the way his father had wished he'd taken to soccer, and the girls swam better than the fish.

Matti surfaced and waited for Emmy and Angel. Once their heads popped up, the girls chattered excitedly about the many schools of fish they'd seen, unanimously deciding to take one more look before swimming back. With that, each of them sucked in a deep breath and plunged below the glassy surface of the sea. It wasn't long before they spotted a couple eels squabbling with one another. The eels seemed like intruders to this coral-lined sinkhole filled with shy, reef-hugging fish. No sooner had the three of them discovered the eels than one struck out sharply and grabbed the other by the neck, swishing it violently until the creature appeared lifeless.

Matti and the girls stared at one another through their masks, and then flipped their finned feet to move on, but it had stirred something in Matti, brought *that night* to the surface of his memory. The night when his father had committed murder. Matti saw flashes of the car trunk, and his father leaning into it. He heard the garbage bag being dragged across cement. He saw dirt flying up into the sky filled with a million winking stars, and remembered feeling powerless to stop it, or change it, or somehow fix it. Matti suddenly felt lightheaded and nauseated. He thought his head might explode. He tried never to think of that night, but he couldn't forget, and the worst of it was he never knew when it would all come rushing back to him. Why now? Why here? Matti kicked hard and darted upward toward the light, surfacing just in time to gulp fresh air before his aching sides burst wide open.

Emmy and Angel had already surfaced. They splashed around, breathing hard, obviously rattled by the scary eels. It worried Matti. They would need to be calmer, breathe deeper, and have adequate energy for the long swim back. If only he could speak, but his mind couldn't remember how, and besides, if he remembered how to talk grownups would ask him about that night. He couldn't ever talk about that night.

"Matti, look! We're so . . . so far from shore . . . I can barely see it!" Emmy stared at the beach behind them while her body bobbed up and down in the gentle surf.

"It's okay, Emmy. You swim good. We be fine." Angel's optimism didn't match her wide-open eyes and the infectious smile that defined her was missing. Matti had come to associate that smile with a joy for life he no longer had. He hated that she looked afraid. He had to do something, so he began to swim slowly, kicking gently with his fins. With his face in the water he breathed through his snorkel tube. He could have set a faster pace, but he wanted Emmy and Angel to follow his lead. He wanted them to see how easily they could cut through the water. Luckily, the wind was still and there was little current to contend with. Angel imitated Matti, staying close behind him, but Emmy was too far back when he surfaced to check. Her kicking was more like thrashing, and she only had her head in the water for short spurts, as if she weren't able to breath through the tube.

Matti circled back, coming up beside her. He began to tread water directly in front of Emmy. She quit flailing around and stared at him. His presence calmed her a little. "I'm s-scared, Matti. I c-can't swim that far! I have a c-cramp in my leg." Emmy's voice was trembling and high pitched. Her eyes had that same helpless stare he'd seen on the poor woman in his dad's car trunk. Matti reached out and carefully positioned her for the backstroke. Emmy didn't resist. He could feel the tension leave her body as she stared up at him. Soon she began to float. Her finned feet surfaced as he felt her muscles relax.

Matti began to pull Emmy through the water. She had the presence of mind to kick her finned feet, which told Matti she'd stopped panicking. Together they focused on moving toward the shore. Matti glanced over and saw Angel already on the beach. "You can do it, Matti!" she shouted. "Just keep on a-comin'!" No sooner were her words of encouragement spoken than a fluke wave washed Emmy's head under. She came up sputtering and began to flail again, screaming this time. She had swallowed salt water, and was coughing, choking, much to the horror of Angel, who looked up and down the shore screaming for help. But not another soul was in sight.

Matti didn't take time to think. He had no time. He couldn't let anything happen to Emmy. She was the best friend he'd ever known. He couldn't let her down, or Diego. And then there was his mother. He must save Emmy for his mother, who trusted him to snorkel alone with the girls, who believed he would keep them safe. She'd always believed in him, unlike his father, who never had.

Matti took a deep breath and plunged beneath the tide. He bolstered Emmy forward with his whole body, all his strength. He knew her head was clear of the sea and could hear her choking between gasps of air. Rising for air himself, Matti took another deep breath and propelled them forward again. He did this half a dozen more times, until the shore was finally near. He was exhausted, but at least Emmy was no longer choking. Angel splashed into the surf and grabbed Emmy, helping her to land. Matti tried to stand in the knee-deep water but kept flopping forward, his legs like jelly. Finally he was able to pull himself onto the beach and collapse in the sand. Emmy and Angel were hugging and laughing. It was music to Matti's ears. He rolled onto his back and just lay there in the sun, breathing hard, letting it warm his aching body. The girls began to hug and kiss him. He didn't open his eyes or hug them back, but he kept grinning. Soon the girls were gathering up snorkel gear and wanting to head back, so they could tell everyone what a hero he was.

Matti wasn't so sure the grownups would be happy to hear they'd gone too far and almost drowned. He would rather have held it a secret among them, but the girls wouldn't have listened, even if he could speak to protest. He stood just a little taller as he walked down the beach, despite his tired limbs. He was sorry they'd gone too far, but proud that he'd saved Emmy. Matti thought perhaps he was not quite the same person. He didn't feel helpless for once. As they walked along the edge of the sea, sopping wet, with the warm sun at their backs, Matti momentarily forgot whatever it was that had held his tongue captive.

CHAPTER THIRTEEN

He was, without a doubt, part of something dark and deplorable.

Nic found himself speechless when Natalie answered the door. How had his undeserving brother won her heart? Suddenly panicked she'd know who he was, beads of sweat broke out on his forehead. Had she seen any recent pictures? Would she figure out the name similarity? How stupid of him to choose Nic Walsh as an alias. Surely anyone in his extended family could figure out Nic was short for Nicholas, and Walsh was his mother's maiden name. He felt inept at this undercover work and was glad he didn't do it for a living. He extended his hand while trying to recover. Natalie's smile gushed such warmth he immediately realized she had no clue who he was. A wave of regret ran over him for having tracked her down while guilt welled up in his throat for taking advantage of Jake and Diego.

"Hello. You must be Nic?"

"Yes. And you're Natalie?" He looked directly into her large green eyes, filled to the brim with vulnerability, and loathed himself for being a Giovanni.

"Please come in. Everyone's out back."

Once inside, her smile lit up the room and made him feel like a traitor behind enemy lines. "Oh, here . . ." He handed Natalie the bottle of wine. "I hope you like it. I've become rather fond of bold Chilean wines." She appeared to be studying him so intently he feared she'd see clear into his mind. If that happened it would reveal a vision of Antonio pacing the floor in anticipation of this fortuitous moment. Nic's confusing thoughts caused him so much discomfort he began to sweat more heavily, despite the ceiling fan directly above him whirling dizzily about.

"I'm sorry, Nic, where are my manners? Let's head out back and get you a cold beer, shall we? You look warm."

He followed her to the yard, wishing he hadn't come at all, but instead had packed his bags and left the island on the next flight. Whatever plans he'd had to secure his trust with the Giovannis had just been crushed like a cigarette butt beneath his shoe. All he could think of was how to undo the damage done thus far, in leading his half-brother to her secret location. Whatever had he been thinking? How could he possibly have considered using an innocent mother and child to secure his share of Giovanni inheritance? This was his excruciating thought as Natalie handed him a beer. Luckily he didn't have to try and recover his ability to speak, because three barefoot children had just run into the yard.

"Daddy!" Emmy shouted, jumping into Diego's arms. "Matti saved me, he saved me! I was too tired to swim back and so he helped me swim!"

"Is this true, Matti?" Natalie asked, looking into her son's eyes.

Angel spoke for him. "Yes, he done save her, for sure! He pulled her along while she did the backstroke and then the wave washed over her and Emmy . . . Emmy went under!" Angel began sobbing.

Emmy picked up where she left off. "I was choking from the saltwater and Matti pushed me into the shore from under the sea. I don't know how he did it." Emmy glanced at Matti, who had turned a bright pink.

"Well, I hope you've all learned a valuable lesson here," Diego scolded, sounding sterner than he looked. In fact, Nic thought he appeared as if he'd seen a ghost. It was quite a silent testimony to the love a father has for his child. Nic wished he'd experienced such love from his own father.

"Oh, we ain't never gonna snorkel that far out . . . ever again, Mr. Espinoza," Angel declared, having regained her composure.

Izzy wiped her daughter's tears away with a loving hand and hugged her tightly, scolding the entire time about how Angel should have known better. Diego chimed in and gave them all a firm but loving lecture, telling them to watch movies and stay out of trouble for the rest of the evening.

With the children safe inside, Diego and Natalie turned their attention back to their guests and the dinner, which the elders announced was nearly ready. Nic watched them interact and wondered if his new partner had fallen in love with his houseguest. There didn't appear to be any romantic overtones on Natalie's part. Perhaps she was still too shaken from her experience with Antonio. Diego on the other hand had already hinted at his feelings for Natalie, and the way he looked at her made that undeniable.

He surmised that Diego was in a lose-lose situation, even if Natalie did have feelings for him. Antonio would never give her a divorce. Indeed, Diego would be lucky if Natalie were to remain on the island, thanks to his dumb luck in finding her through Emmy's portrait. Whoever would have thought he'd be such a great novice sleuth.

The children had gathered in the living room to watch a movie and eat leftover enchiladas, since no one could talk them into trying the traditional island meal. They were impressed by the roaring fire Diego built earlier, now reduced to hot embers, but less impressed with all the strange ingredients elders placed in the Pot of McCoy. Natalie decided to check on them, mainly because she needed a break from the party. She snuggled next to Matti at the end of the sofa, hovered over his Gameboy, while the girls chattered on about which movie to watch. She wasn't angry about Matti's near disastrous adventure snorkeling with the girls. If anything, she was proud of his fast thinking and assertive action to save Emmy, and told him so, whispering it in his ear. She knew they'd never wander so far from shore again and were wiser for having experienced the event.

Natalie petted Matti's hair as if he were the family dog and let her mind wander to Nic. Somehow he reminded her of Antonio. They both had a square jaw and wide forehead. Both were lean with broad shoulders, but Nic was taller. His skin and hair were lighter, and his eyes a brighter blue. Nonetheless their similarities made her uneasy. It was probably just her imagination working overtime, especially considering how paranoid she'd been about the new American partner. As far as Natalie knew, she'd met all of Antonio's family except for a half-brother in Greece. Everything she'd heard about him indicated he was not tight with the Giovannis. In fact, he and his mother were quite aloof from the whole clan. And anyway, what were the odds he'd bond so instantly with Jake and Diego, and have so much in common?

An ancient gong sounded from somewhere in the yard, indicating dinner was ready. The elders had brought the traditional instrument with them for the occasion. It made Natalie smile. Nothing was going to ruin her sanctuary here. She felt surrounded by wild forests, radiant beaches, and old leathery men with spears they knew how to use, should they ever need to. She was one of them now, and felt under the spell of their protective powers, their watchful eyes. She had to let go of her endless, nerve-wracking suspicions before they reduced her to quivering ash, much like Diego's fire, which had finally gone out.

After kissing Matti on the head, she hurried out back to fill bowls with seafood swimming in thickened coconut milk. Izzy stood beside her handing warm tortillas to every guest with steaming chowder. When almost everyone had taken their seat at the long wooden table under the palms, Izzy helped herself to the feast and sat beside Mira. Natalie scooped out her own bowl of creamy goodness and looked up to see Nic.

"I somehow missed the tortillas." He smiled and picked one up off a platter.

"I can't imagine having saved anyone from drowning when I was twelve. You should be very proud of Matti."

Natalie blushed. "I am proud of him. He's a special kid in many ways."

"Diego mentioned that Matti doesn't speak."

Natalie grabbed a warm tortilla with her free hand. "No, he doesn't," she answered, and went to sit down at the far end of the table.

Nic joined her, taking the last seat. "I'm sorry. I didn't mean to pry."

"No, you're not prying. It's definitely an odd situation. Matti's IQ is unusually high, but he pays a price for that in other ways."

"Sort of like having a dark side to his brilliance." Nic was studying her as he said this, and Natalie's cheeks felt warm. Something about Diego's new partner made her feel self-conscious. She'd brushed off any suspicion of him and yet he intrigued her, more than anyone she'd met, prior to meeting Antonio at least. That had been a long time ago, and her instincts for recognizing sincerity had been missing then. She wondered if they were still missing.

"Yes," she responded. "He's always been sensitive and introverted. The older he gets, the more he struggles to find a balance mentally, and then something terrible happened recently to push him over the edge."

"Completely understandable," Nic agreed. "Diego mentioned you have a husband out there somewhere, and that he might have something to do with Matti's condition."

"It's why we're here," Natalie admitted. She wanted to crawl beneath the table, suddenly embarrassed. "My husband has never understood Matti. He wanted to put him in a mental facility, and I didn't."

"How do you like Roatan?" Nic asked, changing the subject.

Natalie was quiet for a minute. She took a sip of wine and observed Nic Walsh, eating his chowder as if he were ravenous, yet his manners were impeccable. He seemed to be a master of conversation, asking the right questions but not digging too deep. She couldn't help but appreciate what appeared to be genuine concern, with polite boundaries. "Environmentally, it's everything you'd expect from paradise—white sand beaches, shimmering emerald water, lush forests filled with bright exotic blooms and small colorful creatures. What do you think of it? You're new to the island too, aren't you?"

"I agree with you. It's like a postcard and you think you're dreaming until the noisy cockatoos wake you at dawn." They laughed. "Diego tells me you paint?"

"Only portraits. Something about the human face fascinates me." She stopped short of telling him his face in particular fascinated her at the moment. "This is delicious, isn't it? I've never had anything quite like it. The coconut milk works well with seafood." Natalie focused on her chowder as if the shellfish in it might come to life and crawl out.

"You're right, the flavors do blend well. It's quite good. I think I'll have seconds." Nic excused himself to get another serving, and when he returned they began talking as if old friends, the initial awkwardness between them gone. Perhaps it was the generous flow of spicy Chilean wines and Honduran beer, or maybe the gentle breeze rustling through island foliage as the sun slowly inched toward the sea. Butterflies dancing between serrated leaves were soon replaced with a chorus of birds, tucked away in the dense forest near where they sat. Nic described his dives with Jake and Diego and Natalie shared the challenges of shopping and learning to cook on the island.

All the luscious rainbow tones in the brilliant sky soon faded away and were miraculously replaced by a luminous star-filled night. Everyone gathered for the cutting of Izzy's famous triple layer fudge cake, which brought spontaneous applause followed by absolute quiet as guests savored the decadent dessert. When the last plate was left with only crumbs, Natalie and Mira volunteered to clear dishes. Izzy had gone home to put Angel to bed while Nic, Diego, and Jake walked to the beach with the elders.

Natalie could see them in the distance while gathering up bowls and wine glasses. They appeared to be smoking something, probably cigars, since Diego seemed to have an endless Cuban supply. Their laughter floated up to the summerhouse as she took the tray of dishes inside to Mira, who had already diligently washed a pile. Natalie grabbed a dish towel and dove in to dry the silverware. "Diego mentioned you and Jake were an item once."

Natalie smiled and raised an eyebrow, surprised at her own boldness, although the wine had surely spurred her courage.

"That's true enough," Mira confessed. "We just couldn't seem to work out the details."

"Too bad." Natalie shook her head. "True love is hard to come by. And it's obvious how you two feel about one another." She poured them each a little wine from the last opened bottle, and they finished the dishes while chattering on about how men and women were incompatible, even before throwing love in the mix. The kitchen was no sooner back in order than Jake came to collect Mira, and Natalie had no doubt they were headed to the Italian resort to spend the night in each other's arms. She suddenly realized there was nothing wrong with her ability to feel desire. Something in her had awakened, at last, after years of numbness.

All alone in the kitchen she watched Mira and Jake walking away through the window and thought about what a mess everything was. Here she sat in Diego's house on fire for his new partner. And then there was the husband back in the States who wouldn't rest until he tracked her down like some sort of animal. She finished off the bottle of wine and threw it in the trash.

Natalie pushed her heavy hair out of her face and fought back tears. Since on the island, she hadn't cried. Stoicism and bravery had been her goal, for Matti. She must be strong for her son. Right now she felt anything but strong. What was most disconcerting at the moment was how her husband was no ordinary businessman. He was, without a doubt, part of something dark and deplorable. How had she missed that? Natalie was certain he'd exposed some terrible aspect of his secret life to Matti, and it had nearly destroyed their son. She recalled Matti's agitation at the site of the fountain. It was the same nervous reaction Matti showed whenever in Antonio's presence. She didn't think perversion was among Antonio's many secrets. No. Something happened on the night before the cement was laid, and it involved the fountain. What did Antonio do? What did he hide in it, or under it?

"It was a pleasure to meet you, Natalie."

She nearly fell out of her chair at the sight of Nic, abruptly appearing to say goodbye, and smelling slightly of cigars as he sat down beside her at the table. Natalie studied his face while thinking about how his voice had aroused her. It was seductively deep and slightly raspy. Antonio's voice had been all hard edges.

"I'm glad I could help celebrate your new partnership with Jake and Diego." She looked Nic right in the eye, hoping to hide the feelings he'd stirred up in her like swirling cherry blossoms in a windstorm.

"Did I hear my name being mentioned?" Diego asked, entering the kitchen.

"Yes," Natalie confirmed.

"Nic, don't be a stranger now that we're in this together up to our eyeballs. I'm sure Nat will be happy to add an extra plate for dinner anytime." Diego grinned, a bit wickedly, and Natalie wondered if he could see through her cool demeanor.

"Well, we should at least have more parties like this one. It was great fun." Nic stood to leave. He thanked them both, but never took his eyes off Natalie, who returned the unreadable but intense look. Then he left, making the room seem emptier than it was, considering that she and Diego were still occupying it. She couldn't remember ever feeling so stimulated by an event. "It was a nice party, wasn't it?"

"Yes, I'd say so. You did a wonderful job of playing gracious hostess. I know what a struggle you had with this, Nat. How hard it was for you to meet this strange new partner of mine from America." Diego chuckled as he poured himself a glass of water from the pitcher on the counter. "I'd say he turned out to be a pleasant enough surprise, wouldn't you agree?"

"If you're asking what I think of Nic Walsh, I think he's a very nice person. You wouldn't become partners with anyone who wasn't."

"I think maybe you found him to be more than just . . . what did you say? Nice."

Natalie felt Diego was enjoying her confusion way too much. Perhaps she had been wrong about his feelings for her. At the moment he obviously found her attraction to Nic quite amusing. A man in love would be jealous, not grinning like the Cheshire cat.

"It's okay, Nat." Diego sat back in the chair and folded his arms. "I've resigned myself to you not having those kinds of feelings for me." He sighed.

"I only want you to be happy. It's hard for me, I'll admit. But it would seem we aren't meant to be."

Natalie struggled with what to say. "I'm not in a position to have feelings for any man. I think you know that."

"You're only human, and a beautiful human at that . . . inside and out. You deserve to love again, and to be loved. Just because your husband drove you so far away he may never find you . . . let's hope . . . it doesn't mean you have to be a spinster for the rest of your life."

Natalie was speechless, for the second time this evening. She rinsed out her wine glass and kissed him on the cheek as he stood there by the counter. "Thank you, Diego, for being my friend." He pulled her to him in a warm embrace. "Don't give up on me just yet," she mumbled into his shirt. Nic and I might only be feeling a connection to one another because we are both Americans. Now I must go to bed. I'm very tired, and Matti will be up early." Diego kissed her on the forehead, his lips lingering there a second longer than necessary. Then silently he left, leaving Natalie to have a fretful night of tossing and turning. Her mind kept jumping from Matti saving Emmy to Nic Walsh and wanting to know him better. Such a relationship could only be destructive for Matti, who already loved Diego . . . and for Diego of course, who would appear the fool for having helped her, for having hoped.

CHAPTER FOURTEEN

Natalie held Sarah's hands and studied her bottomless brown eyes, as if measuring their depth.

Sydney poured herself a cup of coffee and sat down at the nook table overlooking the garden. It amazed Antonio how she was not the least bit self-conscious about her short flimsy nightie. It barely covered her ample breasts spilling out at one end, or her long legs protruding from the other. It made him want to take her back to bed. "Sydney, you have to start putting clothes on before coming down here."

"These are clothes," she responded, looking at herself.

"What if the police show up again unexpected? How would I explain your attire? In fact, how would I explain you at all?"

"You wouldn't need to explain anything. I can slip back upstairs without being noticed." She winked at him. "When they gonna find your little wifey dead, so we can celebrate?" Sydney tucked a lock of blonde hair behind her ear and gave Antonio a pouty look. She continually made it clear how eager she was for a big, new rock on her finger. Once she realized there'd be no walk down the aisle she might burn down his home, with him in it. Antonio believed that to be a legitimate concern.

They both gasped as the doorbell rang. Collecting his composure, he jerked his head in the direction of the master suite. Sydney's face drained of blood and her eyes widened as she took flight across the kitchen. Once she was out of sight he adjusted his bathrobe and answered the door. Antonio sighed in relief when seeing his brother Mario standing there. After a tight hug and long stare, he ushered him into the kitchen for a cup of coffee at the same table he'd just shooed Syd from. It felt odd to be in the same room together after months of distant phone conversations.

"Antonio, why you got that woman hanging around here?" Mario asked, in his typical unpolished manner. It was why Antonio hired Natalie to teach him proper English. He didn't want to sound like a thug with a bad accent.

"How is it, Mario, that you even knew she was here?"

"First of all, I thought like the cops. I nosed around, peeked in the garage and saw the little baby blue convertible with dame written all over it. And it ain't that hard to see through your sheer curtain there at the door."

"Right." Antonio sighed. It would be impossible to come up with an intelligent response for his brother, so he didn't try. There was no logic to his tolerance of this situation with Sydney.

"Antonio, I think that little broad has dulled your brain. We could all go to jail here, bro. You get my drift?"

"Yeah, I get it." Antonio gulped down some lukewarm coffee and nervously tapped his fingers on the table.

"You lose that dame, you hear me?" Mario stood up and began to pace.

Antonio nodded. If only he could "lose" Syd as easily as Mario made it sound. As much as he could never admit it, he needed Sydney. She was the only person who cared about him, even if on a superficial level.

"Listen, Antonio, we got bigger problems than you dumping some broad."

"You mean the peasant woman?" Antonio asked. "Not to worry. They'll never find the body. There's no evidence unless Mattia spills everything to Natalie. Even if he did, she'd have to be willing to return for a trial, which is unlikely. She wouldn't put Mattia through that . . . being instrumental in his father going to prison. No, my only real concern is getting my son back to carry on the business one day, and Natalie, well, she'll get what's due her for making a fool out of me."

Mario slid back into the seat across from him. "Listen, I don't know how to tell you this, but we got more of the same trouble."

"What do you mean?" Antonio asked.

"I mean one of our guys took another kid . . . um, a bit prematurely."

"You're kidding. Didn't you take care of the idiot that got us in this mess to begin with?"

"We never got a clear picture of exactly who did that." Mario shrugged. "All these guys would just as soon take the kids without permission as with it. Money's all they care about. They want their ten percent of each delivered kid."

"Do you have a solution for that dilemma?" Antonio tried to stay calm. He quit rapping his fingers on the table, but then his foot started tapping on the floor. If they had no control over the men in the street purchasing the infants, they had no chance of keeping it all under wraps. It would just be a matter of time before it all came unglued. The most they could hope for, then, would be to get themselves exported before they got arrested.

"Well, maybe I have a solution."

"Maybe?"

"How's Nicholas doing with finding Natalie?"

"I'm not sure. He might be onto something. He should have a few answers for me later today."

"Is the kid still in Honduras?"

"Yes, Roatan. It's an island off the mainland."

"He's been there all this time and no word yet?" Mario seemed annoyed. He'd only met Nicholas once, and never spoke about him like he was family.

Antonio agreed that Nicholas was pushing the limits as a Giovanni. In his mind Nicholas's mother Deirdre was nothing more than a tramp that got lucky. Their old man must have had a serious bout of insanity to marry her. It made him sniff indignantly and catch a lingering scent of Sydney's perfume. Antonio cringed with a *like-father-like-son* revelation. "Yeah, well, these things take time, but if he doesn't have some answers for me soon I'm sending him to a new destination."

Mario poured himself more coffee. "Maybe that destination should be Romania."

Antonio stared at his brother while pouring sugar from a box into his coffee. It was too strong because Sydney had made it. He almost wished he hadn't given the cook time off, but he couldn't trust her not to squeal about Syd being there. People will do anything for enough money. How did Sydney hide her intellect so well? Antonio had seen the diploma in Sydney's ornate den. But then, he knew she had a bone to pick with her mother and father. Nobody tried harder to annoy parents than Sydney, and she did it perfectly with the stupid classless broad routine. Except for craving fine art, there was no trace of refinement in her she hadn't successfully stamped out.

"Why on earth would we send Nicholas to Romania?" Antonio didn't see any advantage to that, especially since he had him searching for his missing family.

"Kinda on we need somebody over there that has a vested interest. I'm seriously thinking you don't wanna go, do ya? Especially with that sweet little tart up there to play around with, while Nicholas does the grunt work looking for the missus."

"Sending Nicholas to Romania can wait until he's found my boy. Think about it, Mario. Having Natalie and Matti out there somewhere is more of a wild card than a bunch of peasants in a poverty-stricken country, halfway around the globe. That is, if Matti starts talking, and there's every chance that he will talk if he continues to be with his mother, especially somewhere safe and far away from here."

"I thought you said your wife wouldn't bring the kid back for a trial?"

"I can't know for sure what she'd do if Matti squeals. If I understood how my wife's mind works, she wouldn't have gotten away from here to begin with."

"For all you know Natalie ran further than Romania with that kid. You might never see them again. No point wasting Nicky-boy on a wild goose chase."

"Let's give him a few more weeks. And it isn't really a wild goose chase," Antonio added defensively. "It was based on an intelligent lead."

"Oh yeah? And what might that be?"

"Nicholas thinks she went with the Honduran because his daughter's portrait hangs in the hallway upstairs. He didn't take it with him, probably thinking that would look suspicious. Nicholas's theory is that if Natalie liked him enough to paint his daughter, she probably trusted him to help her escape from here. Besides, the timing was right. He'd just finished his college program."

"Really! Well, well for Nicholas and detective 101 thinking. Why don't you just send someone else to track him down?" Mario asked impatiently.

"I don't have anyone I trust to do as thorough a job as Nicholas. You want him because he'd be properly motivated to make sure things run smoothly in Romania, well, that's how I feel about him looking for my son. He's got more at stake than anybody outside the family. His whole inheritance to be precise."

Mario slouched in the chair and nodded methodically, like he was mulling the whole thing over. Antonio knew their father had instilled in them a sense of family above and beyond anything else. Nicholas might only be a half-brother, but he was the old man's namesake, and as much as Mario didn't wish to openly admit it, he knew as well as Antonio that their father had a soft spot for Nicholas. He wouldn't want him at risk in a foreign country doing illegal things. It was a last resort and a pretty desperate one. Hopefully his brother would see that.

"Okay, I'll tell you what . . . we'll let Nicholas search for your wife and kid until further notice. I'll figure out a way to track down whoever took this last baby prematurely and make an example of him."

Antonio and Mario shook hands on it. As parting advice, Mario suggested Antonio listen to him and get rid of the sizzling broad in the silk nightie with the hot car before the police got any more upset than they already were.

"Where there's smoke there's fire," Mario suggested. "And there is no thicker smoke anywhere than up in that master suite right now waiting for a fire to break out."

Antonio agreed, and as he watched his brother drive away he realized without a doubt exactly who would get burned by the fire Sydney might ignite.

Sarah Jean sat across the table from Natalie and slowly sounded out the words on the page. She was reading from the American novel *East of Eden.* It was one Natalie never grew tired of hearing read aloud. Sarah Jean was obviously smart despite not having been to school since she was twelve, not to mention sketchy attendance up to that point. Having finished the page, she looked up with those fetching eyes that mesmerized Natalie when first meeting Sarah in Izzy's kitchen. Natalie had already sketched them half a dozen times this morning. Setting the drawing pad down on the table she smiled at her promising pupil.

"Very nice, Sarah Jean. Your reading skills have already improved." Natalie turned the pages back to the beginning of the chapter. "Would you please read it again? Only this time, emphasize the *I* sound every time you see it in a word, whether long *I* or short *I*. Okay?"

Sarah Jean nodded, but before she could begin again, Emmy and Matti burst through the screen door with little Anna Marie toddling between them. "She's hungry," Emmy explained.

"Well then, I guess we better give her a snack." Natalie found crackers, cheese, and juice. She sent the children out back with their mid-morning feast. Once little Anna Marie was seated between Matti and Emmy with a cracker and piece of cheese, Natalie returned to the table to correct Sarah Jean's wrong enunciation of the letter *I*. When it was time for the young mother to leave she thanked Natalie over and over again for her help. Natalie held Sarah's hands and studied her bottomless brown eyes, as if measuring their depth. "Don't mention it, Sarah Jean. I'm only glad I can be of service to Izzy's family after all she's done for me."

"Does Izzy make you potions?" Sarah Jean asked.

"No. But she makes them for Matti, and they seem to calm his nerves, help him focus."

"Maybe it' the island doin' that for your boy," Sarah Jean offered.

"Now what did my English student just say?" Natalie grinned broadly.

"I mean . . . maybe . . . *it is* the island doin*g* that for your . . . son."

"Try *it's*. Contractions are more commonly used than two separate words," Natalie explained.

"Maybe *it's* the island doing that for your son." Sarah Jean smiled proudly at her success and they both laughed.

Out on the porch it took a minute to see where the children had gone, but soon giggles were heard near Harry's cage. Sure enough, they were all there, gathered around Matti. Natalie marveled at her son's tall lanky body, which had never been so tan. His dark silky hair was as unruly as the island itself. The boy had no doubt grown a foot since arriving in Roatan, and although he was every bit as silent as the day they arrived, his confidence spoke volumes. Matti showed absolutely no fear of Harry, who sat on his shoulder and caused Natalie to cringe, but Diego assured her these giant arachnids were quite timid and wouldn't bite unless provoked. Harry was probably quite familiar by now with the hand that fed it, Natalie reasoned, although it gave her little comfort.

"Your boy has that for a pet?" Sarah Jean seemed amused by this.

"I'm afraid so." Natalie sighed.

"You love that child a lot, don't you?"

"Yes. He's my whole life."

"Where's his daddy?" Sarah Jean made no apologies for her inquiry.

"In the States."

"He was a fool to let you go."

"Well thank you, Sarah Jean. But I doubt he sees it that way. Besides, I left without his consent."

"Lord!" Sarah Jean looked frightened for her new tutor.

"He doesn't know where I am," Natalie added.

"Men have a way of finding their women." A vacant look crept into the young woman's eyes.

"I hope he runs out of ideas and gives up."

"Me too, Miss Natalie. Me too." Sarah Jean picked up Anna Marie and kissed the top of her head. She gave her tutor one last fear inflicted look, sending a chill up Natalie's spine, before heading down the rocky path to home.

CHAPTER FIFTEEN

In that instance she felt his pain and frustration with life, and love, and how little control we have over either.

Izzy and Angel strolled across the yard wearing bright yellow sundresses. Their dark skin glowed like melted caramels beneath a cloudless sky. It nearly took Natalie's breath away as she watched them approach, their wild kinky curls bouncing with each step. "We jus' saw Sarah Jean down the road. I's never seen her so excited," Izzy shared while leaning on the porch rail.

"She's a quick learner . . . very smart girl," Natalie added, barely moving in the wooden rocker.

Izzy laughed. "Of course she's smart! She come from the same bloodline as me, don't she?"

"When do I start correcting *your* English, my beautiful island neighbor?" Natalie asked.

"I don't know. Not yet. I got enough to deal with right now." There was defeat in her tone. She sat on the top porch step and sighed heavily, while Angel chased butterflies in the yard. The two women watched until Angel grew tired of running around in vain, unable to catch any winged creatures fluttering about.

"Mama, can I visit Harry?" Angel cupped a hand over her eyes to shade the sun and looked at Izzy.

"Of course, honey. You give that tranchula a big kiss for me, you hear?" Izzy laughed while Natalie explained that Matti had gone down to the beach with Emmy and they had taken Harry with them, cage and all.

"Is it that man of yours?" Natalie asked, while Angel ran back out the gate.

"What troubles do us women folk have, if not their men, Natti-girl?"

"I can think of a few other issues." Natalie fetched them each a glass of iced tea from the kitchen and sat beside Izzy on the wooden step. "What did Sarah Jean mean when she said men have a way of finding their women?"

Izzy shrugged. "When a woman runs off with another man, he searches until he finds her, and drags her sorry butt home again, after beatin' up whomever she done run off with. He beat her plenty too, once she get back home."

"That's different than when island men wander." Natalie raised an eyebrow.

"Uh-huh. The difference is, a woman on the run ain't comin' home to see if laundry's done and dinner's ready. Kinda on she be the one who do that. No, a woman on the run ain't got no thoughts of back-trackin'." Izzy looked at Natalie. "You know that girl, better than anyone. Women who leave ain't playin' 'round. They's dead serious."

Both women fell silent for a minute. There was nothing to add to Izzy's insightfulness about the difference between men and women. They listened to the sea birds overhead and bees buzzing among flowers beside the porch.

"Diego wants me to go boating with him this evening . . . alone," Natalie shared.

"Do he now?"

Izzy's eyes danced with delight, and Natalie had to look away . . . into the horizon. It was embarrassing having Diego pursue her, since she wasn't really single, and especially since she suspected Izzy and Diego had a past. For all she knew they could have a present. The chemistry between the two suggested Solomon wasn't the only one cheating. Yet Izzy seemed genuinely okay with something developing between Diego and herself. Maybe Izzy was wise enough to realize that wasn't going to happen. Maybe that's why Natalie needed to vent about Diego with Izzy. "He wants me to see the sunset from some special cove."

"Oh, I bet he do!" Izzy laughed. "Why don't you let me keep the children?"

"They're old enough to stay alone for a while."

"I know, but they's been wantin' to sleep on my porch. That way, you don't need to hurry back."

"I wish I had those kinds of feelings for Diego, but I don't." Natalie looked into Izzy's untamed eyes that seemed to watch the world go by, like a wild cat perched on a tree limb. They were eyes that didn't miss a thing.

"I know." Izzy returned the stare and Natalie felt her inner thoughts exposed.

"How do you know?"

"It jus' seem like you were swoonin' a bit over that stranger from the States."

"Nic?"

"He be the one." Izzy smiled, slow and wide.

"I was being polite. He is, after all, Diego's new partner," Natalie pointed out.

"There's big diff'rence between polite and pursuit." Izzy laughed.

"Pursuit?" Natalie felt a warm rash cover her cheeks.

"Here on this island when a woman flirts with a man we say she's in season. You's in season, girl."

"That's a terrible thing to say, Izzy." Natalie frowned.

"Hold on there, Natti honey. I don't mean to be makin' you mad or nothin'. I jus' want you to see that you is only human, girl." Izzy stood to leave. "Now let's get them kids off to the café. I need to be startin' dinner for the reg'lars."

Natalie called to Emmy and Matti and sent them packing for Angel's house. The girls were quite excited, and she couldn't detect any protest on Matti's part.

Once Izzy had taken the children to the café, Natalie began to sketch in earnest on the backside of the porch. It was a place she could keep her easel, sketch pads, and paints, without being in anyone's way. Of course, if the sky threatened to release a sideways downpour, she was prepared to haul it all back into the summerhouse. But this time of year the weather was hot and muggy with barely a breeze. A banana tree hung close to her easel, with bunches of green fruit clustered in large shiny leaves. The sweet smell was enticing, especially when mixed with spicy scents from Izzy's café next door. Little green lizards basked on the railing and tiny spotted geckos slept between the porch slats. It was a peaceful and inspiring alcove.

That's where Diego found her, laboring over pencil drawings of Sarah Jean. Some finished sketches of Izzy were lying nearby on a rattan chair. He picked them up and studied the poses. "These are good, Natalie."

Startled, she turned toward him. "I didn't hear you walk up."

"Still want to see the sunset from Pirate's Cove?" He looked up at her from behind the pencil drawings.

"Very much. Izzy took the kids for us. They're all excited about sleeping on her back porch."

"They're spending the night?"

"Yes. Is that okay?"

Before he could answer, Izzy appeared from around the corner. "I thought I might find you two here." In her arms she held a picnic basket, which she handed to Diego. "This here is your dinner. I put some o' my famous corn tortillas in there with chicken and cabbage slaw." Then she laughed. "I also snuck in some chocolate brownies. You can't have a picnic on the boat without some brownies."

"Why thank you, Izzy. You didn't need to do that," Natalie protested.

"I wanted to. You all do so much for Angel and me. Now don't fret none about Emmy or Matti. They be fine with me, you hear? We's havin' a slumber party on the porch." Izzy's eyes twinkled with delight and Natalie marveled at her ability to find joy in the simplest things. "Enjoy your boat ride." She waved goodbye and was gone as quickly as she'd come.

Natalie placed the basket in the back of the Land Rover and Diego set a cooler of drinks beside it. Finally, they left for the dock in West End, and once aboard the boat, headed for Pirate's Cove. They anchored just in time to watch the sun fracture its light between thin, wispy clouds. Lush green hills surrounded a brilliant orange sky. Hordes of onshore birds serenaded them while eating their picnic in the peaceful cove. The chicken was salty and crispy, and a wonderful contrast to the creamy slaw. Izzy's corn tortillas were the lightest and fluffiest Natalie had ever eaten. Her gooey-fudgy brownies made the perfect ending to their picnic in the cove.

"I remember when you taught me how to fish." Natalie smiled. "You brought me and Matti out in your boat, to the other side of the island, that first Saturday we were here."

"I remember. You were like fish out of water. Now you're seasoned fishermen." Diego opened them another Salva Vida.

"Were we really that green?" Natalie laughed.

"Well, let's just say you were awkward with a fishing pole in your hands instead of a pencil or brush. Matti was just nervous, but then he was always nervous. He's like a different boy now."

"He has calmed down a lot, thanks to you and Emmy . . . and Izzy's potions," Natalie confessed.

"I've no doubt the slow pulse of the island and rhythm of the tides have had an effect on him." Diego stared upward, at the darkening sky. "Somehow it seems closer to God here than in most places."

Natalie studied the sky, too, while standing beside Diego at the side railing of the twenty-eight-foot dive boat. "I think fishing has helped. Have you ever watched him? He's completely absorbed in what's he doing, when fishing."

"I've noticed he's a natural at it. Something you certainly are not!" Diego laughed.

"That's true I guess, but you have to admit there's a real art to reeling a line in and out." Natalie nudged him playfully. She'd been careful not to give Diego any misleading signs, yet part of her wanted to fall into his arms and then below deck for a night of lovemaking. She kept replaying the party in her mind. No matter how hard she tried she couldn't get Nic Walsh out of her head. Had her feelings for Diego heightened or was it his new partner causing her restlessness?

Natalie observed how well Diego put himself together. Whether in his everyday jeans and t-shirt, or the khaki shorts and white button down he wore now, Diego looked enticing. He had good taste in clothing and an admirable sense of style, not to mention his rugged good looks and strong, muscular arms. Surely this third-world paradise would be complete with someone like Diego by her side. They could never marry, but that might not matter unless, of course, they were to have children. Natalie smiled. What a strange thought . . . having children with Diego. She laughed out loud as he came and sat next to her on the bow of the boat. "What's so funny?" he asked.

Natalie hoped he would kiss her, against her better judgment, but then she remembered he'd said that she'd have to make the next move. She reached up to touch his wind-tossed hair and their eyes met. His begged for her to embrace him, and so Natalie did exactly that. This time when their lips met she didn't break away but gave herself fully to the moment.

After mooring the boat for the night, they continued viewing stars from well-worn rattan chairs on the front porch of the summerhouse. Quietly they sipped on lemon brandy, made from the lemons off the trees in their backyard. It had a pleasing flavor, sweet and sour all at once. The air smelled of seawater from the shore mist and sand crabs skittering out of their holes. The ocean was like an old friend to Natalie now, illuminated either by moon or sun. She wasn't sure she could ever live without it.

"It was nice of Izzy to have Emmy and Matti spend the night," Diego commented, while gazing upward at the countless stars.

Natalie nodded. "We spend a lot of time out here on the porch, don't we? I've almost forgotten what it's like to be inside evenings. But it is odd to be alone together, without Matti playing his Gameboy and Emmy beside him reading books."

"Emmy's been encouraging Matti to read some of the books she's finished recently." Diego reached over and squeezed Natalie above the knee. "I think he's healing, Nat."

"I hope so, and that he starts reading again soon. He used to read prolifically." Natalie poured herself more of the lemon brandy from the pitcher on the little table beside them. Thinking about the emotional disparity of her son agitated her, especially knowing Antonio was somehow involved.

"This island is medicine for his soul." Diego took her hand and held it in his lap. "You're medicine for my soul . . . and Emmy's. She adores you."

She turned to look at him, really look at the man in the near darkness seated beside her, whom she loved in so many ways, but not in the way he wanted. Maybe Antonio completely ruined her ability to love again. "I don't know what to say, Diego. You know I adore you. You're my hero, and Matti's, but my feelings seem to be numb. Somehow Antonio has frozen my ability to love again. Sometimes I feel brittle enough to crack, as if I might break into a thousand pieces no one could ever reassemble."

"Are you saying I misread your kiss? Because it sure felt like I was kissing someone with feelings."

Natalie smiled. "I love kissing you. You're a very desirable man inside and out, but I have this wall of fear that doesn't want to go beyond kissing . . . all the way to vulnerability . . . which can lead to heartache. I want to build a life of purpose here, and I need to focus on that."

Diego nodded. "Well I'm happy to just relax beside you and enjoy the stars."

Natalie had scooted over in her chair to give Diego her full attention. They were close enough to kiss again, if they wanted to. She recalled their kiss on the boat and it made her warm inside. Then somehow her thoughts jumped to his new partner, Nic, and it made her stomach do a belly flop. This annoyed her a lot. It was irrational to be drawn to a stranger that, for all she knew, might have been sent straight from San Francisco by her incorrigible husband. Obviously, her feelings weren't rational.

"I enjoy just being alone with you, Nat." Diego leaned forward and refreshed his brandy. "I do have other fantasies, of course. But I don't want you to feel any pressure from me. You don't owe me anything."

"I owe you everything. I've never felt so alive as I do here, or so protected. I've fallen in love with your island. I feel as if it's courting me."

Diego laughed.

"No, really. I don't think I could ever leave Roatan. The sights and sounds, the isolation I share with it. I could never tire of tutoring the women here, or painting their proud, courageous faces. Each one is more beautiful than the next, with their bright questioning eyes and silky dark skin."

"So you'll never tutor men?" Diego asked.

"I might. I've even been known to paint them," she added. "You saw the African doctor in my hallway, back in San Francisco." Natalie smiled.

"I have a gentleman for you to tutor, then, if you don't mind. He runs a restaurant in West End. His name is Marlon Romolo. Nic bought a motorcycle from him right after he arrived here. I should take you there, to his bistro. It's very nice . . . wonderful Italian food. He thinks his heavy accent affects his business."

"I'd be happy to tutor him for you."

"I told Marlon what your rates are. He's hoping you'll do it."

"My rates?"

"Yes, I quoted what you charged me."

"I hadn't thought about charging. I tutor the island women for permission to paint them."

"Well unless you want to paint Marlon, and even if you do—he can afford your San Francisco rates. You just said you never wanted to leave the island, and you refuse to let me take care of you forever, so you'll need a livelihood. Maybe you can make it on your own just by selling your portraits, but it never hurts to have a backup plan. Unless, of course, you come to your senses and marry me, in which case I could take care of you better than you ever imagined."

"Diego, I am married, and I don't think Antonio would ever consider divorcing me, even if I were willing to contact him. Besides, I think we just established that I am an ice queen never likely to thaw." She stared into his bright eyes, sparkling like diamonds from the moonglow.

"It might take a while to warm up to the idea of marrying me," he whispered, staring back, "but I would at least like a chance at thawing you out." Diego reached for her hand, squeezed it gently, and let go.

Natalie was stunned at the mention of marriage, so much so that she couldn't address it on any serious level. Maybe in the back of her mind it had occurred to her that Diego wanted them to grow old together in the summerhouse. Maybe she hadn't wanted to face that possibility because it only grew her guilt. "There is no way I could contact Antonio. If he found out where I am, he'd want Matti back, and stop at nothing to get him."

"I beg to differ. I think your husband needs power and wealth more than he needs his son." Leaning forward in his chair Diego took Natalie's hands into his again and looked her square in the eye. "Natalie, I think your husband is making money in some unscrupulous way, maybe to pick up the slack from failing olive groves in Sicily. I don't know. But what I do know is that he is very secretive about his business dealings and seems to have a lot to hide. I believe he would consider it a lucky break to gain the near fortune I could offer him if he's willing to divorce you and give up custody of Matti. It would allow him to end his seedy side-business, whatever it is."

"You would offer him money to do that?"

"In a heartbeat."

"That would be a lot of money, Diego."

"No money is too much to pay for your freedom."

Natalie was speechless. She hadn't considered ever being free of Antonio. Or that he would give up his son. "Diego, why would you offer this, just days after telling me I all but have a crush on your new business partner?"

Diego sat back in his chair as he obviously struggled for an honest, forthright response. “Because I want you to be happy, whatever that ends up looking like.”

Natalie slowly nodded while processing what Diego said, and then she changed the subject completely. “Diego, I’ve seen the way you look at Izzy. It’s a look that tells me you have more than childhood affection for her.” Perhaps the brandy was making her too bold. She studied his face, which had suddenly tensed and looked a bit tormented. Lines deepened on his forehead and appeared at the corners of his mouth. He stared into the darkness, in the direction the sea, and was silent.

Natalie put her hand out to touch his face, caressing it gently. “I don’t mean to upset you. There are just so many thoughts collecting in my mind, cluttering my thinking. I do find you attractive, Diego. I’d be lying to say otherwise.” They were so close Natalie couldn’t resist sliding her fingers from his cheek to his hairline, just as their lips met. His hands tightened on her waist and drew her so near she could feel his heart beating. He tasted warm like the island winds and salty like the surrounding sea, but then he pulled away.

“I think you know how I feel, Nat. It was all in that kiss. As for Izzy, whatever past we may have had doesn’t matter, because she is married and I’m in love with you.”

Natalie couldn’t take her eyes off him, because this new vulnerable side was chipping away at her icy heart. Diego had loved and lost more than once. Maybe he never really loved his wife. Maybe he never really got over Izzy, who must have been his first love, when they were young and the ways of the world didn’t matter. For surely they must have realized their love was doomed from the start. Mixed marriages on the island weren’t tolerated. In that instance she felt his pain and frustration with life, and love, and how little control we have over either. She wanted to take him to her room and make love to him. She *wanted* him. But did she love him? If she was going to sleep with Diego, she would have to be sure first that she was *in love* with him, and not just drawn to what he could do for her physically, monetarily, or in the way of freedom from her past.

Natalie pulled away, sweaty from the Roatan heat and their own desires. Diego looked into her eyes for an indication this was not the end of their date, but Natalie stood to enter the house without indicating anything at all. She turned on the kitchen light and poured herself water from a pitcher in the refrigerator. Then she sat down in the front room. Diego entered the house and locked the door. He sat beside her on the sofa and ran his fingers lightly down her upper arm, arousing a strong desire to simply throw caution to the wind and escort him to her bed, until someone pounded on the door. They both jumped nearly a foot.

It was several seconds before they recovered enough to answer it, rather than just stare in that direction. Diego recovered first and sprung from the sofa, with Natalie right on his heels. Upon opening the door he saw Izzy standing there, barefoot, in cutoff jean shorts and a white cotton shirt that reflected the moonlight.

"Don't you w-worry none 'bout the kids. They's all sleepin' like b-babies," Izzy managed to say, catching her breath between words. "But Harry . . . he's missin'!"

CHAPTER SIXTEEN

She couldn't bear to consider how her night with Diego might have played out differently.

"Missing?" Diego repeated.

"I came over to feed Harry . . . give him a big juicy bug I caught, and he ain't in his c-cage out back."

They all looked at each other, knowing what a tragic scenario that would be in the morning. Without further discussion the three of them hurried to the back porch, where the cage was clearly empty, even under the scrutiny of a flashlight Diego retrieved from a kitchen drawer on the way out.

"Where could he have gone? The door is shut tight and latched," Natalie observed.

Diego opened the cage, and without comment felt under the fresh leaves Matti always placed in there. "Harry has indeed gone missing," he commented.

"Them spiders roam at night," Izzy pointed out. "We could find us a Harry that would do, close to the same size and all," she further suggested. "Of course, we wouldn't try to pawn the new one off as Harry, but at least it would be another tranchula to care for."

"Maybe Matti decided to set Harry free." Natalie glanced in the direction of the forest between the summerhouse and Izzy's café, which is where Harry had been plucked from the ground.

It's certainly a possibility," Diego pointed out.

"But what if he hadn't meant for Harry to be set free?" Natalie fretted. "Or what if he set his pet free only to immediately regret it?" She sat down on the porch swing, crestfallen, wondering if this would set back her son's emotional recovery. Diego sat next to her.

"Natalie, it's just a spider. I bet Matti figured out on his own that it belongs in the wild. He's very intuitive about nature and the delicate balance of things."

The women nodded. That was true enough about Matti. He would save any life of value, or die trying, they agreed. He almost had, in fact, when bringing the girls safely to shore not that long ago.

"I'll let you two be," Izzy said cheerlessly and waved goodbye as she headed back to the café. "I won't say nothin' in the morning," she turned around and added. "You can deal with it however you think best."

Diego and Natalie nodded. Crickets filled the silence with incessant chirping as they rocked on the swing. Natalie laid her head on Diego's shoulder and listened to the palm leaves rustling above them. She looked up through the palms at the crescent moon, thinking that her son, and nothing or no one else, let Harry go. He loved Harry enough to give the tarantula his freedom. If only Matti's father could love them in the same manner.

Diego kissed the top of her head. "I know this is disturbing for you, Natalie, but I also know Matti will be fine. He's probably more aware of what happened to Harry than we are."

"Funny, I was just thinking the same thing." She looked at Diego but couldn't muster a smile. They lost track of time on the swing, where Natalie felt comforted by Diego's presence. She liked feeling the closeness of him. Somehow it made her believe everything would be okay—Harry, Matti, and even herself.

"Natalie, if you need me, I'll be just across the yard," Diego reminded her.

She nodded, realizing she'd never seen Diego's bedroom in the guest quarters out back. They had moved Emmy into the main house, next to Matti's room, where it was cooler and more spacious. It had a ceiling fan, and the summerhouse had air conditioning for especially muggy nights. How gracious of Diego to inconvenience himself in the cramped guest quarters with no air conditioning. Aroused by the scent of his cologne, she was tempted to pick up where she'd left off . . . leading him to her bed . . . but instead whispered goodnight and stood to enter the summerhouse. She could feel Diego watch as she walked across the porch and entered the kitchen. With one last glance, Natalie shut the door and locked it.

She was tempted to run back out and into Diego's arms, while leaning against the locked door, but thought better of it. Giving in to her lust was something she'd probably regret. No. She needed to have her heart in the game. Diego deserved that. He deserved all of her, all of any woman he loved. Everything she'd ever longed for was right there in Diego Espinoza yet for some odd reason, she couldn't just accept his generous offer to love, honor, and cherish her forever.

Sleep came fretfully, after much tossing and turning, but morning serenaded her with sunbeams through the open window. Groves of birds chirped loudly in nearby foliage and everything was the same as usual. She couldn't bear to consider how her night with Diego might have played out differently. They might have been a couple this morning with a future. But instead she and Diego were only inches closer to whatever their fate might be. If only she could know what that was.

Nic had already run on the beach and been to his favorite hangout for breakfast. There was nothing else to use as an excuse for not calling Antonio. One more minute of stalling and his half-brother would descend upon him like a Mafioso gone mad. He hadn't really rehearsed what he'd say, but something acceptable was finally brewing in his head as he made the call.

"Antonio, how are you?" Nic fell back on the bed and stared at the ceiling fan spinning faster than his thoughts.

"Never mind the niceties. What did you find out?"

"I'm sorry, Antonio."

"About what?"

"About your wife and son not being here."

There was a frustrated sigh on the other end. "It figures."

"I was just so sure she probably hitched a ride with her graduate student headed back to Honduras." Nic's stomach began to churn. Lying had never come easy to him.

"Right," Antonio answered sourly. His disappointment echoed through the airwaves. "Why on earth did it take so long to find out she wasn't shacked up with the Honduran? It's not a very big island."

"Antonio, I apologize, but Diego *was* living with some woman and it took me gaining his confidence to be invited to his home and see exactly who. Everyone here is hush-hush about it, and prying would have made me look suspicious. Turns out she's an island girl and quite young. Thus the secrecy."

"Look, Nicholas, Mario wants to send you to Romania." Nic sat straight up and stared at the dresser. "That's crazy. We can't just give up on your family."

"Well, you got any other bright ideas about where they might be?"

Nic wondered if Antonio was as stressed-out as he sounded. Probably the police were on his case. Following him everywhere. Harassing him continually. That was standard procedure when a man's family suddenly disappeared. They may have all but dug up the fountain by now. Nic could visualize Antonio staring at it this very moment. He smiled. Natalie had outsmarted the smug and clever Antonio Giovanni. She was the reason he could barely function at this point. Not a single living person no matter how wealthy or powerful could ever claim such bragging rights.

"I have another lead, Antonio. All is not lost. I figured out Natalie's computer password, and I've been reading her e-mails. The African in the hall painting is someone she stayed in touch with." Nic was grateful he'd brought Natalie's laptop to Roatan so he could tell Antonio he'd recovered all her former communications, and Antonio had no way to double check it.

"You think the African doctor took her in?" Antonio asked, his voice steadier. He was apparently over the initial blow and ready to regroup his search effort. This was exactly what Nic wanted.

"Actually, yes. I've made some phone calls from here and I'm buying a ticket today."

"Good. It's about time. I thought maybe you'd decided to stay there and drop out of the family yourself."

Nic's heart skipped a beat. Antonio had no idea how close he'd come to the actual truth of the matter. Nic wanted nothing more than to stay on the island of Roatan. He saw a future for himself building beach homes with his new partners and affordable housing for native islanders. He'd already decided he'd gladly give up his place in the family hierarchy and any inheritance he'd hoped to acquire by staying on their good side. His intention from this point on was to keep Antonio waiting for news about his wife and son's whereabouts. It was news that would never come, at least as long as Nic was on the case. They would simply never be found. Moving the search to the small remote village in Africa would be the best way to protect Natalie and Matti. He hoped he could convince Antonio he was actually there. They hung up, each encouraged. Antonio had renewed hope Natalie would be found in Africa. Nic had devised a scheme for staying in Roatan. Now it was just a matter of being sure his presence there didn't lead to Natalie's demise, or his own.

Matti stared straight up the tree while hugging it from the ground. He could barely distinguish the coconuts from this angle. He glanced at the burlap bag on the grass beside him, filled with figs and plums he'd already picked for Izzy. She'd sent him out this morning to gather ripe fruit for the day, probably because he awoke long before the girls. He thought about letting Harry go and sadness overcame him, but the spider was obviously not happy trapped in his cage. He ate much less than when first caught, and almost never moved anymore. Matti wanted him to be free again. He tried to think about Harry reuniting with his family and that cheered him up.

The real question was did he have the strength, not to mention the courage, to climb this tree and cut down the coconuts just as he had seen Diego do. He felt the knife in the sheath, tied around his waist. It was a gift from Diego, and his most prized possession. He wanted to make Diego proud and more importantly, he just wanted to know what it felt like to climb so high and cut down your own coconut. Wouldn't Izzy be surprised? With any luck she'd choose not to tell his mother, who wouldn't find it brave or see the skill involved. She would simply be mad at his foolishness. Of course he understood mothers were like that. He loved her for it, but he couldn't be a little boy forever. It was time to grow up.

After climbing a short way Matti hesitated, wondering if his arms and legs would hold him while he somehow shimmied to the top. He was pleasantly surprised by his own strength, but knew it was snorkeling and running on the beach that had made him strong. He barely did anything physical back in San Francisco. What surprised him the most was how he didn't miss home at all, or his father. Thinking of his father made his adrenalin flow and before it got the better of him he bolted up the tree.

Out of breath from the climb, Matti partially rested against the large leaves fanning out from the top of the palm and soaked in the spectacular view. He felt like king of the jungle. Retrieving his knife from its leather sheath was no easy task while clinging to a tree, but he managed to accomplish this. Before grabbing the nearest coconut, he stole one more glance at the view, past the row of houses where Diego and Izzy owned their property, all the way to the farthest shore where the Italian resort was. He had never been there but had heard a lot about it. Some of the women sunbathed without their bikini tops. He would love to visit there one day and see that for himself. Boats were little dots on the sea from his perch in the tree. Without warning the leaf beneath him began to give way under his weight. He quickly leaned over with his knife and sliced at a coconut. It took four more tries before it fell reluctantly to the ground, making a dull thud. Matti hoped he wouldn't do the same.

With aching arms and legs, he slid slowly down the tree, falling the last four feet or so, but not enough to hurt when he landed. He lay stretched out on his back staring at the treetops. It was such a different view from the ground looking up than it had been from the top looking down. He never realized until now that life experience could be as interesting and exciting as reading. Matti picked up the coconut and proudly placed it on top of the other fruit in his bag. He couldn't wait to get back to the café and show Izzy, knowing the girls would still not be up. Izzy said they were giggling long after he had fallen asleep the night before. The burlap bag was heavy and awkward on the return walk, but he didn't dilly dally as he had when heading out. The sun was rising steadily, and Izzy would want her breakfast fruits for the café.

"Oh Laud am I glad to see you, boy! I thought maybe you wasn't comin' back." Izzy took the burlap bag from Matti while giving his hair a rough tousle. It had grown a bit wild on the island, much like he himself. Matti liked the longer hair, nearly reaching his shoulders by now. His mother must have liked it too, since she hadn't subjected him to a haircut yet. He wondered what his father would think and knew immediately that he would hate it, call him a sissy, and demand it be cut.

Matti half smiled. At one time he would have believed he was indeed a sissy if his father called him that, but not anymore. He was no sissy. He had saved Emmy's life, and shimmied up a palm tree to chop down a coconut. He'd loved a pet spider that frightened the willies out of most people. Even Izzy never wanted to hold Harry. Why did his father always come to mind? Would he ever be free from his bad memories of his dad, and that night? Matti thought not, and thought perhaps it would always haunt him, be his punishment for not having the courage to help that woman or tell anyone what happened. And now his voice didn't work anymore. Speech eluded him. Even thinking about talking made his heart pound and his head dizzy.

"Why sweet Jesus, Matti. How'd you get this here coconut?" Izzy pulled it from the bag and held it up. She admired it much like she would a precious jewel and not a hairy coconut still wrapped in its outer green husk. Stooping down to Matti's level, she looked him square in the eye. "Did you shimmy up one of them palm trees for this here prize?"

Matti grinned.

"Your mama would have a fit if she knew." Izzy put it carefully on the table and stared at it some more. Finally she turned toward Matti again and touched his shoulder. He looked up at her, waiting for a verdict. "This here is our secret. You hear?"

Matti nodded.

"But you listen to me, child. If you can shimmy up trees and save little girls, then you surely are thinkin' straight as an arrow. You know what I mean?"

Matti just looked at her.

"There ain't nothin' wrong with your brain, son. You is not the flighty, nervous child that first arrived here with your mama."

Matti stared into Izzy's dark eyes but didn't indicate if he agreed.

"You are whole again, boy. This here island has given you back your sanity. If you can't speak, it's because you *choose* not to." Izzy smoothed back his rumpled hair. "You may not *think* you can talk, but I believe if you needed to, you would. Do you hear what I am sayin'?"

Slowly, Matti nodded.

"It's time you started readin' and writin' again. I hear you's as bright as they get. Be a shame to waste all that."

Matti didn't respond one way or the other.

"Now you get on home, boy. Your mama has somethin' she needs to discuss with you. It has to do with Harry."

Matti hadn't considered his mother finding the cage empty. He felt bad that she'd probably worried all night about Harry's whereabouts. He'd have to make it clear somehow that Harry had gone home, with his blessing. But telling her was not an option. No matter what Izzy said, speaking was no longer something his brain knew how to make happen. What did she know anyway? All her potions and lotions didn't make her an expert on such matters.

No, he could rest assured that speaking painful words of guilt and regret was not possible, not ever. As he ran home, flashes of that woman in the trunk raced through his mind. He covered his ears to the sound of bones cracking and bound limbs flailing. Those sounds and her terror-filled eyes simply would not leave his consciousness. He ran straight to his room and buried his head under a pillow. Matti focused on his climb up the palm tree until he could feel bark beneath his hands and an ache in his legs. He could almost reach out and touch the sea beyond the shoreline, which went on into infinity from his view up in the tree. He could almost forget that lady's sad, frightened eyes, and who had made them that way . . . almost.

CHAPTER SEVENTEEN

Natalie wondered if Matti would ever speak of that night, if it would simply all spill out one day like gutter leaves in a storm.

Nic almost felt good about deceiving Antonio. He had more sympathy for the mouse he'd caught last night with a piece of cheese in a trap than he did for his half-brother. Staring at Natalie's laptop on his tiny desk shoved under the window, he was more relieved than ever he'd had the foresight to bring it with him. It didn't take much convincing for Antonio to believe he'd cracked the passcode and could read her e-mail. He hadn't done that of course. In all likelihood she didn't write e-mails, or she'd have brought the laptop with her. He could ask Natalie in person for information about the African doctor she'd tutored.

He hated not being able to come clean with Natalie but that would open quite a can of worms. Diego, for one, would be furious. Even if he could convince Natalie that he'd changed his mind about helping Antonio and was all about keeping her safe at this point, Diego would never trust him again. Selfishly, he didn't want to pull up stakes and search for a different adventure. At least this is what he told himself—that the island had captivated him, and not the woman he came here to find. It was bad enough that Natalie was married to his half-brother, but on top of that his new business partner had a thing for her.

Nic sat on the tiny front porch of his rented rooms with his feet on the railing and studied the intense emerald green of the ocean. Maybe craving a woman in general was the bigger issue, since he hadn't dated while on Roatan. He missed the sweet scent and soft touch of a woman. Tonight would be a good time to find someone he shared common interests with. Nic put on a clean shirt, combed his hair, and headed out the door toward Sundowners. Only he wouldn't be chatting it up with Ike for once. He'd be focusing on the single women in the room. His goal was to find a nice girl he could dive and drink with, someone who could take his mind off Antonio's wife.

Natalie peeked into Matti's room and saw him sleeping on the bed fully dressed. Giggling girls most likely kept him up half the night over at Izzy's.

She headed to the kitchen and was mixing pancake batter when Emmy came bouncing in through the screen door.

"Harry's gone!" she announced without so much as a good morning.

"I noticed that. Where is the little beast?" Natalie asked.

"Matti let him loose. I saw him do it," Emmy explained.

"Is that right?" Natalie ladled batter onto the griddle as if everything was right in the universe and her heart wasn't in her throat.

"Yep. I think he felt sorry for Harry. He petted the spider for a long time before setting him on a tree out back."

"That must have been hard, but I'm proud of Matti for letting his pet back into the wild," Natalie added, while pouring Emmy a glass of orange juice.

"Ick! Harry was *so* creepy!" Emmy drank her orange juice despite finding memories of Harry disturbing.

"That explains the empty cage." Natalie glanced out the window and saw Diego crossing the yard, heading toward the kitchen—just in time for pancakes hot off the griddle. She added bacon straight from the sizzling skillet and set it in front of him. "Good morning, Diego."

"Good morning. I hope you slept well. I didn't sleep a wink," he added.

Natalie didn't need to answer because Diego turned his attention to Emmy, questioning her about the missing spider. She filled him in on all the details just as Matti appeared in the doorway. He must have heard their voices or smelled the bacon. He sat down in front of a steaming stack of his mom's pancakes, dripping with butter, obviously meant for him. While he poured on syrup, Diego told Matti how proud he was of the decision to let Harry roam free.

"It takes a lot of courage to let something you love go, Matti, if you know it's for the best. I'm sure Harry is grateful."

Matti nodded, seemingly enjoying Diego's approval as much as his mother's pancakes.

"What's on the agenda for today, Nat? Are you tutoring anyone?" Diego asked.

"Not today. When is your friend Marlon coming by to begin his sessions?"

"What about this afternoon?"

"The kids and I are going to the beach this morning while Izzy runs errands, but this afternoon is free."

"Are you sure you don't mind?"

"Not at all, Diego." She sat down to eat and looked directly at him. Their eye contact said more than their conversation had, but Natalie reached for the syrup and tried to pretend nothing had changed between them. Truthfully, she wasn't sure anything *had* changed, but Diego was different somehow. He'd studied her every move since coming to breakfast. It felt like he wanted to reach inside of her brain and pull out her innermost thoughts. If he did extract her thoughts she'd like to study them herself, since she didn't fully understand how she felt about Diego, or anything else lately for that matter.

"I'm going to meet with Nic this morning, get him started with the second crew on building my first design."

"How exciting. The materials must have been delivered to the site okay?"

"Yes, finally."

Natalie thought about Nic organizing the construction crew and managing the building of Diego's first beach house on the shorefront property. It was the design he'd won the award for. Just thinking about Nic's smile made her feel traitorous to Diego.

"I'd like to invite Nic to dinner. What do you think?" Diego asked.

"Why don't you invite Jake, too?"

"Okay, if you don't mind cooking for a crowd."

Natalie smiled. "I'm looking forward to it."

Diego stood to leave. He cleared his dishes and then kissed her on the forehead, lingering there a bit too long, allowing her guilt to set in about looking forward to seeing Nic again. She watched Diego leave in the Land Rover and considered his preposterous idea of convincing Antonio to let her and Matti go. Being free of Antonio and everything he and his family represented would be like freeing Alice from the looking glass. Even before Matti's trauma she'd felt trapped in her marriage. All her dreams had transferred to her son. She was living and breathing solely for him, wanting to be sure he found the happiness eluding her. But she couldn't accept Diego's offer.

Maybe it was this new, challenging environment that kept her from wanting to be indebted to another man, even a good one like Diego. For whatever reason, she was set on steering her own course. She was determined to make a difference in the lives of the women she'd met here, and those she had yet to meet. And then there was her painting. Besides painting the island women, she was ready to branch out and try a few sketches of ocean and sky, jungle and village. She wanted to reveal the delicate beauty of Roatan, along with its dark secrets. Natalie jumped a foot off the chair and nearly spilled the last of her coffee when Emmy and Matti stormed into the kitchen, wearing swimsuits and holding snorkel gear.

"I guess I better get a move on," she commented, rinsing out her cup. She smiled as Angel approached the screen door. "Good morning, Angel. I'll be ready in a minute. You can go on ahead if you want. Here's the blanket, Emmy. I'll catch up with you," Natalie instructed. She watched as all three children rounded the corner of the yard and disappeared from sight. Hurriedly she washed the dishes and went to throw on her swimsuit, tying a silk scarf at her waist, like a loose fitting skirt. She grabbed a sheer cotton blouse to block the sun and somehow managed carrying the art tote, sketch pads, and lunch cooler down to the beach.

A million ideas raced through her mind about what to cook for dinner while she arranged everything beside the blanket on the sand. She anticipated it being awkward to see Nic this evening. She didn't want to examine the effect he'd had on her. The last thing she needed was any more complications in her life, or Matti's. Her attraction to him was probably just a fluke anyway. He was, after all, the only American she'd met on the island. That alone would explain the bond she felt with him.

Nic was ordering men about in Spanish when Diego arrived on the jobsite. They shook hands and Nic filled him in on how things were going as hammers hummed in the background. Soon they were gawking at the view from the one-acre lot, mesmerized by the dazzling sea below the cliff. Both agreed it was an appropriate setting for the award-winning beach house. Jake joined them for lunch at Ike's, where Diego invited them both to dinner. Nic immediately felt odd about it. His blood began pumping harder and the air felt hotter. Seeing Natalie again would be difficult, because his thoughts about her were out of line. The woman wasn't like anyone he'd ever met, although he couldn't identify what exactly it was about Natalie that affected him this way.

He'd spent last evening with an attractive, available woman who'd come to Roatan on her vacation to dive, and to meet other divers. She flirted openly as drinks flowed freely, and eventually invited him back to her resort. Instead, he picked up the bar tab and went home alone. He didn't like the idea of being with a woman whose name he wouldn't remember in the morning. And besides, he couldn't get Natalie off his mind. He knew he'd put her in danger, coming up with this notion that she'd be on the island with her former student, Diego. Throwing Antonio off her trail at this point might not be as easy as he hoped it would be.

Nic focused on work as best he could all afternoon in the relentless Roatan heat. Then he stopped by his rented rooms to shower before dinner. Pulling in a roadside stand on the way to Diego's, he bought a bouquet of flowers. He worried about how hard it must be for Natalie to find herself cooking and cleaning after having a life filled with servants. Regardless, she seemed to enjoy caring for Diego and Emmy, from what he could tell at the Pot of McCoy celebration. It was almost as if the four of them were just a step away from merging into one happy family. For some strange reason that Nic didn't wish to explore, he fervently hoped Natalie and Diego weren't romantically involved.

Natalie sketched Matti, Emmy, and Angel while playing in the wet sand. She was taken aback by Matti's expression. His entire demeanor had changed since arriving in Roatan. Gone were the darting eyes, tense brow, and nervous twitch that came and went from his upper lip. The deeply tanned boy building castles on the beach was smiling broadly. His emerald eyes twinkled from beneath dark, silky hair. Matti was without a doubt calmer. He spent most of his time gathering shells along the shore for his collection, or climbing trees to search for geckos, instead of hunched over the Gameboy zapping aliens. She felt confident that one day, when he had a reason to, he would speak again.

The girls giggled and screeched as they added upturned buckets of wet sand to their elaborate castle. Natalie wished she could hear Matti laugh again. It wasn't something he did often, but she remembered exactly what it sounded like.

"That's good, Natti-girl. Maybe the best I've seen you do." Izzy left a shadow on the paper as she stood there and admired Natalie's sketch. Then she collapsed on the blanket and stared at the sea.

"Done already? I thought you had a longer to-do list." Natalie smiled.

Izzy shrugged. "I did enough for one mornin'. Ain't much fun visiting that side of the island."

"Did you take herbs to your cousins?" Natalie remembered Izzy had a handful of needy relatives who relied heavily on her potions.

"I took it to some cousins, and some nieces. And one auntie. Funny thing is, she gives my medicine to Uncle Keagan, who knows where it come from. But he would never admit I am curing what ails him, let alone say thank you."

"I'm sorry, Izzy, for the way they treat you. Seems like they should be happy for you and Solomon, with the success of the café and all. It isn't like you wouldn't give the shirt off your back to them, if they needed it."

"They think Mama was shameful to have jus' one child, a bastard girl at that. An' now I's a disappointment too, with jus' one child myself, and livin' off the money from Mama's man, who was not her husband."

"They're jealous, Izzy, because you're strong and good, and kind to them despite how they've shunned you. You remind them of everything they're not."

"It don't matter none. What matters is that boy of yours. He's a lot better, Natti-girl. Ain't you noticed?"

Natalie stopped sketching and studied Matti. "I know, Izzy. He looks so . . . normal." Matti had started into puberty. He had shot up half a foot and his dark eyebrows had thickened, but he wasn't so grown up that he minded building sandcastles with two enchanting girls, one on the verge of blossoming into a woman. Emmy had transformed nearly as much as Matti since their arrival on the island. What a magical age twelve always proved to be. Maybe Emmy was why his eyes sparkled, his cheeks glowed, and his mouth was set in a full-on grin as he helped the girls complete their sculpture.

“This island has worked miracles, not to mention your potions,” Natalie added.

“Ain’t nothin’ miraculous about this here island, or my herbs neither. It’s jus’ this child’s no longer in the shadow of what caused him to be speechless.”

Natalie nodded, willing away memories of what brought them here as she began sketching again. The day was too perfect for recalling those events.

Izzy stripped off her skirt and blouse, revealing a hot pink swimsuit. Her svelte body glowed like polished copper in the warm sun as she lay back, covering her face with a straw hat. From beneath it Natalie could hear her slightly muffled voice.

“That boy o’ yours, he needs to be readin’ and writin’ again. Ain’t no reason he can’t do some book learnin’. You hear me, Natti? His thinkin’ is steady as Roatan rain. Be a shame to waste his fine mind you told me he got.”

Natalie nodded, even knowing Izzy couldn’t see her. “I can’t tell you, Izzy, how delighted I am to see Matti nearly whole again.”

Izzy sat up and stared at her, making Natalie all too aware of her lily-white skin covered in a long-sleeved cotton blouse. Her dark hair was pulled into a severe ponytail cascading out the back of a ball cap. She pined for Izzy’s dark skin glistening in the Roatan heat, and wild kinky hair blowing in the occasional breeze.

“Matti’s gonna be jus’ fine, Natalie. Don’t you fret none. Won’t be long now and that boy be chattin’ up a storm with pretty young island girls. You wait and see.”

“Maybe.” Natalie grabbed her water bottle and took a long drink. She finished the sketch just in time. The children had become bored with their sand project and run off to swim. She watched them splash in the water and added, “I’ll start tutoring him in all the major subjects. We can pick up right where he left off when school was out.”

“That’s a good idea, honey. Some kinda routine where he’s learnin’ the way he used to might jus’ bring back his voice.”

“You’re right, Izzy. Maybe it will trigger a reason to talk.”

Natalie wondered if Matti would ever speak of that night, if it would simply all spill out one day like gutter leaves in a storm. She wasn’t sure she wanted to hear what he had to say about it. Part of her didn’t want to know what Antonio had done. She'd never forgive herself for withdrawing into the studio while turning a blind eye to whatever despicable things Antonio had become involved with . . . and probably still was.

CHAPTER EIGHTEEN

Selling her paintings would be like selling little pieces of her soul.

Antonio parked in the garage and slammed his car door, followed closely by the kitchen and refrigerator doors. He downed a bottle of water without coming up for air, crushed the flimsy container, and tossed it into the recycle bin while shouting "Sydney!" at the top of his lungs. After wiping his lips with his sleeve, he went storming up the stairs to find her. She was in the hall, replacing Natalie's paintings with some from her own collection.

"What's all the fuss about, Antonio?" she asked, without looking at him.

"The police have taken up residence at the foot of our hill. Right outside the private gate."

Sydney cocked her head to the side and adjusted one of the pictures. "Taken up residence?"

"In their squad car, Sydney. Not in a house. They have someone sitting there around the clock."

"Why does that disturb you, silly? It ain't like they can do anything about your situation. I mean, no wifey means no charges. Right?"

Antonio stared with dismay at the portraits Sydney had taken down. He had rather liked seeing the same faces every time he entered or exited the upper hallway. "What exactly do you plan to do with Natalie's paintings?"

Sydney shrugged, still adjusting her modern artwork hung in their place. "I guess I'll haul them off to the basement."

"It takes a lot of nerve to replace the art when my wife might be returning!" Antonio glared at her back.

"Why you wanna look at these boring people painted by your ex? And anyway, you and me both know she ain't comin' back!"

"*They* don't know that." Antonio stared out the window at the end of the hallway, in the same direction as the squad car.

"Don't be ridiculous." Finally Sydney looked at him. Her patronizing glare caused his blood pressure to rise. She would be the death of him. He knew she would be. There was a piece of Sydney Beaumont in every corner of his house, his mind—his living hell of a life at the moment. He couldn't take it anymore. Even sexually she was wearing him out.

"Having you here is not the image I need right now. They may not have any hard evidence yet, but they desperately want it. I'm not exactly winning them over with a live-in mistress."

"Calm down, Tony-wony. It ain't as bad as you think. Every time I pass their squad car I get nothin' but big smiles. I think they consider you one lucky guy. That wasn't no crime last time I looked."

Sydney breezed by him, leaving Antonio speechless. He stared at her attractive backside for several seconds before recovering enough to stay hot on her heels. "Sydney, listen to me, we need to talk."

They'd reached the bottom of the stairs and he swung her around to face him. She must have seen the rage in his eyes. Sydney began singing a new tune almost immediately. "Baby-cakes, listen to me. Them cops ain't gonna find no reason to lock you up. There's no crime with no bodies. Anyone's entitled to run off. Of course, taking your son's another matter. Natalie's the one who'll end up in jail if they ever catch the flaky dame. Not you, sweetie."

She nuzzled his neck and her scent excited him. Sydney was an addiction. He might as well be snorting coke or shooting heroin. "Syd, you can't bring any more art over here. It already looks like you've moved in." He stopped there, because she'd started kissing him, invading his mouth with her tongue while pressing voluptuous breasts against his chest. He couldn't help himself from carrying Sydney up the stairs, tossing her on the king-size bed in the master suite, and having fast, rowdy sex with her, exactly the way she liked it. Then he ordered Sydney out of the house while pulling on his pants.

Sydney lay naked on the bed staring at him in disbelief. "What?"

"You heard me. Get out. And take all your art with you."

Sydney sat up and glared at him. "You're kicking me out?"

"That's exactly what I'm doing."

She grabbed her panties from the floor and quickly slipped them on. "Fine then. Have it your way. But don't come crawling back to me. You hear?" Sydney pointed a finger at him and her naked breasts jiggled. Antonio wanted to rip the panties back off and have her again, but he thought better of it.

"Don't worry. I won't be crawling back."

She pulled her tank top over the lovely, exposed breasts and deflated Antonio's second rising. He watched her yank on the tight jeans and almost regretted his decision to give up such a sumptuous piece of ass. Instead of hanging around limp and useless, he exited the room while yelling for her to be gone by dark.

He could hear Sidney screaming obscenities as he entered his den and began reading the mail. Antonio couldn't help but smile. Sydney was too stunned and angry to retaliate despite her clever mind that never quit. Sex was her best weapon, and he'd just had a wonderful round of it. She'd be long gone before he felt the urge again. He only hoped in a few days he wouldn't want to go crawling back.

Natalie dropped her art tote on the porch and flew into the house. She had just enough time to shower before Marlon arrived for his first tutoring session. She hoped he wouldn't be early. Matti was still at the beach with Izzy and the girls, and truthfully, Natalie wished she were, too, but she couldn't turn down someone Diego referred to her. Improving the lives of the island women was all that she cared about. It was her one burning desire at the moment, but she didn't have the heart to let Diego down or disappoint him—not after all he'd done for her.

It wasn't that the women of Roatan weren't bright. They'd just left school too soon. Education wasn't a priority. Not yet. Before Natalie was done with them it certainly would be. It all boiled down to self-esteem. Until they saw themselves as something other than a prize for men, nothing about their lives would change regardless of reading and math skills. She knew once they could earn a living, their priorities would be different.

Natalie returned to the porch in a bright blue sundress just as a man entered the back gate. She assumed it was Marlon. He was a short, stocky man with graying hair and a nice smile. His appearance suggested wealth. The restaurant Diego said he owned must have been doing well. He wore light-colored trousers and an open weave button-down shirt. It wasn't tucked in, but it looked expensive. When he came closer, Natalie saw that he wore a Rolex watch and a large diamond ring, opposite his wedding band.

"You mus' be Natalie." He held his hand out and she shook it.

"Yes, and you're Diego's friend, Marlon. It's a pleasure to meet you."

"I hope I'm not impose' to ask for your tutor me."

"Not at all." Natalie thought his thick accent quite charming. It suited his demeanor.

"This is . . . how you say . . . quite nice," he commented, studying the sketch of the children Natalie had drawn on the beach this morning. "Who are they?" he inquired, still admiring the sketch.

"The boy is my son, Matti. The girl in the middle is Emmy, Diego's daughter, and the other little girl is Angel. She lives next door at the Internet café."

"Oh . . . goodness. You mean Izzy's child."

"You know Izzy then?"

"Oh yes. She bake bread for my café. Delivers twice a week. Never met daughter. Looks much like mother."

Natalie nodded. "Izzy told me she bakes for a few restaurants in West End."

"I collect art, you know, me and Justine. Do you sell work?" Marlon asked.

"I've done a few portraits on commission, and I hope to sell my work in some of the shops here," Natalie added.

"Can I see?"

"I don't have paintings ready to show, but here are more sketches." She collected her drawings from the back of the porch and handed them to Marlon, watching as he thumbed through the pile. The sketches were like a visual journal of her time on the island. There was a drawing of Izzy standing at the door with a basket of avocados, and a sketch of Sarah Jean in Izzy's kitchen looking tiny and tired, with Anna Marie balanced on her hip. It was painful to look at the somber drawing of Izzy, her eyes flashing hurt and anger at Solomon's unfaithfulness. Several were of Matti and Emmy on the porch swing—Matti with his Gameboy and Emmy with a book, or both of them eating ice cream. Some of the sketches she'd forgotten about and it felt empowering to have a history here. Roatan was no longer a temporary refuge. It was home.

"Please, show finished work, when ready."

"I'd be happy to." Natalie smiled and put the sketchpads aside. She spent the next hour helping Marlon with his English. He read from East of

Eden, just as Sarah Jean had done, while Natalie corrected one consonant. Next time, they would add another. He was pleased she could help him and agreed to come every Monday and Thursday for his lesson. When the session was over he mentioned his interest in her artwork again. She watched him walk down the beach, and wondered if she could really sell her art. The many sketches that read like journal pages would come alive on canvas, in oils. Her emotional investment by then would be tremendous. Selling her paintings would be like selling little pieces of her soul.

Once Marlon was out of sight, she shifted her thoughts to dinner and began scurrying about the kitchen. Natalie planned to have Diego throw lobster tails and steaks on the grill. She made fresh tortillas and cleaned ears of corn to roast. Yellow island potatoes baked in the oven while she chopped onions and cilantro for the salsa. When everything was ready she went to freshen up for her guests and check on Matti, who was back from the beach. He sat on the porch swing reading a book. She didn't know why it hadn't occurred to her sooner that Matti was ready to focus on reading. He'd been watching movies for some time now. When first arriving on the island his eyes looked blank while viewing the screen and his twitches were evident as he stared straight through the television set. However, lately, the movies Emmy and Angel frequently stuck into the old VCR held his attention.

In fact, everything about Matti seemed quite normal, other than his lack of speech. He behaved like a typical twelve-year-old boy, something he honestly hadn't done in San Francisco. Something about the island had been magical for him, piquing his curiosity through its many timeless mysteries regarding treasures of the sea and creatures in the forest. Countless species swam or crawled, flew about, or stealthily stalked their prey.

She stood at the screen door and stared at the back of his head. Natalie thought about how attached he'd become to Izzy and Angel, and of course, he was quite bonded at this point with Emmy and Diego. It disturbed her because she was already thinking about moving out of the Espinoza summer home. She had imposed long enough, and she couldn't see herself marrying Diego anytime soon, even if something finally developed between them.

Natalie sat down beside Matti. He didn't look up and she didn't disturb him, her own thoughts lost in what Marlon had said earlier regarding interest in her artwork. It was something to give serious consideration to, since she had no hope now of making much money tutoring. The women she was passionate about teaching could not afford to pay. Art was her only other possibility for a livelihood on the island. She and Matti looked up when Diego's Land Rover pulled into the driveway. Their jaws nearly dropped as Nic swung in behind them on a motorcycle.

Jake and Diego were laughing as they slammed the SUV doors. She enjoyed Diego's laughter, especially since Antonio never found anything amusing. She'd stepped off the porch to greet everyone and noticed Matti's eyes were glued to Nic's motorcycle. As if Nic could read the boy's mind, he asked him to come and check it out. Matti peered up at her and she motioned for him to go and see it for himself, which he did without a second coaxing. Before she'd given a cold beer to Diego and Jake, Matti was seated on the bike wearing Nic's helmet.

"Looks like you got a willing passenger there, Nic." Diego nodded toward the bike.

The men all looked at Natalie. She turned and studied her son, sitting on the black Harley wearing a bright red and yellow helmet two sizes too big.

"Can I take him for a short ride?" Nic asked. "I promise to be careful," he added.

Matti's eyes lit up with anticipation.

"Yes, of course. I'm sure you'll use good judgment," Natalie cautioned.

Nic handed the boy his spare helmet, which fit better, then he positioned himself in front of Matti and started the engine. They rode off slowly, with everyone watching. Once out of sight Jake went looking for chips and salsa while Diego lit the outdoor grill. Natalie poured herself a glass of the wine Jake had brought, thinking she would need it to get through the evening. Nic had only been on the premises five minutes and already endeared himself to her by exciting Matti with a motorcycle ride. She secretly yearned to be Matti right now, riding along the road parallel with the beach.

They returned in ten minutes or so, with Matti absolutely beaming. Natalie believed it was actually painful for him not to speak. She thanked Nic for thrilling her son with the special ride.

"It was my pleasure. He's a great kid. Oh, I almost forgot . . ." Nic walked back to the motorcycle, opened the leather compartment beside the seat, and pulled out a stunning bouquet of local island flowers. He handed them to Natalie. "This is for having me to dinner."

"They're beautiful, but you shouldn't have." Natalie smiled, and marched off to the kitchen in search of a vase. When Nic caught up to her she handed him a Salsa Vida and placed the flowers on the table. Everyone gathered on the backside of the wraparound porch and dipped warm tortilla chips fresh from the oven into the salsa she'd made earlier. Izzy had shown her how to cut and bake the day-old tortillas for chips. Natalie was more grateful than ever for Izzy's expert instruction. This dinner party would probably have been a disaster otherwise. She poured herself more wine and watched Diego rearrange the hot coals.

"I need to prepare my tortillas," Natalie remembered, and excused herself from the porch. Nic followed her inside and leaned against the door jam. He watched as she heated a cast iron skillet and placed a perfectly round tortilla in it, feeling proud of how well she'd learned to roll the dough until just the right thickness.

"Who taught you how to make tortillas? Nic asked.

"My neighbor, Izzy."

"Is that the exotic looking woman I met at your party?"

"Yes. Izzy and her husband run the Internet café next door. Angel is their daughter," Natalie added.

"I see. She's one of the little girls Matti helped swim to shore after snorkeling out too far. Has Matti saved any damsels in distress lately?" Nic asked.

Natalie looked at him and grinned. "No, thank goodness. He's managed to stay out of dangerous predicaments."

Nic took a long drink of his beer, watching Matti through the screen door. He was kicking a soccer ball around the yard while Jake and Diego hovered near the grill roasting ears of corn. "He seems a lot better than last time I saw him, Natalie. That nervous look is gone."

Natalie glanced out the screen door at Matti running after the soccer ball. Her face was just inches from Nic's, and she could feel him staring at her. It aroused desires she shouldn't be having, at least not for Nic. "He's much calmer, and more focused. If he'd just talk . . ." She looked up at him. For several seconds their eyes locked, as if trying to read one another's minds.

Natalie was glad they weren't alone, because she had an irrational urge to kiss him. Without a doubt, she believed he shared that feeling, but then Nic shifted his gaze to Matti. "I hope he does speak soon, but I'm not sure that can happen without some kind of therapy."

"I know." Natalie forced herself to leave the doorway and finish the tortillas.

"Diego tells me you painted his little girl, Emmy, but the portrait is back in the States." Nic stepped over to the counter where she was working.

"That's true. I had it hanging in my hall with a few other paintings."

"Really? Who else did you have hanging there?"

He sounded genuinely interested. Natalie wondered if he collected art. He didn't really seem the type. "Just some of my students, the more interesting ones."

"Men or women?"

"One of each. I painted our maid, because she is determined to improve her English skills and go to college. I feel bad that I'm no longer there for her. I was going to be a reference when the time came and help her sort through red tape. I'm sure she'll be eligible for some type of scholarship."

Nic nodded. "You said you also painted a male student?"

"Yes. I did a portrait of Faraji. He was a medical student when I knew him. Dr. Faraji returned to his village in South Africa as soon as he earned his degree. He was a splendid man, quite the scholar. His stories about the village he grew up in were fascinating. We had long discussions about science and geography, but his personal stories about Africa were my favorite."

"I'd love to hear those stories some time. Africa intrigues me. I plan to visit there one day," he added.

"Well, in the meantime, you can put the tortillas on this plate, after they cool a bit." She handed him a blue china plate with a green cloth napkin. Side by side they each did their job until Nic had placed the last one on the plate.

"Thanks, Nic, for your help."

"It was my pleasure." Nic grinned and Natalie nearly forgot there were other people there for dinner, but then Diego came barging in the screen door. He quietly piled the roasted corn on a serving dish and placed it on the table. Jake was right behind him with the steaks and lobster tails. Natalie retrieved her twice-baked potatoes from the oven and told Matti to wash up.

"Where's Emmy?" Jake asked as they all sat down at the table.

"She's eating with Angel, next door at the Internet café," Diego shared. "Emmy is a fan of Izzy's fried chicken, and she's not fond of steak or lobster."

"Good to know she'll be a cheap date for some lucky guy in a few years," Jake commented. Everyone laughed, and Natalie was grateful he'd put everyone at ease. Diego hadn't looked pleased when walking in on her and Nic in the kitchen, but now he was smiling. It helped alleviate her guilt, knowing Nic had mesmerized her in a way that must have been obvious. It was clearly a mutual fascination. She had no idea why they were so drawn to one another, or what to do about it for that matter. Her feelings had never been out of control like this before, certainly not when meeting Antonio.

During dinner Natalie shared stories about Africa that had been told to her by Dr. Faraji. Nic had prompted her, but everyone enjoyed the stories. She wasn't suspicious of Nic's inquiries. Nothing about Nic felt threatening, other than bringing out dangerous desires in her. After dinner she insisted the men retire to the porch where an ocean breeze had picked up. Natalie thought the heat in her kitchen was especially stifling on this particular Roatan evening. She poured herself more wine and tried to focus on putting the food away.

CHAPTER NINETEEN

She'd draw the inky outline of boats through shadows of dusk and the night surf crawling on the shore, beneath a crescent moon.

Antonio sat alone in his den staring outside at the fountain. He continued to stare at it while answering the phone. The sound of trickling water was supposed to be soothing, but it gave him chills, as if someone's jugular were spewing out their life's blood. Was he losing his mind? Surely he hadn't grown a conscience. What disturbed him most about his paranoia was the need to examine the water several times a day, half expecting it to turn a telltale pink. The Romanian woman's pleading and horror-stricken eyes still haunted him. Antonio listened to the gurgling water through the open window and felt cursed. As long as the fountain was there, he'd never be able to forget.

Pops's voice on the other end of the phone startled Antonio back to reality.

"Hello my son! How are you?"

"I've been better, Pops. How are you?"

"Not so good either. We need to resolve this . . . dilemma . . . with Natalie and Mattia."

"I know that, Pops. Nicholas is working hard on it."

"So Mario tells me. Until that little woman and my grandson are returned to their proper home, the police will continue to scrutinize the Giovannis. Do you hear me, Antonio?"

"Yes, Pops, but what more can I do?"

"You can assure me when Nicholas brings back your son, and that artist mother of his, you won't let either of them wander off again."

Antonio didn't mention that his Bay Area thugs were offered a reward for Natalie's death, so she wouldn't be returning . . . as if she would want to. Envisioning her at the bottom of the bay sandwiched between two concrete blocks gave Antonio some pleasure for that very reason. He understood his father's concern. Their family had a lot going on that was at risk for exposure. Antonio wished the police had never been alerted to the situation. Matti's school had contacted authorities out of alarm when Natalie and Mattia disappeared without a word. Why didn't the school accept his explanations? Lots of eccentric people ran off to foreign countries on an impulse, especially the type that could afford Mattia's private school. "I don't think Natalie will cooperate with your plan, Pops. When's the last time you held a woman hostage in her own home?"

"Antonio, it's all about negotiating. You threaten her plenty, but you promise her a quiet divorce if she stays put long enough to get the cops off our backs."

"And how long do you think that will take?" Antonio was careful to keep his tone pleasant and respectful, even knowing the cops would never be *off their backs*, as Pops put it. As for Natalie, if she did return, she'd fall prey to a most unfortunate and fatal accident. He would see to it himself.

"The police will leave your doorstep when you once again reflect the happy little family that you are," Pops added.

Such an idea made the hair stand up on Antonio's neck. His old man actually wanted him to produce a happy little family for the police. They hadn't been that to begin with, and now Natalie wouldn't trust him any further than she could throw him. If he thought reconciliation possible, he wouldn't be plotting her murder. He would much rather ravish her luscious body than bury it six feet under. However, the likelihood of that ever happening again was more remote than the possibility of inviting Sydney back to the house. "I'll see what I can do, Pops. Okay?"

"You will do this, my son. You will show everyone what a happy family you have. Just like Mario will run the Romanian operation with no more mishaps and Nicholas will find Natalie and Mattia. He'll return them and you . . . Antonio, will appear overjoyed. Everyone does their job, and we have no worries."

"Right, no worries. Just one big happy family, huh Pops?"

"I'm counting on it."

Antonio rolled his eyes, said goodbye, and hung up. The rushing water outside his window became deafening. It roared louder than a storm at sea in the dead of winter. And when he looked into the water flowing down the tiers, he could have sworn it had a pinkish tint.

Natalie poured herself the last of the bright Chilean wine Jake had brought to dinner. It did her heart good to hear Matti giggle as the men played soccer with him in the yard. After much fun and many impressive moves by everyone, Matti kicked the winning goal. She couldn't believe her son was playing soccer, let alone scoring the winning goal.

Once they'd caught their breath Jake and Diego slipped into the kitchen to cut the Key Lime pie Izzy had dropped off earlier. She'd made "a whole mess of 'em," as she put it, mostly for café patrons, but some she took to restaurants in West End. Natalie wondered if Romolo's bistro bought Izzy's pies. She'd have to wait until tomorrow and ask Izzy. Matti sat on the porch steps to eat his and Natalie sat beside him. The men could be heard laughing in the kitchen.

Nic soon emerged through the screen door and leaned on the railing. "This is a perfect island evening, isn't it? There's such a nice breeze out here," he added.

"What was everyone laughing about in there?" Natalie asked.

"Nothing really." Nic smiled. "I think they're leaving for Ike's bar."

Diego stepped onto the porch and announced that he and Jake were headed to Sundowners. They invited Nic to come along, but he declined.

"Thank you for the wine, Jake." Natalie hugged him goodbye and looked at Diego, who told her they wouldn't be late.

Nic and Natalie watched as the Land Rover pulled away.

"It isn't like Diego to visit Sundowners mid-week," Natalie commented.

"I think he's just happy," Nic reasoned. "His award-winning home is coming together nicely. It means a lot to him, finally being an architect."

Matti had gone inside, and it felt awkward to be alone with Nic on the porch, so Natalie gathered up dessert dishes and went to check on their star soccer player. When she returned Nic was sitting in a rattan chair finishing his beer.

"Thanks again for taking Matti on that motorcycle of yours," Natalie commented. "Judging from his smile, I think it must have been quite exhilarating."

"Want to see for yourself?" Nic asked.

"I've never been on a motorcycle," Natalie confessed.

"Well, if you've never been on one, I think it's about time." Nic winked at her.

"Are you sure about this?" Natalie felt like a kid at Christmas. "What about Matti?"

"He'll be fine. I'll go ask him to stay put while we're gone."

Nic went looking for Matti in the house and Natalie tried to talk herself out of such foolishness. She wanted to blame Jake's bottle of wine for being so absurdly excited about a motorcycle ride, but she really couldn't. The shiny black machine and its raw, untamed power had excited her before opening the wine. Stepping off the porch she walked over to the bike and ran her hand along the cool metal. Natalie could almost feel her hair blowing straight back when Nic appeared beside her. Without a word he climbed onto the bike and she slid into place behind him. He revved the motor a few times, handed her the spare helmet, and took off.

The beach ran parallel to the road and the sun had just begun to set, spewing blood orange and ripe mango across the sky. The colors soon melted into the sea and swirled about in puddles of raspberry and plum. Natalie was quite sure it was the most magnificent sunset God had ever created. Maybe it was the wind in her hair and all that power purring beneath her that helped make the sunset so special. Her ride was even more of a thrill than she had anticipated. Nic was an expert driver, making the machine perform like a sleek panther barely touching the ground while gliding across it. She snuggled closer and held on tighter, feeling perfectly giddy from the wind and the wine.

Nic slowed down and skillfully maneuvered onto the beach. He pulled up to a deserted dock across the sand and came to a stop. Neither said anything as they watched the last crumbs of faded color drop below the tideline. The moored boats became mere shadows and lines with the dusk, reminding Natalie of ink drawings. Nic helped her off the bike and together they walked down the beach. She removed her sandals and went ankle deep, while Nic sat in the sand and watched.

Stars appeared in the sky and reflected off the calm sea. Natalie still felt tipsy and wasn't sure if it was from her breathless ride or the stunning night. She collapsed on the sand next to Nic and had no idea how to thank him for this moment. Of all the new and notable things she'd done since coming to the island, nothing compared to this. She turned toward him, hoping to find just the right words, but then she realized how close he was. Before she could recover he leaned forward and kissed her. It wasn't timid or sweet as she imagined it should be—not at all. Like the night itself, his kiss was filled with fiery passion.

They didn't come up for air until their better judgment got hold of them. Pulling apart they simply stared at one another, as if they'd wanted that kiss from the moment they'd met. Natalie broke the spell to smooth her rumpled clothes and hair, and to prevent doing something she might regret. Without a word they collapsed on the sand to star gaze and Nic spoke as if nothing had just happened. "I looked through your sketches on the porch . . . while you were cleaning up dinner. I hope you don't mind."

"Not at all." Natalie was so relieved Nic didn't want to discuss the crazy chemistry between them that she almost laughed.

"I'm not really knowledgeable about art, but I enjoy your work. I feel as if I know the people you've sketched, just by how you've sketched them. It's uncanny the way you capture their feelings and personality."

"My sketches are as alive to me as the people I'm sketching." Natalie was certain her images of tonight would become sketches. She'd draw the inky outline of boats through shadows of dusk and the night surf crawling on the shore, beneath a crescent moon.

"I think you'll make a decent living on the island with your artwork, and your tutoring," Nic added.

"I'm not so sure. I have this crazy notion to tutor island women, for free of course, so they can get jobs and make a better life for themselves." Natalie sat up and stared into the moonlit surf. "I plan to ask if I can draw them in return. So if I do make a decent living here, it will be from my sketches and paintings."

"I have no doubt you'll sell everything you paint or draw." Nic sat up beside her and their faces were dangerously close again. "I plan to build affordable housing for local islanders, so it would seem we have such foolishness in common."

Natalie quietly admired his strong jawline and large, deep-set eyes. His face would make an intriguing portrait. Every line and crease seemed to reflect a moment in time worth knowing more about. "Why would you do that?" she asked.

"I should have been as poor as the scantily clad Hondurans here on this island. My mother was no better off than theirs, until a rich man married her in a weak, irreversible moment of midlife crisis."

"And so you want to be Robin Hood," Natalie summarized.

"I suppose," Nic admitted.

"I'm sure I was poor growing up, but it never felt like it. My mother found love in the floodlights, as a ballet dancer in a traveling theater troupe. The dancers became my family and I never wanted for anything—except a real home with a white picket fence." Natalie laughed. "I ended up with a mansion in the hills of San Francisco and was completely miserable. If it weren't for Matti I'd have left Antonio years ago."

"I'm glad you left him. He doesn't deserve you."

Natalie wasn't listening. She could feel his breath on her face, and still tasted that kiss. It made her want more . . . and it made her want to run away down the beach.

"We should get back," Nic suggested. He helped her up from the sand and they walked in the dark to the bike beside the dock. The ride home was every bit as thrilling as the ride there had been. The Harley purred like a cougar and exuded a controlled power unlike any Natalie had ever experienced. The only difficult part of the ride was having it end. When they arrived at the house she slid off the leather seat and kissed him on the forehead. "Thank you. It was wonderful."

"Would you like to take an island tour on Saturday?"

Natalie smiled. "I'd love to."

"Can I pick you up around noon?"

"Noon is perfect."

She didn't move a muscle as the Harley drove out of sight. Then she stared into the darkness where it had disappeared. Natalie still saw Nic's broad shoulders and narrow hips driving away, still felt the wind rushing through her hair. Somewhere in the distance crickets brought her back to earth. She checked on Matti, who'd fallen asleep with a book on his chest. Curling up in one of the rattan chairs on the front porch, she waited for Diego. It seemed like an eternity ago when he'd left with Jake for Sundowners. In that short amount of time her perspective had changed drastically. It wasn't long until he pulled into the drive and sat beside her on the porch.

"When did Nic leave?"

"You just missed him."

Diego nodded, but had nothing more to say.

"Nic gave me a ride on his motorcycle, while Matti read a book in his room," Natalie confessed. She thought it best to come clean up front, hoping she'd feel less guilty that way. "We watched the sun set over the ocean and then came back."

"Did Izzy say what time Emmy would be home in the morning?" Diego asked, changing the subject.

"I'm assuming after breakfast." Natalie stopped stargazing and turned to look at him. "The girls are very good friends, aren't they? Like you and Izzy."

"Or you and Nic," Diego added.

"I barely know Nic. I'd hardly call us close friends. Whereas you've known Izzy your whole life."

"Length of time doesn't matter. You've only seen Nic twice, and yet I'd give our last coffee plant bathed in the blood of my ancestors to have you look at me the way you look at him."

Natalie was speechless. She stared at him through the darkness between them, but he was focused on the stars above. She wondered how many Honduran beers he'd downed with Jake at their little post party in the open-air bar. Surely every swallow that trickled down his throat was fueled by indulgent self-pity. It was so unlike Diego to be negative and introspective. "Is it the same look you reserve for Izzy? Not that I would judge, but it seems to me you share a dance of mutual desire, in your body movements—and the way your eyes meet."

An army of crickets cheerfully chirped in the distance while she waited for him to form an answer, not blatantly bathed in denial. How could he in good conscience expect hard and fast truths from her if he was unable to reckon with such realities himself? Diego left for the guesthouse without so much as a goodnight, while Natalie sat quietly in the rattan chair until dawn.

CHAPTER TWENTY

She wanted to cry because her days were numbered in Diego's summerhouse, amongst all this joy that could not last.

Nic couldn't sleep, mainly because he couldn't wrap his brain around the situation he'd gotten himself into. He was falling for a woman who literally fled the country to hide from his half-brother, suspecting him to be the lowlife that he was. Antonio would rather place his son in an institution than risk the boy's voice returning. Not to mention that messy little murder shoved under the fountain in his front yard, because of an illegal baby trade with a former soviet country.

It was true that fate, if not Antonio himself, had placed him in this precarious position for which he was undeniably thankful. He couldn't help but admire and respect Natalie while feeling protective of her at the same time. No one in all of history exemplified the fragile albeit strong damsel in distress better than she. Why not just come clean with her, he reasoned, and together they could go to the police? Authorities would then discover the body beneath the fountain and send Antonio to prison. His father and Mario might do time for their part in the baby trade, which would no doubt come to light during the murder trial. On the other hand, ratting them out would be more than a little risky. In the end they might find a way to pull him down the rabbit hole along with them.

He went to grab a bottle of water, opting for a shot of tequila instead. Nic poured it into a drinking glass and took it, along with the bottle, out to his tiny front porch. Collapsing into a canvas deck chair, he stared up at the stars. Nic poured himself another shot and thought about viewing those same stars not that long ago with Natalie. He decided either the tequila or that kiss, still on his mind, was fogging up his thinking. The only thing perfectly clear was how he'd managed to double-cross all the people he cared most about on the island. None of them were likely to be forgiving when they found out who he really was, especially not Diego or Natalie. He downed another shot of tequila and threw the glass at a tree in the yard. It broke without a sound and fell to the dew-covered earth. Nic returned to bed, but still couldn't sleep. Instead he stared at the ceiling fan and thought about how beautiful Natalie had looked wading in the water on the beach earlier.

If he were honest with her, she'd see him as someone who wormed his way into Diego's life under false pretenses, with every intention of exposing her location to Antonio. On top of that he was a Giovanni. Natalie had crossed time barriers to escape the Giovannis. She'd left everyone and everything she knew behind and was prepared to start a whole new life in order to protect her son.

It would sound shallow and be embarrassing to admit his motivation for coming here was to secure his place among the Giovannis so he could be certain of the inheritance due him. As a child he would have done anything to know his father's family better, but it had been his mother's mission to protect him from his heritage. Now he understood why.

Receiving his inheritance didn't seem worth the price he was paying for it. What had he been thinking? Perhaps he played no part is his brother's hideous crime, or the shady business causing it, but certainly, his first concern should have been to protect the innocent—not help the guilty. He didn't want to leave the island. He'd already acquired property to start his housing development, and after talking with Natalie this evening, he thought he might designate the homes for island women trying to make it on their own.

There wasn't any way he'd be able to stay if the truth came out. It would be impossible to call the island home if those he cared most about would never speak to him again. On the other hand, he couldn't live a lie. That wouldn't be fair to Natalie or Diego. He'd have to find a way to tell them.

Nic finally dozed off and dreamt about building his homes, swinging a hammer beside the island men he would pay to help him—until rudely awakened by his cell phone. It was Antonio whining into the long-distance airwaves.

"How's Africa, Nicholas? I hear it's hotter and muggier than Roatan."

Nic sat up in the bed and leaned forward on his arm. His head hurt, and his situation was rushing back with intense clarity. "Yes, it's hot here."

"Have you located that village doctor yet? The one my wife tutored?"

Nic cleared his throat. "Um, no, it would seem traveling to his village is a little harder than you might think."

"How are you going to get there . . . on an elephant for God's sake?"

"I'm waiting for a private plane to take me."

"Pops called."

That came out of the blue, but Nic was grateful to change the subject from his location to anything else. "Really? How is Sali anyway? Taking all this in stride?" Nic knew better. The old man hated having anything out of order. He'd loathe this entire fiasco Antonio was smack in the middle of.

"Pops isn't happy. Neither am I. The sooner you get my son back to me the better off we'll all be."

"Right. I'll call you in a few days, once the plane has made its mail route and dropped me off. Shouldn't take long to locate the good doctor once I'm in his village." There was silence on the other end of the phone and Nic feared Antonio wasn't buying his blatant lies.

"Let's hope this is the end of the road," Antonio finally said.

"I have a good feeling about this," Nic assured him. After they hung up he considered how angry his brother would be if he knew Natalie and Matti had started a wonderful new life on the island. More importantly, he considered how angry Natalie would be when she found out who he was, and why he was there. If there was only one thing Nic could be certain about, it was that his lies were bound to catch up with him.

At dawn a chorus of birds serenaded Natalie, dozing in the rattan chair. She watched the sunrise through low-lying fog and then went inside to make coffee. After a hot shower she checked on Matti, who was still asleep. Grabbing a cup of the special blend Diego kept in endless supply, she curled up on the porch swing. It wasn't long until Diego joined her, with his own steaming mug. Not a word was said about the night before. They listened to songbirds in the plum trees until Diego finally spoke.

"Izzy and I have loved each other for as long as I can remember. Why does it matter? She's native born of mostly African heritage. I'm not. You've been here long enough to understand the implications of that."

"So you and Izzy have never expressed your love for one another?"

Diego chuckled. "Do you mean have I ever slept with her? No. How could I have slept with Izzy knowing I'd never be able to make an honest woman of her? Neither of our cultures would have accepted us, and more importantly, neither of our families."

"So you each found someone else."

"Yes. And I loved Amanda. Perhaps not in the same way, but I did love her. I know Izzy loves Solomon, so it all turned out for the best."

"Solomon is cheating on her."

Diego shook his head. "I'm sorry to hear that, but I'm not surprised. Most island men aren't faithful."

"It's sad that Solomon doesn't love her completely the way you might have."

"Please, Natalie. It doesn't help my ego to tell me what a great husband I'd make when you obviously want no part of being married to me."

"I think you'd be settling for second best, Diego."

"Not true. I love you more than you will ever know, regardless of any unfulfilled fantasies I might have about my good friend and neighbor. It's clear to me, however, that you're interested in someone else. I promise to stay out of your way."

"Diego, I can't be involved with Nic Walsh while living under your roof. It wouldn't be right, and anyway—I don't want to be involved with anyone." Natalie paused there, not sure how to share with him what she'd been thinking about all night. Finally she took the plunge. "Your friend . . . Marlon . . . is very interested in my artwork. I'm going to focus on completing a couple paintings as soon as possible. I need to see if I can really sell them." She turned sideways in the swing to give Diego her full attention. "If I can make enough to live on every month, then I can take the money I saved from my tutoring in San Francisco and buy a little place on the island."

Diego nodded slowly. "Of course your work will sell, of that I have no doubt. And you know that you're welcome to stay here as long as you wish, but I understand why you want to leave."

"It isn't what you think, Diego." Natalie gently turned his face to look at her. "I need to prove to myself that I can be the independent woman I'm convincing these island women to become."

"That's very noble of you, Nat."

"I am hardly noble. I just want to help them make a better life for themselves. There are so many of them, Diego. I haven't told you yet, but word of mouth has already brought me two-dozen women eager to be tutored. They all want to get jobs and improve their lives."

"Where are you finding room for so many eager pupils?" Diego asked.

Natalie smiled. "We're meeting on the beach, under some shade trees. Izzy told me I'd reach more women if I held the tutoring sessions somewhere in the open. That way no one has to feel like they're imposing on me. The women bring baskets to weave and laundry to fold—whatever portable jobs they can do while learning. It's very guilt free for them that way, and the little ones can play in the sand or wade in the water." Natalie could hardly contain herself, now that she'd finally shared with someone what was happening on the beach with the island women. "Izzy didn't want me to tell anyone. She's afraid if the word gets around, someone might put a stop to it."

"So this is what you've been up to while I'm on the construction site? I agree with Izzy. I'm concerned, Nat, about what the men will do when they find out."

Natalie shrugged. "I'm not. From what I've seen of Izzy's family, most of the men would rather hang in the background and complain as opposed to actually doing anything about it."

Diego laughed. "True enough."

Matti stood at the screen door and Natalie noted he wasn't holding his Gameboy. It was progress. In the past he wouldn't have considered standing alone at the door and peering out at them. He would have stayed in bed playing his Gameboy and probably would have starved to death before letting anyone know he was hungry.

Natalie went inside to make breakfast and Diego followed. Emmy soon joined them. The little thrown-together family ate their bacon, eggs, and toast while talking about everything and nothing, except for Matti, who watched and listened. He looked so happy that Natalie thought it quite a victory. She wanted to cry because her days were numbered in Diego's summerhouse, amongst all this joy that could not last. A second victory this week was having the island women multiply on the beach like fish and loaves in the Bible. She felt a sense of satisfaction with her new life, and it felt good indeed.

Natalie spent the rest of the day composing a painting from her sketch of the kids on the beach, except for the two hours midday when meeting with Roatan women on the beach. All of them had agreed it would be called a gossip session, an excuse to do a few chores by the sea and let the kids play on the shore. No one planned to breathe a word of all the reading, writing, and math skills they were learning on the portable chalkboards Natalie brought. There weren't enough for everyone, but they shared and took turns. Izzy spoke about Natalie wanting to sketch her students, and rather than being hesitant as Natalie had feared, they were grateful to repay her for the tutoring.

By the time evening rolled around, she felt more hopeful about her future than she had in quite a while. It was all because of Diego, who had agreed to bring her to Roatan in the first place. Without his help there was no telling where she'd be right now. Maybe she'd still be in the hills of San Francisco and Matti would be in a mental ward. It was foolishness to think she wasn't as dependent upon a man as ever, but in this case, Natalie couldn't have been more grateful.

Natalie put a lot of thought into packing a lunch Saturday morning. She wanted to properly thank Nic for the island tour he was about to take her on. She'd been looking forward to it ever since he and Jake had come to dinner earlier in the week. Nic was making her nervous for completely different reasons than he had before meeting him. She was annoyed with herself for thinking he might have been sent by Antonio. Fortunately, she was feeling less paranoid every day. If Antonio hadn't figured out where she was by now, chances were he never would.

It did surprise her that Antonio hadn't put the pieces together. Surely he turned over every stone in the wake of her mysterious disappearance? The daughter of her Honduran student was hanging in their upstairs hallway, and he had returned to his homeland. The more she thought about it, the more she wished she could have figured out a way to remove Emmy's portrait without it looking suspicious. Unfortunately, removing it probably would have been an even bigger clue to her whereabouts. The whole subject was exasperating.

She put water bottles in the backpack, and a nice Chilean wine. Maybe she'd confide in Nic her original suspicions about him being sent by Antonio. They could have a good laugh about it. Suspecting him of working for her husband seemed silly now. Nic Walsh might be somewhat mysterious, but he was no bounty hunter. She had met men that would probably do anything for a price, and they were nothing like Nic. She suspected every one of the men who had frequented Antonio's office to be nothing short of underhanded in their business dealings. They wore flashy suits and never smiled or engaged in small talk with her. Their hushed discussions with Antonio always involved expensive liquor, consumed behind closed doors. She had no proof Antonio was dealing with unscrupulous men, but she was convinced that olives weren't his only business. Natalie shuddered as she cinched the backpack shut.

Sitting on the porch steps waiting for Nic, she recalled her days back in San Francisco filled with tutoring, sketching, or painting—followed by long lonely nights. Antonio had always been disappointed she didn't fit into his life well. She'd never wanted anything to do with any of it—certainly not the parade of creepy men coming and going at all hours, or his activities on the docks which he never cared to discuss. Something not nearly as wholesome as olive oil was probably being unloaded from their ships, and maybe if she'd made any effort at all to find out what, Matti wouldn't have somehow come face to face with it.

She watched Nic pull up on the bike and wished she'd asked Antonio, just once, what exactly it was he worked so hard at hiding from her. She also wished she'd kept Matti home a bit longer before sending him to Izzy's, so he could see Nic and maybe take another short spin on the bike. Diego was taking Matti and Emmy to camp this afternoon at Anthony's Key, and she already missed her little boy, growing up too fast before her very eyes.

Walking down the driveway shouting a friendly hello, Natalie decided she would never get involved with anyone again without full disclosure. She'd need to know every detail of their past, every fact about their present, and even their future goals and dreams. No more mysteries and lies by omission. If she were fortunate enough to find true love it would be with her eyes wide open.

"Looks like we're going to eat well." Nic took the well-stuffed backpack from Natalie to place in the side compartment, after pulling out her helmet.

They both climbed aboard, and Natalie's heart began to pound in her chest as she felt the power surge beneath her. It was intoxicating soaring down the road on such a sophisticated machine. Living in Antonio's San Francisco mansion had been suffocating compared to the breathless freedom she felt here on the island. Nic and Antonio couldn't be any more different. Although physically they shared similarities, in every other regard they were like night and day. Nic had a great sense of humor and Antonio never laughed. Nic was an engaging conversationalist but seldom spoke about himself, whereas Antonio's conversations centered on him.

Natalie relished the wind on her face and the gulls circling out at sea, dipping down to feast on whatever school of fish had wandered near the surface. The long ride curved steadily upward and at the highest point, Nic stopped at a pullover. He snatched water bottles and binoculars from the side compartment of the Harley and they walked to the edge of the cliff, which overlooked the shoreline. Natalie couldn't take her eyes off the view while Nic adjusted the binoculars for her. She was impressed with how they made distant sailboats and fishing vessels sharp and detailed. You could even see the reef surrounding the island in dark jagged shadows beneath the shallow surf.

"Have you been snorkeling?" Nic asked.

Natalie nodded. "Diego takes us near the house on Saturday mornings, or off the dive boat when fishing."

"I want to take you and Matti snorkeling in a cove I've discovered, tucked away from tourists. It's brimming with sea life and the coral there is stunning."

"I'd like that." Natalie handed the binoculars to Nic. "If Matti had his way he would investigate every square inch of this island, and the surrounding sea."

"I don't blame him. I love exploring this island myself."

Natalie couldn't help herself from staring at Nic while he looked through the binoculars. There was something so familiar about him, but she had no idea why. She was sure they'd never met before. Perhaps it was the square jawline that mirrored Antonio's. Nic's hair was a reddish brown in the sun, not nearly as dark or curly as Antonio's, but so similar at the hairline. Antonio had a younger half-brother living in Greece, and she suddenly wondered what color his hair and eyes were. Natalie couldn't remember his name, if anyone had ever mentioned it. He'd only been referred to as the son from Sali's midlife crisis. She couldn't imagine why she was thinking of him. Was she really that paranoid? Natalie was annoyed with herself, hoping she wouldn't spend the rest of her life looking over her shoulder and questioning everyone she met.

"You look lost in thought." Nic had put the binoculars down and Natalie was suddenly embarrassed for having stared. She looked away, out to sea.

"I'm sorry, Nic. I just have a lot on my mind."

"That's funny . . . because all I can think about is you. Focusing on anything else has been a struggle ever since I came to dinner, and you took your first motorcycle ride." Nic grinned. "Our time on the beach just keeps replaying in my head."

"That's one of the things I can't get off my mind. I couldn't wait for today to get here." Natalie smiled at him. "I've been looking forward to this island tour."

"Well, let's get on with it then. I'm excited about that lunch you packed," Nic added. They clinked their water bottles together and took one last drink before getting back on the road.

CHAPTER TWENTY-ONE

Neither one had the energy to exit the vehicle and carry on as if important relationships weren't shattering right before their very eyes.

When they reached the north side of the island, Nic stopped at a picnic area. Natalie had put a gingham tablecloth in the backpack, which he spread under a broad-leafed palm. Nic opened the wine and poured it into small stemless wine glasses Natalie had wrapped in the tablecloth. They feasted on shredded chicken rolled in flour tortillas with avocado and tomato, and a salad made from yellow island potatoes. Homemade salsa and corn chips rounded out their lunch. For dessert, she surprised Nic with Izzy's brownies, dropped off this morning on her way to deliver baked goods in West End.

Nic couldn't comment enough about the brownies, and Natalie was once again indebted to Izzy. It was easy to see why Diego was so impressed with her, and hard to understand why Solomon would take a woman like Izzy for granted. Aside from her intellect, ambition, and industrious nature Izzy was high spirited, loving, and kind. What man wouldn't consider her the ultimate fantasy? Who could ever long for more? It had to have something to do with island ways concerning power and prestige. Men refused to treat women properly in order to hold themselves in higher esteem—not unlike many societies of the world, including her own.

When they'd finished eating, Nic poured them more wine and moved a little closer. They'd taken off their sunglasses and Natalie was startled by how blue his eyes were. "Have you ever been married?" she asked.

"No."

"Have you ever been in love?" She took a sip of wine and kept a steady gaze on his blue eyes. Nic didn't look away. He seemed to be up for the challenge of personal questions.

"I thought I was a couple times, but I've since realized love is an entirely different beast than what I'd encountered in past relationships. I think those were more about lust."

Natalie took a bite of brownie as she considered his answer. He really was an honest, open book. Nic put the wine bottle down and made sure it was balanced on the grass beside them. "Did you love Antonio?" he asked.

Natalie carefully considered her answer. "I didn't know what love was when I met him, and I think maybe I falsely identified the emotion. I confused it with longing for a family and security. All the things I didn't have growing up."

Nic nodded appreciatively. "Are you in love with Diego?"

Natalie stared at the stemless crystal in her hand. "I don't know. What I do know is that Diego is very special, and I care deeply for him."

"That says it all. You wished you loved him, but you don't."

"I'm not so sure about that. Maybe I'm just pushing love away because my marriage was . . . so unfulfilling."

"Maybe," Nic agreed. He put his empty wine glass down beside Natalie's. "Or maybe you just want to love him, because he's in love with you."

"What makes you think so?" Natalie asked, flustered by his comment.

"It's pretty obvious, don't you think? And I feel terrible about that because Diego is my friend and all I can think about right now is kissing you."

Natalie could feel her cheeks turning red and had no idea how to respond to that. Fortunately she didn't have to, because Nic pulled her close for a long, slow kiss. It aroused her to the point of breaking away before losing control right there in the park and having her way with him on the gingham tablecloth. "Nic, if we don't leave right now I'm afraid we won't leave at all."

He smoothed her hair back, which he'd messed up quite a bit while running his hands through it. "I agree, and that would be a shame because I have so much more to show you." His eyes sparkled in the sunlight and Natalie was quite sure she'd never forget this moment, because it was as clear to her as the gulls squawking on the beach that she was falling in love with him.

Izzy packed the herbal concoctions in Sarah Jean's leather bag, the same worn pouch she had been using ever since first coming to the café for the potions.

"Now listen here, cousin. You be sure to keep it quiet where you got these here medicines. Solomon's been on my case about it. Seems your daddy's been harassing my man about it whenever he sees him in Coxen Hole." Izzy rolled her eyes.

"I'll try to hide them. Daddy comes to Sunday dinner a lot, and he likes to snoop around in my cabinets, probably looking for your potions . . . so he can scold me," Sarah added.

"Why you think he even cares?" Izzy asked, not expecting an answer. "Ain't like my herbs is gonna do anything but soothe whatever ails you."

"I don't know why my daddy and Uncle Ray are so stubborn. I've tried to tell them they shouldn't hold a grudge against you for wanting to better yourself, with the café and all, but they won't even discuss it . . . let alone listen to me."

"It ain't about the café, Sarah Jean. It's about the wedding money I got from my daddy. But if I tried to give them some, they'd run me off the island for sure." Izzy shook her head. "Pride. It's all about pride, and keepin' us womenfolk in our place." Izzy looked Sarah Jean straight in the eye. "That's why it's so important you keep on with that tutorin'. Listen to ya!" Izzy smiled. "You sound jus' like my friend, Natti-girl. She makin' you quite the smart soundin' woman."

Sarah Jean nodded enthusiastically. "There's lots more women coming for tutoring down on the beach, Izzy. I spread the news around just like you told me to."

"Good." Izzy laughed. "Wait till all them young island girls get themselves jobs and don't need no man. Them island boys be singin' a new tune then."

They both laughed.

"I just wish they wouldn't blame you for who your daddy was, and what he did for you." Sarah hugged her cousin and Izzy thought she couldn't agree more. All the respect she earned from strangers with her Internet café, and all the comforts her inheritance had provided didn't erase the misery of being shunned by her own family. There was little solace in tourist acquaintances.

"Your daddy and all the rest know my door is always open and I try to help any of you's I can with my medicines. Ain't nothin' more I can do than that." Izzy kissed Sarah Jean on the top of her head and walked her to the door.

"No, but there's plenty I can do. I'm going to learn everything the tutor has to teach, and then I'm going to get me a job and leave that no-account man of mine. I'm going to help change things on this here island. You watch and see." Sarah's eyes were on fire, flashing with determination. They hugged again, and Izzy had tears running down her face and into Sarah Jean's hair.

"I knows you will, Sarah Jean. You gonna change things fo' sure. You and the tutor." Izzy chuckled and wiped her tears away. "That be my Natti-girl. She gonna change all our lives, Sarah honey. Now you get on home and read that book she gave you. Read until you know every word in it. You hear me?"

"I hear you." Sarah Jean grinned from ear to ear, and then she ran home, never slowing her pace until out of sight. Izzy hoped she would stay strong for the road ahead, because that's what it would take to change anything at all.

Sarah Jean had barely left when Solomon came strutting up the stone walk. He winked at Izzy as he walked past her and pushed open the screen door. Izzy followed him into the kitchen. She leaned against the doorframe while Solomon explored the contents of the refrigerator.

"There's chicken in there, on a plate in the back."

Solomon set the plate on the counter without so much as a glance at Izzy. He snatched a tomato from a hanging basket nearby and an avocado from another. Solomon sliced through them, peering up at Izzy occasionally. She was still leaning against the doorframe with her arms folded. Neither of them spoke until Solomon had wrapped his chicken, tomato, and avocado into a big flour tortilla and grabbed a Salva Vida from the fridge. "What you starin' at, girl?" he asked finally, just before taking a big bite of his island-style sandwich.

"Nothin'. I'm jus' wondering where you been all night."

Solomon didn't answer. He took a long drink of the beer and stared into space, probably to avoid the hurt in her eyes. She unfolded her arms and slipped up beside him at the counter. "Is there nothin' I can do to keep you all mine? I ain't never said no to you, Solomon. I ain't got fat or mean, neither. I be thinkin' those the only excuses a man has for cheatin'."

"Hush now, woman. A man does what he was born to do," Solomon proclaimed.

"And what's a woman put here to do? Jus' have your chil'ren and wash yo' shirts? Give you all their sweet love and not be sad when it ain't enough?"

"Somethin' like that," he answered, still staring into space, eating his chicken wrap.

"I don't think it was God who made them rules. I think it was a bunch of drinkin', cheatin' island men."

"You leave me be, Izzy. Ain't your place to tell a man what his needs are. Yo' place is right here in this kitchen, cookin' for me and all them customers who jus' love you and your food. Why can't you be happy I come home at all?" He leaned on the counter and looked her right in the eye. His large brown eyes didn't look angry, not at all—in fact, they seemed to be flirting with her. "I meet all your needs, Izzy girl, don't I? When you ever not been happy with my manly services?"

"It ain't that I'm not happy with your lovin'. It's sharin' your love with other women I object to." Izzy's voice was hard and unyielding. She was annoyed with his making light of the issue. Solomon stood to his full height and stared down at his wife, who wasn't much shorter than him. He was tall by island standards, but so was Izzy. It was clear that Izzy pushed her limits in many ways besides height, which she suspected unnerved Solomon. Grabbing his chicken wrap in one hand and his beer in the other, he stormed out while letting the screen door slam behind him.

Izzy walked out to the porch and put a hand up on the railing as tears began to stream from her eyes. She watched his truck speed down the road in a cloud of dust and thought maybe she'd pushed him too far this time. Maybe he would never come back. It seemed likely he would, considering the setup he had. Most island men, although just as prideful, didn't have as much to walk away from. On the other hand, native islanders were a stubborn breed, and Izzy was no fool. Solomon could easily live in conditions one tenth as desirable for the rest of his life just to prove he was the one in control, regardless of who held the purse strings.

Matti, Emmy, and Angel came storming up the porch steps less than a minute later. Angel asked for toasted cheese tortillas on their behalf and Izzy quickly wiped her eyes. She told them to go wash up while she made their lunch. Staring blankly at the griddle she methodically assembled their toasted cheese tortillas and turned them to heat the other side. "After lunch, we is goin' to Anthony's Key with Diego, to check you all in for summer camp," Izzy informed them. She was happy to dismiss her hurt temporarily and talk about how much fun it would be for them to sleep in cabins near the Bay of Dolphins and learn about the reef that surrounds the island.

"You all get to swim with them dolphins," Izzy told them.

"Will we get to feed them, too?" Angel asked.

"I's bet you do," Izzy answered.

The kids had been looking forward to camp for a long time. Matti's eyes brightened whenever the subject came up. It was mostly for tourists staying at the resort, but Diego and Izzy knew the resort manager. They'd grown up with him, spending hot, lazy summers swimming and snorkeling until dusk. He was from the mainland, like Diego. Native islanders didn't run with the rich kids from the mainland, but Izzy had found herself a real gem in Diego. He'd become her first friend and then her best friend. Diego included her in everything he did during those summers on the island, and none of his buddies seemed to object.

Izzy sat on the porch while the kids ate inside. She thought back to those carefree summers and couldn't recall when she'd fallen crazy in love with Diego. Maybe it was love at first sight, since she couldn't remember a time when she didn't love him. Izzy couldn't imagine what their lives would be like if they'd become a couple. There wasn't any place at all she'd have fit in to his world. It made her wish she didn't love him, because it was such a painful thing to love somebody you couldn't have. She was lucky to have found Solomon, whom she loved differently, but nonetheless she did love him. Izzy wiped away more tears as quickly as they fell, thinking that she didn't have Solomon either . . . not completely. No, she had to share him with whatever island girl he might fancy. It wasn't right, but there was nothing she could do about it. That much she knew for sure.

Just as lunch was over, Diego's Land Rover pulled up. He sat beside her on the porch and must have noticed Izzy was not her usual self. He asked what was wrong and she shrugged it off, not willing to share her marital burdens. Grabbing Angel's suitcase and sleeping bag she threw them in the back of Diego's Land Rover, next to Emmy's and Matti's. Izzy was quiet on the ride to Anthony's Key while the girls chattered nervously about camp. Diego answered their questions as best he could, glancing at Matti occasionally, who sat between the girls with a big smile on his face.

Once they arrived at the resort it didn't take long for the children to check in and join other campers, already swimming in the resort pool. The three of them would be roommates, despite gender differences. Diego had convinced the counselors of Matti's need to be with his close friends because of his muteness. Nic had recently rented one of the bungalows across the bay and agreed to be an emergency contact. Izzy was glad Angel wouldn't be around asking where her daddy was, since Izzy suspected he might not be home for a while, if at all.

On the ride back to the café Diego kept the conversation light. He didn't pry into what was upsetting her. Izzy was grateful for his thoughtfulness. It was all she could do not to breakdown and make an embarrassing scene. No one could ever know how humiliated and helpless she felt about Solomon's running around on her. When they pulled up the drive Izzy invited Diego to stay for dinner. He didn't need to be asked twice, and Izzy wondered if he'd had a falling out with Natalie. They never seemed to have angry words between them, but then Izzy remembered Natti-girl was spending the day with Nic. In all her misery she'd forgotten. That had to be taking its toll on Diego. She looked at him, really studied the man for the first time since he'd come for them earlier. "When's Natalie getting back?" she asked.

Diego looked out the windshield and sighed. "I don't know."

They sat in the Land Rover for another minute, each lost in their own thoughts. Neither one had the energy to exit the vehicle and carry on as if important relationships weren't shattering right before their very eyes. "Come on, Diego. I's give you my best table and fetch you a beer while I git ready for the evenin' crowd." She leaned over and kissed him on the cheek.

"You got yourself a deal." He winked at her and they climbed out of the Land Rover, slamming the doors behind them. Diego sat under a shade tree on the large café deck, while Izzy charmed customers and laughed along with them while serving their dinners. She kept Diego supplied in Salva Vidas and brought him her famous chicken dinner. Shortly after that she sat with him to eat something herself, since the dinner rush had tapered off.

"Diego, this here's the first time we had a meal alone together since you moved to the island."

Diego smiled. "I'd hardly call this alone. He glanced at other diners. Some were barefooted locals wearing straw hats, and others were tourists in flipflops.

"You know what I mean. Jus' you and me at this here table eatin' dinner."

"I haven't seen you eat much," he commented, and they both looked at her nearly untouched plate."

"I'm not hungry, I guess."

"Why don't you tell me what's bothering you? I'm the kind of friend you can confide in," he added. Diego put his fork down to listen.

"I don't know what kind of friends we are," Izzy answered honestly, staring into the Roatan sky. It was a beautiful rosy pink, from the sun starting to set.

"Old friends . . . lifelong friends . . . at least, that's what *I* think of you as," Diego answered.

"We got a funny way of showin' that, don't ya think? I mean . . . we ain't spent time together since we were teenagers snorkelin' right over there." She nodded down the beach and Diego glanced longingly at the shore. Customers paying to leave pulled Izzy away for a minute. Finally the deck was empty, except for her and Diego, who still stared down the shore, lost in thought. She slipped back into her chair and took a long slow look at him.

"Ain't Natti-girl comin' back at all tonight?" Izzy asked, feeling guilty about stirring up the pot. It wasn't like they didn't see the writing on the wall when Nic first came to dinner. Sparks between him and Natalie had nearly ignited into flames before their very eyes. Still, she felt sorry for Diego. He was so obviously smitten with his houseguest and former tutor.

"I have no idea," Diego answered. "Where's Solomon?" He glanced about as if first noticing Izzy's husband was nowhere in sight.

"He's away for a while."

"Is that why you've been so sullen?"

"Like you jus' figured that out," Izzy commented, wondering how Diego could be so dense. Natalie had probably shared all about Solomon's unfaithfulness.

Diego shrugged. "It did occur to me that he might be causing your distress."

"Don't matter none. It ain't like I got the only unfaithful man on this here island. Far as I know, ain't none of 'em don't wander."

Izzy did her best to catch up with Diego's drinking, downing a cold beer in record time. He leaned forward in his chair and studied her, causing Izzy to feel warm all over. Despite the near darkness, she believed he could see clear into her head and know what she was thinking about him. The truth was that Diego had been her fantasy ever since she was twelve years old. A dark fantasy she could never share with a living soul.

"If I were married to a beautiful and amazing woman such as yourself, Izzy, I would not be wandering. Solomon must need his head examined."

Izzy grinned nervously, a reaction to hide her simmering libido. She had never been this alone, and this frank with Diego in a long time. "Maybe I ain't any good under the sheets. You don't know why he is elsewhere tonight," she joked.

Diego reached out to touch her wild, wavy hair. She was all too aware of how different it was from Natalie's silky, trimmed locks. But then, they were as different as day and night in every way. Izzy felt sure Natalie never had the kind of wicked thoughts about Diego she was having, and then suddenly he was pulling her to him, kissing her forehead . . . her cheek, her mouth. Izzy pulled away and looked into Diego's eyes. She hoped he wouldn't regret this once he sobered up, because they'd both had quite a few Salva Vidas. Grabbing his hand, she pulled him toward the beach until they were walking down the shore, stopping several times to kiss again—long, hard, messy kisses with their hands everywhere. Once they caught sight of Diego's boat they nearly sprinted to the dock, like-minded in their need for a private place alone together. The snug little bedroom off the galley would do quite nicely for that . . . and it did.

CHAPTER TWENTY-TWO

By the end of the hour-long swimming spree it was clear Matti had a special way with his finned friends.

Natalie applied the final brushstrokes to her painting of the children playing on the beach. The idea of selling it to Marlon had been her motivation. She'd never completed a painting from start to finish as quickly as this one. It was without a doubt her best work. Perhaps the island breezes had influenced her brush strokes, or maybe the gulls cheering her on from overhead. In any case, selling it to Marlon would be a bittersweet triumph.

One reason she'd completed the painting in record time was not having any interruptions. The children were at camp and Diego had taken that opportunity to be away. He'd slipped in and out all week without breakfast, and said he'd be working late. Maybe he thought it would be awkward spending time alone together, considering the way they'd left things between them. It made her feel a lot less guilty about spending her evenings with Nic. They'd been inseparable since last Saturday when they'd toured the island on his Harley. Natalie smiled at her memories of that day. It had been such an exciting, scenic ride. Their picnic lunch had been a lot of fun, but it couldn't compare to dinner. They'd sat for hours and just talked, until the restaurant closed. Not wanting to leave, they took their conversation to the beach and finished a second bottle of wine sitting in the sand, under the stars.

Life was taking another fast turn, and she liked it. Even her guilt about hurting Diego was fading, especially since he wasn't around enough lately to cause her to fret about it. She was excited to show her completed work to Izzy, who hadn't been around much either. Izzy had greatly admired the sketch it was taken from, and Natalie couldn't wait to show her the painting.

She hated having to sell this portrait of the children. Their glowing faces were smiling in the forefront, while sand and sea merged in the background. If she wanted to move out of Diego's summerhouse and into a place of her own, she'd have to relish the opportunity to sell her work rather than mourn the loss of each finished piece. Just looking at the painting made her miss Matti. Natalie recalled how he would barge into her studio after school and chatter on about something he had read or learned in school. God, how she missed his voice . . . his thoughts and opinions. Staring at his face between the girls on the wet canvas made tears well up in her eyes.

A voice startled Natalie and she swung around to see Marlon, who was all smiles. She'd forgotten about his tutoring session.

"Beau-tee-ful. My wife . . . she love." Marlon sat down heavily on a deck chair and stared at the painting.

"You think so?" Natalie smoothed back her hair and hastily sat across from him, with as much cheeriness as she could muster. Truthfully, she was exhausted from her nearly nonstop painting the last few days.

"Her birthday . . . is tomorrow. Let me buy for her."

"The oils are still wet, I'm afraid." Natalie gave him an apologetic look.

Marlon shrugged. "How about I bring her to see, and we take home when dry?"

Natalie didn't answer right away. "This painting . . . is of my son and his friends," she finally said.

Marlon rubbed his chin with stout fingers, assessing the dilemma. "I pay you ten thousand dollars."

Natalie stared at him. "Why would you pay so much? It isn't like I have a name for myself."

Marlon laughed. "You make name. I do not doubt, and I know my wife love this." He leaned forward in his chair, closer to Natalie. "I need your beau-tee-ful art . . . to make things right. We have troubles lately." Marlon's hazel eyes were soft and pleading. Natalie determined him to be quite the businessman. He certainly knew how to get what he wanted, including these tutoring sessions she couldn't turn down because the request came through Diego. Part of her was pleased that he admired her work and was willing to pay such a ridiculous price for it, but somewhere deep inside she regretted having met him. It was a silly way to feel, especially since he was going to make it possible for her to buy a home.

"How could I refuse your generous offer? I'm flattered you think my work is worth that much money, and I hope it makes your wife very happy." Natalie tried not to feel anything as Marlon whipped out his checkbook, paid for the painting, and left. He was too excited to wait for tutoring and needed to ask Justine when he could show her the birthday present.

It was just as well. Neither of them seemed to be in the mood for tutoring. Natalie had a sudden urge to visit Matti. She couldn't wait a minute longer to see him. Maybe she'd stop by Nic's cabin to discuss property and housing. If anyone knew what was available on the island, Nic would. He'd been studying the market while determining what land to acquire for his housing project, and what his affordable homes would cost to build. As excited as she was about selling the painting, she was equally sad, but didn't wish to dwell on her sadness. She needed to suck it up and make herself celebrate. She grabbed a bottle of wine on her way out the door and hoped Nic would be home to help drink it.

Antonio paced back and forth in the kitchen, wishing his arms were not empty night after boring night. He was tired of flirting with available women at the health club or on the golf course. Natalie's mysterious disappearance had not helped his social status. Many appeared standoffish or looked at him with suspicion through their smiles. Sydney, on the other hand, didn't care that his wife and child were missing. He could hear Syd shouting not to come crawling back—over and over again in his head as he peered out the window for the tenth time. The squad car was still at the bottom of the hill. The officers obviously believed he was responsible for the disappearance of his wife and son. Ironically, he was more perplexed as to their whereabouts than the police.

Antonio began pacing again. He had himself worked up over more issues than just an unsatisfied libido. He was beginning to think his half-brother was a terrible sleuth. It had taken Nicholas six weeks to find out they weren't on the island of Roatan. Now he was in Africa but hadn't been to the right village yet. Antonio thought perhaps he should go to Africa himself and help track down the doctor in question. Nicholas would no doubt be annoyed that he was coming. He'd think the trust in him was waning, and truthfully it was—at least where competency was involved. Helping Nicholas find Natalie and the boy would give him the perfect opportunity to take care of the situation himself. If something happened to his wife in a remote African village, there wouldn't be much scrutiny regarding the incident. Next time he spoke to his brother he'd get more detailed information about his exact location.

Besides finding Natalie and Mattia, he had the dilemma of how to get a woman in his bed. His options were limited. At this point a call girl was the only solution. Antonio collapsed in a kitchen chair and reached for his phone to dial the old service, still in his contact list. After negotiating a tall voluptuous blonde, he made himself a stiff drink. When the doorbell finally rang, even the couple of drinks he'd had couldn't avert his nervousness. Not answering the door at all came to mind, but then, he'd paid a large fee for his impulsive idea. He opened the door on the second ring and looked a blue-eyed platinum blonde in the eye. He asked her in, poured her a drink, and began to chuckle when realizing how this would look to the cops at the bottom of the driveway. At least they would conclude he didn't have a live-in mistress. They'd probably assume he had a blonde whore fetish.

She wasn't the euphoric upper Sydney always proved to be, but she was better than watching porn again on the Internet. The next morning Antonio couldn't stop thinking about Sydney while watching the well-paid call girl sort out her rumpled clothes. They were still on the living room floor where he'd peeled them off the night before. Barely a word had been spoken between them the entire night, so not saying goodbye didn't seem unusual. He watched as she walked to her car and exited past the cops at the end of the lane, thinking the only solution to his misery was convincing Syd to take him back. Meeting someone new was tedious, and whores were uninspired. Besides, Syd was perfect for him. He understood the woman, whereas he had never understood Natalie. His wife would have been repulsed by the real Antonio Giovanni, if she fully understood who her husband was. Sydney, on the other hand, found his darker side exciting. Why hadn't he realized this sooner?

Antonio began scheming what he'd bring as a peace offering to Sydney. He spent the rest of the morning picking out expensive diamond earrings and a necklace to match. Next he visited the florist. Unfortunately, his ex-mistress wasn't home when he rang her doorbell holding small, exquisitely wrapped packages and blood-red roses. After arriving back at the mansion, he set the bribery gifts on the table in the foyer and buried himself in paperwork. He pieced together the sketchy information given all too infrequently by Nicholas and decided it was enough to pull off a surprise visit to his half-brother. Antonio was suddenly motivated to track down the doctor hanging in the upstairs hall—where he'd rehung the portrait after Sydney left in a huff with her modern art in tow. Packing for a quick trip to Africa conveniently helped take his mind off Sydney Beaumont.

Swimming with dolphins, Matti surmised, was even better than snorkeling with tropical fish weaving between his legs. He didn't know why Emmy and Angel were squeamish about it. The other kids were equally overwhelmed, laughing and darting about nervously in the water, scaring the dolphins away. Four of the boys about his age were visiting from the States. They seemed awkward and unsure of themselves, just like he had been back home in San Francisco. Matti hated how his father always pushed him to be better at sports. He didn't miss anything about his life in San Francisco except perhaps his time in the science and technology labs at school. Other than that, he loved his new island home surrounded by the sea, cushioning out his father and his father's world.

Matti had bonded with the gentle mammals instantly. From the moment he stepped into the water they had nudged him deeper until he was swimming beside them, as if a long-lost brother. Everyone looked on enviously, including the camp counselors, who were also the dolphin trainers. It was the most exciting thing he'd ever done—better than having a tarantula for a pet or cutting down a coconut. It was even better than riding a motorcycle. The only thing he could think of that would be better than swimming with dolphins, would be for his mom to marry Diego. Then they could be a family. Emmy would be his sister, and Diego would be his dad.

He still felt like a failure since he hadn't attempted to save that poor woman. Matti recalled how much he had been afraid of his father that night. The only thing that frightened him on Roatan was a storm brewing with all the intensity of a hurricane, only to end up a hard, refreshing rain. He never tossed and turned on the island like he had back home. Here he slept a deep peaceful sleep and awoke with a ferocious appetite. Instead of dreading getting ready for school, Matti looked forward to breakfast each day with Diego and Emmy, and his mom. He didn't feel as if he were failing them, even though he didn't speak. They loved him the way he was.

Matti couldn't believe how much he looked forward to whatever new adventure each day at camp would bring, and for that matter—each day on

Roatan. He felt no envy for these boys that would return to the States after their family vacation, and to their private schools with the bullies and peer pressure. School had always been a constant reminder of his inferiority in all ways not related to academics. While deep in thought about all these things, Buck, the largest dolphin in the pod, suddenly catapulted Matti clear out of the water. Instinctively, Matti arched his arms and dove back in. At first everyone in the bay and on the shore stared—stunned at what had just happened. But then they all broke out into cheers and applause.

Matti couldn't help but grin with pride. What an exhilarating feeling—being tossed into the air, and then applauded for diving back into the water! He concluded anyone would naturally do the same thing if a dolphin chose to throw them into the air. No big deal. What was a big deal, however, was having Buck treat him as if a trained performer. Matti glanced at the counselors to be sure he wasn't in trouble. They were scratching their heads and smiling at one another. Matti was delighted they didn't seem to mind his shenanigans with the gentle mammals.

By the end of the hour-long swimming spree it was clear Matti had a special way with his finned friends. The counselors had been speaking amongst themselves the entire time Matti swam with Buck and the other three dolphins. The pod led the way into each of their tricks, and Matti had been up for the challenge. Instinctively, he'd figured out the expectation, and it helped that he had seen the dolphin show with his mom and Emmy, Izzy, and Angel. When finally tired from such intense focus and physical antics, he swam to shore. His cabin counselor, Tanner, helped him out of the dolphin bay. The other kids at camp cheered and clapped. Some came forward and told him the show had been amazing, while a few of the kids patted him on the back.

The attention was more overwhelming than learning tricks with the dolphins. Matti had never received positive attention from other kids before, except for Emmy and Angel when guiding them to shore after snorkeling out too far. Otherwise, rude remarks and stares from classmates had been the norm. Matti had learned to enjoy being ignored. It was never his goal to be noticed. It seemed to be more of a byproduct when sharing knowledge about subjects he had researched—which always ended badly. He vividly recalled the many aches, pains, and nasty bruises received in dark hallways or sunny courtyards when no instructors were nearby. Social media had been a literal entourage of unkind and downright threatening remarks, and so Matti had avoided those popular sites among his peers.

"Matti, you have a gift. I think you and Buck could be quite a team in the dolphin show," Tanner added. The other trainers agreed. "Buck likes you, and he's the lead dolphin. For some reason he wanted to do the whole routine with you." Tanner shook his head. "I have no idea how the two of you communicate so well, but somehow you knew what to do every single time." Matti nodded his head, knowing exactly where the dolphins performed. When here for the show he had watched them follow a boat from the bay where they trained, to a bay surrounded by covered bleachers. There was a gift shop, and vendors that sold snacks and cold drinks at the performance arena. What an exciting idea . . . to be part of the show he had absolutely loved. Oh, how he'd envied the trainers in the water with the dolphins, doing silly tricks to make people laugh and amazing feats to impress them.

"If it's okay with you, I'll talk to your mom about it," Tanner offered up. Matti nodded and grinned excessively while the other trainers laughed at his enthusiasm. Before heading into the recreation facility, Tanner encouraged Matti to join the campers, who were already eating lunch. Matti, however, couldn't think about food. He sat at the edge of the dolphin bay, still dazed by the thought of being in the show. If his mother would let him perform with the dolphins, he would be the happiest boy alive. It would be great to make Emmy laugh and his mom proud of him. Maybe he would even talk again one day, if never having to mention the unspeakable events leading up to his amazing new life.

Natalie tried not to think about what she had just done, accepting an obscene amount of money for a painting that pulled at her very heartstrings. How would she ever forgive herself? On the taxi ride to Anthony's Key she was grateful Matti didn't know about the painting. He would never question her selling it, but surely it would hurt a little to know she'd wanted the money more than the portrait of him with Emmy and Angel. She dared not consider what he'd think of her if he knew moving out of the summer home was her ultimate goal.

She took a water taxi from Anthony's Key to the camp across the bay and was ecstatic to spy Matti with the dolphins. He was sitting on the side of the training bay and it was all she could do not to run up and hug him. She decided it might not be a wise entrance for a middle-school mom, but she'd never been separated from Matti for such a long time. Nonetheless, the days had gone by so quickly. She was grateful that her son was not only thriving in the camp environment but excelling. Tanner couldn't say enough good things about Matti when she'd called regarding this visit, and he was elated she could see for herself what Matti was doing with the dolphins.

Natalie shook hands with Tanner, who asked her to sit in the bleachers with the kids for a special dolphin performance, starring Buck and Matti. She grinned and looked at her son, who was grinning back. All the camp kids were excited about this second show, which had been finessed a little in the last couple hours since lunch. Everyone else had gone paddle boarding just offshore from the resort, while Tanner helped Matti tweak his routine with the pod.

Tanner asked everyone to quiet down, and with no more ceremony than that, he signaled to Buck with a whistle. The biggest dolphin Natalie had ever seen came up under Matti. She could hardly believe it when he rode on the back of Buck to the middle of the dolphin bay, with the other three dolphins following behind. The pod was obviously an eager supporting cast, accepting Matti as if he were one of the seasoned professionals.

Buck slipped out from under Matti and swam away, while the remaining three circled him until Buck came swiftly back, lifting Matti up out of the water—far enough to form a perfect dive for landing! After enthusiastic applause the dolphins formed a single line in the water and Buck came up between Matti's legs, lifting him onto his back. They wound around the bay, intermittently standing on their tail fins in unison. Matti would wrap his arms around Buck and simply hold on when he rose up out of the water. Next, the impressive mammals came alongside each other and swam together as one unit. Matti straddled the two middle dolphins, standing with one foot on Buck and the other on Max, balancing there while the dolphins swam the length of the training bay. Natalie couldn't believe the sparkle in her son's eyes when riding Buck back to shore, or the admiration he received from the camp kids, who were cheering and clapping the whole time. It meant more to her than the agile way in which he did the three stunts.

When Tanner pleaded for him to star in the dolphin show, Natalie was more motivated by the pride it would give her son than anything else. She asked Matti if he indeed wanted to be a part of the show and train each afternoon with the four dolphins. The pleading look on his face said it all. After signing some papers as to his earnings and conditions for working, she visited a little longer with Matti, Emmy, and Angel. The girls chattered on about how amazing Matti was with the dolphins. They were beaming with pride for him. As for Matti, he never stopped smiling. Tanner pointed out that it had been quite an exciting day, and everyone should wash up for dinner.

Natalie reluctantly left the camp, taking a water taxi to the other side of the resort where Nic's bungalow was. Poised to knock on the door she tried to push away Emmy's questions at camp about her father. Natalie assumed Diego was busy with his building projects. In truth, she had no clue where Diego was spending his time of late. For all she knew he was indeed working on the job sights or running around purchasing supplies. After business hours was another story. He'd insisted she not cook while the kids were at camp, and so she could only assume he was frequenting his favorite bars along the beach, or bistros in West End.

According to Sarah Jean, Solomon and Izzy had a falling out and Solomon was shacked up with Jessica. Could Diego and Izzy be together? Natalie couldn't bring herself to believe that, but it was certainly possible regardless of Diego's denial that he would cross that line with Izzy. Why else did he avert eye contact when passing through the summerhouse for one thing or another? And why hadn't he made any effort at a real conversation since dropping the children off at camp? Natalie had thought he was upset about her day with Nic on the motorcycle. It didn't take long to surmise Diego might have his own set of circumstances to sort out.

She stared at Nic's door and suddenly lost her nerve to knock on it. He had said to be sure and stop by, when visiting Matti at camp, but did he really mean it? She hadn't texted him ahead of time in case she changed her mind, but now here she was, standing on his front porch. Nic's Harley was in the driveway, and it reminded her of the two rides with him. They were the most wonderful experiences she'd ever had. Just thinking about those rides gave her the courage to knock.

CHAPTER TWENTY-THREE

It was time to become the strong empowered woman she was teaching island women to be.

Nic answered his door and looked pleased to see Natalie standing there with a bottle of wine. "To what do I owe this honor?" he asked.

"I was in the neighborhood." Natalie smiled at him.

"Visiting Matti at camp?"

"Yes," she admitted.

"I had hoped you'd stop by." Nic escorted her in and gave a tour of the bungalow, which was mostly filled with Anthony's Key furnishings. Natalie was impressed with the few possessions Nic owned. He had a collection of miniature Harley Davidsons proudly displayed on a built-in shelf and told Natalie it had been a hobby since he was a teenager. His mother shipped them out to him recently.

"Did your mother ship these books?" Natalie asked, picking one up off another shelf. It was *The Sun Also Rises* by Ernest Hemmingway. Glancing at the rest it was clear Nic had most of Hemmingway's books, if not all. She ran her fingers across hardcover bindings of *The Old Man and The Sea*, *For Whom the Bell Tolls*, and *A Farewell to Arms*. Another dozen of his lesser known novels lined the shelf.

"Yes. She shipped all my personal things because I don't plan to ever leave this island," Nic confessed.

"Which Hemmingway novel do you like best?" Natalie inquired.

"It depends on my mood." He opened the sliding glass door and ushered her out. "You admire the view while I open the wine," he suggested.

Natalie stood at the rail and realized his bungalow was directly across the bay from where the dolphins performed. She still couldn't believe Matti was going to perform with them. When Nic joined her with the bottle and two glasses on a tray, they toasted to his new living quarters. Afterward he confessed staying in the bungalow was temporary, until he either bought or built himself a home.

"I don't know if I'd ever want to leave. This is quite a view you have," Natalie commented. "I can almost see the kids at camp from here."

"How's Matti doing over there across the bay?" Nic asked.

Natalie put her wine glass on the table between them. She looked Nic right in the eye. "They've asked him to perform with the dolphins."

Nic grinned. "You're kidding?"

"No, really. The dolphins seem to have taken to him, especially the lead dolphin . . . Buck. Apparently Buck treated Matti as if one of the trained performers from the minute he entered the water."

"What a sixth sense that boy has." Nic shook his head, as if pondering Matti's giftedness.

"I have no idea why the dolphins bonded so easily with Matti, but the feeling is mutual. He's obviously transfixed by them." Natalie stared across the bay intently, recalling the amazing show she'd seen earlier in the practice bay.

"I haven't known Matti for long, but the boy seems to have blossomed here."

"You're right," Natalie agreed. "He's a different kid on this island. Matti's never excelled physically like he does here."

"Has he always had a way with animals?" Nic asked.

"Yes. His father is allergic to dog and cat dander, so Matti had hamsters and white mice over the years. Trained them to do all kinds of tricks." Natalie laughed.

"Now he's had a pet spider bigger than those little white mice, and he rides on the backs of dolphins," Nic added.

Seabirds along the shore caught Natalie's eye as she finished her wine. "Can we walk along the beach?" she asked.

"Of course." Nic set his wine glass on the table beside Natalie's and they meandered along the edge of the bay, where fish laid their eggs in the thick protective turtle grass and schools of minnows darted about. It wasn't long until the sun had set and lights from Anthony's Key lit up the resort, reflecting off the water and trees.

"You'll never guess what else happened today." Natalie almost pinched herself to believe it was really true. "I sold a painting . . . to Marlon."

"Is that the first painting you've sold here on the island?" Nic asked.

"Yes. And no one saw it. The kids are at camp and Diego's been busy with work. I painted it in record time, but then, I've had a lot of solitary hours . . . with Matti at camp."

"At least Marlon lives here on the island. We'll have to invite ourselves over so we can view your first island masterpiece." Nic winked at her.

"You won't believe what he paid for it." Natalie sat down on the sand, still warm from the sun.

"Money is no object to him," Nic commented, sitting beside her.

"He bought it as a birthday present for his wife. Nic, he paid me ten thousand dollars. He was desperate it seems, for the perfect gift."

"I don't doubt it. Justine hasn't seemed very happy lately, at least not the last few times I've seen her at the bistro," Nic replied.

"Do you think I could buy something small and cozy with that much money for a down-payment?" Natalie asked.

"Why don't you buy Diego's house with the floor plan he got his award for?" Nic suggested.

"Are you serious?" Natalie thought he was joking. "Even if the down-payment was acceptable, I might not be able to make the mortgage payments."

"With that much money for a down-payment, you'd have a reasonable mortgage. I know what your skills are worth. It won't take long, and the island will be your oyster," Nic told her.

"I don't know." Natalie ran her fingers through the sand. "I can't assume my paintings will sell for what Marlon was willing to pay, and eventually the savings I brought from home will run out."

Nic leaned back on his arms and studied the half moon rising over the water. "I can buy the house outright from Diego and Jake, and that way you'll never have to worry about the mortgage payment. You can make payments to me when you're able. It's an impressive design. No wonder Diego won an award for it." Natalie didn't say anything. She just stared at the moon glow on the water and let him continue. "It has a slate stone piazza in the middle and a copper sculpture of sea turtles. You could never begin to touch a house like this anywhere else in the world for such a reasonable price."

Natalie stared at him in disbelief. "Why would you take a risk like that on me, when you could buy it for yourself?"

Nic grinned. "I plan on spending a lot of time visiting you." He reached out and took her hand. "Even if that doesn't happen, I want to help you get settled here, after everything you've been through."

Natalie had no idea how to respond. "We should walk back. It's getting late." She headed toward his bungalow down the shore and Nic put his arm out to stop her. He pulled her close and kissed her. When he broke away, he led her to the bungalow. They leaned against the sliding glass door on the deck and kissed again, until Nic opened it and ushered her in. The moon lit up the room in a dreamlike state as Natalie stood there, looking at Nic, who was waiting for her to make the next move. She could say goodnight, grab her purse and leave quietly in the dark—but everything inside of her resisted that rational plan. Her pounding heart refused to cooperate with reason. This wasn't about rationalizations or anything close to reasonable thinking. This was about more feelings than she'd ever had for any man. Exploring those feelings was more about keeping her sanity than losing it. She took a step closer and kissed him on the chest, where his shirt was unbuttoned. Then she led him through the moonlit bungalow, past the miniature Harleys and the Hemmingway books, to the master suite at the far end.

They didn't resurface until gulls screeched loudly outside the window, fighting over fishermen's castaways from nearby boats. Peering through the blinds at the rising sun they saw lots of vessels bobbing in the calm sea with their lines and nets extended. Natalie had never seen anything like it. It was a fascinating scene. She turned to look at Nic and decided she found him equally fascinating. Natalie put on one of Nic's shirts while he made coffee. They took their steaming mugs out to the deck chairs beside the bay and she curled up in his lap to drink it. They watched the fishing boats until nets were pulled in and lines reeled tight for the day. It was only then that she left, after a long parting kiss.

"Wait," Nic called out as she reached the water taxi that had pulled up in front of the bungalow. "Let's meet for lunch at . . . say, noon . . . at Marlon's bistro. I'll have some figures ready and give you a tour of Diego's beach house afterwards."

Natalie grinned. "Okay. I'll see you then, but I never said I'd buy it."

She took the water taxi to the other side of the resort and a land taxi back to Diego's summer home. She had the driver let her out when close enough to see Izzy's café. It was time to have a heart-to-heart with her neighbor.

Marlon couldn't believe how beautiful the painting was, or how well he pulled off the birthday event. What went wrong? Just last night he was staring at the stars with a wife half his age, and twice as pretty as the first two Mrs. Romolos had been. He'd taken Justine by to see the exquisite portrait of the children in oils and then toasted her birthday with all their friends and his best Chianti at the bistro. He served her favorite meal of hazelnut encrusted halibut, basil linguini with Portabellas, and lemon cheesecake complete with birthday candles. The night ended with some of the best sex he'd ever had on so much booze, and now she was gone.

He'd barely been out of Justine's sight for five hours while tending to the breakfast crowd, and then returned to a skeletal shell of a home. Original art, expensive Oriental rugs, and brass candleholders—anything of value that could be boxed and shipped was missing, except for the larger pieces of furniture and everyday disposable items. Most heartbreaking of all, the masterpiece his tutor painted as a birthday gift for Justine was missing, after having just been delivered.

Marlon shook his head. To think that Natalie had brought Justine fresh flowers in a gorgeous, native-made vase as a neighborly gesture. She didn't know his wife and yet was so thoughtful. Who knew he'd be jilted just hours later? His heart was beating so furiously he thought it might explode any minute. Marlon sat heavily in a chair, his feet on the bare hardwood floor where once a beautiful silk rug had lain. Who was he kidding? It was only his money and exotic location for the bistro that had won Justine's heart. Once she tired of the remote island that offered no sophistication other than what a few entrepreneurs could provide, she was probably set on leaving with the first hard-body diver that would have her. Marlon's biggest regret was Justine taking the portrait of the tutor's boy and his friends. He would miss it. And chances were it would be ruined during shipping, since the oils were still damp. So much for wooing younger women. All that money for a painting, now gone like the wind of a Roatan storm.

On the long flight back to San Francisco Justine chided herself for bringing the oil canvas of the Roatan children. She feared it would always remind her of Marlon. It had been packaged so the wet paint wouldn't touch anything else in the crate. Something about the portrait had deeply touched her, and she couldn't bring herself to part with it. Marlon on the other hand, she was more than happy to part with. It was a hard lesson, but one Justine had learned well. Being wealthy on a secluded island was pointless, at least in terms of glamorous nightlife or high-end clothes shopping. Anything bought on the Internet cost more to ship than to purchase, and unless it was suited for hot, humid weather you wouldn't be able to wear it. If she could have gotten the stubborn Italian to move back to his home country, or at least back to San Francisco where she was from, she might have considered sticking it out for a while . . . at least long enough to outlive him and inherit his millions.

Justine stared out the plane window at nothing but clouds while recalling her few travels with Mr. Rich Bags Romolo in the last few years since they'd married. She had bought some beautiful things on those trips, most of it salvaged on her way out the Roatan house door, thanks to the short stocky natives who put everything in crates and hauled it to the ship docks. Ironically, her favorite item was a birthday gift from the very man she was leaving. She knew exactly where she would hang the painting when she got home, and hopefully Marlon wouldn't come looking for it. All he really cared about was getting *laid* on his secluded island, and running his bistro, where he drank bottles of Chianti with all his island buddies late into the night. At least she waited long enough to get the exquisite birthday present.

Natalie was disappointed to find no one at the Internet café. A sign in the window said: "On vacation. Will return Sunday." How odd. Izzy had said nothing about taking time off while the kids were at camp. Natalie wondered if Solomon's leaving had anything to do with this. She worried that somehow Diego was involved. Maybe that's why they had been like ships passing in the night. For that matter, she hadn't seen Diego at all the last couple of days. Of course, she wasn't home herself last night, which brought details of her time at Nic's bungalow rushing back—causing her to feel warm all over. She left Izzy's porch and went home, trying not to think about whether Izzy and

Diego finally gave in to their feelings for one another, which could no doubt be a train wreck for both of them in the long run.

Natalie called out Diego's name when she opened the door, but he wasn't there. She grabbed a bottle of water from the fridge and went straight to her studio space on the wraparound porch, picking up where she'd left off on her portrait of Izzy holding a basket of avocados. At this point it was just an oil wash done in earth tones of burnt umber and raw sienna, an outline of Izzy's flattering African features. Natalie missed her heart-to-heart talks with this sublime creature on her canvas. It was hard to believe she barely knew Izzy when doing the sketch that inspired the painting. If only she could keep the portrait when finished, or give it to Izzy as a gift, but her priority at the moment was to secure a home for her and Matti. It was time to become the strong empowered woman she was teaching island women to be.

Izzy stared at the calm water from the tiny cabin galley. Diego had left for the day, and soon she would brave the trip back to the café to see if there had been any sign of Solomon. She wondered what the rumor mill had to say about her mysterious behavior, or if anyone had noticed where she spent her long hot nights. Was Solomon gone for good? Even if he did return, his pride would never allow him to stay if he found out she had retaliated with an affair of her own. Men were like that. Turnabout was not fair play in their rulebook. Gathering up her tote bag Izzy climbed onto the dock. She'd never regret her time spent with Diego. It seemed as if she'd dreamed about sleeping with him her whole adult life. And every second had lived up to her wildest imaginings.

Choosing not to take a taxi, Izzy zigzagged across the dirt and gravel roads toward the café, her heart feeling heavier with each step. As much as she had relished and savored these long sweaty nights in Diego's arms, she did still love her husband. Angel deserved a mother and father that didn't put their selfish desires first. If there was any way she could resolve her issues with Solomon, she intended to do exactly that.

What kind of future could she have with Diego anyway? She'd never be accepted or fit in to his world. If he insisted, and she was not at all sure that he would, then he would be an outcast from his own society. If she truly loved him, and strangely enough, she had always loved Diego, then she couldn't possibly cause him that kind of burden. Izzy knew in her heart God had made her to love only Solomon, and it was her sinful nature rearing its ugly head that allowed her to love the wealthy, powerful, out of reach Diego.

Now she would most likely burn in hell, having made her fantasies sizzling realities. Why couldn't Natalie have fallen madly in love with him? Diego deserved a good woman like that, with no devilish thoughts that made Satan himself blush. Despite her guilty conscience Izzy couldn't wait to meet Diego for dinner at Ike's and make sweet love again all night—sneaking down to the docks after dark, so as not to be seen by any nosy neighbors.

Nic would need to tell that truth to Natalie, *and soon.* The whole story of exactly who he was. In fact, it might already be too late. Could she ever forgive him for not confessing his mission, not to mention his bloodline? He drummed his fingers on the table and wiped his brow yet again as he glanced nervously at the bistro door, waiting for Natalie. He couldn't tell her here, in the restaurant, but how could he talk real estate with this huge issue churning in his stomach? No, he'd have to hold off about the house and take her somewhere private. They could walk along the docks. All the dive boats would be out for the day.

Shaking his head at his own idiocy, Nic wondered how it was he'd finally fallen in love and it just so happened to be with his sister-in-law. He was poised to leave, too shaken to see Natalie for lunch after having spent all this time berating himself over the whole ordeal, when he looked up to see her standing there in the doorway. He stood to greet her and forced himself not to run out the door—straight to the airport and all the way back to the States . . . any state where no one knew him.

CHAPTER TWENTY-FOUR

You listen here, missy . . . you is nothin' but dust off the Roatan roads.

Justine admired her birthday painting, recently placed in a heavy wooden frame and hung over the mantle. She couldn't believe she was back in her own country, unpacked and ready to continue where she'd left off. Except for the painting of the kids on the beach there was nothing to remind her that she'd been married to Marlon. Her unique pottery collection, hand carved by local artists, was something she put together herself while meandering through art galleries on the tourist strip in West End. She spent hours picking out her stunning jewelry collection as well. All hand crafted from wood, stones, and sea treasures found right there on the island. She stared at the impressive birthday present while waiting for her bridge club to arrive and wondered if she could ever view it without remembering her birthday and the huge smile on Marlon's face when showing it to her.

Soon the doorbell rang, and the garden patio was filled with giggling high-pitched voices and tinkling glass. The bartender Justine hired for the evening had mixed lemon-drop martinis for all the ladies, who couldn't wait to hear about Justine's two-year tropical island adventure while peering over rooftops, down the hill, in the San Francisco neighborhood. When most of the appetizers were gone from the silver trays, everyone gathered in the front room to play cards. The group of bridge players had attended college together in the Bay Area, but what had bonded them more than anything else was their love of art. Justine was very pleased to show off the jewelry and pottery collection she'd put together over the two years, the artwork she had collected during her side trips from the island, and of course—the birthday painting over the mantle, done by Marlon's tutor.

Nothing else seemed to stand out quite as dramatically as that painting. Everyone found it striking, between the young carefree faces in the foreground and the rich cyan sky in the backdrop, melting into a white sand beach. Justine noticed that her closest friend and confidant over the years looked especially impressed by the artwork. In fact, Sydney Beaumont announced she *had* to have it at any price and grinned as if the Cheshire Cat himself. Fortunately, Justine was in a melancholy kind of mood and inclined to sell it for a reasonable sum. It reminded her too much of Marlon, and so she was happy to be rid of it.

Izzy had barely arrived back at the café when there was a knock on the front door. Usually the café was open, with a sign that said to come on in. People either sat in front of a computer along the wall to use the Internet, or at a café table where they waited to be served a meal. But then she had put that note on the door saying she was gone for a while and hadn't taken it down yet. Who would knock anyway, with the sign on the door? Only someone who must have seen her enter the café. She decided she better answer it and was surprised to see two of her uncles standing there. Uncle Roy and Uncle Ray were her mama's older brothers. With Izzy caught off guard, they spoke first. "Well, hello there, Missy Izzy. Ain't you gonna let yo' family in?" Uncle Roy asked in a flat tone.

"We won't be takin' up much o' your time, girl. I can see from the sign you is not really here," Uncle Raymond added.

"Why this sudden change of heart to come see me? Especially since I ain't open fo' business right now?" Izzy asked.

"We got somethin' to say that can't wait," Uncle Roy responded, staring at Izzy from the other side of the screen door.

Reluctantly, she let them in.

They sat down and made themselves comfortable while Izzy volunteered to get cold drinks. She came back with two Salva Vidas and set them on the table. Then she sat down and waited for her uncles to spill whatever was on their minds.

"Ray here saw you with that Espinoza neighbor of yours at dinner in one o' them West End cafés." Roy didn't look at Izzy after he said this. Instead he took a long swig of the cold beer.

"So what? Diego and I been friends since we was little kids." Izzy folded her arms defensively and hoped her panic didn't show. The last thing she needed was rumors about her and a rich coffee plantation man, especially if she wanted to patch things up with Solomon.

Uncle Roy leaned forward in his chair and glared at Izzy. "You didn't look like jus' friends to hear Ray tell it, sittin' there all cozy like, sippin' some kinda 'spensive wine together."

"It ain't none o' your business what my relationship with Diego is," Izzy answered, staring back at her Uncle Roy. "And it sho' ain't your place to worry none 'bout it."

Roy glanced at Ray, as if for moral support. He took another swig of beer and slammed it down on the table harder than need be. "As long as you a part o' this family, it sure do matter. It's bad enough folks think you deserted your own kind. I ain't gonna have 'em talkin' about you bein' some rich man's cheap thrill, you here?"

Izzy squinted at him in a defiant way and said nothing, her temper teetering on the edge of no return.

"It bad enough yo' mama was kept on the side by a mainlander, and you be a bastard anyway, but that is no reason to flaunt yo' brazen ways you got from our sister and make us all laughin' stock to poke fun at and spit on."

Izzy stood up to her full height. "You listen to me, Uncle Roy, my mama loved that man and she didn't know he was married for the longest time 'cause you men folk is so good wit' yo' lies. Still, he musta loved her or I wouldn't of got a big weddin' check fo' a gift, and the truth be known, that's what's eatin' at your craw . . . not who it is I am spendin' my time with." Izzy walked over to the door and opened it wide. "Iffin' you cared about me at all, I might listen to you as a loving niece, but I got no time for a couple o' men with chips on their shoulders so big they walk bent over and think they too good to be my family. It be diff'rent if you visited my café 'cause you all proud o' me and my success."

Uncle Roy stood up slowly, and Uncle Raymond followed his lead. Strutting to the door, Uncle Roy stopped within inches of Izzy and stared her down one last time. "You listen here, missy . . . you is nothin' but dust off the Roatan roads. Don't be thinkin' you some big business gal . . . better than yo' family down the ways, 'round the bend from these here rich folk."

"I woulda gladly given you some o' my wedding monies, were you to ask. Even now, I be generous with my profits where family is concerned. If only that family really considered me to be one o' them."

Uncle Roy and younger brother Raymond walked on out, their heads held higher than Izzy had ever seen them, with nothing more to say. They strolled down the road and when nearly out of earshot Uncle Roy turned to view Izzy, still holding the screen door wide open.

Uncle Roy shouted, "You stop sendin' them potions to my daughter for my granchillen . . . you hear me, Izzy?"

"I hear ya, Uncle Roy, but that's between Sarah Jean and me." Then she added, "You all come back any time. And I be servin' you a meal if you want. You is always welcome. Pass the word now, you hear?"

Uncle Roy looked at Raymond, and then both men chuckled. Izzy continued to watch them walk down the road and when they were out of sight, she slowly closed the screen door. Leaning against it, she took a good look around . . . from the café tables she'd sewn the cloths for herself, to the refurbished and well-used computers along the wall. What good fortune she'd had to build this thriving business. Thanks to her daddy, but who was she kidding? It was Diego and Mira that gave him the generous backpay. They knew what her daddy would do with the money, seeing as her mama was dying of malaria at the time and it was right before her wedding to Solomon.

Tears ran down Izzy's cheeks as she sank to the floor in a heap, wailing and moaning. But then she stood up tall and proud, and smoothed her vibrant green sundress. "Damn you, Uncle Roy . . . and Uncle Raymond too!" Izzy shouted to the empty room. "I ain't sorry for none of it. Not for this here home and business o' mine, or who my mama was, or my daddy. I ain't sorry for knowin' Diego, and I sure as rain ain't sorry for lovin' him!" Izzy stared out the screen door at dust clouds in the road, rising off the hard, dry earth and whispered under her breath, "Maybe I *am* dust off the Roatan road, Uncle Roy . . . 'cause the harder you tries to knock dust down, the higher it rises."

Natalie silently observed each hopeful face during her tutoring session on the beach this morning and secretly wished she could help them in more ways than tutoring. Every personal story told during their time together revealed the same situation of being trapped in poverty with too many mouths to feed, and a roaming man that did as he pleased. At least they would soon have skills to make a living for themselves, either to leave their husbands or help support their family. Teaching them reading, writing, and math gave Natalie a sense of joy and purpose well beyond all her tutoring of the past. Her heart broke daily for these young mothers who, aged by the burdens they carried and lifestyles they endured, appeared much older than they were.

Diego's pantry was stocked with canned tomatoes, homemade salsa and jams, hand-dipped candles, and dried flowers. She'd received baskets of fresh fruit off their backyard trees and vegetables from their gardens. All gifts of gratitude from these bright, industrious women who gathered daily on the beach beside the grove of coconut palms where Matti, Emmy, and Angel played with the younger children in the shallow surf, or built castles with them in the sand.

Natalie walked between little clusters of women and gave them new math problems or different sentences to write on the chalkboards they shared. Some were reading out loud to one another and she listened in. For a magical couple of hours weary expressions transformed into knitted eyebrows of careful focus. When their lessons were done for the day each face softened into a satisfied smile for what had been accomplished. Natalie observed one young girl called Norma to be especially bright. She absorbed everything taught in record time. Her big brown eyes were on fire with life and she had endless questions about the United States. Norma had somehow managed not to marry or become pregnant yet, but at nearly seventeen, her window of time to be single or without child was limited. If luck would have it, maybe Norma would be the first one to break tradition and get a job—be free and independent until of an age to determine her own fate. She reminded Natalie of Izzy with her cocky confidence and sharp wit. She laughed openly and was kind to everyone, helping those who struggled with the lessons.

On this particular day it made Natalie miss Izzy more than usual, because she hadn't come for tutoring since the kids went to camp at Anthony's Key. Natalie wondered when her wandering friend of late would come back to the beach sessions, or over to the summerhouse for a visit. She'd seen Izzy walking down the road toward the café early one morning. She had also seen her special friend slip out into the last remnants of dusk, to walk back down the same dirt road. Natalie suspected the travel worn path came and went from the dock where Diego moored his boat. She suddenly wondered who was watching Angel. It wouldn't be like Izzy to leave her alone all night, even though she was nearly eleven.

Soon the last young mother left the beach and Natalie hurried back to the wraparound porch to put finishing touches on her second painting. It was a portrait of Izzy holding the basket of avocados she'd brought by when they first met. Natalie stood back to admire her work and was pleased with the final result. She poured herself a tall glass of iced tea and took one to Matti, who was sitting under a shade tree studying one of his textbooks. Natalie shook her head in amazement at how she never needed to prompt that boy to study. "I'll be back in a minute, Matti. I'm going next door to the Internet café." He looked at her with questioning eyes, but Natalie had nothing to add. She needed to see for herself what was happening at Izzy's place.

A young woman appeared behind the screen door the minute Natalie shouted hello through it. She was barely old enough to be swelling with the child in her belly. "I live next door," Natalie explained. "I'm here to see Izzy."

The young woman introduced herself as Theresa Rose while opening the screen door. "You can call me Rose," she added shyly. Natalie smiled and handed her the jar of plum jam she'd grabbed from the pantry shelf before walking over. Rose offered her a glass of lemonade, which Natalie said would be wonderful, thinking it an excuse to stay a minute. They sat together at Izzy's wooden table in the large kitchen, where only those who knew Izzy came and went from. It was on the backside of the café and Internet computers.

While sipping their lemonade Natalie learned that a married man had gotten Rose pregnant, and then she had been asked to leave the neighborhood—by the same relatives who had turned their backs on Izzy. Of course, Izzy then welcomed her cousin with open arms to stay for as long as she wished. "The man who got you pregnant should be the one asked to leave," Natalie told Rose. It made her all the more determined to equal the playing field with her educational efforts for island women. "If you need anything at all I'm right next door," Natalie added.

She didn't ask where Izzy was, or how Angel was doing. She could see Angel playing with baby chicks in the yard and thought Izzy was probably delivering baked goods in West End. At least, that's what she hoped Izzy was doing. It was none of her business as to what her friend and neighbor might be doing each night from dusk until dawn. She doubted Izzy had confided in Rose anyway. The girl had enough problems of her own. Surely she knew

Solomon was shacked up with Jessica, since this rumor was everywhere on the island. There had been no rumors about where Izzy might be spending her time, or Diego for that matter, but Natalie no longer had any doubt as to where they were each night—and what they were doing. It worried her. Izzy's indiscretions would be viewed entirely differently than Solomon's, and Diego wouldn't escape unscathed either. She said her goodbyes to Rose and emphasized her desire to help the girl if she should need anything. "Tell Izzy I was here, and that I miss her terribly," Natalie shared, before heading out the door.

It was entirely too quiet when she returned to the summerhouse. Angel was with her new nanny and Emmy had gone to the mainland to spend time with her Aunt Mira. How convenient for Diego and Izzy. With Emmy on the mainland and Rose at the café, they could extend their hot summer affair for a bit longer until reality demanded common sense from them. Solomon had not been seen anywhere near the café since the kids went to camp. Thus the heated nights of rocking Diego's boat in the Caribbean . . . but Natalie had no intention of judging them. How could she? Every late afternoon while Matti swam with the dolphins, she occupied Nic's bed on the other side of Anthony's Key. Just thinking about it made her blush. Had everyone's common sense been swept away on an ocean breeze?

Staring at the portrait of Izzy with her basket of avocados made Natalie's heart ache for the days when she first arrived on the island. Everyone was busy with the daily routine of living, sharing fun times and frustrations alike. Now they were all scattered to their guilt-ridden corners of self-involved desires, which could blow up in their faces. And more than likely would. Diego could lose his fine reputation in the community as a man of integrity. Izzy could lose her husband, whom Natalie knew she loved despite her recent behavior, and she could possibly lose Angel if Solomon was vindictive enough. Island men had a shameless double standard. And then there was her situation with Nic. She could lose him because of her inability to commit. Even more frightening was how her feelings for Nic might affect Matti. Natalie put away her paints and called a taxi to take them to Anthony's Key for dolphin practice.

On the way there she thought about her lunch with Nic at the bistro, after their first night of lovemaking. He was somehow different—distant and awkward. When showing the beach house that day he had been unusually quiet, even a bit melancholy, until he took her in his arms beneath the palm tree of the oceanfront home and kissed her. Afterward he explained that loving her had overwhelmed him, never having been in love before. Then it all made sense and she assured him of being equally overwhelmed, and afraid of a broken heart herself. Natalie pointed out that he could leave her eventually and rightfully so, since she had no way of committing to a relationship with an estranged husband out there somewhere. She couldn't be sure that had appeased him, because even now he would look at her with vulnerability in his eyes, or maybe a touch of fear—she couldn't be sure which. It made her wonder if he knew something she didn't.

Sydney lay sprawled across the deep gold fabric of her antique four-poster bed. Lying there grinning widely she studied the only painting that adorned the recently redecorated room. What a fabulous find! Its beauty was unrivaled by any that she owned in her vast collection, of which she was quite proud. Not only was the oil brushed in a lavish style, but the subject matter was more scrumptious than even the artist could have anticipated. There wasn't any doubt in Sydney's mind about who the dark-haired boy was in the center of the canvas. She rolled over and giggled into the plush comforter. "How perfect is this?" she asked herself. "I have Antonio's son right here on my wall and know where the kid has run off to with his tramp of a mother." She wondered what in the world Antonio was thinking to marry someone raised by an unwed woman in a ballet troupe. An English tutor, no less! How *common* was that? And how nervy of him to break up with her, when she came from some of the best lineage San Francisco had to offer.

Sydney sat up and squeezed a pillow to her chest while staring at the portrait of Matti. It was just too funny. Antonio had told her that Nicholas would finally earn his keep by finding Natalie and Mattia. It had irked Tony-wony that his old man favored the half-brother who didn't grow up as a Giovanni. Sali had brought him into the business right after college and didn't care that he spent as much money as he made selling olive oil. Now Antonio was being double crossed by him. There was no other explanation for him being in Roatan all that time and coming up with nothing. No doubt he was somewhere smiling about the entire incident. Maybe he was screwing the illusive Natalie. That would be even funnier. But she didn't laugh at the thought. The whole subject was annoying to say the least.

"Who needs you anyway, Antonio!" she shouted at the pale peach walls. Falling back on the regal bed she stared at the painting once more and reminisced about making love to other men right here, while Antonio's son looked on with those large green eyes of his. She rolled over and buried her head in the pillow. "It serves you right, Antonio . . . *you bastard,*" she whispered.

CHAPTER TWENTY-FIVE

Adding notches to his particular gun handle appeared more like shooting himself in the foot.

Diego headed to Coxen Hole for the day based on the rumor that Solomon was living there with Jessica. He met up with a few of his diving buddies at a hole-in-the-wall hamburger joint and casually inquired about where Izzy's husband might be found. Coincidentally, his diver friends said they'd just seen Solomon enter the food market across the street, with a woman half his age. Diego nodded and stared out the window at the market, wondering what he would say to Solomon. He couldn't very well confront him in the store. Hopefully Solomon would head to a bar for a few beers afterward. This was common procedure for islanders when visiting Coxen Hole. The women would meander through specialty shops once their basic supplies were bought, while the men drank in the bars.

He paid his bill, said goodbye, and left to lean against a post outside the food market and wait for Izzy's husband to exit. Diego didn't know if Solomon knew about his time spent with Izzy on the dive boat but assumed not. It might have been a foolish assumption, and one he would pay for with a hard right to the chin the minute Solomon appeared. He would, after all, deserve it. Standing there in the dust and heat gave him time to stew about his guilt. It was bad enough he let his lust for Izzy consume him but being in love with Natalie made the entire affair inexcusable. It helped somewhat knowing Izzy was also very much in love with her husband, regardless of those long sweaty nights in the bedroom beside the galley on the dive boat.

Diego was grateful Izzy agreed they should end their tryst, in the best interest of Emmy and Angel. Not to mention for their own sanity. Now it was imperative he do everything possible to reunite Izzy and Solomon. He was hoping to talk some sense into Izzy's husband, but the last thing he wanted to do was further alienate the man from his estranged wife. Diego wiped his brow and tried not to see the recurring vision of Mira returning with Emmy, only to find him eating dinner on Izzy's café deck alone last night. Typical of his sister, she had not stuck to the agreed time and place for returning his daughter, who begged her aunt to bring her home. Mira had not taken it personally, since she thought a month might be too long for Emmy to be away. According to Mira, Emmy missed Matti and Natalie as much as she had missed him.

Once Emmy had gone to bed, there was no bypassing his sister's scrutinizing look regarding him and Izzy. Mira didn't ask about Izzy, however, she asked where Natalie and Matti were. He told her they were on a late-night excursion with Nic, who had bought a boat recently. He added that Solomon was temporarily occupied elsewhere and Angel, who had eaten earlier, was watching movies with Izzy's cousin Rose. Unfortunately, it was obvious to Mira that the situation was a lot more complicated. She cautioned him about the small proximity of everyone on the island, and the even smaller thinking of those who lived there. Rumors would spread like wildfire. She warned him that it could be disastrous for the innocent, such as Emmy and Angel, whereas the adults involved would deserve their tar and feathering should it come to that.

It was a point well taken. Diego wished he hadn't been so self-righteous with Natalie on the porch that morning, indicating he would never cross a forbidden line with Izzy. In the end he had not only crossed it, he had completely succumbed to it. *Sweet Jesus* . . . he had to pick up the pieces and make everything right again. He couldn't live with himself if he had destroyed Izzy's marriage, regardless that Solomon might already have done that by shacking up with Jessica.

His entire life he'd looked out for Izzy. He was elated about the success of the Internet café, never doubting Devante would give his backpay from the coffee plantation to Izzy. Anyone who knew Devante realized how much he worried about her, especially since Izzy's mother had just died of malaria. Diego watched Solomon walk out of the market with his arms full of bagged groceries. There was a young island girl in cut-off jeans at his side—Jessica, no doubt. Solomon placed the groceries in the back of his pickup and headed down the street in the opposite direction of his young companion. Diego followed close behind and entered the corner bar right after him.

Antonio hesitated to push the button on his computer and run the credit card for the ticket to Africa. He glanced at his luggage sitting on the bed, wondering if it was a bad idea to join Nicholas in his search for Natalie and Mattia, especially since he had no intention of letting Nicholas know he was coming. Africa was, after all, very far away and probably another dead end. Why should they think Natalie followed anyone she happened to have painted? It sounded more like a bad mystery novel than reality.

If only he could get more out of the trip than determining his half-brother to be incompetent. Maybe he could not only convince Sydney to forgive him but to come along. How crazy was that idea? He picked up one of the small, beautifully wrapped boxes on his desk and then set it back down. His purchases, he decided, wouldn't be enough to get Syd back. She'd keep the earrings and matching necklace but kick him out after opening them. No, he needed something more substantial to win back her heart. Antonio grabbed his wallet and headed out the door. On the way to the jewelry store he rationalized that he couldn't actually become engaged to Syd until his missing ex showed up dead, but maybe a diamond ring would at least get her to forgive him. Otherwise there would be nothing to look forward to but a string of whores parading through the house.

By early evening he arrived once again on Sydney Beaumont's doorstep, with a tiny glittering gift in hand and more blood-red roses in the other. Nothing else would do, since blood red was Syd's favorite rose. He prayed this would be a winning combination and that he could play his ace before Sydney threw him out. Antonio closed his eyes and rang the doorbell. No one answered, so he rang it again, and began to tap his foot lightly, forcing himself not to look in the windows. Finally, the door opened and there she stood, looking prettier than ever. God how he missed those sensual lips, perfectly painted in baby pink.

"Well, if it ain't the devil himself! What brings ya to my humble abode, Tony-wony? Need someone to kick around and don't wanna get a dog?" Sydney asked, with not the least bit of a smile on her face. It wasn't the reaction Antonio had hoped for, but it was better than what he had anticipated. He sighed deeply, took a long breath, and asked if he could come in. Sydney stared at him, her look of disbelief turning slowly into confusion. "What for? Surely you don't think I'd take you back?" She rolled her eyes with annoyance.

"Sydney, I can't tell you how much I've missed you. It was wrong of me to lose my patience, but you have to admit I've been under a lot of stress, what with my wife and kid missing for so long and the cops on my back."

"Enough!" Sydney held her hand out to halt his conversation.

"These are for you," he added quickly, handing her the roses and holding the small gift as temptingly as he could.

Sydney sniffed the roses indignantly while glaring at the little glimmering box. "Well, maybe you could come in for a minute and apologize proper like." She opened the door wide and he slid through it sheepishly. Sitting side by side on the couch in the front room, Sydney laid the flowers on the glass tabletop and stared at the tiny package Antonio had set in her lap. For a few awkward seconds neither spoke, and then he went in for the kill.

"I can't get you off my mind, Syd. I'm so sorry I lost my temper that day. Believe me, I have regretted it ever since. I'm leaving for Africa in a few days, and well, I want you to come along. That is, if you can find it in your heart to forgive me."

Sydney just gawked at him.

"Please, open it." He nodded toward the gift.

Looking down at the shimmering box, she opened it without any more coaxing, ripping off the expensive paper somewhat un-daintily. With shaking fingers she lifted the lid to reveal a large square-cut diamond. She screeched. "Oh my goodness! It's beautiful!" Giggling nervously Sydney pulled it from the satin holder and stuck it on her finger. Holding her hand up, she wiggled the diamond just enough to make it sparkle. Antonio couldn't believe how good the rock looked on her finger. And it wasn't all that painful spending a large chunk of his money on Sydney, like he always feared it would be. In fact, it made him horny. Reaching over to kiss Syd, he was pleased to discover it had the same effect on her. Within seconds they were tangled together in a most erotic way. He picked her up from the couch and carried her into the bedroom where he didn't bother to turn the lights on. They were naked within seconds.

All night they carried on as if newlyweds until dawn's first light appeared at the window. Then Sydney snuggled up against his chest and began to snore lightly, so he too shut his eyes and slept for a while. When he popped them open again several hours later, the room was flooded with sunshine. Staring blankly into space for a minute he noticed Sydney had redecorated. He squinted to focus on the new painting directly across from him. He couldn't quite see it from the bed, but it was most definitely a portrait of three half-grown children, somewhere on a beach. The longer he stared at the picture, the more curious he became. It seemed to him that the boy sandwiched between the girls had a strong resemblance to his son. Sydney had awakened while he lay there wondering about the uncanny likeness, and left the bed saying she had to pee.

Antonio pulled his trousers on to examine the oil painting close up. Standing inches from the piece of art he could not believe his eyes. If this wasn't his son, then it was a cruel attempt at forgery. And one of the girls looked very familiar. Antonio rubbed his forehead and thought back to his argument with Sydney about removing paintings in the upstairs hallway. One was of a little girl . . . *this* little girl! Only she was older in the masterpiece before him. Antonio walked over and stared blankly out the window, trying to remember more about the girl in the hallway. Her father was the Honduran that Natalie had tutored . . . right up until Mattia saw the unfortunate murder and all hell broke loose. He heard the toilet flush and then Sydney's electric toothbrush turn on as he dashed back over to the painting. Antonio stared at the glistening white sand and painfully blue sky, done in bold oils.

They were in Roatan. That half-brother of his probably knew all along and was stringing him out for a sucker. He more than likely wasn't in Africa at all. God only knew where he was . . . but clearly, Natalie and Mattia had been busted. And by a painting Natalie did herself, no less. He scrutinized the initials in the corner of the canvas and sure enough, they were Natalie's long loopy letters . . . two *N*s for Natalie Northcross.

The toothbrush had shut off. Antonio heard the shower running. He wondered where Sydney got ahold of this painting. Obviously she enjoyed knowing where his family was, while he didn't. All this time the crucial information about his missing wife and kid was staring right at her from the goddam wall, and yet she never felt the least bit tempted to tell him. Antonio was dressed and out the door before Sydney could have lathered up her platinum-blonde hair. He was on a plane to Honduras that afternoon. The leather bags were crammed with lightweight clothing, and his wallet with cash—to buy an illegal firearm on the remote, nearly lawless island.

Diego ordered a drink, being careful not to glance at Solomon, who downed half his beer in one gulp. They were only a couple bar stools apart, but

Solomon hadn't noticed him yet. Rumor had it that Jessica's father died recently, and Solomon had been living in the house he left her. Jessica had also inherited the vegetable truck everyone bought produce from. Apparently he'd raised Jessica alone and there was nobody to contest her inheritance.

No wonder she'd been happy to hook up with the flirting Solomon, feeling lonely and scared with her father gone, or maybe feeling cocky and independent with the old man six feet under. Either way, what didn't make sense were Solomon's motives. There wasn't a smarter or more attractive native-born woman on the island than Izzy. True enough, island men considered trysts to be nothing more than notches in a gun handle, but most island men had wives who were raising half a dozen children in near poverty conditions. They relished any form of escapism from excessive fishing expeditions to shameless cheating with girls who were barely of age.

This was not the case for Solomon, who shouldn't have messed with the best deal going. Adding notches to his particular gun handle appeared more like shooting himself in the foot. It didn't gain Solomon respect, admiration, or empathy from his peers, who envied his marriage to Izzy. Solomon was as bright as he was well built, so why would he toss his brains aside and mess around with Jessica? Even going so far as to shack up with her, so he could live in a home and run a business worth considerably less than what he left behind?

Solomon ordered another beer, while laughing and cutting up with the bartender. Diego continued to study him, pondering what was going on in that head of his. Finally he made his move, scooting over to the seat right next to Solomon, who turned and saw Diego for the first time. "What you doin' here, man?" he asked in a friendly manner, which was a huge relief to Diego. It meant he knew nothing. Of course, it was strictly paranoia that allowed Diego to think he could know anything. He and Izzy had been so careful, and checked the island pulse every day to be sure there were no slip-ups in their secrecy.

"I'm cooling off. It's hot out there." To prove his point, Diego emptied his beer and ordered another.

"Man, you got that right!" Solomon laughed.

"I haven't seen you around much lately." Diego smiled, to defray any accusatory insinuation.

"No, I guess I ain't been at the café for a while," Solomon admitted, his jovial expression turning somber.

"You're a good neighbor, Solomon, so I'll speak my mind." Diego paid for his second beer while Solomon waited to hear what he had to say.

"You know me and Izzy go way back."

Solomon nodded. "I sure do."

"Well, then you know I am fully aware of what a good woman she is, I mean, besides the fact there's no prettier girl on the island, she's also smart."

"Right." Solomon took a long, slow drink, as if contemplating that.

"I have to tell you, friend, the rumors are flying. I mean, there she is all alone, and so easy on the eyes."

"What rumors?" Solomon asked.

"You know . . . the typical kind. That this man or that man is trying to turn her head during dinner by flirting shamelessly with your very vulnerable woman, left by herself while you're doing whatever it is you need to be doing. I'm sure you wouldn't leave her alone otherwise. What husband would leave a wife like Izzy alone for any length of time unless they had to? Right?"

Solomon played with his sweaty beer bottle, staring at the label. "Right," he finally answered.

Diego gave all that very little time to actually sink in before continuing. "A feisty woman can sure be a handful." He chuckled, and Solomon nodded, still staring at his bottle. "I bet sometimes you wonder who's actually wearing the pants, rather than just taking them off . . . you know what I mean?"

"You got that right." Solomon glanced at Diego, as if wondering how he knew so much.

"I bet Izzy can be a little bossy and overbearing at times," Diego added. "But a smart, beautiful woman is totally worth the trouble, isn't she? It's a lucky man who has a wife with brains, beauty, and an inheritance in the bank. I mean, look around, Solomon. Do you see anybody else here that lucky?"

Together they skimmed faces in the half-filled bar.

Diego finished his beer and set the bottle down assertively. He leaned into Solomon and whispered, "I'd get home if I were you, Sol. Somebody's going to snatch up that amazing woman of yours, right out from under you. Don't let it happen, you hear? I like you both too much for that."

Solomon nodded slowly in agreement while he stared straight ahead at the liquor bottles lined up on a shelf behind the bar. He appeared to be thinking in overdrive.

Diego put his hand on Solomon's massive back and slapped it firmly while adding, "I got to go, neighbor. I hope whatever business has taken you away from home will be done soon." Then Diego leaned in and whispered, "Don't believe any rumors, Solomon, about your Izzy. She's a rock. I've taken the liberty of checking on her occasionally, and trust me she loves only you, and can't wait for your return."

Diego was back out in the sunshine and nearly to his vehicle before he even exhaled. Leaning on his Land Rover he took a deep breath, wiped his sweaty brow, and wasted no time getting out of Coxen Hole.

CHAPTER TWENTY-SIX

Matti screamed out loud for no one to hear but the wildlife, hiding behind lava rocks and tree limbs.

Natalie thought it odd that Marlon didn't want to talk about his wife, or where she had hung the birthday painting. Aside from his evasiveness about Justine, however, the conversation went very well. She was thrilled with Marlon's idea of displaying her work at the bistro. Local business owners and tourists alike often frequented the authentic Italian restaurant. Natalie did express concern about her canvases leaving the country with tourists, specifically Americans. She shared with him that her estranged husband did not know where she was, and she needed to keep it that way. Marlon didn't pry, since Roatan was known for its ability to swallow up people not wishing to be found. He agreed to tell Americans the artwork was already sold, should they ask.

Marlon had already viewed the portrait of Izzy with the avocados, still hanging on the front porch easel, and loved it even more than the painting given to Justine. He was excited about showing it, and her future work at his beloved bistro—but something was obviously troubling him despite his excitement. He couldn't focus on his tutoring session and had left early. Maybe his pretty little wife was giving him grief about something. Justine did seem rather distant when they'd met.

"Well, would ya jus' look at that!" Natalie turned around to see Izzy standing on her porch, admiring the portrait of none other than herself, displayed on the easel. "It's jus' gorgeous, girl. You do nice work!" Izzy beamed as she stared in awe. "Do I really look that good?"

"Better. I couldn't quite capture your special aura that mesmerizes people, but I tried." Natalie gave Izzy a tight hug.

"I'd say yo' work is mo' than a little flattering." Izzy laughed.

Natalie made them each a cup of tea and scolded her neighbor for being so scarce in the past few weeks. They sat at the kitchen table just like old times, and neither knew where to begin their conversation. They knew precisely what the other had been doing, and why, but talking about it was another matter.

Finally, Izzy broke the silence. "You's in love with Nic, ain't ya, Natti-girl?"

"Yes," Natalie admitted. "God help me, I do love him."

"Then you has already forgiven me for my time with Diego."

"There's nothing to forgive."

"Then why can't I forgive myself?" Izzy asked. Her expressive eyes reflected the turmoil churning deep inside. "I love Solomon. I want him back."

"It was Solomon who strayed first." Natalie squeezed her hand. "Maybe you didn't need to follow his lead, but extenuating circumstances sometimes yank us along."

"True enough," Izzy confessed. "Still, it ain't like me to be so weak."

"Are you sorry for what happened with Diego?" Natalie asked.

"How could I be?" Izzy looked straight into Natalie's eyes, and saw complete understanding. They were both married women but had powerful reasons for straying. "Anyways, I think I am mo' willin' to take Solomon back now that . . . well, it ain't right for the pot to call the kettle black, you know what I mean?"

"You and Solomon belong together, Izzy." Natalie poured her more tea. "As far as I can tell, nobody knows about your time spent on Diego's boat. I've tutored a lot of women lately, and not one has mention anything other than Solomon foolishly shacking up with Jessica."

"Good. Then they don't know nothin' 'bout me and Diego, 'cause trust me, girl, iffin they did . . . you'd hear about it."

Before they finished their tea, Izzy promised to return to the tutoring sessions on the beach. Natalie told her about Norma and together they brainstormed how to get that bright young woman a job to support herself, before some man got a chokehold on her dreams and strangled hope right out of her.

Matti calmly treaded water and waited. He watched Buck dart across the bay and then back again, anticipation mounting until finally the silver streak came up beneath him. Matti was lifted clear out of the sea and twisted his body into a perfect dive formation. Like a knife through butter, Matti shot beneath the surface. When his head popped back up, he swam to the side of the dolphin bay. "That was impressive, Matti. You make it look so effortless, and yet you've only been working on this trick a couple days." Tanner kneeled beside Matti. "Listen, you've been working so hard, and tomorrow night is your first big performance. Why don't you call it a day on that high note?" Tanner looked at his watch. "It's only a half hour until practice is over. Is your mom around here somewhere?"

Matti nodded. He remembered his mom telling him what Nic's cabin number was. She'd been visiting with Nic every afternoon during practice, returning to the dolphin bay for the last thirty minutes to watch him, and cheer. Matti liked Nic, but he worried that maybe his mother shouldn't spend so much time with him if she was going to marry Diego. He knew she would need a divorce first from his father in San Francisco, but he figured there must be a way to get one.

Putting on his shirt and shoes he grabbed his backpack and headed toward Nic's cabin. He had never been there, but he knew it was on the farthest point of the resort. He took the trail that led to the appropriate cabin clusters. It was lined with thick foliage on either side, but then opened onto a clearing. Some of the cabins faced the performance arena while others faced the open sea. Matti stopped in front of number seven, wondering what his mother and Nic did in the cabin while he swam with the dolphins. He only knew that Nic went to his jobsite before the sun was up and had worked a full day by the time dolphin practice began.

Trotting up to the door, he knocked softly. There was no answer. He walked around to the back of the cabin and stopped dead in his tracks. In a glance he saw the spectacular ocean off the point, and two beach chairs side by side with a little table between them, but Nic and his mother were not sitting in chairs beside the sea. No, not even close. They were standing near the edge of the water, and they were kissing. Not like how his parents had kissed, which was seldom. No, this was how they kissed in the movies. Matti just froze. He stared at them and couldn't help himself. They were in their swimming suits and were soaking wet. Watching them kiss made him very uncomfortable. He turned around and leaned against the cabin, feeling embarrassed and sad and upset all at the same time.

It was clear Diego would never be his father. Nic was obviously very special to his mom. It was more than Matti could stomach at the moment, having all these feelings hit him at once. He turned and ran back along the winding trail, leaving it at one point to sit against a fat palm tree. Breathing heavily, he wondered how his mother could do this to him. It was true that Nic was nice enough, but Diego was like the father he never had. And then there was Emmy, who was the sibling he'd always wanted. Deep inside he didn't want to admit it, but he wasn't wild about the idea of his mother ever really needing anyone but him. It was fine for her to laugh with Diego during breakfast and dinner, but what he had just witnessed with Nic was disturbing. Out of pure frustration Matti threw a rock as far as he could. Birds squawked in the trees all around him, and a little green lizard darted for safety.

He decided he simply wouldn't go back. Who needed them? He was madder than he could ever remember being. And at everyone, except maybe Emmy, whose father had failed to win his mother's heart. *Damn you, Diego!* And damn Nic too . . . offering a ride on that shiny new bike and then stealing his mother right out from under him. He was angriest of all with his mom and felt completely betrayed by her. He wasn't exactly sure why, but that's how he felt all the same. Matti screamed out loud for no one to hear but the wildlife, hiding behind lava rocks and tree limbs. He sat there simmering with anger for the longest time, unaware that his scream had been the first sound he'd made since that night, long ago, in San Francisco.

Antonio turned off his cellphone and waited for the plane to finish preparing for takeoff. He arranged his pillow ten different times and tried to focus on how he would go about tracking Natalie down once he arrived—anything but think about what was happening at Sydney's house. He made it perfectly clear the murder should look like a byproduct of robbery, and they should take all the valuable art to back that theory up. He didn't give a rat's ass what they did with it, as long as the Roatan piece ended up at his mansion.

As he drifted off to sleep he considered what a shame it was to snuff out Sydney, but she knew way too much at this point, should the authorities choose to question her. And since she had proven not to be trustworthy, she might actually go to them first. In any event, it wasn't like she didn't deserve it. At least he'd told his men to shoot her fast and clean, after which they should grab the painting from Roatan, heist the rest of the art, and ransack the place. By the time he found Natalie and snuffed her out as well, there'd be little left to do but bring his son home and maybe move back to Sicily. Just in case some overachieving cop tried to blow the whistle on him. Stupid police. He wondered how many tax dollars were wasted on the time they'd spent at the bottom of his hill. He watched from his window as the plane left the runway and was grateful the island of Roatan didn't have much in the way of law to contend with.

Natalie showed up right at the end of Matti's dolphin practice. She tried not to let her mind linger on the goodbye kiss from Nic, before showering and running out the door after their swim. Slightly alarmed to hear practice ended early, she smiled and said she'd look up by the ice cream vendor for Matti. She didn't see his dark mop of hair anywhere around the vendors, or in the empty bleachers. He didn't turn up at the little store either, where tourists got cold drinks and munchies while waiting for the water taxi. Remembering Tanner had said Matti nodded when asked if he knew where to find her, Natalie wondered if he'd walked to Nic's cabin. She sprinted down the path to the cabins, calling out Matti's name and scanning the forest on each side. Not seeing her son anywhere on the way, panic began to set in as she knocked on Nic's door.

"Is Matti here?" she asked, out of breath.

"No. Should he be?" Nic looked puzzled.

"I gave him this cabin number in case he would ever need it, like today, when getting out of practice early. But apparently he chose not to come here. So now I'm wondering where he went."

Nic grabbed his bike keys and came outside. "Let's check everywhere again." Natalie nodded, not really sure what else to do. Nic slowly drove his Harley down the path instead of the road, asking the few bicyclists and hikers they saw along the way if they'd seen anyone of Matti's description. Next they visited the management of Anthony's Key, who gladly agreed to speak with employees, warning them to stay alert in case someone of Matti's description was spotted anywhere on the grounds. Nic and Natalie took a water taxi to the camp cabins and practice bay. They checked in with Tanner and the other trainers, who promised to keep an eye out.

"Maybe he walked back to the summerhouse," Nic suggested.

"But I told him to come to your cabin if he got out early," Natalie answered.

"Maybe he did, and I didn't hear him knocking. I was in the shower right after you left," Nic added.

"Let's just hope he shows up at Diego's house," Natalie said in frustration. She shook her head, as if to shake off all the unpleasant possibilities. Matti was, after all, a very smart kid and quite a resourceful one. Since moving to Roatan he had steadily become more self-sufficient until even she was amazed by how adapted he was to his environment. He was no longer timid and frail, he was strong and confident. Although a gangly adolescent, he'd put on height and weight since arriving on the island, to the point that she rarely thought of him as a little boy anymore, and at twelve, he really wasn't. Still, her heart leapt into her throat at the mere thought of all the things that might have happened to him.

Nic and Natalie arrived at Diego's summer home only to find no one there. Nic called Anthony's Key on his cell phone to be sure he hadn't turned up at the resort. He hadn't, but they promised to keep searching. Natalie went next door to see if Izzy had seen Matti or might know where he was. Izzy didn't know anything but called Angel inside along with Emmy and asked the girls. They hadn't seen Matti while on the beach collecting shells all afternoon. It was decided they would split up and comb the grounds behind the café and the shoreline further down from where the girls had been. Natalie thanked them for helping, returning to the summerhouse just as the Land Rover parked in the driveway. She ran up to greet Diego as he exited his vehicle.

"Have you seen Matti?" she asked.

"No. Why? Is he missing?" Diego glanced at the porch and saw Nic standing there.

"Yes. He got out of dolphin practice early and no one's seen him since."

They walked up to the porch together while Natalie told him that Emmy and Angel were checking the shoreline, and Izzy was combing the grounds out back.

"Hello, Nic." Diego offered his hand when stepping onto the porch. They hadn't seen each other since Nic began dating Natalie, although they'd talked business frequently on their cell phones.

Nic shook his hand and filled him in on the search at Anthony's Key.

Diego pondered this. "Were arrangements made should he need to get ahold of you during practice?" he asked, looking at Natalie.

"He was to come to Nic's cabin," she answered.

Diego took a good look at Natalie, who felt guilty and awkward.

"Might he have seen something there that would disturb him?" Diego inquired.

Natalie glanced at Nic, who chose to be silent. "We swam the whole time, on the point behind Nic's cabin," she explained. "We wouldn't have heard a knock on the door, but Matti is a smart boy. He would surely have come around back."

"I hate to ask this . . ." Diego looked directly at Natalie. ". . . but do you think his father might have somehow discovered where you were and come for him?"

Natalie sat down in a rattan chair, her knees feeling suddenly weak. "I have no idea," she answered. "But if Antonio has taken Matti from me, then we need to check the airport, now, before he leaves the island." She suddenly felt nauseated.

"I'll go," Diego offered. "I know the officials at the airport. Maybe I can find out something." No sooner had Diego turned the key in the ignition than Natalie put her head in her hands, trying to think clearly about what to do next. Nic knelt beside her.

"Natalie, listen to me . . . there isn't any way Antonio has taken Matti."

She looked up at him, feeling more miserable than she ever thought possible. "How can you know that?"

"I know."

Natalie studied his face. "What aren't you telling me?" she asked.

Nic hesitated before answering. He pulled up the other rattan chair and sat in it, taking Natalie's hands into his and looking her right in the eye.

"This is a terrible time to have to explain this, but . . . I've spoken with Antonio recently, and he is *not* here . . . or even aware that *you* are."

Natalie was speechless. She continued to stare into his . . . *very blue eyes* . . . not steel grey like Antonio's, *but the same eyes* nonetheless. She touched his cheek and ran her hand up through his thick brown hair . . . yes, the hair had fooled her most of all. It wasn't black Giovanni hair . . . but the hairline was the same. "You're Antonio's little half-brother, Nicholas, aren't you?" she asked, already knowing the answer.

Nic observed Natalie's stunned gaze, focused on his features. He closed his eyes and sighed deeply, then looked directly at her. "Yes, I am Nicholas," he confessed. Nic reached for her hand, but she pulled it away from him. "Natalie, listen to me . . . please. It's true that originally I came to the island at Antonio's request, but once I met you, my heart wouldn't let me betray your cover. I was so impressed by your courage, and by Matti. I saw what an amazing son you have. I decided I couldn't let my half-brother take him from you. It would be wrong to return Matti to San Francisco. As for you . . . I had no idea you'd be so together, so focused on a new life, and for all the right reasons. From the moment I met you all I wanted to do was protect you both. You have to believe me."

She made no effort to speak or move, suddenly horrified by her own idiocy. How could she have been so blind? So naïve? *So stupid!*

"Natalie, please . . . I've been trying to find a way to tell you all this."

Natalie laughed, and stared at him in amazement . . . at his face, a face she should have placed immediately. Where had her common sense been all this time? "Do you expect me to believe that?" she asked, standing up to distance herself from Nic. Leaning against the porch rail she looked at him coldly. "Just when, Nicholas Salvatore Giovanni, do you think you'd have gotten around to telling me you were my husband's little brother? Maybe after the next time we made love . . . while holding one another through the night, naked and intertwined?

Nic stood up but didn't try to approach her. "Listen to me, Natalie. I beg of you." Nic ran his hands through his hair in frustration. "When you answered Diego's door that day we met . . . all I could think about was, God, you had such a warm smile and intelligent, vulnerable eyes. I suddenly hated myself for having found you . . . for agreeing to look." He slipped beside her at the railing and looked out to sea while she gripped the rail, as if to hold her up, and stared at the very door where they had met. "You have to believe me when I tell you that Antonio thinks you're in Africa. For that matter he thinks *I* am in Africa, and that I found nothing here but good diving."

"Roatan . . . Honduras, Africa . . ." Natalie stood up straight and turned to stare at Nic, right beside her. "The paintings in the hall. You guessed where

I was through the portrait of Emmy. I knew it! I should have done something with the portraits but removing them would have only made their subject matter more suspicious." Natalie began to pace across the porch. "Maybe if I would have taken them all down and brought them with us . . . maybe then it would only have looked as if I had no intention of returning." She stood still and stared at Nic. "I don't think it ever would have occurred to Antonio to even suspect the portraits might tell a story of where I could have gone to feel safe and be far away." She paused there, and studied Nic's broad shoulders—his narrow torso, just like Antonio only Nic was taller. He had longer legs. His mother's gene pool had given nice advantages to Nic . . . especially the bright blue eyes, admirable height, and creative thinking. Antonio didn't have a creative bone in his body.

"I confess, it was my idea," Nic answered honestly.

They studied one another, and Natalie wondered how she had missed it, his more than coincidental resemblance to the Giovanni clan. She clearly saw the remorse on Nic's face, but it didn't sway her anger in the least.

"I don't expect you to forgive me Natalie . . . at least, not right now. But I *will* find Matti—I promise you. I won't let Antonio touch a hair on his head. I'll make sure you're both safe, and that he never discovers where you are . . . *so help me God.* It's the least I can do and would have done anyway, even if I hadn't fallen in love with you."

Natalie didn't respond. She swiped at a few tears and turned to stare at the Roatan sky, as clear and blue as the painting she had done of the children on the beach. "The portrait!" she blurted out. "The picture of Matti on the beach with the girls that I sold to Marlon—for his wife's birthday present! He was acting very strange here yesterday," she added.

"Strange how?" Nic asked.

"Strange . . . like maybe his wife had left him. She seemed so distant when I delivered the canvas, and I know they'd been having difficulties. It's why he bought her the special birthday present to begin with." Natalie's hands began to shake with fear. "She was from the Bay Area. I remember Marlon telling me that once. It disturbed me a little. What if she knows Antonio? All those rich people in the Bay Area are a tight social group." Natalie was pacing, talking to herself more so than to Nic, whom she couldn't even look at—she was so angry with him and disappointed in herself for letting her guard down. It served her right, for even considering having a relationship with someone so soon after her disastrous marriage . . . with its horrific outcome.

"I'll head to the bistro right now and find out exactly where the painting is," Nic offered. "If you're right, Antonio might have discovered where you are." Without waiting for a response, Nic left. Natalie watched his Harley head down the dirt road and when he had disappeared from sight she realized that her whole body was shaking, as if having a very bad dream, one that she couldn't wake up from.

CHAPTER TWENTY-SEVEN

Sometimes he thought the island itself was magical, that the moods of the sea and ways of the forest had transformed him.

Izzy, Angel, and Emmy were searching the beach and surrounding area. Employees were still looking for Matti at Anthony's Key. Diego was investigating the airport, and Nic was finding out where the painting had gone. Natalie's and Matti's peaceful lives on the island, where they'd felt safe and protected, had crumbled into chaos and fear. She sat in a rattan chair on the porch, trying to calm down while thinking in overdrive. When Matti was let out of dolphin practice, she was still swimming with Nic at his bungalow. Diego had wondered if Matti saw something that might upset him. Would it upset her son to realize she and Nic were more than friends? Natalie saw flashes of her kiss on the beach. That would definitely disturb a sensitive adolescent boy, especially knowing how fond he was of Diego.

What a damn fool she had been. Selfish, gullible, stupid. Falling for the very man that had come to collect them. But there was no time to dwell on her idiocy. She had to *think* . . . where would Matti go if he were angry and contemplating running away . . . wanting to make her worry and suffer—exactly as she was doing? And then it dawned on her.

Izzy swatted a fly on the back of her sweaty neck and entered the café feeling discouraged and frustrated. Where could Matti be? Chances were he had his favorite places for alone time that no one knew about. Surely he would come back when he got hungry, or lonely enough. There were occasional violent crimes on the island, but they always had to do with money or infidelity. Children were not preyed upon unless it was a teenage girl seduced by some witless cheating husband, like what happened to poor Rose. Now that was all too common indeed.

She wished Rose were still here to help look for the boy, but she'd moved back home to her mama's house. Sometimes the womenfolk got their way with the men. In this case, Rose's mama threatened to leave too if her baby girl couldn't come home. And no doubt she meant business. Men always knew when they'd lost the upper hand. Too bad they didn't lose it more often, Izzy thought. She poured herself a glass of iced tea and shuttered, realizing Natalie would also be in danger if that evil husband of hers had come for them. Izzy looked up just in time to see her own husband walk through the kitchen door. "Solomon! You done scared me witless sneakin' up like that!"

"What you been doin', woman? I seen Angel and Emmy runnin' down the beach lookin' frantic this way and that, and you traipsin' back from the woods all hot and upset."

"It's Matti. He's been missin' for a couple hours now."

"Couple hours ain't nothin' for a boy his age."

"Matti ain't the type to jus' run off and not tell his mama where he is," Izzy commented, wondering why Solomon was here. She thought he looked good, and suddenly wasn't angry with him anymore. Instead she felt a rush of guilt for her time spent in Diego's arms, being licked and touched in every conceivable place. Oh how she'd relished each long, sweaty night of Solomon's absence. "Besides," she added, hoping her cheeks weren't fire red, "he disappeared in a kinda funny way, right after he got let out early from dolphin practice."

"Dolphin practice?"

"Yeah. That boy got himself a job doin' tricks wit' the dolphins at Anthony's Key." Izzy laughed. "He one interestin' chile, that one!"

"I'll help look for the boy." Solomon stared at Izzy with his eyes all big and somewhat sad, like he wanted to say more, but didn't know where to begin.

"That be great," Izzy answered, and then she walked closer to him, looking right into his vulnerable brown eyes, those same eyes that had always filled her with desire. Diego became a distant memory with her next heartbeat, their sin-filled hours something to sweat bullets over on her knees in church, and then dismiss forever as if it never happened. "Whatcha doin' here anyway?" she asked, hoping he would say what she wanted to hear.

"I missed you, Izzy. Ain't no other woman for me but you," he confessed, not taking his eyes off her.

"What about Jessica?" she asked, annoyed at the sinful pleasure he'd found in her. But what the hell, Izzy thought, she and Diego had met Solomon and Jessica's sizzling touches second for scorching second.

"I was stupid, Izzy. It ain't never happenin' again, I promise. If you jus' take me back I's ready to love only you, woman, forever this time. You can cut me up in little pieces and feed me to them sharks out there hoverin' near the edge of the reef otherwise." He glanced out the front window, across the kitchen on the far side of the café, which was still closed to business. Izzy was planning to open it in the morning. Now putting the sign back out front would be like a new beginning for them . . . together forever . . . all their mistakes forgiven and forgotten. She would trust and believe that, because she wanted to with all her heart.

"Solomon, you knows I ain't feedin' you to no sharks, silly man." Izzy stepped into his loving arms. They embraced like both had been on a long journey down the wrong trail and had finally found their way back to each other. She wondered if he felt the same peace of mind she did, standing there in the kitchen of their Internet café feeling like newlyweds again. This business had been their dream then. One built together until old man Satan came calling and made a disheveled mess of things. After a long involved kiss they tore themselves apart, resisting temptation to seal this new pact in the bedroom. No, they couldn't do that while their neighbors needed them. They'd make up properly after Matti was home safe and sound. Both agreed all would not be well on their little piece of island paradise until then.

Izzy filled Solomon in with who was searching for Matti, and where. They decided to break up, and each look somewhere new. Solomon would drive to Coxen Hole to ask around and see if anyone had news of a stranger in town, or strange happenings that might involve Matti. Being a native-born islander, there wasn't much that got past Solomon. He knew all the locals intimately. Not just their name and business, but their family and interests. Izzy would go to the restaurants in West End where she catered her bakery goods, asking the same sorts of questions. They agreed to meet up in a couple hours right back here in the café kitchen and compare notes.

Diego used his influence with every known official at the airport. All his effort produced nothing. Antonio must have had a fake ID if he was on a recent incoming or outgoing flight. This didn't surprise Diego, considering his own methods for getting Natalie and Matti into the country. He didn't feel at all good about the situation, mulling it over on the way to his award-winning beach home, where Jake was overseeing some finishing touches. Nic had bought the house outright, and Diego wondered if he were planning a future there with Natalie. It hurt more than he wished to admit, but it wouldn't help anybody to be a sore loser. He wanted to warn Jake about Matti's father possibly having kidnapped him. As unlikely as it seemed that Antonio discovered where they were, it seemed even more unlikely that Matti would run away. Nonetheless, odds were it was one of the two. Children never disappeared on the island. They weren't preyed upon for reasons that might come to mind anywhere else.

He hoped Matti *had* run away, rather than his father taking him. The boy had become so strong and self-reliant during his time on the island, away from his father's negative influence. And then there was Natalie. She'd be devastated if she lost her son. He seemed to be the driving force behind everything she did. Matti was her whole life . . . until recently, when becoming involved with Nic. That alone might be why Matti ran away. He'd obviously never shared his mother's affections with anyone else before, but Natalie deserved to be happy. Matti would come to understand that in time. He could empathize with the boy, since his own world had spun out of control once Nic entered their lives. It was obvious from the first encounter that the two of them had more in common than a home country. Diego wished he'd been able to talk to Matti about the developing relationship between his mother and Nic Walsh. Everything had escalated so quickly, and now it would seem that all their lives were affected. Chances were if Matti had run off, he'd get over it soon. What boy his age would miss the opportunity to perform with dolphins? His first show would be tomorrow night. Surely he would come to his senses and be there, unless his father had intercepted him.

Antonio rented a Jeep at the airport and hoped that would allow him to blend in with the scenery. He briefly regretted not having chartered a private plane, but fortunately his false identity was not questioned. He kept his ball cap low on his forehead in case he should run into the very people he was looking for. He needed the element of surprise on his side. He tried not to finger the gun in his pocket, purchased from a local man who had a whole armory to choose from. The wad of cash had gotten him a very nice piece, with a silencer to add when necessary. It did so help to have friends in low places . . . or at least, connections to them.

As he drove toward Diego's home, using information cajoled from a waitress at a beach bar, he wondered why he didn't just hire someone to kill his wife and return his son. It would have been a lot safer, and more practical. But then, it would also deprive him of dealing with Natalie personally. He cursed at the humid, sticky air streaming through the open window of his rented Jeep. What a fool he had been to go along with Nicholas's blatant lies. He would give his half-brother exactly what he deserved, as soon as he'd retrieved Mattia, and Natalie was lost somewhere in the Caribbean. If he was lucky, her body would become dinner for a shark and no evidence would resurface. Once he moved back to Sicily this nightmare could finally begin to fade from his memory. He would get Mattia a drill sergeant nanny. By the time the boy became a man he would be a solid Giovanni, completely set straight as to who the bad guys really were . . . including his deceased mother and Uncle Nicholas, both of them double-crossing scum.

Antonio pulled up to Diego's home. It was a charming and solidly built house on the edge of a white postcard beach. Not far down the road stood a newer structure, also charming, and probably the Internet café the waitress spoke of. They were approximately where she had said they would be, give or take a mile of beach frontage.

Pulling out his fine new weapon, Antonio attached the silencer. His plan was flawless as long as it all went quickly. He could be back off this island with Mattia before local authorities figured out what had happened. With any luck, it would be a while before his wife's remains washed up on shore, shark or no shark to help dispose of her.

Scrutinizing the deserted shoreline, he decided chances were good no one would see him take off down the beach with his estranged wife. He had no doubt Natalie would cooperate if she believed Mattia's life were at risk. Women were gullible. He'd make up something really good to get her out on a boat. He'd seen plenty of fishing rentals in West End, just one water taxi ride away. Rumor was the Hondurans who drove the water taxis were mostly drug runners anyway. It would be easy to pay one off and have him swear he never saw Natalie. Once she was overboard, he'd really do some fishing . . . for the whereabouts of his son. Then he'd slap his parent custody papers on anyone protesting their exit. Mattia would be on a plane with him long before his wife's remains were recovered.

He decided to lie low for a short time and monitor activity in the area. Parking his Jeep inconspicuously among other vehicles at a public beach, Antonio walked back to the house through the jungle behind the property. The foliage was thick and high until near the home, where a clearing had been made and was surrounded by flowers with breathtaking blooms. Definitely Natalie's handiwork, he thought, and leaned against a thick, bushy palm tree, waiting patiently to seize his moment.

Matti heard Emmy calling his name from the dock and was torn between not showing his face and coming out to greet her. It was, after all, Emmy's secret storage space behind the galley where he'd chosen to hide out. They'd barely been on the island a week when Diego and Emmy brought him and his mom fishing for the first time. Matti remembered being nervous and twitchy, not able to focus on anything but that poor woman's muffled screams, her struggling, and then the sound of her neck breaking. He still saw visions of his father leaning over the trunk, forcefully pushing down, while grunting and jerking his body in swift downward thrusts. And the woman's bound legs kicking against the side of the trunk. It was hideous, simply hideous. Yet Matti was tortured by knowing he'd done nothing to stop it—nothing at all.

He recalled Diego showing him how to bait a hook, throw a line, and catch a sea bass that day. He could still hear Emmy giggle in delight as he reeled in his first fish, and Diego laugh his hearty laugh while teaching him to clean it. Catching a fish had chased the demons away for a short while. That evening Izzy had given him an herbal concoction and he was able to sleep all night for the first time since everything happened. Matti didn't know if it was those strange roots and herbs Izzy mashed up with her mortar and pestle or learning how to fish that made everything bearable. Sometimes he thought the island itself was magical, that the moods of the sea and ways of the forest had transformed him.

Emmy's voice was getting closer and he feared she wouldn't leave until she'd done a thorough search. She knew him well . . . knew that if he were going to hide somewhere on the island, this would be his first choice for a safe place. How many times had they hid in this storage compartment when

Diego brought them fishing? The space wasn't tall enough to stand in, but they could see out the vent well enough to spy on anyone moving about the deck. An old sleeping bag covered the floor for soft padding. Emmy would lie beside him and read books while Diego and his mom lounged about the deck, their lines lazily dangling in the clear waters near the reef, just beyond the coral beds.

Thinking of his mom made him feel bad for causing her this worry. But he simply couldn't face her right now. He needed to sort out this situation. Every night he prayed for her happiness, especially since it was his fault she had to leave their home and her students, the shelves of books, baskets of paints, and half-finished canvases—all left behind, along with their way of life. Because he wasn't brave enough to tell what his father had done, or to stop him from doing it. Nonetheless, he thoroughly regretted her meeting Nic. It had spoiled everything.

From the sound of Emmy's voice, Matti knew she was in the galley right outside the entrance to their secret storage area. She'd have to climb on the small table against the wall, where they ate on rainy mornings, to pull up the horizontal door. Their secret space was only inches away from the miniature sink, two-burner stove, and half-size refrigerator. Even though the space was not lit, Emmy would know he was there the minute she pulled up the hinged door and peeked in. Sunlight was streaming through the angled vent and would expose his silhouette among the shadows. Sort of like his mother's laughter exposed her feelings for Nic, ever since the first time he came to dinner. Why did it anger him to see his mom happy, especially since he'd prayed she would be one day? He knew why of course . . . it was his own selfishness. He wanted her to love Diego. Suddenly he felt foolish for being such a child, for wanting everything his way, and wanting his mom to love only him.

CHAPTER TWENTY-EIGHT

Were certain things going to happen regardless of anything one did or didn't do to prevent them?

Matti wondered what Emmy would say if he told her his true feelings. She would be upset with his selfishness, he decided, even though she wanted him for a brother as much as he wanted her for a sister. She would say they could always be friends. And she would be right. As if on cue, Emmy lifted the camouflaged opening to the secret storage compartment. "Matti! What are you doing in here? Everyone is so worried. Half the island is looking for you!" Emmy scolded.

Crawling out of his hiding place, Matti sat on the bench protruding from the wall beside the built-in table and took a good look at his best friend. It was wonderful to see her, but he doubted his expression conveyed that. Somewhere below his joy he had an oppressive feeling, like life was about to change again. Just thinking about his mom and Nic kissing on the beach made him uncomfortably warm. Only in his wildest dreams . . . of which he'd had a few lately . . . could he imagine such a kiss as that, and still, it exceeded anything he'd imagined. To think his mom had those same kinds of feelings was, well, embarrassing. Emmy slid onto the bench across from him and folded her arms. "Matti, everyone's worried about you. What happened to make you hide here like this?"

Matti shrugged. Emmy didn't really expect an answer. She understood him so well she would figure it out for herself.

"It's because our parents are acting crazy, isn't it? My dad's been gone a lot lately, and your mom, well, she's been painting nonstop and tutoring so much. It's like she wants to teach every single island woman reading, writing, and math. What's up with that?"

They both giggled.

"The painting she did of Izzy is really good. Your mom is a real artist. I wish we could've seen the painting of us. I mean, geez, she sold it so fast. That's really weird she didn't keep it. Don't you think?"

Matti nodded.

"And she's been seeing a lot of that Nic guy, hasn't she?" Emmy said this rather carefully, her eyes studying him as if she expected something in writing to appear on his forehead. "I think they're really sweet on each other."

Matti just stared at her. He was sure that she knew what he was thinking. Emmy was excellent at reading his thoughts. He wondered how she did that, because he rarely knew what she was thinking. Sometimes he would just watch her while she looked at the ocean, or when she sat in trees with him spying on geckos, but he simply had no clue what was going on in that head of hers. Nonetheless she always could tell what he was thinking. Women were like that. His mother always knew his thoughts too, maybe not as completely as Emmy, but well enough. If he could read his mother's mind, he wouldn't have been blindsided by her feelings for Nic, and then seeing them kiss like that wouldn't have jerked his brain around so much. Girls were lucky to have this ability. Maybe they weren't as physically strong, but they sure could read minds.

"I was hoping my dad would marry your mom," Emmy confessed. "I'm pretty sure that won't happen now," she added. "I wonder if there's anything here to eat." Emmy got up and began opening cabinets, looking for a snack. "Wow, the pantry is bare. Dad needs to restock this place." Emmy looked at Matti. "I'm gonna get you some food, okay?"

Matti nodded, but didn't smile. He didn't feel like smiling, even though he was hoping Emmy would offer to bring him food. He was hungry. The hike from Anthony's Key to Diego's boat took a lot of energy. The few snacks he had in his pack were eaten on the way. And then there was the dolphin show. He was torn between staying lost and making it to his first performance tomorrow night. How could he miss it? But then again how could he watch his mom sitting there beside Nic? That would scream at him how his life was going to drastically change. No more summer home, no more Emmy to hang out with all the time. No more thinking Diego might be his dad someday.

"Matti, listen." Emmy slid onto the bench again and this time she leaned forward so their eyes were only inches apart, as if he could hear her better that way. "I'm gonna go get food, and I want you to think about not being mad at your mom, okay? I mean, I know you love my dad and all, but you can't expect your mom to just fall in love with whomever you want. It doesn't work that way. Nic is a really nice guy. You need to give him a break." Emmy peeked out the galley door, as if she expected to see a posse on the other side demanding Matti return home.

"I'll be back soon." She glanced at Matti, who nodded. "I promise not to tell anyone either. Cross my heart and hope to die . . . well, no adults anyway. I might have to tell Angel 'cause she can be a pest sometimes." She gave him a serious look and he nodded again. He could trust Emmy with his life. He hoped she knew that.

And then she was gone.

He wondered how she got so smart at only twelve. Here he was the same age and he didn't know half as much as she did. He might have been a genius in the eyes of some, but Emmy was just plain *smart.* Like she had a sixth sense or something. He crawled back into the hidden storage space and drifted off for a short nap, hoping she would bring Izzy's chocolate chip cookies and his Gameboy when she returned.

Nic left the bistro with his mind awhirl. The disappearance of Matti was getting more complex by the minute. Justine had taken Natalie's portrait of the children to the Bay Area. What were the odds Antonio would know or see Justine? Just in case, he called Antonio at the mansion. While he waited for his half-brother to answer, he thought about the irony of Natalie's own artwork possibly exposing her, through a client recommended by Diego. All the clever coverups he devised to detour Antonio from Roatan might be rendered pointless. Did fate really have such a stubborn hold on their lives? Were certain things going to happen regardless of anything one did or didn't do to prevent them? It certainly would seem so. Hopefully this phone call to Antonio would dispel such a preposterous idea.

"Hello, this is the Giovanni household. May I ask who's calling?"

Nic hesitated. Why was a strange man answering Antonio's phone in his private den? "I work with Antonio."

"I'm sorry, he isn't here. May I take a message?"

Nic wasn't sure what to say. Should he expose who he was? What if his brother was onto him and this person knew it? On the other hand, he wouldn't get any information at all if he didn't come clean with his identity. At least the value of shock reaction would say a lot. "This is Nicholas,

Antonio's brother. With whom am I speaking?" There was silence at the other end for an uncomfortable few seconds in which Nic questioned his honesty approach.

"Hello, Nicholas. Yes . . . Antonio has mentioned you. I'm Matti's doctor. You can call me Henry. It seems he plans to bring the boy back here in the next few days. He doesn't know how you could have missed finding Natalie and Matti on that island off Honduras, but apparently an art collector friend of his had a recent portrait of the boy hanging in her home."

Nic slammed the wall beside the bistro with his open fist and cursed under his breath. "What did my brother say exactly?"

"Just that a painting of his son was hanging in the home of a Sydney Beaumont. He also said it was obvious Natalie had painted the portrait and it was definitely an island setting. Considering how many islands there are in the world, I'm not sure why he was so certain it was Roatan, since you didn't find her there after all your efforts. Are you still in Africa?" Henry asked.

Nic was at a loss for words. Antonio had to know he'd been made a fool of, but apparently he didn't wish to share that with Henry. "Yes, I'm still in Africa . . . and there are a lot of beaches in the world," Nic agreed. "How wonderful Matti has turned up on one. Let's hope it's the right one. I didn't discover any evidence of him or Natalie in Roatan, but I am an amateur at these things. Henry, why are you answering my brother's private line?"

"Antonio wanted me to examine Matti when he arrives, but that's not why I'm here now, of course. He asked me to check on the portrait of his son and put it in a secret vault behind a closet in his den. I thought it might actually be him on the phone. I also wired a prescription to give Matti if he seems agitated on the trip home."

Nic made the jump from Marlon's wife Justine to this Sydney woman. They obviously knew each other, and Henry had mentioned Sydney was a friend of Antonio's. "The painting was a gift, then, to my brother from this Sydney?"

"Um, possibly." Henry coughed. "Miss Beaumont was the unfortunate victim of a burglary and homicide recently. Lots of her art was taken. She had a fine collection, according to the newspaper. Anyway, this particular painting was spared because she . . . already had it in a safe place for Antonio to pick up. Anyway, I think you need to ask your brother whatever else you wish to know. I have no way of reaching him, but surely he'll call you soon."

"I'm sure he will." Nic ran sweaty fingers through his hair and took a deep breath of hot, sticky air. "I'll return to San Francisco if he actually found Matti. This is a dead end here anyway." Nic just stared at the street in front of him after they hung up. At least if Antonio called Henry he'd be told little brother was still in Africa and had come up empty handed. You never know, he might choose to believe stupidity rather than deceit was at play here. Somehow Nic doubted that. The bigger question was why this Sydney turned up dead. He didn't buy a coincidental robbery shortly after Matti's portrait was discovered. Probably, his brother had other issues with Miss Beaumont. Hell hath no fury like a Giovanni scorned.

Natalie watched from her kitchen window as Emmy met up with Angel midway down the beach. They walked past Diego's house and entered the café together. The girls either had nothing to report, or they didn't wish to share whatever information they had. The camaraderie between the three children was endearing. If the girls knew where Matti was hiding they wouldn't be inclined to rat on him, but if they had found him to be in danger they certainly wouldn't hesitate to get help. Natalie hoped they had found Matti and were just keeping his location secret, which would mean her son was safe and well cared for by his friends. She had a strong feeling that place might be Diego's boat. An eerie feeling had caused her to freeze up at the kitchen window and simply stare at the beachfront, rather than heading to the boat in search of Matti.

While standing there, she berated herself for not catching the end of dolphin practice like usual, even though Matti had been told frequently to come to Nic's cabin if let out early. And she was where she said she'd be, at Nic's cabin. Unfortunately, every time she did the math, it placed Matti there right about the time she was kissing Nic on the beach, which is why she knew that in all likelihood her son had run away. If he hadn't run away, then all other options were much scarier. The scariest of all being that Antonio had come looking for them. That would mean he'd seen the portrait of Matti and the girls, which she had sold in order to secure them a home on the island. There was too much irony in all of that to dwell on at the moment. Right now she needed to focus on finding her son, regardless of where Antonio was.

Not much time had passed until Emmy reappeared on the beach, wearing a backpack and heading in the direction of her dad's boat. Natalie was glad she'd kept watch for a while, not really sure what she was waiting to see. She certainly didn't want to face Diego or confront Nic in her harried state of mind. Natalie left the house convinced Emmy had the best idea for locating her son, if she hadn't already found him.

Staying close to the foliage on the edge of the beach and pacing herself well behind Emmy, she followed her son's best friend, who was obviously bringing supplies to the boat. Emmy had probably packed Izzy's chocolate chip cookies always kept in a large mason jar on the café counter. Everyone knew they were his favorite. Knowing Emmy, she had a deck of cards in that backpack, along with some books, and maybe even Matti's Gameboy if he'd left it at the café. Wisely, Emmy hadn't come to the summerhouse, so Angel must have lent her the backpack and helped her fill it.

Natalie wondered what she would say to Matti while following Emmy down the beach. It didn't take a rocket scientist to know how he felt about Diego, who spent more time with her son in one week than Antonio had in his entire life. Fishing on the boat, snorkeling, eating meals . . . just kicking the soccer ball around the yard. Diego had been a real dad to him. She wished she had talked to her son about Nic. He deserved to know the status of their relationship. Maybe if she'd shared how she felt, Matti wouldn't have been shocked to find them kissing—if that's what had upset him enough to run away.

How do you talk to a twelve-year-old boy about feelings you don't understand yourself? From the first time she saw Nic standing at the door, something inside her had stirred. It wasn't fear or curiosity. It was a sense of already knowing him, yet she'd never met Antonio's younger half-brother. At first she thought his resemblance to the Giovannis was paranoia on her part, because it was subtle. But the more she got to know him, the more she realized that something in her was simply drawn to something in him. He was an attractive man but lots of men were appealing to look at and they hadn't commanded her attention. Nothing about Nicholas indicated he was anything but a good person, struggling to find his path in life, just like she was doing. The boat came into view and she watched Emmy climb onboard.

Natalie had figured out that Matti was hiding in the storage unit off the galley. That's where he always hung out with Emmy when they'd had enough sun. It occurred to her that Matti was probably safer there than anywhere else on the island if Antonio had come for them. She stared at the dive boat bobbing in the water and thought about how it was her fault if Antonio was on the island.

As angry as she was with Nicholas, she had to admit he'd protected her location. It was obvious that he intended to stay in Roatan. Nic was behaving as the rogue family member he had a reputation for being. In fact, he didn't seem to be any more of a Giovanni than she was. He'd even hired Norma recently to help coordinate suppliers for the homes he was building in addition to his business with Diego. It was endearing that Nic was going to dedicate some of those homes to women who wanted to leave their men. Nonetheless, she wasn't sure she could ever trust him again. It wouldn't have been that hard to tell her who he was during the weeks they had spent together. She couldn't think about that right now. She couldn't allow herself to fall apart and give in to her feelings of betrayal. If she did she might never recover. Natalie hadn't been aware of how much she completely loved Nicholas until the moment she discovered the awful truth about him. To dwell on it would affect her focus right now, which needed to be on keeping her son safe.

Natalie continued to scan the beach in front of the dive boat from the palm tree she stood beside at the edge of the sand, where the forest began. She sat down for a minute and tried to come up with a game plan to keep Antonio from finding them. Leaving the island and uprooting Matti was not an option. Her work here wasn't finished. She was so proud of how the more determined women had excelled at their lessons. It was exciting to help them write resumes earlier today and discover that many of their daily tasks would transfer well into island jobs. With the addition of their newly acquired education they would be more than a little competitive among island men. And besides, running from one location to another for the rest of her life made no sense. She needed to make her stand here and face down her bully of a husband.

Several minutes went by and Natalie hadn't seen any activity on the beach. She also hadn't thought of what to say to her son or what to do to keep them safe from Antonio, but she couldn't wait another second to see Matti. She walked out on the dock and climbed over the railing of the boat. It was time to apologize for being a very absent mom recently between her painting, tutoring, and Nicholas—whom she had no idea how to tell Matti about, considering his real identity.

Antonio watched as some kid walked down the shore and then entered the Internet café. It wasn't long until she left the café and headed out across the beach again with a backpack. The girl looked about the same age as Matti, and he wondered if they knew each other. Maybe it was Diego's kid from the portrait, but she was too far away to tell. Right about that same time a woman came out of Diego's house and stood on the front porch, watching the girl walk down the beach. He wasn't sure at first if that was Natalie. She had her hair pulled back and a ball cap on. The milky white skin he remembered so well was tanned. He'd never seen Natalie in cut off jean shorts and a skimpy white tank top. After watching her walk a few yards down the shore he was certain it was his long-lost wife. She had a recognizable gait—graceful with long strides. His adrenalin began to flow, and he started to sweat. Damn this Roatan humidity he mumbled beneath his breath. Antonio adjusted the binoculars he'd brought in the pocket opposite his shiny new weapon, which he checked again before following Natalie. He walked up along the road, among the foliage for as long as he could. From there he observed her head toward a dock with a boat moored beside it.

The boat was fortunately docked alone, and all other boats, which he assumed were mostly for commercial diving, were down the shore another half mile or so. Antonio assumed the boat moored alone on the private dock belonged to Diego. His island informant had called him not long ago with lots of details about Diego Espinoza, including where he was at the moment. His informant was a friend of the guy who sold the superb weapon, albeit for a phenomenal fee. Considering what he was paying him and the general lack of scruples these guys had, not to mention any lack of camaraderie with rich coffee plantation heirs, he trusted the information he was getting.

Maybe Diego would soon be headed to his boat for an evening cruise with Natalie. It would be the perfect scenario. Antonio couldn't believe his luck. He would snatch up Natalie and secure her in the galley, then head out to sea, and call Diego from offshore on his fancy satellite phone. He knew Diego had one too, and even had the number thanks to his greedy informant. He'd demand Diego bring his son to him ASAP if he ever wanted to see Natalie alive again. Then he could kill them both. Espinosa deserved to die for helping Natalie run off with his kid.

The only hitch might be if Nicholas were still around somewhere, but so far his informant hadn't come up with anything. Diego had a new business partner, but his name was Nic Walsh. It wasn't much of a stretch to go from Nicholas to Nic, and Walsh sounded familiar although he couldn't recall why. Still, no one knew for sure where he'd come from. It seemed unlikely Nicholas would be a business partner on an island where his missing sister-in-law and nephew were, unless he just happened to love taking extreme risks.

On the other hand, Nicholas did have a history of building houses in Mexico with Giovanni money. Once he had cooled down about discovering where Natalie and Mattia were, Antonio wanted to believe Nicholas had been too inept to find them on the island. His informant had said that there was very little information about Espinoza's houseguests. The man had kept who they were and why they were there quite secretive. It made Antonio want to believe Nicholas was in Africa smoking dope with some chief to get information about the missing wife and son, rather than double-crossing his own Giovanni blood. The more he thought about it the more he doubted Nicholas would choose to stay on this little third world island and risk losing his substantial inheritance.

Mainly, Antonio hoped Nicholas was not Nic Walsh because he didn't want to contend with him being here. Antonio scowled. He hated having the disadvantage of not knowing where his inept half-brother was at the moment. He watched Natalie step onto the dock and stare at the boat. He made a quick call to his informant, telling him to keep looking for information about Diego's partner, Nic Walsh. He offered the sleazy Honduran a big bonus for getting ahold of two seats on the early morning flight to San Pedro Sula. Then he hung up and crossed the beach as Natalie entered the galley of the boat.

CHAPTER TWENTY-NINE

Izzy stared at Nic, deep into his eyes, as if the key to waking up from this nightmare could be found there.

Diego's cell phone rang the minute he returned to his Land Rover, after finalizing plans with Jake regarding the beach house built from his award-winning design. He didn't recognize the phone number of the person calling, but he did recognize the voice and it caused every muscle in his body to tense up. "Hello Diego. This is Antonio Giovanni. You have a very nice boat. It rides quite smoothly. Oh, and I believe I have someone here that is currently your house guest." There was silence as Diego pondered his worst nightmare coming to fruition. Before he recovered, Antonio continued. "Natalie would like a few words with you." There was a rustling sound and then he heard Natalie's voice, shaky and weak.

"Diego . . . can you please . . . bring Matti . . ."

Diego had no time to respond before Antonio was on the line again.

"Bring me my son and Natalie is all yours. However, if you don't bring me my son she'll be fish bait. Either way I couldn't care less. I'll get my son with or without your help. Oh, and I have a few spies out there, Espinoza. If you try to mess with me, Natalie loses."

Diego wished he could yank Antonio through the airwaves and strangle him, but he focused on staying calm when answering. "You can't raise your son from prison. I suggest you not do anything that might cause your arrest when you return to shore."

"I suggest you believe me when I say you won't ever see Natalie again if you don't bring Mattia in the next thirty minutes. And I'll know if you alert anyone. It would seem the law on this island is easy enough to pay off."

Diego quickly deduced that Natalie must have known he couldn't bring the boy to Antonio. Otherwise she would never have cooperated with the phone call. That might mean that she, and she alone, knew where Matti was. "I'll be there with the boy in an hour," Diego answered, untruthfully. "I can't collect him and get to the boat any sooner, but if you hurt Natalie, there won't be an exchange. I have my own spies to rival your informants. Consider it an advantage of being a local," Diego added. Antonio laughed, and it made Diego's head throb from a pent-up desire to beat him unconscious.

"Come alone, Espinoza, if you want to see your tutor alive. Meet me straight out from what the map calls Bodden Point. Make sure no one else is with you. Don't be late. Natalie is depending on you."

He hung up.

Diego stared at the phone for a minute, a million thoughts racing through his mind. Nic had a boat fully loaded with scuba gear. One of them could climb aboard behind Antonio and catch him off guard. Diego looked up from his phone and scrutinized the area outside his windshield. He believed Antonio was bluffing about paying off local authorities, but it couldn't hurt to be cautious. Next, he dialed the best diver and only hope he had for getting Natalie back safely.

Nicholas had just hung up from speaking with Henry in San Francisco when Diego called. "I have some very bad news. Natalie's husband is here and he's holding her hostage on my dive boat, at Bodden Point. He wants Matti . . . in exchange for Natalie."

"He doesn't already have Matti?" Nic asked, relieved.

"That's right. Ironic, isn't it? We wouldn't have suspected Antonio was on the island, if Matti weren't missing."

Nic wanted to smash his cell phone into the same wall he had slammed when speaking with Henry. Diego had no idea what Antonio was capable of, or that he never intended for Natalie to live once he found his son. For that matter, Diego didn't know he was Antonio's half-brother and had come to the island with every intention of finding Natalie and Matti, whom Diego had risked everything to protect.

"Nic . . . let's meet at your new dive boat in ten minutes and try not to be seen by anyone. Do you have fresh tanks and extra dive gear onboard?"

"Yes . . . that's a great idea. We can take him by surprise."

"Exactly. Do you own any firearms?" Diego asked.

"I do. Very nice ones. And waterproof packs for diving with them."

Nic stopped by Diego's summerhouse on his way to the boat in case Matti had returned home. It was lucky he'd purchased the dive boat, which he'd barely had out to sea, other than one evening with Natalie and several dives with Jake. Of course they had no intention of bringing Matti to Antonio, but it would be good to know where he was. He quickly looked around inside the house and called for Matti several times, nearly shouting. As he headed back out the door he met Izzy and Angel on the front porch.

"Have you found Matti?" Izzy asked. Her eyes were bigger than usual and were filled worry and fear.

"No," Nic answered flatly. He decided to be straight with her. "Izzy . . . I have some disturbing news. Natalie's husband is here, and he's holding her hostage on Diego's boat. He wants to swap her for his son." He glanced at Angel, wondering how much the child understood, but her expression told him she probably understood plenty.

Izzy's face tensed up. "So her husband *is* here, but he don't have Matti?"

"That's right. Matti must have run away as we suspected. Did any information about where he might be turn up on your search?"

Izzy stared at Nic, deep into his eyes, as if the key to waking up from this nightmare could be found there. "No, not a single clue," Izzy answered.

"Diego and I are going out on my boat to bring Natalie back," Nic assured her.

Izzy nodded. "You be careful, hear?" She put her arm around Angel, pulling the child close. "I didn't know you had a boat," she commented.

"It's fairly new. Thank God I have it." Nic swallowed hard. "This would be easier if we knew where Matti was."

Izzy looked at Angel. "Where's Emmy, chile? She was searching this beach with you."

Angel stared up at her mama. She glanced at Nic and then back at Izzy. "Emmy and Matti . . . they's on the boat. In the secret place." Angel began to cry. "Emmy found Matti there . . . she took him snacks . . . and books . . ." She tried to catch her breath, while Izzy and Nic stared in disbelief. "Emmy tol' me not to tell," Angel confessed. She turned and clung to her mama's long flowery skirt and began to sob.

Izzy knelt down to console her. "It's okay, baby. You's only doin' what Emmy asked."

Nic left them alone to comfort one another and rushed to meet Diego at his boat, relieved that he'd put his pistols in the special vault installed off the galley. He thought they'd be safer there than in the bungalow where the small safe was flimsy. He had heavy-duty waterproof bags on the boat that would keep the guns dry for a short dive. God willing, they were prepared to take Antonio by surprise the minute they reached Bodden Point.

Natalie had just stepped onto the dive boat when someone grabbed her from behind and put a hand across her mouth. The minute he spoke a chill ran up her spine. "Hello darling. How've you been? Still painting, thankfully. What a nice portrait you did of our son and his new friends. Where is Mattia, by the way?" Natalie tried desperately to free herself by jerking about and kicking. She screamed beneath his hand, but all her efforts were pointless against the tight grip. "Settle down, sweetheart. I know you're excited because you missed me. I'm sure you meant to send a forwarding address, didn't you?" Antonio dragged her below into the galley. "I'm going to take my hand away so you can tell me where my son is. If you scream, I'll break your neck and find him without your help. Do you understand?" He stared into her eyes and she stared back, praying the kids would not come out of hiding. Then he released his hand, but not his hold on her. She gasped for air. "Where is he?" Antonio demanded.

"In one of his . . . usual places. I'm not . . . sure exactly," she spit out between gulps of air.

Antonio let go of her and slapped Natalie so hard she fell against the wall. "Are you lying to me? I bet your precious Diego knows where he is. I bet he could find Mattia rather quickly knowing your worthless life was on the line." Before Natalie could recover he grabbed her again but didn't cover her mouth this time. Natalie could feel her lip swelling and tasted blood. "Scream and I really will break your neck," he whispered. "Yours wouldn't be the first I've broken. Just ask Mattia about the woman beneath the fountain."

Natalie gasped. She was stunned to finally know what had caused Matti to retreat within himself that night. Tears sprang to her eyes recalling how agitated he became whenever near the fountain. What a horrendous experience for him to witness. His father had killed a helpless woman and dragged her to a shallow grave where cement would soon entomb her forever. Staring straight ahead at the door to the storage unit she prayed again that the kids would not come spilling out. "I'm going to call your housemate and you better hope he cares enough about you to bring my son here on the double."

It felt as if he'd loosened his grip a little and without a second thought Natalie kicked him in the shin as hard as she could. He winced with pain as she dove for the stairs to the deck, but Antonio recovered in time to grab her again. He pulled her back into the galley and wedged her between himself and the counter. Natalie was well aware that Emmy and Matti were less than two feet away. Asking Diego to bring Matti here would be pointless. She cooperated with his phone call, but then tried once more to slip from his grasp. Antonio hit her in the back as she pulled away. Natalie fell, knocking her head against a corner of the sink. Just as everything went black, she prayed he wouldn't find Matti and Emmy, and that Diego would get there soon.

Nic opened the vault in the galley of his boat and pulled out the guns. After that he assembled dive gear for himself and Diego. He had just finished when hearing footsteps on the deck. With gun in hand, he waited at the entrance of the galley until a familiar face came around the corner. "It's me," Diego shouted. "Let's get going."

Nic started the engine and headed out to sea, wondering how to tell Diego about his news. Once they were cruising steadily toward Bodden Point, he filled him in. "I have information about Matti." He glanced at Diego, standing beside him at the wheel. "I saw Izzy at your place earlier. Angel was with her and shared where he's hiding out." Diego had been keeping watch for Bodden Point, but he shifted his gaze to look at Nic. "She said Emmy found Matti in the storage unit of your boat." Nic gave this a minute to sink in.

"He's on the boat? With Natalie?" Diego's eyes widened.

"Yes. And so is Emmy."

Diego looked as if someone had punched him. "Emmy's on the boat?"

Nic nodded affirmatively.

"God no, she can't be." Diego stared at Nic as if looking for some indication it was all a lie.

"They're smart kids," Nic reassured him. "Smart enough not to get caught, since obviously Antonio has no idea they're on the boat."

Diego studied the shoreline, looking for Bodden Point again. He didn't have a response, but Nic was well aware of how Emmy was his whole life. The sun was getting low in the sky as they neared their destination. It would be setting just as they climbed aboard Diego's boat. Nic hoped that would be to their advantage, and that his brother hadn't hired a few hit men to help pull off his plan. He realized this might be his last opportunity to come clean about his true identity. "There's something else I need to tell you."

"What?" Diego asked, not appearing to be interested.

"My name isn't Nic Walsh." The words nearly caught in his throat.

That got Diego's attention. He turned to look at Nic.

"My mother's maiden name is Walsh. She was Salvatore Giovanni's second wife. Antonio is my half-brother." Diego stared at him as if he didn't believe it, while Nic quickly informed him of where his loyalties were. "I despise my brother, and my father."

"Then why are you here?" Diego looked dazed and confused.

Nic kept a steady gaze on the horizon as the boat cut through the water. His guilt wouldn't let him look at the man beside him. "I was sent by the family to find Antonio's wife and son, but once I did, I couldn't expose their location." He finally looked at Diego. "And then I fell in love with them."

Diego sighed. He pulled his ball cap lower against the setting sun. "I've hated you for that, even though I can't really blame you," Diego added.

"I want you to know that everything between us, except for my identity, has been honest and real . . . more real than the rest of my life." Nic looked Diego right in the eye and wondered why the man didn't just beat him up, because he deserved it.

Nic slowed down as they approached Bodden Point.

"Why would you agree to search for Antonio's family if you despised your father and brother?" Diego asked.

"Half-brother," Nic corrected.

"Okay. Half-brother."

"I was being selfish. Basically, I wanted to secure my full inheritance. It was the main reason I agreed to go into the family business after college. I knew that someday soon my old man would die, and I would get what was due me for putting up with him."

Diego grinned. "Well truthfully, my intentions for bringing Natalie here were also selfish. Only what I coveted was the woman you stole from me."

Nic pulled into a cove so as not to be seen by Antonio. "I'm really sorry about that," he confessed.

"No you aren't," Diego countered. They glanced at one another for a few intense seconds and then broke into laughter. It was an emotional release sorely needed. Together they made haste to drop anchor and then scrambled to put on dive gear while discussing what was a loose plan at best. Details could not be narrowed down when attempting mutiny against a maniac. Once the firearms were safely packed inside their suits they shook hands and lowered themselves into the water, tank first.

CHAPTER THIRTY

She reminded him of Sleeping Beauty from the fairy tales, lying there peacefully with blood-red lips.

Matti and Emmy hugged tightly, tears mingling together on their faces as they lay barely breathing. Straining their ears to listen they stared at one another with wide eyes while events unfolded in the galley. Matti was not surprised that his father had found them, especially since the possibility had always been there in the back of his mind, where he had purposefully shoved it. It sounded like his dad was pushing his mom around, but it would do no good to expose himself and Emmy. He couldn't overpower his father anyway. His mother would want him to lie low and be smart about the situation. He only wished he had a weapon of some sort.

Matti pulled away from Emmy, who watched as he examined the vent opening onto the deck. It was a metal unit that could be lifted out. If he removed the vent, they could crawl onto the deck. He glanced at Emmy and hope sparked in her terrified eyes. Matti looked around for something to push it out with. He grabbed one of Emmy's hardcover books and wedged it between the vent and boat wall, which loosened it enough to be pushed out. He glanced at Emmy again, who nodded her approval of the unspoken escape plan. Matti lay back down and stared at the ceiling of the storage unit. They hadn't heard any voices for a minute or two, but then Matti felt the boat pull away from the dock. His thoughts kept shifting back to that night in San Francisco. Between that behavior and this, he concluded that his father was a psychopath. Matti covered his face with his hands. How could he have hidden in here while that maniac was shoving his mom around? He only hoped he was doing the right thing to wait for a chance to overtake him.

It seemed to Matti like it would be impossible to save Emmy and his mom by himself. He needed help, even if it only meant the element of surprise. Maybe he could sneak out and find something to hit his father with from behind. He sat up and looked over at Emmy, who was peering out the vent. Her face was streaked with tears and he wished he could tell her all hope was not lost. He'd think of something . . . and then he remembered that Diego kept a revolver onboard! It was in the bottom drawer beside the sink. Matti scooted over and studied the door as if he had ex-ray vision. If he snuck out while his father was above deck steering the boat, he could grab the gun from the drawer.

Emmy had been watching him carefully. She looked so frightened it worried him. He thought of the portrait in the hall back in San Francisco, how it had calmed him to see her smiling face in his hour of need, after his father had *murdered* that poor woman. Somehow he had to put that smile back on her face. He couldn't let anything happen to Emmy. Matti suddenly felt courageous. He put his hand on the hatch that opened into the galley and imagined jumping down to get the gun, climbing back into the storage compartment, and then onto the deck through the hole where the vent was. With any luck he could shoot his father before he got caught. Matti wished he'd tried harder to shoot rats in empty crates on the shipping docks. Then at least he'd have a feel for how to hit what he was aiming at. The boat stopped moving. His father would be busy putting the anchor out—perfect timing to grab the gun.

Matti opened the hatch and jumped down into the galley, where he immediately saw his mom lying on the floor beside the sink. She was as pale as the sandy white beaches, and blood had pooled beside her head. Matti knelt down and felt for a pulse on her neck. He couldn't detect one, so he felt for his own to be sure he was checking in the right place. His was throbbing full-speed. Again he pressed two fingers to her neck and thought there was a faint pulse this time. He couldn't be sure it wasn't wishful thinking. If she didn't get help soon, it might be too late. Matti grabbed a kitchen towel off the counter and carefully wrapped it around her head, pulling it as tight as he could. He secured it with a knot and looked at her face, really looked for the first time. She reminded him of Sleeping Beauty from the fairy tales, lying there peacefully with blood-red lips. Ever so gently, he kissed her on the cheek.

"Matti," Emmy whispered, with her head sticking out of the storage unit. "Hurry."

Tearing himself away from his mom was the hardest thing he had ever done, but there was no other way to save her and Emmy. Matti quickly opened the bottom drawer where the gun was stored. He grabbed the revolver and a box of bullets sitting beside it, handing both to Emmy before crawling back into the storage unit. They stared at one another. Matti felt as helpless and afraid as Emmy looked, but he forced himself to snap out of it. Carefully he lifted the revolver from her lap and opened the box of bullets. After some fumbling he figured out how to put them in. He practiced holding the gun in his hands while aiming it out the vent onto the deck. There was nothing left to do but wait.

Antonio stared straight ahead and watched the sun get lower in the sky. It shouldn't take Diego this long. How hard could it be to borrow or rent a boat? And he had to know where Matti was because he didn't say otherwise. If Diego believed there were men out there spying on him, then surely he'd get here straight away with the boy. Especially since he thought Natalie's life depended on it. Feeling impatient Antonio called his informant, who couldn't seem to get any information on Nic Walsh other than that he was a newcomer to the island. He was staying at Anthony's Key, but had recently bought the house he was building with Espinoza and Banderas. The informant suspected Nic Walsh was an alias. Regardless, no one knew where he was at the moment. That was disconcerting news. Next he called Henry, who informed him that Nicholas had checked in to say Africa was a dead end. Henry expressed his surprise at Nicholas not knowing Antonio was in Roatan. He also confirmed the painting was safely in the vault, and he'd wired a prescription to the clinic in San Pedro Sula for Matti. It was a mild sedative, just in case he seemed agitated for the trip home.

Antonio gave Diego a call. There was no answer. He scanned the distance looking for a boat. Suddenly it dawned on him that Diego was a diver. What if he hid the boat in a nearby cove and was planning to arrive from underwater, unannounced? How clever would that be? Not clever enough. Antonio laughed out loud. Diego obviously didn't know who he was dealing with. By the time it was all over, he'd regret having brought Natalie to the island in the first place. Thinking about his wife gave him an idea. Maybe he could use her for a human shield. She'd give him the edge he needed to shoot first, since it was obvious Diego had no intention of politely handing over Mattia. Antonio was a little surprised by that. Surely Diego would be happy to exchange a boy that wasn't his for the damsel in distress he'd helped disappear without a trace, at least until she started selling her paintings to people in the Bay Area. He found that amusing, and only hoped she wasn't dead yet.

Returning to the galley he saw immediately that someone had wrapped a makeshift bandage around Natalie's head. Antonio stood still and carefully observed his surroundings. After scrutinizing the area, he realized a storage unit was next to the tiny kitchen. Leaning against the wall beside the unit, he aimed his gun and opened the hatch. Even in the dim light Antonio could clearly see that a young girl about Matti's age was crouched down in the storage unit. She screamed just as he reached inside to grab hold of her. Antonio yanked her out and held the kicking, screaming adolescent tight against his body. While putting a hand over her mouth he realized it was the girl he'd seen earlier on the beach. He decided she'd do just fine for a shield. Nothing like a helpless teen for armor.

Antonio took a good look at her, while squirming in his arms, and remembered the much younger version hanging in his hall at home. That painting was why Nicholas got the cockamamie idea to check Roatan in the first place. "Listen kid. If you want to get through this alive, don't test me." He peered into the storage unit again with his gun aimed everywhere he looked. It was empty but rose-colored light from the setting sun was streaming through an opening in the back. It looked like a vent had been removed. "Were you going to crawl out that vent? Or did somebody else already do that?" Antonio asked, without removing his hand from Emmy's mouth so she could answer. He exited the galley while holding the struggling girl in front of him and stopped at the outside corner of the boat. Antonio scrutinized the panoramic ocean view and cocked his gun, anticipating Diego's appearance from the water at any moment.

If someone had exited the vent, it had to be a pint-sized person like the girl. A full-grown man wouldn't fit through the opening. Diego's kid must have been planning to escape through it after hearing his struggle with Natalie in the galley earlier. Nothing else made sense. The kid just froze up with fear and never ran out the vent opening as planned. That conclusion was a load off his mind. Now he just had to wait and see where Diego emerged from. His adolescent hostage wouldn't quit squirming as he strained to hear company coming, so Antonio slapped her hard across the face. The girl passed out and went limp just as a figure emerged on the far side of the boat, near where the vent would be. Pointing his gun at whoever it was standing there, Antonio shouted, "Shoot, and you'll kill the girl!"

At that same time a man in a wetsuit climbed onto the railing with a gun in his hand. Antonio was pleased to see it was Diego. "Welcome aboard, Espinoza. It looks like your kid beat you here." Antonio was beaming at the thought of blowing away the man who helped his wife double cross him. *Never mess with a Giovanni* he mumbled under his breath as he cocked the hammer. Diego tensed while balancing on the rail, his gun aimed straight for Antonio, until he saw his daughter. "You should have done as you were told, Espinoza, and I could trade your kid for mine." Antonio didn't wait for a response. He shot Diego, who fell head first onto the deck with a loud thud.

"No!" someone shouted, just as Antonio approached Diego and removed the gun from his hand. It was the person still silhouetted against the setting sun, on the far side of the boat. The girl in his arms had come to and bit Antonio on the hand before slipping away. He cocked his gun to shoot her as she ran, but it was he who fell at the sound of a gunshot. Antonio felt blood gushing from his chest just before passing out. When he came to, Mattia was staring down at him. The boy was holding a gun with trembling hands. In that instant Antonio realized Mattia had escaped through the storage vent and had been on the boat the whole time.

"Listen . . . son . . . I . . . had . . . no choice."

"Yes, you did. You always have a choice." Matti cocked the gun and pointed it shakily at his head. "You hurt Mom." His voice was clear and steady.

"She fell . . . was an . . . accident."

"No. You meant to hurt her." Matti stiffened and aimed more determinedly.

Antonio struggled to catch his breath. "You . . . won't shoot. Put the . . . gun down." He made a sudden, focused effort to grab the boy and knock the gun from his hand, but someone intervened and threw him roughly back onto the deck. Excruciating pain shot through Antonio as he looked up to see Nicholas, standing beside Mattia. Antonio laughed. It hurt like hell, and he spat out blood. With his last breath he whispered, "You . . . deserve . . . each other."

Nicholas took Diego's pulse and noted where the blood was seeping through his wetsuit. "He's going to be okay, Emmy. It's not a serious wound." Nic hoped he was right. He was grateful his brother had such bad aim. It worried Nic that Diego was still unconscious. He probably landed on his head when falling off the railing. Hopefully it was just a minor concussion.

Emmy looked at him through her tears. "Matti's m-mom is below deck, and sh-she's hurt bad."

Nic gave Emmy a tight hug, told her to keep an eye on her dad, and joined Matti in the galley while on the phone. He requested a rescue helicopter to be sent from San Pedro Sula, along with the authorities. Nic gave their Bodden Point location and then hung up. Kneeling beside Natalie he checked her pulse. She was very pale. "Did you do this?" he asked, looking at Matti, while adjusting the makeshift bandage around her head.

Matti nodded.

"Well I think you just may have saved her life." Nic looked at Matti, who was still shaking and holding the revolver loosely in his hand. Nic reached out and gently took it from him. "She is breathing, Matti. I know it looks bad, but honestly, I think she'll be okay. Diego, too. It's too soon to say for sure. It couldn't hurt to say a few prayers." Nic studied the boy. "Do you realize you're talking again?"

Matti nodded. "Yes."

Nic grinned, despite their grim situation. Both of them turned their attention to Natalie, who was clumsily reaching up to feel the bandage on her head.

"Mom!" Matti laid his head on her chest, just as she opened her eyes.

Natalie set a shaky hand on his tousled hair. "You're . . . talking." She closed her eyes again, but tears were running from them.

Matti lifted his head and looked at her. "Will she really be okay?" he asked.

"I think so, Matti. I honestly do."

"Will Diego be okay, too?"

"I believe he will. It appears to only be a flesh wound."

Matti stared at the gun Nic had stuffed in his wetsuit pocket. "I killed my father," he confessed, showing no emotion.

"You were courageous enough to do what needed to be done, and if you hadn't shot him, I would have," Nic added. "You just beat me to it. Look at me, Matti." Nic put his hand on the boy's chin and raised his face until their eyes locked. "You saved Emmy's life. I would have been too late. That split second made all the difference. Never forget that." Nic hugged him tightly and said a silent prayer for the helicopter to get there soon.

CHAPTER THIRTY-ONE

Nic studied the boy looking up at him and realized how the frail, nervous lad he'd originally met was gone without a trace.

Nic sat in the crowded stands and cheered louder than anyone. It was such a rush to see Matti out there being a star. He seemed to be in his comfort zone with the dolphins. He was so proud of his nephew, hanging in there because the show must go on, as Diego had pointed out to him at the hospital. Besides, there was nothing at all he could do for his mother or Diego. They simply needed time to heal. Both were out of Intensive Care, and Mira had probably brought Diego home by now. Despite having spent the night and half of today at the hospital, Matti's performance was flawless. Of course, he dedicated his first show to his mom and Diego, who'd brought him to this island paradise to begin with.

Nic whistled loudly and applauded after Matti performed another trick as if he'd been doing it his whole life. "That's my nephew, you know," Nic said to the tourist sitting beside him. He intended to care for Matti while Natalie recovered, and tried not to think about what would happen after that. There was a good chance Natalie would never speak to him again, and he wouldn't blame her.

Mira would be staying at the summer home to care for Emmy and Diego while he recovered. Nic had observed Mira and Jake holding hands while sitting beside Diego's bed at the hospital. It looked as if this unfortunate incident had brought them to their senses. Nic had a strong feeling that they would be planning a wedding as soon as Diego fully recovered. It was expected that physically, Natalie would be fine. Recovering emotionally from Antonio's attack would be harder, but Natalie was a strong woman and had already proven as much by moving to Roatan to protect Matti. The women she had been tutoring were coming one at a time to sit by her bedside and read to her from the books she'd given them. No doubt Izzy had organized it. He felt quite miserable, knowing what a mess he'd caused by coming to the island in the first place and then feeling compelled to stay.

The show was over and everyone heartily applauded. Nic waited in the stands for Matti as the tourists filed out. He had told him the truth about who he was and why he had come to the island during the longest night of their lives, waiting outside Intensive Care. Matti seemed to have forgiven him. At least, he didn't indicate otherwise. Diego had also been forgiving, when Nic shared with him on the boat while heading to Bodden Point, but Natalie might not be so willing to dismiss his lies about who he really was. All he could do was wait and see. Mario had been arrested in the wee hours of the morning for his involvement with the illegal baby trade through Romania. Salvatore was also in custody, in Sicily. Apparently, his father and brothers had been under surveillance for some time. Mario had come clean about the murdered woman beneath the fountain, and sometime during their long night together, Matti had shared seeing it happen.

When Nic called Henry, he'd recommended an estate attorney for Antonio's holdings that would now go to Natalie. As an afterthought, Nic had Henry ship the painting of Matti, Emmy, and Angel. He knew Natalie would be thrilled to get it back. It would be his get-well gift for her. While he was at it, he had the portrait of Emmy from the hall shipped to Diego. Everything else could be placed in storage until Natalie was ready to decide what to do with the house.

The stands had emptied and Nic sat alone to wait for Matti, wondering how different things would be if Natalie had been in this very spot yesterday waiting for her son. But then, that was the most frustrating thing about life. There was no erasing the past. If he could push a rewind button, he'd go back in time and tell Natalie who he was that first night at his bungalow, so she could make an informed decision about their growing relationship.

Matti came and sat beside him, having showered and dressed to leave. "Your mom will be so proud of you when she watches what I recorded on my phone." Nic put his arm around the boy and hugged him close. "Let's go see her."

"Okay," Matti agreed.

They took the motorcycle to the ferry. Standing at the rail on the boat ride over, Nic shared his plan with Matti. "Diego won't be at the hospital when we get there," he began. "Mira took him home this afternoon. That's good news, right?"

Matti nodded in agreement.

"She's going to stay in your mom's old room, and watch over him and Emmy for a while," Nic added.

"Where will Mom stay?" Matti asked.

"Well, I was thinking maybe you could stay at the house I just bought, the one Diego designed." He paused there waiting for some reaction, but Matti was silent. "We could go by Diego's place later tonight and pack up your things. Maybe Mira could pack your mom's stuff, and she could crash with us at the new house. At least for now, Matti, until your mom is able to decide for herself where she wants to live."

Matti still had nothing to say. He was staring out to sea, probably thinking it all through. Nic knew it had to be hard for him to realize his time in Diego's summer home was over. That was the past now. As soon as Natalie was recovered enough to take care of herself and Matti, he would move out and let her buy the house, if that's what she wanted. Money was certainly not a problem for her now that Antonio was gone. The house was in a good location for tutoring, and quite suitable for an artist, with a generous loft on the top floor overlooking the Caribbean. Perfect for a studio, and just to be sure it was, Nic had put in extra touches any artist would need in the way of flooring and counter space. He'd also installed several skylights, to see the stars Natalie loved so much.

"We won't stay there once she's well?" Matti asked.

"I hope you will, but maybe not. You'll be there at least as long as it takes your mom to recover."

"You aren't going to marry her?"

Nic thought this question quite painful, and not one he really wished to face. But he owed Matti the truth. He put his hand on the boy's shoulder, while they studied seagulls flying noisily beside the ferry. "I'm not sure your mother will want to marry me. You see, Matti, I didn't tell her I was a Giovanni until you ran away and we thought your dad might have come for you. Now she doesn't trust me, and I don't blame her."

"But you saved her life," Matti pointed out, looking up at him.

"*We* saved her life," Nic corrected. "You, Diego, and I all contributed to her rescue . . . even Emmy played a part." They looked out to sea again, at the waves and the gulls gliding about. "Would you be okay with it, if we married?" Nic asked. Matti shrugged. Nic turned the boy to face him and looked directly into his emerald eyes . . . Natalie's eyes. "Either way, I love you both very much, more than anything on this earth, and I will do everything in my power to make her comfortable while she is recovering." Nic nearly choked up and paused to regain his composure. "A view of the sea right outside her window should help. Your mother loves the sea," he added.

"I know," Matti agreed. "Nic?"

Nic studied the boy looking up at him and realized how the frail, nervous lad he'd originally met was gone without a trace. In his place was a taller, stronger, more confident version of that broken kid he'd first laid eyes on. "What, Matti?"

"I wouldn't mind if you married Mom and became my dad."

Nic didn't know what to say. The words would have caught in his throat anyway. He simply nodded and hugged Matti to him. Side by side they watched the ferry land and hurried onto the dock, eager to see Natalie. Hopefully she would be awake, so they could tell her all about the dolphin show, and Diego's finished beach house with the skylights and ocean view, where she would be recovering. Nic hoped it would be a new beginning . . . for the three of them.

ACKNOWLEDGMENTS

First and foremost, I want to thank my daughter Anna who lived on the island of Roatan, allowing me the opportunity to spend time there and learn the ways and moods of this tropical paradise. Observing her navigate nail-biting adventures are memories I will always cherish.

A special thankyou to my granddaughter Taryn Alyse, whose youth and wisdom contributed exactly the right input. I am confident that one day she will be writing books and God willing, I will be around to read them.

As always, my daughter Sasha has had the last say in editing before handing off to my publisher

I want to thank Shauna Berry, my new Napa friend who is now off on an exotic adventure of her own. She has left an imprint on this book with her wise counsel. Shauna blesses every life she touches, and I am grateful to have her in mine.

Thank you to those few but mighty friends I made while living in Colorado. Rene Villard Reid, Carol Spaulding, and Elaine Taverrite Atkins, you have all enriched my life tremendously. I am humbled that you took the time to share your thoughts about the book. You helped me shore up every weak word.

I am ever so grateful for Ladd Woodland, who has done the cover art for all my books. He is a gifted designer and has greatly enriched my life with his humor, art, and friendship.

Finally, I wish to acknowledge my friend Eldon Thompson. He has enthusiastically (and tirelessly) read and reviewed all my books. Eldon is the author of a very distinguished fantasy trilogy, and I excitedly anticipate his next genius series. Eldon is an exemplary person in every way, and I am blessed to know him.

ABOUT THE AUTHOR

Award-winning author Kathryn Mattingly has taught writing at four private colleges. Aside from her literary suspense novels and short-story collection, Kathryn's work can be found in numerous small press anthologies and print magazines. She currently lives in a one hundred and sixteen-year-old house in Napa, California, with her husband, their two cats, and a resident spirit named Genevieve.

Made in the USA
Middletown, DE
28 September 2019